THE WEAVING

H.J. Eliot

Acknowledgements

Special thanks to my friends
in the Westside Writers Group:
Laurie, Peter, Adrienne, Rudi, Rupert and John,
for your expert critiques and kind encouragement.

Thanks also to those brave souls who took
a look at the first draft:
Pat, Jim and Tim.

Chapter 1 – New Orleans

She hesitated just a moment, then stepped out from the shadowed doorway, her eyes half-lidded and unfocused. Light fell on the street's uneven brick pavement from a single streetlamp a few doors down. The balcony over her head was graced with a wrought iron balustrade, and as she stepped out from its shadow, the broken light played over her curves like moving waves. She stopped on the block of limestone that was the doorstep to a small bar, waiting for the people in the street to turn toward her. Behind her, still in the shadows, stood a man, his hat concealing his face.

She stood unsteadily in high-heeled boots, weaving a bit. Her long black hair fell past her shoulders and swayed with her body as she languidly revolved in the uneven light. Heavy black eyeliner concealed any expression in her eyes, and her red mouth was slack and moist, smiling slightly. She raised her long white arms over her head, waving and entwining them like two snakes. She arched her back and undulated, baring her fishnet-sheathed body to the late-night crowd. The netting stretched across her breasts and the sequins flashed as she drew a slow arc with one hip, up and around, then with the other hip, up and around. Her body drew her onlookers' eyes like the swing of a hypnotist's pendulum. She stretched like a cat and undulated once more, relaxing. One arm drifted down, caressing her hair, her breasts and her hips.

She lowered her eyes and caught the eyes of a man in the street. A gray-haired, gray face a long way from home, under a red baseball hat with a slogan. A big-livered belly, doomed anyway. He wore an expensive suit jacket with a convention tag over a Drunk in NOLA t-shirt, and he stood alone. She noticed the bonus, a couple of heavy rings and a Rolex. That's the one. She crooked her finger at him.

"C'mon, honey, you know you want it."

The knot of frat boys watching grinned and nudged each other until she turned her knowing smile toward them. They glanced away in embarrassment and moved off down the street.

She focused on Mr. Red Hat, who had moved closer. "How much you got to spend, cowboy?"

"A hundred."

"Sugar, you can't even look at me for that."

"One fifty."

"Give you some business for two hundred…real slow." She leered and winked and started to turn away, keeping her limbs languid. She stepped down off the stoop, stumbled and caught his arm.

"Ooh, I must be high – help me stand up." She leaned into him, brushing him with her nipples. Her hair swung forward and across his face. He stared stupidly and reached for her.

"Come on in, honey, we'll have some fun." She took his hand and pulled him up the step with her eyes.

They reeled into the club. It was tiny, a real dive, with black walls and a gouged and grubby oak bar. "Buy me a drink, sugar?" She did a slow sashay to the far end of the bar, then turned and lifted one long leg after the other as she slid onto a barstool. She pivoted toward him, leaned forward and beckoned with one finger. She wore white lace gloves with frills at the wrists, an incongruous girly touch.

For an hour Mr. Red Hat was buying, drink after drink. The bartender was expert and kept the liquor flowing. After a while the bartender slid down the bar and elbowed her pimp, the only other person there. "Just look at the wad this fool is toting – Jesus, he can't even tuck it away anymore. She keeps up like this she's not even gonna have to open her mouth."

"That's my bitch," the pimp grinned.

None of the three men saw her nursing her drink and pouring it out on the sticky floor. None of them noticed the hilt of the poniard, a small dagger with a square cross-section, at the top of her vinyl boot. She sat swaying on the barstool, smiling and running her lace-gloved finger up and down Mr. Red Hat's arm.

Suddenly he lurched to his feet and announced thickly, "I want some action, baby."

"Right this way, lover."

She took his hand and led him through the beaded curtain at the back of the bar into a room with a lurid red glow. With a lithe and graceful movement, she slid the jacket off his shoulders and dropped it on a chair. He stared stupidly as she slid down, then up again, snaking one leg around his waist and caressing his crotch. She pulled his t-shirt up and over his head and halfway down his arms, exposing his pathetic belly. She unzipped him, then stepped back, smiling, and bit open a condom package, her eyes never leaving his. She slipped the sleeve on his hard-on and fondled his prick, then sucked it hard for a moment. He grinned and groaned and his eyes rolled. She stood up and stepped away again, still holding his prick. He stumbled after her as she led him through another door into the alley.

"What the hell are we doin' here?"

The question died with the dagger in his throat and he fell heavily as she jumped aside, quick as a cat, yanking the shirt off his arms ahead of the spurt of lifeblood. She stripped him expertly: shirt, pants, condom, rings, shoes and hat were gathered quickly and tossed behind a box. Damn she was good at this. She grabbed the bankroll, stuffing it expertly in her sequined thong. The cell phone she didn't touch. Then she slipped to the side of the door.

She didn't have to wait long. Ten minutes later the pimp came out to collect and she sliced him neatly. He started to make noise but she strangled him, lithe and strong as a tigress. She collected the rest of the evening's earnings from his wallet and added them to her stash. His gold chain and rings she dropped with the clothes. Then she strolled back inside and spoke to the bartender.

"Andre wants to talk to you."

"What for?"

She shrugged. "I don't know, he said come outside."

She followed him out and leaped on his back as he started to scream, but it came out as a grunt, as the dagger slipped between his ribs and twisted. She dropped his body with the others.

She collected Mr. Red Hat's shirt and pants. She wiped the makeup off her face with the shirt, then slipped his clothes on over her nakedness. His sneakers went on her feet and her own boots, kimono and wig were rolled up and tucked in the pants to fill out his paunch. And the condom, DNA-laden – *don't forget that*. Her hair was twisted up under the red hat and the bill covered her eyes. She scanned the scene to make sure nothing was left behind. Slipping back in the door, she picked up the jacket, shrugged it on and transferred the loot to a pocket. She eased behind the bar and emptied the till. She slipped the small glass she'd used into a pocket. *Good, no more witnesses. That's enough killing for tonight.*

She slouched heavily out the front door, hands deep in the pockets of the too-loose pants, just one more old drunk in the Quarter. Same guy who'd followed that nice piece of ass in there.

"Must have worn her right out," the frat boys joked, "'cause she didn't come back out." They pulled on their beers and looked down the street toward another doorway. The cop she passed looked right through her.

Here in the Quarter you can act drunk in the street and nobody cares. She shambled down the street, mouthing deeply slurred words, lurching toward tourists and watching them flinch. *This is too much fun*, she thought, *cut it out before you get caught.*

After a few blocks, she turned into an alley, scrambled over a fence and snaked between buildings. She left the Quarter, heading west to Tulane Avenue. She paralleled the avenue but stayed in back alleys until she came up behind the Goodwill store. There she picked the lock on the back door and slid into the darkened building. She fumbled through the sorting room and came out into the dark, cavernous store. She knew the layout by heart, and it didn't take her long to find a great pair of construction boots. She slipped the poniard and its sheath neatly down in the boot cuff to hug her calf. She explored the rest of the store, picking up shirts to layer and jeans that fit her better. Everything else she stuffed into a shopping bag.

Back outside in her new outfit, she followed the railroad tracks west into River Rouge, past the airport and then on up toward St. Charles. Near one of the bayous she slipped under a fence into a junkyard, slid down a dirt pile and picked up enough rocks to weigh down all the clothes she would discard. Only after she'd tossed them in the canal with a splash did she peel off the white lace gloves. Such versatile stuff, lace! It could lure a man to his doom and ensure there were no fingerprints.

The transformation was complete. She looked like a young boy now, as she followed the tracks westward toward the lake. When she heard the slow, creaking approach of a freight train she ducked behind a bush until it was almost past, then chased alongside it. Grabbing a handhold, she swung up between two cars and wedged herself securely.

Two hours later she jumped off at the outskirts of Baton Rouge. She made her way to the north side of the city near the barge terminal. After walking several more blocks, she knocked on a door at the side of a brick warehouse.

Steps approached the door. A large dog growled deeply and a voice called out.

"Who's there?"

"Miss Andrea, it's me." A pause. "Jamie – from New Orleans."

The door cracked to the length of a chain and a woman said, "Step into the light." Jamie stepped back and pulled off her hat. Her blonde hair tumbled around her shoulders, limp and dirty.

The door closed again, then swung wide open. Jamie stepped into an embrace. Andrea was short and buxom, a soft, comfortable black woman of late middle age. Her hair was up in braids and she was dressed comfortably in a caftan. Her hug was a sweet balm to Jamie's weariness. The smell of jambalaya and cornbread filled the apartment, and Jamie realized how hungry she was.

"Come on in, honey, sit down. It's been a while."

"It sure has. It's so good to see you. But I can't stay long. I need to get going early."

Jamie held her hand out to the dog, fingers down, so he could sniff it. Satisfied, he backed off and sat down.

"That's a good dog you have there."

"He sure is. Do you know he's a quarter wolf? Saved my hide a couple of times already. Got him off of a gal in Georgia who raises 'em up in the hills there. Best damn protection I ever had." She chuckled. "You want to hear some stories?"

They walked into the kitchen. Andrea handed down some plates and both of them scooped jambalaya from the iron skillet. Jamie poured molasses over the square of cornbread and grinned at her friend. They took out beers and sat down at the tiny kitchen table. They shared tales, some of them invented, and laughed long and hard. Jamie said nothing of her recent adventures. After a while she stifled a yawn.

"Oh honey, you must be tired. I'll fix up a bed. You go clean yourself up. The towels are in the cupboard in the bathroom there. Use anything you see. There's a spare bathrobe on a hook in my bedroom – the purple one."

Andrea laid flannel sheets and a wool blanket on the sofa while Jamie showered. Jamie stood under the hot water for a long time. It was good to wash off the memory of the day. She came out toweling her hair. The two women hugged good night, and Jamie crawled naked into the bedding and, this time, slept deeply.

In the morning Andrea pulled out the backpack and skateboard Jamie had stashed in her closet on her last visit. She packed some food and a canteen of water into it, along with the extra clothes and a poncho.

Together the women climbed the five flights of stairs to the roof of the warehouse and crossed over to the pigeon cages.

Jamie reached into the second cage, seizing a large gray pigeon. The bird fluttered as Jamie held its legs and stroked it, then held it against her cheek. She fastened the clip around its leg and looped it through the ring she pulled off her finger, the one adorned with Celtic knotwork and a single lion's head. She kissed the ring and purred to the bird.

"Go home now, Sweet Pea." She tossed the pigeon upward, where it fluttered into the morning sky, circled high above her and set off west.

At the door, the women hugged each other and Jamie slipped out, walking down the street at first. Then after turning a couple of corners, she set down the skateboard and stroked it forward.

Chapter 2 – Louisiana

Three days later Jamie woke slowly in the woods, savoring the smell of the earth and last year's oak leaves. She ate a bagel left over from last night and drank from her canteen. She built a small fire to burn up the silly lace gloves, an unnecessary but satisfying little ritual. She mentally checked off anything that could surface to betray her. She decided that only the gold jewelry and the cash would be a problem now, so she kept it in a small bag in a pocket, ready to drop or fling in a second.

Jamie had left Andrea's house in Baton Rouge at dawn three days ago. With a long, loping swing of her leg she'd sent the skateboard rolling down the gentle slopes toward the Mississippi River. Then she followed River Road north along the river, passing through the industrial parks and refineries to the Huey P. Long Bridge on Route 190. This bridge was designed to support railroad tracks, but it had narrow automobile lanes hung off each side of the trestle superstructure. Even after the auto lanes were widened in the 1990s, however, there was still no room for shoulders or breakdown lanes – and certainly no room for a skateboard rider. But Jamie knew this bridge, and she knew that only five trains passed over it each day. It was just a matter of timing her run across the railbed after the noontime westbound freight train had passed. The bridge was over a mile long, but she traversed it quickly, bending low and trotting between the rails. She hoped no one noted her passing, and she was relieved to reach the western end in less than twenty minutes. She scrambled down the earthen embankment from the tracks and headed north again, getting away from the highway.

When she struck the Mississippi again, it was at a meander that twisted almost directly east. Travelling upriver, she headed west, following the edge of the flood plain on small roads. Where the pavement was smooth, she used the skateboard. Where her route was a dirt road, she walked. Toward midafternoon, she walked through Alfords, a crossroads farming community. From there she headed northwest on even smaller routes toward New Roads, bypassing the oxbow lake called False River, a curve that the Mississippi had long ago abandoned. She spent the second night after leaving Andrea's in a woodlot with a stream flowing through it. She had followed the stream into the woodlot, hoping to find a pool to cool off in. Instead all she found was muddy farm runoff, which she didn't dare drink. She didn't bother to wash, and drank only from her canteen. As she scouted the creek, she came across a deer blind. Off-season, it was a perfect place to hide. She climbed up into it and spent the night.

Far behind her, New Orleans was frantically looking for the Bourbon Street Slasher again. He was described as a black man, heavily muscled and menacing. The motive was obviously robbery. Later when Jamie was told this news, she felt a twinge of guilt that those guys had been pulled in, victims of being in the wrong place at the wrong time. But that was the way of the world – people see what they want to see. Nothing she could do would have saved those poor souls from the misfortune of being born black and male, in a city that valued its tourists more than its citizens.

Jamie's talent lay in showing the world someone they recognized, then shifting like a shape-changer into another guise. Now she traveled as a teenage boy in a flannel shirt, a nondescript feed cap, jeans and boots. This morning she had rolled through New Roads and LaBarre, using the back roads she had memorized, looking like a kid out for some weekend exercise. Her route took her closer to the Mississippi again, and she smelled it before she saw it – a slightly fishy odor, competing with the smell of newly turned earth. The rendezvous point she was headed for was an abandoned grain elevator at a railroad siding outside of Morganza. She'd have to wait until evening again, but she'd stay out of sight until she saw the pickup.

Meantime she'd eat only what she could buy in convenience stores or small groceries, not risking the length of exposure of a restaurant meal. She knew that waitresses had long memories. She'd been one herself once, blending into the background and reading the customers carefully. *Show them what they want to see, say what they want to hear.* She recognized the acute skills of good waitresses, and she couldn't risk being a stranger in town that they'd remember later. She didn't buy from farm stands either, where the old folks were keen observers. The counter clerks at the 7-11 were another matter, poorly trained teenagers attuned only to their iPhones. She could barely catch their attention to ring up the sale.

Now she sat at the top of the grain elevator as the sun sank, lighting the clouds from underneath with brilliant fuchsia and purple. To the east, the wide meanders of the Mississippi reflected the sky. The fields in the river bottom were beautiful with pale springtime green, early cotton and lush swaths of winter wheat. It would be a good year for fruit after all the rain. The rivers were back up to where they should be and the land drank deeply. A good year for growing.

11

The truck slowed and pulled into the gravel siding and the headlights blinked once and went out. She climbed quickly down the rung ladder and circled behind the truck, recognizing the rotted fenders. The dog in the front seat wagged a welcome and her friend Bonnie leaned over and gave her a kiss as she climbed in. "Hi, honey, I heard you done good. What was it, eight?"

"Eleven. I got three this last time."

"Damn. I gotta do some math now – they're comin' in from all over."

"Yeah? Not much on the news."

"Well, that's 'cause you're so damn good." Bonnie chuckled, "Them peckerwoods up there in Washington just can't piece it together. You and them other gals got some real invisibility goin' on. Glad you're back safe, Miss Jamie Lynn." She winked and grinned, then reached in her jeans pocket and pulled out Jamie's Celtic lion ring. "Here you go, sweetheart. Your ticket home. Sweet Pea brought it in day before yesterday."

The truck started up with a grumble and swung out onto the road. They drove in companionable silence, the windows down and the wind smelling sweetly of rain. Jamie looked over at Bonnie's profile, loving the wrinkles around her eyes and the one heavy dark braid draped over her shoulder. Bonnie drove easily with her elbow out the window, reaching down to work the stick shift as the truck labored up into the Kisatchee National Forest north of Alexandria. Jamie loved to ride this pickup – always had – especially in the early evening, perched on the grubby bench seat with her boots up on the dash. Used to ride that way with her Dad before he went off and got killed in the war. She ran her finger over the dash and picked up the red Ozark dust and tasted it. *It's been too long.*

The night deepened and they pulled onto the interstate, still headed northwest. The lights came and went, hypnotizing and regular. Jamie nodded and finally lay her head over on the tolerant dog. He was a backwoods mutt that had lived at the farm forever. He licked her face once and she smiled and slept.

She woke up once as they passed around Shreveport. Bonnie left the interstate and drove straight north toward Texarkana, then angled northeast toward Little Rock. At Hot Springs she turned north to pass through the Ouachita National Forest. Descending from that highland, she drove further north into the Ozarks. For another hour she followed two-lane roads past sleepy towns and small farms. The road wound between widely spaced homesteads, some buildings neat and well-kept, others succumbing to the pull of monstrous mounds of kudzu.

As her head became heavy, Bonnie thought about waking Jamie to ask her to drive. But Jamie slept on, snoring lightly. Bonnie had hoped they'd get home tonight, but as the fatigue beat on her, she realized they wouldn't make it. Instead, she decided to cut off onto a gravel road, going up steep switchbacks into the Ozark hills. She knew this road and the people who lived here, and she knew a safe place to spend the night.

The truck bounced to a stop at the iron gate of the old MacAvoy cemetery. The engine dieseled for a few seconds after Bonnie shut it off, as if it couldn't believe it could finally quit. Bonnie pulled the emergency brake on, yawned, settled herself and slept, curled up on the other side of the dog.

Chapter 3 – New Orleans

The New Orleans medical examiner's office had been a busy place lately. The discovery of the three latest victims of the Bourbon Street Slasher had turned up the heat on Dr. Henry's team. Conventions were pulling out of the big hotels and tourism was way down. Unless this guy was caught there would be hell to pay at city hall.

Late at night the lights blazed in the morgue as Dr. Henry's assistant, the diener, moved the latest murder victims onto slabs. The diener was a short but muscular young man, trained in autopsy details, but also strong enough to lift and position bodies all day, and all night if need be. His boss, Dr. Henry, the medical examiner, was older, with white hair and a calm, imperturbable manner. A city as large as New Orleans could afford to hire a real medical doctor for this position – unlike the poorer communities throughout the state, who elected their coroners regardless of medical training.

Tonight both Dr. Henry and the diener wore their full protective gear of scrubs and aprons, along with face shields, surgical masks and gloves. The photographer wore a lab coat and surgical mask and gloves, but he stood back until summoned. In fact, this was the photographer's first experience in an autopsy lab, so he was a little out of his depth and full of questions.

"When I ask you to step forward, I'll show you what I want," instructed Dr. Henry. "Most of your shots should be as close up as you can get them, but every once in a while, I'll want a full-torso or full-body shot. Got it?" The photographer nodded. "And the rest of the time, you take one step backward, and you protect your camera. Things will squirt." At that, the photographer retreated hastily.

Working together, Dr. Henry and the diener autopsied the bodies, one after another, working with the photographer to catalogue the fatal wounds. Dr. Henry pointed out a close-up he wanted. "See those edges? That's some kind of a square-shaped blade. Nothing I'm familiar with."

"Whatever it is, it's sharp as hell. He would hardly have felt it." The photographer sought confirmation. "Am I right?"

Dr. Henry nodded. "Yep, you're right. Man, what a way to go. I thought I'd seen it all."

"And why was this one guy stripped?" asked the photographer, pointing to the first table. "It doesn't make any sense."

Dr. Henry shrugged. "Like they said, robbery. Maybe this poor fool was uncooperative. As for the others, word is that pimp had a lot of bling on him. And a lot of dough."

There was silence for several minutes as they continued to work.

"So what happened to the hooker? If there was a pimp, where's the hooker?" The diener challenged the others, and they looked up at him. "Just asking."

Dr. Henry looked grim. "We'll find her in a bayou next week, probably. They would've tossed her in somewhere after they were done with her. But warm as it's been, it won't take long for her to float. You can bet on it. If the gators don't get to her first."

The diener, with all his experience, looked queasy. "Jesus. Sorry I asked."

"What do you mean?" asked the photographer.

"I mean she'll float. Her body will fill up with gas and she'll just pop right up. Not pretty." At that, the photographer blanched and took another step backward.

"Look, let's just get through this." Dr. Henry stepped on the foot pedal to start the dictation machine again. "Stab wounds to neck and thorax. Left side, count three wounds, maximum depth four point two inches. Carotid artery severed."

It took Dr. Henry over two hours to describe all his findings on the three victims, and for the photographer to capture images of all the wounds. The diener took fingerprints, blood samples and swabs as Dr. Henry directed, in hopes the pathologists could identify anything. There was, however, no doubt as to the cause of death for all three victims.

When Dr. Henry finished, he placed a call to the police department. He spoke with the chief for several minutes, describing the most pertinent details. "The stab wounds have a square cross-section," he concluded. "I'm convinced this must be some kind of Chinese weapon. You'd better send the undercover guys out to hunt through those voodoo shops again – see what they've been importing along with their fridge magnets. I'll have the written report to you tomorrow."

The team completed the autopsies and closed the body cavities. The diener covered the corpses and wheeled them back into the cooler. Dr. Henry finished dictating his autopsy report and uploaded the audio into the queue for transcription. Tomorrow it would be filed with the city, the state and the FBI.

In a small town in Utah a medical transcriptionist named Lucy Blaylock downloaded the audio of Dr. Henry's autopsy report from the transcription service she worked for. It turned out to be an interesting case, three murders in the same bar in New Orleans.

Lucy worked from home at night after her boys were in bed. The job didn't pay well, but she could do it while the kids were asleep, and the reports would be ready for signature in the morning. Nowadays they wanted fast turnaround, and unless you're willing to work Indian hours, you don't get any work at all. Indian pay, too, practically. She was paid by the line – they called it "incentive pay." But what choice did she have?

Lucy had been supporting herself and her family ever since her divorce. She had a bachelor's degree in bioscience, but that was the last thing this little town needed. She had followed her college sweetheart to this godforsaken place, had three kids, and then everything fell apart. Her husband became distant and abusive. After several attempts to patch things up, she finally decided to file for divorce. He had money and she didn't, which is why she battled his lawyer in court, by herself, pro se. Of course, the result was that she was outmaneuvered by her husband's attorney. To avoid paying child support, he insisted on joint custody. The judge ruled in his favor, which meant that the divorce settlement restricted her from moving anywhere. If she did, she'd lose custody of the kids completely. So, year in and year out, she stuck it out in this place she called Bumfuck, Utah.

For the first few months after their divorce, her husband would take the kids when it was his turn, returning them unbathed and hungry, and carrying their dirty clothes in a bag for her to launder. After half a year, the kids told Lucy they didn't want to live with their dad at all. She went back to court to claim full custody, but lost again to his aggressive lawyer. So here she was, caring for them morning and afternoon, sleeping while they were at school, and trying to make a living by typing all night.

After typing Dr. Henry's report, Lucy uploaded it, smiling at the hefty line count. At 8 cents per line, that would mean she'd earned – she worked it out – $10.20 for the last hour. Her face fell. *Shit. I'll never pay for the propane now.* She could see the gauge on the propane tank outside her kitchen window, and it looked like maybe a week's worth was left. She thought about finding a second job, one that she could do while the boys were in school. OK, maybe she could work the lunch line at their school. Maybe she could sleep for three hours in the morning before going to work at the school, and another three hours in the afternoon. Then take care of the kids when they came home, and type all night. That'd work, sure. She felt an ache in her throat. Then she put her head in her hands and gave in to tears. After a couple minutes, her sobbing slowed. Then she looked up, saw the time, and got back to work.

After uploading her typed transcripts to the service, Lucy printed a copy of the pertinent parts of the New Orleans medical examiner's report on onionskin paper. She did not include victims' names or even the examiner's name, just the location and the findings that could cue law enforcement to identify a modus operandi. She did the same with several other reports from other cities, printing just the essential parts on onionskin. Sometimes she printed the toxicology report in a poisoning; sometimes it was the location and details of wounds in an obvious murder. She added the rest of her autopsy reports from all over – Los Angeles, New York, Houston – all of them describing unique methods of murder. Lucy liked to think of herself as a counterintelligence agent, collecting all the data that law enforcement had, allowing her sisters to always stay one jump ahead of the law.

Since she was an expert transcriptionist, working for an agency that understood the value of specialization, it hadn't been hard to create a niche handling homicide autopsies. Other women she had mentored had done the same. Together, they created a hidden conduit of information from across the country, all flowing to its central destination.

She pulled out a yellow card-shaped envelope and addressed it to Maybelle Barker in a small town in Arkansas. She had a stash of these old colored envelopes from when she worked stocking cards in convenience stores, another starvation job. But waste not, want not – this big box of dog-eared envelopes was just what she needed now. And that old box of onionskin paper, saved from her mother's house when she died, that was handy now, too. That stuff dated back to carbon copy days, but it allowed her to pack a lot of pages into a birthday card. Just before she sealed the envelope, she stopped. She jotted a quick message on a sticky note: *Please send more seeds.* She planted it front and center on the sheaf of papers.

She sealed the envelope and put it in her purse to post from a box tomorrow. Last, after checking that the transcription service had received her work, she deleted any trace of the reports from her computer. Despite the espionage she was engaged in, or maybe because of it, she was very careful to adhere to HIPAA rules. She closed her computer down and yawned. A good night's work.

Chapter 4 – Washington, D.C.

At the FBI Washington Field Office, in the Office for Public Affairs, a middle-aged secretary named Mary Anderson typed out her minutes from the strategy session of the Office of Public Affairs. The meeting had been called to review crime statistics in urban centers. Chicago was the center of attention because of the gang violence. As a result of the strategy session, a press release would be prepared about combatting youth gangs in Chicago and L.A.

Toward the end of the meeting, the last presenter mentioned reports of isolated armed robberies and murders of johns in urban red-light districts. These incidents had been reported in a few cities nationwide. Mary's boss, Doug Williamson, the Assistant Director of the Office of Public Affairs, started to pick up his papers and remarked, "No news there."

The speaker continued. "Some of these murders have taken place in upscale downtown development areas, even close by convention centers. There's no identifiable common modus operandi. So far, the Uniform Crime Reporting Program has determined was that these are random crimes, not the work of serial killers."

Mary, taking the meeting minutes, listened carefully. There was a brief mention of the Bourbon Street Slasher but no specific news from LA, New York, Houston or the many other cities she guessed the sisters worked in. *So it hasn't filtered up here at all – good job, ladies.*

After the meeting wrapped up, Mary stepped outside at 10 a.m. sharp for a smoke break, although she didn't smoke. She went out to meet up with her friend Samantha, who worked in the

Criminal Investigative Division. Mary wore a nondescript tan raincoat over her business suit, as it was still chilly in D.C. in March. Her short gray hair was covered with a scarf.

Sam looked full of news and grinned at Mary. "The latest dashboard shows sex trafficking dropping off in *all* of the major cities – wait'll I show you the graph." She tapped her purse. "Well, except L.A. There's still a huge flow of girls from Mexico. Those poor kids."

"Same old shit," Mary nodded. "Some slick asshole promises them school or nanny work with a rich family. Before they know it, they're riding a truck north and they wind up in Los Angeles, strung out on crack and whoring away in some back room."

"Yeah, that is the truth. They can't go to the cops 'cause they're illegals. Nobody even knows they're here. And a year later they're dead, either overdosed, beat up by their pimps, or they kill themselves. We seriously need to fix this shit."

"Well, let's get at it. Give me what you got." Sam stubbed out her smoke and the women walked back inside to the ladies' room. They went into adjacent stalls and Sam wordlessly passed Mary the charts under the stall wall. Mary stuffed them in her purse and the women left separately.

Back at her desk on her lunch break Mary pulled out her seed company catalog. She loved leafing through the lush photos of perennials and shrubs. This company was an old-fashioned nursery somewhere in Arkansas that specialized in heirloom vegetables and gave out personal gardening advice. She pulled the order form from the center of the catalog and carefully filled it out. She ordered some ornamental grasses, and in the Comments box noted that she wanted to change the look of her New Orleans style garden this year to something not quite as showy, more native. She also wrote that she had decided not to change her other plantings this year – they were blending well. Then in the Ask the Gardener section she asked for advice for a persistent weed that she recognized from her visit to L.A., some kind of invasive species coming up from Mexico.

"Looks like we have a resistant strain here, she wrote. "It's especially showing up in urban areas, towns and cities. I saw it when I was out there. Do you know how this is spreading? What can we do to wipe it out?"

She laid the line graphs Samantha had passed her under a blank sheet of tracing paper. Using colored markers, she carefully traced the lines, then labeled each line discreetly with initials to identify cities. She titled the drawing "My Garden." Her sketch appeared to show the various heights of plantings and how they followed the slope of her hill down to the right. One line, however, slanted upward, and she labeled it "L.A. weed problem!" in red. Then she slipped Sam's charts into her purse. Later that day she would burn them in her fireplace at home. Doug Williamson walked in and she smiled brightly at him as she folded the order form into its envelope.

"Getting my seed order in for spring!" she chirped. He smiled indulgently and asked her for coffee and the meeting minutes.

"Right away, sir." She hurried to type out the meeting minutes, making no note of the speaker's last comments before the meeting ended, about the murders at convention centers. She was sure that Williamson wouldn't notice the omission.

Chapter 5 – Ozarks

At dawn, Bonnie's pickup turned the last corner of the mountain road and bounced into the Barkers' front yard. As she opened the door and let the dog jump out over her, Jamie savored the smell of lilacs. It brought back memories of long spring days spent wandering the hills and building forts in the underbrush or high up in trees, safe places where girls could play undisturbed. As a child, she and her friends used to spy on people or create trigger traps to warn them if people were approaching. Who knew those tricks would come in handy now?

Jamie picked up her backpack and headed up to the porch, then turned back, offering, "You need some help there?" as Bonnie struggled with the old pickup's tailgate latch.

"I got it." The tailgate crashed down. "But help me with them crates up in there." Bonnie jumped up into the pickup bed, pulled back the canvas tarp and handed down the empty wooden crates to Jamie. She pointed, "Pile 'em on that wheelbarrow and tote 'em up to the barn. We'll be fillin' 'em again this year, for sure!"

Jamie loaded the fruit crates on the wheelbarrow and pushed it up the slope and into the barn. Inside, the space was cavernous, and the dusty air was shot with sunbeams coming through the chinks in the siding. She saw the swallows' nests high up in the rafters and guessed there were young ones up there, from the chittering and swooping of the birds. She sniffed the fresh hay smell and closed her eyes for a moment. Then she opened her eyes and got to work. She added the crates to the tall stack already there and went back for more, until the pickup was empty.

Bonnie jumped down and slammed the tailgate shut.

"Well, come here, gal, give me a real hug." Bonnie gathered Jamie into her arms and kissed her, then held her for a long moment with their cheeks together. She pulled back and ran her hand through Jamie's hair. Jamie reached up and cupped the back of Bonnie's neck. They looked hard into each other's eyes. Bonnie's searching stare dissolved into a grin and they hugged again.

Jamie wrinkled her nose. "Phew, I stink. I need a bath."

"Me, too, honey. Let's go swimmin'."

"Well, I need to go in and say hi to Maybelle and the kids. It's time they got up. And I'm hungry."

Jamie picked up her backpack and skateboard and lugged them uphill toward the house. It was a long, low, rambling place. The paint was peeling in places and the porch steps were worn smooth. A large lilac bush, covered with blossoms, leaned out over the yard. The old dog, fed and watered now, slept in its shade.

Further back, between the house and the barn, stood the dovecote, a small round tower built of native limestone blocks, cut smooth and fitted tightly. A band of smooth adobe circled the tower near the top to keep the cats and weasels out. Above that, the pigeonholes were full of nesting birds, brooding on clusters of eggs. The air was thick with their thrumming.

Jamie stepped up on the porch of the house and the screen door opened. Maybelle stood in the doorway in her housedress and folded the girl into her arms. Maybelle's face was creased with sunburn and wrinkles, and her gray hair was gathered into a bun. She was of medium height and somewhat stout, and she moved stiffly on arthritic knees.

"Glad you're back safe, honey, so glad you're back safe."

"Aw heck, Maybelle, you know I can take care of myself –
that town was easy compared to some. How are the little ones?"
She walked in and peered around the kitchen looking for
something to eat.

"Go wake 'em yourself and wash up. I'll put breakfast on."
Maybelle grunted and turned back to the stove.

Jamie walked back through the narrow hallway to the kids'
rooms. "Hey, y'all, get on up outta bed. Your gramma's got
cornbread on."

She was met by screams and two little kids piled out of bed
and knocked her over. "Jamie, Jamie, Jamie! Jamie's home!"
She rolled around with them on the floor, then pushed them off,
sizing them up. The littlest one, Ellie, was a pretty black 4-year-
old girl, a former foster child whom Maybelle and Jim had
adopted. Buddy was a gangly 6-year-old boy, another adoptee,
the son of Maybelle's niece. His mother had, several years ago,
succumbed to an opiate overdose, and Jim and Maybelle, his
only living relatives, had taken him in.

"You two are growin' so fast, I hardly knew who you were!
My goodness!" Jamie looked up at Arlene, who had just
appeared in the doorway. Arlene was the teenager in the family,
Maybelle and Jim's granddaughter. "And you are getting taller
by the minute, honey! How did that happen?"

Arlene blushed and fidgeted. "I don't know, Auntie. It just
happened."

Little Ellie, rocking on Jamie's lap, held her nose and hooted,
"Ooo Jamie you stink."

"Yeah, you do!" Buddy let out a whistle. At that, Arlene
laughed.

"Don't mind him, Auntie. He just learned to whistle and he
has to show it off all the time."

Jamie pushed the kids off. "Give me a break, we've been driving all night. I'll wash up after breakfast." She led them all back to the kitchen and over to the slate sink. She grabbed a dishcloth and pumped water onto it, gave each little face a swipe, then ran the rag over her own face and around her neck. "Arlene, you set the silverware and I'll get the plates. Quick now."

The little kids scrambled into their chairs as Arlene set out forks and knives and Jamie set down plates and plastic cups. She poured cider while Maybelle dished out breakfast: cornbread with syrup, grits, ham and eggs. Plenty! Jamie hadn't eaten food this good in a long time. Bonnie came into the kitchen and poured coffee for the women, then joined them at the table.

Jamie looked around. "Still a lot of empty chairs. When are the rest coming in?"

"Jim's off fetching Ta'quisha and Anita's picking up Angela. That's all we've heard from yet. But they'll be here. Some we'll get at the Greyhound tomorrow." Maybelle leaned on the table and sat down heavily. "Oof, these knees of mine. Glad some of y'all are back to do some work for a change. Can't keep doin' it all myself, you know."

Jamie grinned and winked at Bonnie across the table. "Not right yet we ain't. We got some catchin' up to do."

"But Jamie, can you fix my hair?" Arlene begged.

"Mine too!" Buddy echoed.

"Okay, all three of you," Jamie sighed. The she clapped her hands. "Take your dishes to the sink and get that syrup off your hands."

They rushed to comply, drying their hands on their shirts. Then they scrambled back to the bedroom, Arlene herding the

26

two younger kids down the hall. Jamie collected beads and barrettes, then sat down on the springy braid rug with Ellie in front of her. Bonnie leaned on the doorway, amused.

Jamie glanced up at her. "Well, don't just stand there, give me a hand!" With a shrug, Bonnie sat down and brushed the other kids' hair before Jamie finished the styles. Arlene got her blond hair arranged in two reverse French braids that fell down her back, finished with bows of black velvet ribbon. Ellie's springy black hair was transformed into a neat maze of cornrows and braids with a bead on the end of each one. Buddy's hair was sculpted with scissors into a short cut except for an exaggerated Tintin topknot dressed with olive oil.

"Lucky you kids don't have to go to school down the valley," said Jamie as she stood up. "You can wear your hair however you want and nobody's going to make fun of you." They admired themselves in the mirror. The two youngest started arguing.

"Okay, okay!" Jamie laughed, "Next time I'll cut Arlene's hair short, put cornrows on Buddy and two long braids on Ellie. How's that?"

Bonnie smiled and clapped her hands. "And now it's time for y'all to get reading. Get your books and get on back out to Gramma. Jamie and me need to get goin'."

Bonnie had a towel wrapped around soap and shampoo, and she grabbed Jamie's hand and pulled her out the back door. They trotted down the path, laughing.

"Gotta run faster'n them kids if ya wanna be alone!"

It was half a mile to the river and another quarter mile upstream to the swimming hole. Bonnie and Jamie had helped build it ages ago, and the rocks still held – well, except in one spot where a boulder had tumbled down, allowing a sluice of water to escape.

"I been waiting for you to get here," Bonnie said, "I couldn't lift it myself." They looked around in the woods for a sapling and cut it down with the hatchet Bonnie carried. They cut it into two poles. Then they stripped out of their clothes and hunkered down with the poles levered under the rock.

"One, two, three, heave!" The boulder rolled obediently back into place, damming the stream again. They rolled a few more limestone rocks into place as reinforcement. Finally, the women climbed over the wall and sank into the deep pool above it. Jamie's blonde hair fanned out and floated around her head as she gazed up through the leaves. *Jesus, this is livin'!* Bonnie dipped under and came up, flinging a high arc of water from her dark hair.

"So how y'all been all winter? Did you miss me?"

"Honey, I been achin' for you. And I've been real careful. Always used condoms, always had gloves on, never got no needle sticks, never even cut myself, which was a piece of work considering how them pigs squealed and flopped around. My body is my temple." Jamie smiled and did a slow turn, then laughed and fell back into the water.

"And a real purty one at that. Come on over here and let me wash your hair." Bonnie sat on a rock with the water up to her waist, while Jamie nestled into her lap and let her massage the shampoo into her hair. Bonnie's hands kneaded Jamie's neck. "My lord, gal, you got some knots here. Let me work that out." She hummed and stroked Jamie's neck and shoulders, then slid her hands down her arms and breasts. "Come on up here in the sunshine, sweetheart."

They dipped under one more time, then waded to the shore hand in hand. They both slipped on the clay bank and splashed down. "Ah shit, that gets me every time. I gotta remember to get out over yonder."

Jamie threw her head back and laughed aloud. "You are a sight! Look at your butt!"

"Yeah, what about my butt?"

"Well it's kinda slimy now."

"Show me." Bonnie turned her butt toward Jamie, who reached out and stroked the wet clay down both hips and between them.

"Come on, come on, quit playin'."

"What's your hurry? I'm gonna make you wait for it. I'm in charge now."

Later they lay on their backs. Bonnie turned on her hip and grinned at Jamie. "Damn, that was worth waiting for."

"You look like some kinda hoodoo. What a mess!"

They slipped back into the water and rinsed off the clay, then washed again and stepped out on the other side of the stream where the rock shelf was smooth and warm in the sun. They rolled the towel up as a pillow and shared it, heads together and bodies spread out on the rock. They dozed as the trees sighed overhead and the sun twinkled through the new leaves.

Jamie opened her eyes. Then she sat up, arms stiff behind her, and stared past Bonnie into the woods, her eyes open but not seeing.

Bonnie rolled over and watched Jamie for a minute. Finally she asked, "What's goin' on?"

Jamie looked at her. "Nothin'...." And lay back down.

Bonnie moved over and cradled Jamie's head on her thigh. She stroked her hair and started to knead her shoulders again. "Tell me what it is."

"I wisht I didn't kill the bartender."

"What happened? Tell me about it."

Jamie's voice was low. "I meant to kill that fat bastard. And I sure as hell meant to kill that pimp." She paused. "But the bartender...?" Her voice trailed off.

"What did you know about him?"

"I didn't know much. I don't know if he had a family or anything. Maybe he did. Maybe he treated some woman nice. But he sure was an asshole to me." She went on. "He himself, he wasn't abusing anybody. But he was givin' them a place to do it. I don't know." She paused again. "I keep thinking, wondering if there was any way to leave him out of it."

"You're tellin' me he was part of the setup there," Bonnie countered. He's part of the chain we're tryin' to break. If he was getting' money from it, he's guilty."

"Well, yeah, he was."

"And he was a witness."

"Yeah, he was."

"So he had to die. We can't leave no witnesses."

Jamie's mouth was a grim line. She moved her head off Bonnie's lap and rolled over on her belly, head faced away, eyes closed.

"Hey, come on, honey," Bonnie cajoled. She reached out.

Jamie slapped Bonnie's hand away and withdrew further. Bonnie sat still.

Several minutes passed.

Finally, Jamie lifted her head. Bonnie was staring at her, a stricken look on her face. Jamie melted. "Oh hell, girl, it's not your fault. If it's anybody's fault, it's mine. I coulda planned it better."

"Well, I'm thinkin' that woulda been close to impossible." Bonnie paused. "But I get it. You don't wanna hurt anybody you don't have to."

"No...I don't. But shit!" Jamie sat up, angry. "There were girls who died, young girls, 'causa these assholes. All over the Quarter, dyin'..." Her eyes filled. "No, I'm not sorry. Not at all. Goddammit. I want to scare the shit out of 'em. So they never touch a young girl again. And they never let a pimp into their joint again." Her finger stabbed the air. "That there was his fault, goddammit."

Bonnie stayed silent.

"You know what I want to do? I want to make it so that every man who thinks about steppin' out thinks twice. I want him to think that any piece of ass, any woman or child even, might just kill him. For no reason. Rip! – that's it! He's gone!" Jamie grimaced and looked away.

Bonnie reached out. "Shhh, shhh. It's okay." This time Jamie didn't flinch back, but neither did she move closer. "We do get revenge," Bonnie whispered. "That's what we do. Remember that."

Jamie rolled over and laid her head on her arms and closed her eyes again. Bonnie sat there and watched her, at a loss. *Leave it be, leave it be.*

The morning sun sifted down through the early foliage onto the two women, who lay still. Jamie slept, while Bonnie stared at the treetops. There was no sound but the chitter of spring peepers and the deep *glunk* of a bullfrog.

Chapter 6 – Ozarks

The blacksmith forge was some distance behind Maybelle and Jim's house, behind the greenhouse and barn, set away from the other buildings in a clearing of its own. This farm was settled by folks from the old country, who knew how a stray spark could threaten nearby roofs. There wasn't so much danger of that now, since the cedar shake roofs had been replaced with corrugated tin. Still, the distance from the house and barn also muffled the sound of the forge, and kept the toxic dust away from the kids.

Babs, the blacksmith, was hard at work forging a new weapon, a knife with a wicked edge. Babs was tall and muscular, almost masculine looking, especially behind the leather apron and the face shield. Adding to that image was her very short haircut, almost a buzz cut. If you'd asked her, though, Babs would tell you that haircut was a safety measure. But she'd say it with a smirk and a bit of a challenge in her eye. A challenge that told you not to challenge her.

The blade of the knife she was working on was made of nickel and iron forged together. The two metals were heated and pounded out, folded, pounded out, folded, again and again. The process was long and exhausting, but it yielded beautiful pattern welds in almost iridescent stripes. A blade forged in this way could bend and spring back, making it indestructible in close combat. As a final touch, Babs tempered the knife to a fine hardness and honed it to a razor-sharp edge. She always made the hilt of the knife broad, to protect the thrusting hand and allow the knife to be twisted and pulled out. This knife would never snap inside a body and leave evidence behind, and the unique cross-section would again baffle the medical examiners. Babs smiled and quenched the blade.

Babs stepped out into the air and pulled off her safety glasses and mask. She called to her apprentice, "Take a break!" Kelly, her apprentice, stopped pulling and eased the bellows chain up, then came out the door as she pulled off her own mask. The huge bellows sank down, its last gasp of air scattering sparks from the forge. The women tossed off their leather aprons, walked over to the well and drew water, pumping it over their heads and into their mouths.

"Man, my feet are hot, too," Kelly complained. She was shorter than Babs, but just as muscular. She stood unsteadily, blinking in the sunshine. Her face was red as a beet.

"Well, take off your boots for a minute. Nobody says we have to die of the heat." Babs peered closely at Kelly. "Say, you don't look so good. Sit down." Babs grabbed up a t-shirt from the bench outside the door and wet it down, then wiped Kelly's neck and arms. "Okay, lie down." She laid the wet t-shirt on Kelly's chest, examined her face, then dashed down the path toward the barn.

She swung around the corner and grabbed a rope hanging at the corner of the barn. Overhead, a large brass bell swung and tolled. Faces appeared at the door of the house.

"Heatstroke!" Babs yelled, "Help me carry her."

Arlene dashed out of the house. Maybelle followed as fast as her knees would allow. They followed Babs back up the path to the shop, and as they came out into the clearing, Bonnie and Jamie, summoned by the bell, dashed from the path on the other side. Between them they lifted Kelly's limp form and carried her down to the cattle trough in the pen. They stripped off her clothes and lowered her into the water. Her eyes opened and she struggled with them. Then she relaxed and sank back into the cool bath.

"Easy now," said Maybelle, "cool down now." She held up Kelly's head and continued to daub her face with the wet t-shirt. Arlene found a dipper and poured water over her hair. After a while, Kelly's red face turned to white and she started to shiver.

"Okay, get her out now," said Maybelle, and they heaved her out and lay her on the grass in the shade. One of the women went to fetch a towel. Arlene got a glass of clean water and held it to Kelly's lips, while Jamie lifted her up to drink.

"How much water have you been drinking?" demanded Babs. Kelly rolled her eyes at her and mumbled. Babs asked more slowly, "How much water did you get?" When Kelly didn't answer Babs marched back to the shop and looked around the bellows for Kelly's water bottle. She found it and grabbed it up.

Back under the tree by the barn, Babs held the water bottle up so Kelly could see it. "Half full. How many times have you filled it this morning?"

"Just the once," Kelly admitted. "I'm sorry."

"Well, I'm sorry, too. I should have reminded you to drink more. It was my fault. I was on a roll and I forgot about you." Babs took Kelly's hand.

Kelly, wrapped in the towel, squeezed Babs's hand back. "It's okay. I learned my lesson. Can I have my clothes back?"

Maybelle, embarrassed for Kelly, handed her clothes to her. "You'd better lie down for a while. How's your head feel?" Then turning, with a gesture of her hand and a look on her face, she shooed the others away.

"Wait a second," interrupted Babs. "I need some help. I'm out an apprentice for this afternoon." She looked around at the women's faces and her eyes fell on Arlene, her hand raised tentatively, fingers wiggling with excitement. "Well, what are you grinning at? Tuck those pretty braids up, get a water bottle of your own, and let's see if that mask will fit you. With your permission, Gramma." Arlene twirled around to face Maybelle, her eyes bright.

"Well, all right," Maybelle sighed and shook her head. "Book learning can take a break today. And we did agree that once she was tall enough, she could start. And here she is, 13 years old last week." She nodded to Babs. "She's all yours. But I want to hear her recite the safety rules for the forge before she goes in there."

Maybelle set her hand on Arlene's shoulder and sent her toward the house. "And go get your boots, girl. You sure can't go in there barefoot."

That afternoon the work in the forge continued at a brisk pace, with Arlene manning the bellows and Babs working at the anvil. Several more knives were fashioned, each with a different profile. Three of the blades were simply reforged into a different cross-section while the handles remained the same, a procedure which saved some time. By the end of the afternoon, they had made six new untraceable knives.

The last project of the afternoon was simpler – melting down gold. Babs placed necklaces and rings into a crucible and maneuvered it into the forge with tongs. Then she took a turn at the bellows, while Arlene took a break outside. When the gold had melted, she poured it into a mold with small, unmarked, ingot-shaped cavities. This was left to cool while the two walked down the hill toward the big hall for dinner.

"Well, what did you think of that?" Babs asked Arlene. "Was it as exciting as you thought it would be, working in the forge?"

"Well, maybe not," answered Arlene as she rubbed her tired shoulders. "At least not that part. I want to learn to forge. Pumping bellows is too hard."

Babs laughed. "Well, that's the way in, sweetheart. Until your arms are built up you can't hope to swing a hammer. Stick with it and when you're strong enough, we'll teach you the other stuff. But you at least know one thing – the safety rules. And how much water to drink."

"Yeah, okay. Can I come back tomorrow?"

Babs smiled. She had another apprentice.

Chapter 7 – Washington, D.C.

Two weeks later, back at the FBI Office for Public Affairs, Mary Anderson sat across from her boss, Doug Williamson, listening to him describe the problem of conference cancellations. His pasty face grew red as he pontificated, stabbing his desk with his finger.

"National and international conferences are the lifeblood of American cities. Every trade organization and every academic discipline holds them, every year. We can't have people murdered when they go to conferences and go out for a little fun! This is a multi-billion-dollar industry, and the media is starting to report these incidents. If we can't put a lid on it, Congress will call for an investigation of what's going on." He glared at Mary across his desk.

"Yes sir, Mr. Williamson, how can I help?" Mary asked.

"I want you to put together a webinar and audioconference with FBI regional directors from New Orleans, LA and New York City. I want this to happen this month. We need to appoint a task force. We need a strategy. For crissake, the election is coming up this year. That's a hell of a lot of people coming to the major cities. Hell, they're going to be swarming over Iowa and New Hampshire. Everyplace they go, they'll be looking for some fun. How in hell are we going to keep 'em safe?"

Mary asked him to name the directors he wanted to bring in. He replied that he wanted representation from every city over 600,000 in the U.S. "Oh, and Anchorage and Honolulu," he added. *What the hell*, she thought, *does he think I can work miracles?* She sighed. *Well, maybe I can.*

She went back to her office and clicked into the secure FBI personnel database. She opened the shared calendaring system to do a preliminary schedule check. Then she printed out the names, phone numbers and contact information of the admin assistants in each region's FBI field offices. One of them she had to research to find.

Mary used her next break with Samantha to ask if she knew the admin assistant she was looking for, a woman named Deborah. Sure enough, Sam could vouch for her.

"I know her. She is a sister. Don't worry."

After her break, Mary got to work and ran a preliminary calendar screen. Then she called each of the admin assistants, adding them to the conference call one by one until they were all connected. They worked through the calendars until they found a two-hour block of time, five weeks away, when most of the directors could meet via webinar and audioconference. When the call was over, Mary made a contact group of all the assistants for later communications. Then she sent a memo to them, listing the details of the upcoming audioconference, including the time in all six time zones, so they could add it to their bosses' calendars. She promised briefing papers soon on the background of the request.

As each of the assistants received Mary's memo, they reserved conference rooms and ordered audiovisual assistance. They drew up lists of those who should attend, and started blocking calendars. In the Office of Public Affairs here in Washington, Mary knew she could rely on her friend Tammy, the AV tech, to set up the conference room with a recording device to capture every word.

At their next one-on-one, Mary asked Williamson if she should solicit agenda items from the meeting invitees, and he agreed.

She smiled as she thought how easy it was to gather intelligence in her position. She was the liaison and organizer, the assistant who puts the important people in the room.

And Mary knew there were tens of thousands of women like her. For every executive in a corner office, there is a Gal Friday who keeps his life running, and who has access to every secret memo and the minutes of every closed-door meeting. As a matter of fact, she probably is the secretary in the room who records and transcribes the minutes and composes the agendas. Mary smiled. She imagined a vast army of intelligent but underpaid sisters inside practically every office of government and business. She knew where their loyalties lay, and it wasn't with their bosses, that's for sure. When talking to each other, they never gossiped about their bosses because they didn't need to – they could practically read each other's minds.

The few assistants who held actual loyalty to their bosses were easy to detect. Their second-hand snobbery and deluded protectionism came across in their voices. Some were even high-profile spokeswomen, spouting their bosses' lies as if somehow they were more credible coming out of a pretty female mouth. Mary avoided dealing with those ones if she could. If she had to work with them, she manipulated them with subtle flattery. *Funny how flattery works*, she thought. *The more a man thinks of himself, the blinder he is to manipulation. And when his assistant lives in his reflected glory, she can be flattered just as easily.*

With the summit meeting scheduled, Mary concentrated on sussing out who would be picked to run the task force. Of course, a task force would be necessary – nothing happened in the FBI without a slew of meetings. Her job was to run through the resumes of the likely candidates, and schedule them for interviews. Mostly men, of course, but with a few women sprinkled in, even a few women of color. The hiring protocols required diversity at the interview stage. Mary hated calling them to come in. She felt horrible doing it, setting up false hopes in people, knowing that the task force director chosen would always be male, always white, always full of himself. After all, as Williamson reminded her, it's important that the new guy fit into FBI culture.

On break the next day, Samantha scoffed at Mary's news about the new task force.

"So they're starting to notice that the johns and pimps are getting offed. That's big news. Not the epidemic of children being sucked into sex trafficking in the first place. Well, let them pull all their intelligence together, and we'll know what they have."

"We'll know it before they have time to analyze it themselves," Mary added. "And get this: they've already done the hard work of coming up with an acronym. Well, actually, Mr. Williamson gave it to me to do, so I suggested we call it the Operation for National Entertainment Venue Recovery and Renewal. The short title is Operation NEVRR." Mary grinned. "He liked it. On the report, I'll subtitle it Protective Policing of Entertainment in Conference Cities and Resorts."

Sam's mouth opened. "P-PECCR! Damn, you're good! Once it's printed, it'll be too late." She threw back her head and laughed.

Mary spent the rest of the afternoon sifting through resumes for the task force lead position. She put together a folder of the best candidates; that is, the ones she knew Williamson would look favorably on. Some were career FBI staff, and some were MBAs from outside the agency. She had a hunch that Williamson would favor the new MBAs. They were always more glib and articulate, and he favored those skills over technical crime-solving expertise. After all, this was the Office of Public Affairs, not the Intelligence Branch. By the end of the day, she had a decent-sized sheaf of resumes, sorted in order of likelihood. She knew he'd only look at the first three or four, anyway.

Williamson had left for the day by the time Mary took the folder of resumes into his office. She placed it front and center on his desk with a sticky note identifying it. She also brought a handful of cruise schedules and left them on the end tables by the sofas in his office. She had marked a cruise to the Bahamas in the third week of September with a blank sticky tag.

Predictably, the next day Williamson noticed the brochures and picked them up. Before lunch, he approached Mary with the Bahamas brochure in his hand.

"I'd like you to call my wife and tell her about this cruise. Get her to check her calendar, then book us on it. September would be a great time to get out of town," he chuckled, "because we don't have to take the kids along." Mary mirrored his chuckle.

Mary dutifully called his wife, who sounded thrilled and agreed to the cruise. Mary proceeded to make all the arrangements and reservations, and delivered a complete itinerary, starting at his very doorstep, to her boss.

The following day, it was Mary's turn to inform Williamson of her vacation plans.

"I'll take the same two weeks you're taking off. You wouldn't want to have to use a sub from the typing pool, I'm sure. And I wouldn't want to inconvenience you in any way. This will work out well for both of us."

Williamson agreed with Mary, impressed once again that she seemed to read his mind so well, and accommodate to his schedule so willingly.

Mary didn't need to use the story she'd prepared – that she'd be going to a harvest folk festival in Tennessee. Since her boss didn't ask, she didn't have to use that fib. *Always better to give no information than to lie,* she mused. *Mark Twain had it right: "If you tell the truth, you don't have to remember anything."*

Mary's actual plan, of course, was to meet with Maybelle Barker and the others at the farm in the Ozarks in September. By that time, she would have learned all there was to know about Operation NEVRR. She planned to take details of the FBI's strategy with her to that meeting, tucked in the corners of her mind. *A college education is never wasted,* she thought to herself.

Chapter 8 – Washington, D.C.

The Operation NEVRR summit webinar and audioconference went off as planned. Doug Williamson used the first half hour to outline the problem. Several recent sensational stories of murders in convention cities had caught the public's eye, in Los Angeles, New Orleans and Las Vegas. In each case, it was suspected that the victims had engaged prostitutes and had been robbed, although there was no other similarity between the cases. Murder weapons had not turned up, and in some cases the mode of death was difficult to discern. No useful DNA evidence had been found.

As usual with his presentations, Williamson had asked Mary to do the research, put it into a PowerPoint, and write his script for him. She enjoyed this part. To assemble the presentation, she created complex, uninterpretable Excel graphs, lots of them. The titles of the slides were long but acronym-heavy, as were the names of sources. She gave Williamson 45 slides to work through in his allotted half hour, so each slide was on the screen for less than a minute, not even time enough for his audience to comprehend the data presentation. She cut and pasted excerpts from news stories from all over the country, as well as from academic journals, much of the material irrelevant and obscure. It was a magnificent data dump, guaranteed to induce boredom. It was also guaranteed to feed that secret feeling of inadequacy that renders an audience mute.

For Williamson's script, Mary inserted plenty of multisyllabic jargon, Lean training terms and directive statements. As usual, the more bombastic and decisive he sounded, the more he liked what she'd written. There was a Task Force Mission Statement, a Smart Art network chart of participating government agencies, and a timeline with sequential objectives and deliverables. For each objective there was an assigned sponsor, a process owner, and various consultants from academia and business, all of them high-level.

Mary enjoyed the work of creating a presentation immensely, piling it on and ensuring that Williamson would run over time. Since he never rehearsed his presentations, running over was guaranteed. At the end of this presentation, she tasted success when he came to the end of his talk and asked for questions.

"We'll take questions if you have them. Let's go to the phones," announced Williamson. Mary signaled to Tammy, the AV tech, to unmute the phones. There was no sound.

"Are we connected?" asked Williamson. Tammy nodded. Nothing. He looked at her again.

"Yes, we are connected, Mr. Williamson." There was a long, uncomfortable silence from the unseen audience, with some clearing of throats. Then there was the unmistakable sound of a toilet flushing at the other end of the line.

"Well, then, if there are no questions, we'll just end with this," concluded Williamson hastily. "Operation NEVRR will be launched this month. We will distribute electronic copies of today's presentation to all of you. We will be in touch over the next few weeks about our new task force lead. Signing off." Williamson walked quickly away from the podium, his face red, leaving Mary to collect the thumb drive.

Back in her office, Mary smiled as she started on the report that would be published in two years' time, a further embellishment on today's work, but including the contributions of the participating agencies, all reproduced in their entirety and carefully indexed in the table of contents. The footnotes and bibliography would run to dozens of pages. She already had the illustrations assembled. The frontispiece would be a photo of a gleaming city skyline with a harbor in the foreground. This would cover two full pages, on glossy paper, with the 14-point text of the opening paragraph overlying the water. Inside the report would be artistic shots of restaurant meals, wine glasses, musical extravaganzas and casinos. The report would emphasize the safety, security and attractiveness of America's conference venues. She could write it today, she decided, and so she began.

Chapter 9 – Ozarks

The countryside eased into spring, and the days grew warmer on the mountain. The red dirt rose in clouds of dust as each new crew of women, as well as a few men, arrived at the Barker farm.

Jim Barker, Maybelle's husband, and Ta'quisha Alberts, one of the long-time residents, had arrived the last week of May with a school van full of girls and some boys, scooped up off the streets and from shelters in L.A. and other cities. Several shelters had sent selected women along. These girls would spend the summer working in the orchard and fields, eating on the porch of the big house, and sleeping in bunkhouses and smaller buildings across the field from the barn. The community of women on the farm would mother them back to health, with the assistance of a few medical students out of the University of Arkansas Medical School at Fayetteville. It was hoped that the hard work, clean air, fresh food and spring water would nourish their bodies and renew their spirits.

Meantime, in communities all over the country, elaborate and sometimes secret plans were being made to re-house the girls and women in the fall. Some would be guided toward citizenship and jobs in their new towns. Many would re-enter school. Tutors and coaches from local colleges would nudge them toward literacy and beyond. Some of the girls would be helped to emigrate to Canada. And some of the stronger ones would be allowed to go back to the cities they'd left. This time, though, they would not be left to the mercy of traffickers. This time, they'd be protected by cadres of women who would watch over them, who would raise them like their own daughters. Each year the network grew stronger.

On the farm, Arlene, in addition to her duties at the forge, was assigned to work with Malik Varayeva, a teenager who had traveled in with his older sister, Irina. They were orphans, refugees from the war in Chechnya, rescued on the streets of Newark, New Jersey, where both had been lured into the skin trade. They arrived on the farm with Angela, who drove down from New York City.

As Arlene started to work with him, Malik was silent and watchful, but obedient. Arlene demonstrated the work of tending the farm's small herd of dairy cows. Malik spoke little English, but Arlene gesticulated and pointed and he picked up the tasks quickly. Together the teens drove the cows and their calves out into the upper pasture in the morning, and brought them back to the milking barn in the afternoon.

Arlene taught Malik to watch out for bears and wolves on the mountain. Ever since these predators had been reintroduced to the Ozarks, they had become a menace to young calves and lambs. Two years ago, several lambs had been carried off, and since then the women had erected a fence around the upper pasture. Arlene and Malik patrolled the perimeter and checked that the wires were taut. Arlene carried her Grandpa Jim's lever action 45-70 rifle loaded with heavy shells. Buckshot wouldn't have been enough to stop even a small bear.

One day in late April, Malik found a curious tuft of coarse fur caught on the barbed wire, along with evidence of digging under the fence. The next day, he and Arlene made a hunting blind out of brush, downwind from that spot, and lay there for the whole afternoon. Just at dusk, as they were about to give up, they heard scuffling and grunting, and suddenly a family of feral hogs trotted into the clearing outside the enclosure. Arlene aimed and fired five times and dropped two giant hogs and a smaller shoat. The rest of them scrambled out of range. Together, Arlene and Malik rounded up the skittish cows and calves and drove them home, then rallied a crew of women and some wheelbarrows to harvest the pork.

Several women butchered the large hogs and boiled down the hides. The meat was hung in the smokehouse, where the fire was stoked with fresh apple wood.

The small shoat was spitted whole and roasted over an open pit the next evening. This became an occasion for celebration, a welcome break from the season's heavy work. Bottles of mead were broken out and platters of baby summer squash, greens and cornbread were laid out. The bread was spread with new butter and honey, and the celebrants ate until they were stuffed. Then they unpacked their guitars and drums and finger cymbals, and danced until the dew settled and the fire died.

Malik and Arlene stood together and accepted the women's thanks. When Malik's sister Irina bit into her serving of pork, she beamed at him and his eyes shone back with pride. Their healing had begun.

A month before, Irina, two years older than Malik, had started to work in the peach orchard. She had some knowledge of horticulture from growing up on their farm in Chechnya, and she surprised the orchard boss, Kristin, with her ability to graft branches onto rootstock. She also was good at pruning. She was tall and had good reach, so she set to work with the pruning shears. Her command of English was much better than Malik's, so she was able to teach the others some of the nuances of pruning. She emphasized opening up the center of the tree, and keeping the water sprouts and drooping branches trimmed right back to the scaffold branches. After a week of working with Kristin and two other women, Irina asked for more pruning tools. Kristin brought some of the teenagers and even some younger kids in to help. The orchard began to look better than it had in years.

Chapter 10 – New York

At BGS Capital Advisers, an investment firm in New York City, a hedge fund manager named Rick Gregory was in charge of several accounts. Some accounts bought and sold options on commodity grains like corn and soybeans, betting for or against weather scares in the Midwest. Before the recession ten years ago, several of the accounts he handled bundled mortgage contracts. Back then, home mortgages had been bunched together and sold as mortgage-backed securities to investors, and the same kind of bets could be placed for, or against, their future value. Rick joked with his assistant Sandy that there was no difference between a grain bin of soybeans and a city's worth of houses. Once they're poured into the same freight car, who cares where they came from? His job was to watch the markets and place his bets. To him, the farmers who grew the soybeans and the people who lived in the houses were so far below his line of sight as to be invisible.

His assistant, Sandy Smith, originally from Indiana, had a better idea of the contents of grain bins and small towns, but she hid her knowledge beneath an urbane exterior. She dressed well and smiled at Rick's jokes. She was decades older than him, but she had a deferential manner that conformed to what Rick, as a young MBA, expected.

Rick had graduated from the University of Pennsylvania's Wharton School of Management, the number-one ranked finance MBA program in the country, with several case competition wins and a good internship at Bear Stearns to his credit. At school, he had taken full advantage of the group project instruction style that was the norm at Wharton. At the beginning of every school term, he had sought out the foreign students with the best computational, research and analytic skills, and flattered them into joining his group. Then, as they divided up tasks, he offered to be the one who would do the final edit on the group project, and do the presenting in class. As the only native English speaker in the group, the editing and presentation tasks suited him best, and his partners knew it. They exchanged their research and analysis for his final polish and flashy presentation, and everybody was happy. He won his position at BGS Capital Advisors by using that same confident and polished persona, along with a bravura resume, and he bargained well for his salary and benefits.

Rick inherited his assistant Sandy from the previous hedge fund manager, and he relied on her research as he had on his partners' work in business school. Only this situation was even better, because with a little bit of flattery and a small raise, he figured he'd won Sandy over completely. He didn't even have to pretend to treat her as an equal. She served him well and was a credit to him in every situation.

One area in which Rick relied on Sandy was in the allocation of his profits to BGS's tax home on Grand Cayman in the Cayman Islands. The firm operated both in New York and on Grand Cayman, and a portion of the profits were declared in each location. Of course, it made sense tax-wise to declare the majority of profits offshore. In fact, BGS Capital Advisors had this division of profits down to a science, and Sandy was the one who directed where the money was deposited. When Rick first explained this scheme to Sandy, she had some reservations about it.

"I want you to declare 85% of BGS Capital's corporate profits as being earned in Grand Cayman, and 15% here in New York," Rick instructed Sandy. Then he thought a moment. "No, make that 95% in Grand Cayman and 5% here in New York. I think we can get away with that."

"Is that legal?" Sandy asked.

"Sure, it's legal. It's whatever we declare it to be," he answered, waving her away.

Sandy didn't venture to ask, *is that ethical?* That was a question that wasn't even relevant at this company. As they set up the corporate structure, the firm had even taken the precaution of incorporating under another name in the Grand Caymans; there it was called Flight Incorporated.

Sandy also had the task of shielding Rick Gregory's income. She declared Rick's salary income in Grand Cayman, and just a portion of his "unearned business income" in New York, thereby helping him to escape most federal and New York State income taxes. Rick relied on her skill to manage this allocation, and in fact he rarely examined her figures.

As a matter of fact, no one watched what Sandy did, as the Cayman Island accounts were beyond the reach of U.S. regulators or auditors. That is, they were not under scrutiny yet, but Sandy knew the day was coming when it would all come unraveled. Depending on who won the next election, new international banking laws were likely to be put in place that would make this kind of thing hard to hide. She knew she'd have to work fast to get her plan in place. *Luckily, I'm not alone*, she reminded herself.

In managing Flight Incorporated's finances, Sandy Smith worked directly with a woman named Maria Cruz, in the office in George Town, Grand Cayman. Several years back, after Maria and Sandy got to know each other, they found themselves sitting in Maria's kitchen, sharing a bottle of wine. They'd been talking about the poverty level on the smaller islands in the Caymans, and in cities across America. And they'd been speculating about how far the money they handled every day, Flight Incorporated's money, would go if it could be spread around. That day they determined to do something about it. *But how?*

"I'll show you how," said Maria. "Work this problem for me. What is $198,344 plus $72,240?" Sandy grabbed a pen and did the math on a napkin.

"Um, that's $270,584," answered Sandy. She looked at Maria quizzically.

"Good. Now what's $189,344 plus $72,240?" Maria asked. Sandy worked it out on her napkin again.

"It's $261,584. What are you getting at?"

"OK, now, what's the difference between $270,584 and $261,584?" Maria asked. "You can do that one in your head."

"The difference is $9000. So what?" Sandy asked.

"That's what we skim off when we turn around the 8 and the 9 in the first number. Simple. And defensible if it's ever caught." Maria smiled.

Sandy slowly nodded her head. She saw the genius of this method: a small transposition error, when multiplied by the billions of dollars that passed through their hands, would amount to a substantial sum. This time she didn't ask herself, *is it ethical?* She was prepared to do whatever it took to alleviate the crushing poverty they both saw.

From then on, as BGS Capital Advisors profits were wired to George Town, Maria deposited them in several banks, per Sandy's instructions. Most of the money went into Flight Incorporated's primary account. But Maria and Sandy had set up several secret accounts to absorb the revenue they skimmed off. After several years, growing in the secret accounts tax-free, it had become a real nest egg, and it was completely invisible. If one of the errors ever came to light, it could have been easily explained away. But the errors were infrequent and had never been noticed. Sandy and Maria were cautious and conservative. They never fell in love with the money itself, never got sucked into the allure of the game. They knew that the dollars were going to sisters who would use them frugally, so they didn't need tremendous amounts. By now, in fact, the interest alone on the money in their accounts had become quite a revenue stream.

In the meantime, BGS Capital Advisors management was content to let the offshore account, under the moniker of Flight Incorporated, accumulate most of the firm's wealth for now. It was possible that with the new administration in the White House, rules about repatriation of profits would be relaxed, and the treasure could be brought back to the U.S. without additional taxation. At least that was the promise... but why bother? After all, how long could the good times last? And why bring it back at all? For now, BGS was concerned about keeping the whole Cayman Islands operation off the radar of the U.S. Department of the Treasury, so communication between the New York and Grand Cayman offices was kept to a minimum.

Once a year, Sandy traveled with Rick Gregory to the office in George Town on Grand Cayman. This trip was booked as if it were a vacation, and Rick's family even came along. Sandy, being single, did not have anyone to bring, but she didn't mind. It left her more opportunity to meet with Maria privately. In packing for the trip, Sandy filled her checked bag with gifts for Maria's extended family, plus clothing and shoes for the orphanage on the island. At the check-in counter Rick had to lift the women's large suitcases onto the scale. He grunted as he lifted the luggage.

"Why do you women have to bring so much clothing? We're going on vacation, remember?"

"What, you want me to spend resort time doing laundry?" his wife shot back. "Get over it!"

Sandy merely smiled. Her big suitcase was for another purpose entirely.

On Grand Cayman, Sandy met with Maria while Rick took his family to the beach and played golf. Sandy and Maria went over the income from their secret accounts, and decided how much to disburse and to where. They sat together over coffee in Maria's apartment and wrote out a list.

"Let's send an anonymous gift to the Safe Harbor shelters in New York. How about two hundred thousand?" asked Sandy.

"Sounds okay to me. Can they use that much?"

"I'm sure they can. They have a dozen shelters just in the boroughs alone."

"Okay. But that's a lot of money to send all at once. Let's space that out some. And let's send some money to Chicago and LA as well. And Atlanta can use some."

Together they worked through the priorities, assigning money amounts to the various shelters and advocacy groups. Sandy had brought with her a handwritten list of shelters, their addresses, and notes she made about them. All of her information had been obtained through her on-the-ground contacts in the cities, and for each shelter she had the name of a trusted contact, a woman who would know what to do with a package of cash arriving from an anonymous source. And who would know not to expect such a windfall on a regular basis.

Sandy and Maria were careful not to set up a pattern that could entrap either themselves or their beneficiaries.

The last name on Sandy's list was Lucy Blaylock, a medical transcriptionist who lived and worked in a small town in the middle of Utah. The five thousand dollars they were sending to her would fill her propane tank and buy groceries for a few months. They figured this money would allow Lucy the latitude and time to train more transcriptionists to specialize in autopsies and pathology reports. To enlarge the sisters' intelligence network.

After making the list of what they planned to disburse, Sandy and Maria divided the total amount in two. At the bank Maria withdrew half of the funds from their secret accounts, and Sandy withdrew the other half. They still hadn't even touched the principal this year – it was still growing.

They took the cash back to Maria's apartment, divided it out, and packaged it up. The packages would be taken to the post office, a couple at a time, over the next week. The return address on the packages was a post office box rented under an assumed name. Maria handled the keys.

As they finished the last package, Maria folded her hands and looked at Sandy.

"We really should be wearing some pirate hats, you know."

"Ah, well, we can't be that obvious. But we can still have a jigger of rum, can't we?"

"Sweetheart, we can have a whole bottle." She stood up and went to get it.

During this year's visit, Sandy and Maria also finalized their plans for the big payoff a few months from now, when all of Flight Incorporated's assets in Grand Cayman would be wired to banks in Panama, Bermuda, Switzerland, Ireland and Singapore. Sandy and Maria's task for the past few years had been to set up groups of women in each of these countries to receive and launder the funds after the distribution. This planning work would be complete by the end of the summer. The final stroke – the transfer of the firm's assets – would happen next January.

Of course, once Sandy and Maria had succeeded in sending away all of the firm's assets, the two of them would need to disappear completely. This took some careful planning as well. Sandy had already purchased a small house in a village in Uruguay. Surrounding it were several acres of rich ground, where she planned to grow a vegetable garden. There were a few mature pear trees behind the house, and she imagined stringing a hammock between two of them. She would lie there looking up at the sunlight twinkling through the leaves overhead, drowsing or reading, as she pleased. She'd never have to listen to another siren or jackhammer, or ride a jostling subway train, ever again.

For Maria, the preparation was a little more complicated, as she would need to move her family. She cared for a granddaughter, all that was left of her family after the child's parents tried to emigrate to the United States. They had left Argentina fourteen years ago, and she had not heard from them since. Nine years ago, she and her granddaughter, Eva, moved from Argentina to Grand Cayman, where Maria started to work for Flight Incorporated. Eva had grown up and graduated high school, and now was employed as a maid with a wealthy family. Maria was working on getting visas for both of them, under a new last name, to Uruguay. They would move with Sandy to her new home, and make further plans from there. It wouldn't be long now.

In the meantime, Sandy and Maria continued their usual practice of moving money around. According to the U.S. Customs and Border Control rules, a traveler is allowed to mail or carry ten thousand dollars into the U.S. at any time; any amount over that requires a customs declaration form. Consequently, Sandy always bought handcrafts during her visit to Grand Cayman. Traveling back to the U.S., she concealed cash inside the handcrafts, sometimes sewing it inside stuffed animals or under hatbands, other times stuffing it into odd pockets in her clothes. Some she left loose in her purse, ready to count out if questioned, and that stash never exceeded $10,000. For the trip back, she dressed in colorful, loose clothing, with sunglasses and odd accessories. She occasionally dropped things or had trouble with her sandals or handbag or scarf, creating delays and testing the patience of the customs officials, who did all they could to hustle her through.

Back in New York, Sandy got in touch with the sisters who managed the safe houses and distributed the cash from her suitcase to them. It wasn't much, but they stretched it as far as they could to keep the places going. She contacted the other recipients, in person or through intermediaries in the network, to tell them to expect packages in the mail. Then she settled back into her routine in the New York office, efficiently supporting Rick Gregory. He never suspected that the firm was short several hundred thousand dollars a year.

Chapter 11 – Washington, D.C.

In the FBI Office of Public Affairs, the interviews for task force lead on Operation NEVRR were proceeding well. Initial phone interviews had been conducted with Doug Williamson. Afterward, Mary listened to the recordings of the phone calls. Mary had, of course, provided Williamson with the questions to ask. For once, she had written simple, straightforward questions, designed to elicit meaningful information from the candidates. As she expected, though, the candidates' answers all came back in the form of rehearsed sound bites, memorized in business school recruiting seminars, virtually indistinguishable from one to the next. It was no surprise that Williamson came to her afterward and asked her to review the resumes again to narrow the field. She carefully chose the most inflated resumes, the three-pagers, to go with the slickest sound bites she'd heard. Perfect candidates.

After reviewing the selected resumes again with her boss, Mary invited his three top picks back in for second-round interviews with both Williamson and his boss Andrew Jones, the Associate Deputy Director. Again, Mary supplied Williamson with the questions to ask.

Tammy installed a temporary bug in the conference room, and later dropped off a thumb drive of the recorded interviews to Mary. Mary carried the thumb drive home contained in a tampon wrapper, although the cursory handbag inspection at the FBI building exit hardly merited that caution.

She listened to the interviews over wine at home, chuckling at the predictable questions and rehearsed answers. The question "What would you bring to this department that sets you apart from other candidates?" elicited this answer:

"I am thrilled that you invited me here today, and I'll tell you why I'm a perfect fit for this position. As Task Force Lead, I would bring a unique set of leadership skills and values, attributes that have served me well in my eighteen years in the communication and public relations arena. In my last two years with the RGM Group, my communiques and tweets rated over one million likes and thirty thousand retweets per year. As a Lean Six Sigma Black Belt, I have experience in operationalizing change management to interface with the public and satisfy customer demands. I have successfully managed large-scale projects of up to eight million dollars, spanning multiple years and achieving sequential strategic milestones. Every project I have been entrusted with has been completed under budget and ahead of time. In short, I believe in thinking globally but acting locally. I assure you that I could very quickly pull together a dynamic, empowered team to collaboratively engage with this very pressing problem." Mary sighed. *Every damn one of them the same as the last. What a crock of shit.*

On Tuesday, Williamson informed Mary that he and Andrew Jones, the Associate Deputy Director, had decided to hire Bill Ames, a recent Dartmouth Business School grad with prior Army service. She remembered his answer to the question, "How would you design security for conference and entertainment venues?"

"Obviously," Ames had replied, "we need to increase the number of security staff, to make our presence very visible. An armed and vigilant patrol presence would provide the sense of protection that our VIPs expect. And we will use every method of crowd control and vetting at our command. No one will penetrate our perimeter."

"Good, that's what we want to hear," Andrew Jones had muttered. Williamson had nodded in agreement.

The following morning, Williamson directed Mary to get back to Andrew Jones's boss, the Deputy Director, to endorse his choice of Bill Ames as Task Force Lead on Operation NEVRR.

A week passed. On Wednesday afternoon Williamson called Mary into his office. He was visibly upset. He stood behind his chair, his face red. His jowls quivered over the edge of his collar and his expensive suit was rumpled.

"I can't believe they did this to me!" He glared at Mary.

"Did what, sir?"

"Andrew Jones. The Associate Deputy Director. He told me I could hire Bill Ames. And now look!"

"I'm sorry, I don't – "

"He put a woman in instead. A Negro woman!"

Mary said nothing.

"A fuckin' quota filler." His sneered. "Here – it says, 'We need to strive toward a more diverse workplace, especially in our outward-looking departments.' Look at that!" Williamson flung a letter at Mary. She scanned it quickly. Stapled to the upper corner was a photo of an attractive black woman, her hair pulled back tightly, in dress uniform. Mary guessed she was in her 40s.

"Yes, sir. It says that they're hiring Vanessa Woodside." Mary read from the letter. "She comes from ten years in management in the Intelligence Branch. Here in Washington. Before that she served two stints in combat in Afghanistan. And before that she was a teacher." Mary looked up.

"Yes, but can she run a task force?"

"It says she was the administrative director of an intelligence department for the last 10 years."

"Yeah, but can she make a PowerPoint? Can she speak to a group?"

Mary almost said, "I make your PowerPoints, sir," but she bit her words back. Instead she said, "I can assist her, sir. We won't have any problem. I can handle it."

"Fuckin' quotas. I'm sure they're happy about this." Williamson ticked off two fingers. "They filled the female quota and the minority quota both together. How fuckin' clever." He stopped for breath and glared at Mary again.

Mary pretended to mirror Williamson's indignation.

"Well, yes, this is a surprise. But I'm sure we can bring her up to speed. I can handle it."

Williamson smacked the back of his chair.

"See that you do. See that you handle *her*. Now get out."

Mary left his office, somewhat rattled. Even for him, this was quite the outburst. To herself, she wondered what Vanessa was made of. Whether she could withstand this job.

Two weeks later Mary met Vanessa on a Monday morning. She arrived a little before 7:30 a.m. with a briefcase, out of which she took a few family photos. There was a photo of Vanessa with another woman, maybe a sister, and another with what appeared to be her parents, and one in uniform with her army platoon. But no boyfriend, husband, or child. Mary was full of curiosity, but didn't pry. Vanessa could divulge her family structure on her own time.

Mary helped Vanessa settle in and complete her credentialing and orientation, then gathered the office supplies she'd asked for. Mary didn't need to explain the cybersecurity system. As an agent who'd risen through the ranks, Vanessa was well versed in FBI procedures and protocol. As they worked together through the morning, Mary realized that her own work load would not balloon as she supported Vanessa. She'd been afraid of that.

Vanessa's new position as Task Force Lead had been created without any additional support staff, which was not surprising to Mary. Many times, over the years, Williamson had assigned her extra projects and extra responsibility with no increase in pay, no upgrade in title, and no additional staff. Mary expected no better this time, so Vanessa's obvious competence, independence and self-sufficiency were a great relief.

Throughout the morning Vanessa was brisk and a little nervous, Mary thought. As noontime came, Mary invited Vanessa to join her and Samantha at the cafeteria for lunch. As the three women ate the institutional iceberg lettuce and cold salad trimmings offered by the food service, Vanessa confessed that she usually carried her own lunch. Mary and Samantha laughed out loud and looked at each other.

"We do, too… we were just testing you," laughed Mary, and the wink she sent Vanessa was the welcome she needed. The three of them vowed to meet in the lounge from then on, whenever lunch meetings didn't interfere.

Then they spent the rest of the hour talking pets, kids and grandkids, showing off photos and sharing family stories. Mary sensed some wariness from Vanessa. The only photo she showed was of her platoon in Afghanistan, and she didn't say anything about her time there. Mary realized there was a gulf between them that would be tough to traverse. But there were tentative signals of trust as well. She reminded herself to go slow. *You can't be too careful.*

Chapter 12 – Ozarks

On the Barker farm, the small tractor and its implements had worked their magic in the hayfield at the beginning of June, and the barn filled up with sweetness. The hay would be fed to the cows and sheep through the winter, when the pastures were under snow. Luckily, in this part of the country the snow never lasted long.

Long rows of squashes and pumpkins had been planted, along with sweet corn, tomatoes and beans. The women were kept busy hoeing between the rows and thinning the plants where they needed it. In the meantime, the kids picked wild raspberries from the edges of the fields, eating most of what they picked, but still bringing some home to be made into jam.

July came, and the peaches ripened on the trees. The orchard was located up on the bench of the mountain. The mountain itself was one of those long rambling plateaus of the Ozarks, formed of flat-lying limestone and eroded over eons into natural terraces. From across the valley, a traveler could make out the pale bluffs circling the mountain, stained black where the iron-rich water seeped over them. Invisible from a distance were the small entrances into caves in the mountainside, well concealed behind heavy brush. Only a few of the women knew where those entrances lay.

The bench, a wide, level terrace of land, went clear around the mountain, with a bluff below and a bluff above it. On the south side it widened to 800 feet, plenty of room for an orchard. This orchard had been planted over a hundred years ago and had been nurtured by the Barkers for generations. When their peach preserves business caught on, they had expanded it, and now the newer trees were coming into fruit. In the early spring, the soil on the bench warmed quickly, protected as it was from northerly winds. The high bluff that backed the bench absorbed the sunshine and radiated warmth back to the vegetation below. Two natural artesian springs bubbled all year long, and tubing ran from them down through the orchard. The trees never lacked for moisture, even when the summers turned hot and dry.

The only road up to the bench was a winding, steep, single track, and the only vehicle that could reach the orchard was a Jeep with heavy-lugged tires. This vehicle was only used on the mountain and had never had a license plate on it. It could haul the utility trailer, but the two would have to be disconnected and repositioned at the upper end of the road, as there wasn't enough turning space in the orchard for both hooked together.

The road had never been graded by machine, nor had gravel ever been hauled in. Instead, men and women with sledgehammers had broken up the soft limestone into cobbles, laying them carefully in a tessellated pattern like a Roman road. In some places, the road ran over broad shelves of bedrock, heaving up out of the mountain like the backs of petrified whales. The road was crowned in the middle, with ditches on either side and runoffs every few feet and at every switchback. Every spring the rain and snowmelt would gouge the red clay road in one place or another, and the mending crew would go out to repave the small gullies. With each year's tending, the road had grown stronger and more solid. Yet to the untrained eye it looked like a winding dirt track, nothing to risk a car's undercarriage on.

Overseeing the work in the peach orchard was Kristin's job. She had arrived seven years ago with her husband Erik. They had moved east from Oklahoma, from the flat wheat fields to these beautiful mountain plateaus. Their home was half a mile down the road from Maybelle's and Jim's. Connecting the two homesteads was a steep overgrown path. If necessary, Kristin or Erik could run up that path faster than a vehicle could navigate the switchbacks on the road between the two houses.

Kristin had graduated from Purdue in 1985 with a degree in agriculture, just in time for her family's farm in Iowa to succumb to debt. The farming crash left no survivors that year. The family home, equipment and land had been auctioned off, and her brothers and sisters scattered to Midwestern cities. Her parents lived a sad, reduced life in the Lutheran retirement home outside Sioux City, Iowa. Kristin herself, unable to find a job as an agronomist, had drifted into waitressing and administrative assistant work, eventually settling into a desk job at a USDA Farm Service Agency in Pryor, Oklahoma. But for years, as she raised her family, she longed to get out into the fields again. Now the kids were grown, and Kristin felt the old pull in the springtime, when the smell of the rain and the soft sunlight lured her to the garden. She and Erik would celebrate the first really warm nights by camping in the back yard overnight, a sweet remembrance of their first nights together.

Seven years ago, Kristin's friend Mildred told her about a fruit and seed business in a small town, over the state line from Oklahoma, in Arkansas. Kristin and Erik decided to look it up on their way through to Blanchard Springs Caverns for vacation. It was supposed to be somewhere in the same vicinity, somewhere near the Buffalo National River, nestled in the limestone plateaus of the Ozarks. They couldn't find anything about it on the web, so they decided to drive the minor highways through the mountains and ask around. All they had to go on was a brand name: Barker Farm Seeds and Preserves, with a P.O. box in a small town.

The two-lane road they chose was spectacular, winding precipitously around bends between towering bluffs on one side and nothingness on the other. Kristin watched the caution signs while Erik drove. Each yellow sign showed a squiggly arrow. As soon as Kristin judged they had reached the tip of the last arrow, a new sign appeared to show the direction of the upcoming hairpin turns.

Finally, Erik pulled abruptly off the road at an overlook, thankful to be able to release the wheel. They stepped out and stood by a low stone wall, looking out over the broad valley and distant mountains, as low clouds moved into the hollows below them. The colors shifted as the light faded. The mist in the hollows turned a deep purple, while the setting sun, hidden behind gold-rimmed cloud banks clustered on the horizon, shot shafts of light straight across the sky. Kristin and Erik stood transfixed for twenty minutes, watching the slow approach of evening. Then they turned back to the car, and Kristin took the wheel for the rest of the way.

They drove down the steep two-lane highway into town, wary of the 15-mile-per-hour speed limit posted on the last hairpin turn. They parked next to the courthouse, a large, square, three-story building constructed of roughly hewn limestone blocks. At the top of the building, the blocks were turned vertically, creating a ragged stockade-looking outline against the sky. Wooden benches were placed on either side of the entrance doors, and in front of the benches were small piles of wood shavings, left there by the whittling knives of old men. Opposite the courthouse, in one of the stores catering to tourists, Kristin and Erik found preserves and canned peaches labeled

Barker Farm. They bought some and asked the young lady how to find the farm. She didn't know where it was, but she called her grandmother out of the back room of the store.

Gramma came out, wiping her hands on her apron, and sized the two of them up. They explained that they were trying to find their way to a peach farm – was this Barker Farm the one?

"Maybe, but you won't find your way out there tonight." The old lady quizzed them about why they wanted to find it, asking more questions than Kristin could easily answer. Finally seeming satisfied, Gramma suggested they put up in the small motel down the road and come back in the morning. "I'll get my grandson to run you out there in the morning. I want him to pick up some eggs for me."

Kristin and Erik found the motel at the bottom of the hill, a long, low, cinder block structure. The entrance was lit by a worn painted sign reading "Foster's Motel", with a single neon stripe around the edge of it. They parked at the office and entered through the screen door, dodging the moths that circled around the light above it. The office was empty, but they could hear a TV in a room behind the desk. Kristin rang the bell on the worn wooden counter, and an elderly woman came out to greet them. She looked a little surprised to see them.

"Can we get a room for tonight?"

"Just one night? Where y'all comin' from?"

"We're just passing through, although we might end up staying for two nights," Kristin explained. "We're just interested in the area."

"Not much to see here, but you're right welcome. My name's Lurleen." She reached a thin hand across the desk.

"We're Kristin and Erik. We're from Oklahoma. We're on our way to Blanchard Springs, but we're taking our time. Pleased to meet you."

Lurleen turned to a pegboard and reached down a key hanging from a plastic tag. "You're in room number 5. That'll be twenty-eight dollars for the night, if you're paying cash."

Kristin and Erik paid and moved their car. The room was stuffy but clean, and the air conditioner wheezed into motion when they turned it on. After a little while they decided it was too noisy and they opened a window instead. The breeze had cooled and it carried in the night sounds of cicadas and whippoorwills. Kristin and Erik listened contentedly and drifted off to a sound sleep.

In the morning, they ate breakfast at a café on the square. The jar of jam on the table had the Barker Farm label, and Kristin scooped some onto her toast. The jam was sweet and soft, with big chunks of peach flesh. As they sat in the sunny window, they watched a young man cut across the road and enter the café. He looked around and spotted them, the only strangers in the place. He walked up and introduced himself as Jody, and said his grandmother had sent him over to find them. "She says y'all want to find the Barker place. How come you're lookin' for it?" Again Kristin explained that she was interested in seeing the orchard and where the peaches came from. She didn't confess that she was looking for work, as she hardly dared admit that to herself.

Jody looked down at the toe of his boot and considered Kristin's answer. Finally he said, "I'll meet you down at the motel in half an hour. I need to talk to Lurleen about it afore I take you up there." He shuffled and seemed about to say something else, then abruptly turned and left the café.

After he left, Kristin looked at Erik with a raised eyebrow. "These people are pretty provincial, aren't they? Why is it so hard to get directions from them?"

"Oh, well, I guess if we want to see the place, we have to do it at their pace," replied Erik. "Why are you so eager, anyway?" He looked searchingly at Kristin, sensing something in her mood.

She sighed. "Haven't you ever wanted to settle down in a place like this, with these mountains all around?" She gazed out the window at the tree-clad hillside behind the courthouse, then turned back to him. "I'm tired of the flatland. Now that you're retired, can't we pick up and leave Oklahoma and come to someplace like this?"

She put her chin in her hand and toyed with the spoon by her coffee cup. "What if, even, they could use an agronomist? Maybe I could work there." She was surprised to hear herself saying the words, as if a spell had come over her. A truth-telling spell.

Erik looked at her as if seeing her for the first time. She was his wife, with gray hair braided back into a bun, but she was also the shy blonde tomboy he knew back in high school. Suddenly he too was struck by a restlessness and an odd new springtime mood. *What if... and why not?*

Kristin and Erik left the café and walked four blocks back to the motel, walking hand in hand. They gathered up their stuff, left a tip for the maid, and packed the car. The motel office was at the end of the concrete porch, the screen door under a faded tin awning. When they walked in, Lurleen stood behind the counter, folding towels. Jody turned and saw them, muttered "Howdy" and walked out.

"Don't mind him," Lurleen said. "He just don't see many strangers. Tell me again where you're from and where you're tryin' to get to?"

Kristin explained that they were passing through from Oklahoma, but were looking for a place to retire. She caught Erik's amused look and plowed ahead, "What I mean is we're looking for work. Work that's interesting. That's why I wanted to find out about this fruit and seed farm." She faltered and looked down at the floor, then up at Lurleen. "Mildred Robinson told me to find this place. She told me to ask for Maybelle Barker."

"Well now, now we're gettin' to it. If Mildred sent you, that's just fine. I'll have Jody run you up there. Your little car," she gestured out the window at it, "wouldn't make it across the first crick." She walked around the counter and put her head out the door. "Jody, you go on up and get your truck. I want you to take these nice folks up to see Maybelle." She turned back to Kristin and Erik, "That's Maybelle Barker and her husband Jim. Jody will take you on up. But there's just one thing. Do you have any electronics on you, a cell phone, somethin' like that?"

Surprised, Kristin said, "Yes, I do, actually. We carry this when we travel. We share it." She pulled out of her purse an ancient Motorola radio-style phone. "It used to have an aerial but it broke off." She laughed, "So Erik duct-taped a darning needle on the back of it and it works just fine. It's all we need."

Lurleen laughed out loud. Then she sobered and said, "But you can't even take that up there. That's them Barkers' rule... no electronics on the farm. You'll have to leave it here, either in your car or in our safe here. Which would you rather?"

After a moment's hesitation, Kristin decided to leave it in the safe, wondering at herself as she did so. Erik said nothing. Sometimes events are so bizarre that all you can do is go along. Yet even as he thought that, he felt something like relief to leave the damn thing behind.

Jody pulled a small pickup around the front of the motel. It was originally green, but so covered with red dust that it was hard to tell. As Kristin and Erik climbed in, they searched for seatbelts but found none. Kristin's knee hit the stickshift that stuck straight out of the floor. Jody apologized, "You're just gonna have to move your knees thataway." He smiled then and said, "Glad to meet y'all."

The truck pulled out of the motel lot and up onto the main road. They drove across a rusty trestle bridge over a placid, slow-moving river on the far side of town. On either side of the water, broad shelves of bedrock and stretches of round river stones formed a wide, dry valley. The morning sunshine was already baking the clean stones and filling the air with a sharp vegetative tang. At the edges of the stony expanse, willow roots clung, holding back the hollowed clay banks from collapsing completely. Debris was snagged higher up in the willows and witch hazel that lined the river, testifying to the height of the spring flooding. Small islands of stubborn, exposed shrubbery were surrounded by isolated pools and stony flats. Birds and snakes hunted their prey in the meandering watercourse.

After the road left the bridge, it started to climb steeply. For several miles it twisted upward. Jody drove with his window open, and Erik rolled his down also. The light blinked alternately between deep shade and brilliant midmorning sun as they drove past deep forests, then rounded corners to broad vistas. Suddenly Jody turned off the road, seemingly right over the edge of the highway. Kristin's heart jumped before she realized that he'd turned onto a gravel switchback. The new road dropped suddenly in the opposite direction than they'd been traveling. They descended for a mile into another broad valley. At a shallow stream, they drove across a sunken concrete roadbed. Water arced from the truck's wheels on either side as they forded the stream. Beyond the crossing, the stream meandered across the valley. Something glinted in the sun along the watercourse, something that Erik and Kristin couldn't identify. Staring harder, they made out cars slumped sideways into the stream, rusted hulks with windows busted out, but still showing bright paint colors here and there.

"What in the world...?" asked Erik. "What are those cars in the water for?"

"What cars? Oh them," answered Jody, "Them are to keep the water from cuttin' in any farther."

He slowed the truck and pointed out how the cars were slung over the side of the stream on the outside edge of each curve. "When they get too old, we just push 'em into the stream where we need some shorin' up. Then we push some dirt over them. You ain't never seen that before?"

Erik and Kristin just shook their heads. As they stared, a groundhog poked its head up out of the window of a car door. It used to be the passenger door of a sedan but now pointed up at the sky. Kristin looked sidelong at Erik and suppressed a comment.

Further across the valley, they passed a small weather-worn house with a broad front porch. A man sat with his chair tipped back against the front wall, boots on the porch rail, smoking. He raised a hand in greeting to Jody, who raised his hand in reply.

The man stared keenly at Erik and Kristin. Kristin shivered. Suppose they had tried to come up here without an escort? Kristin guessed they wouldn't have gotten this far.

That afternoon, seven years ago, they had arrived at the farm and visited for a few hours with Maybelle and Jim. Jim and Jody had taken them up to the orchard in the Jeep, and Kristin fell in love. Here on the high bench the sun was a different quality, the shade beneath the trees deeper, the hum of bees mesmerizing. The sharp smell of daisies at the edge of the orchard brought back memories of endless childhood summers in Iowa. She walked beneath the trees, noting some suckers shooting up that should be pruned, some withered limbs that needed to come down. There was evidence of peachtree borer as well, and she asked Jim about it. He confessed that the problem had been around a while, which is one of the reasons they had to sell a lot of the peaches as jam. Only the unblemished fruit could go out to the farmers' markets.

Later they sat down in Maybelle's kitchen over lunch and lemonade. They exchanged addresses and phone numbers. Kristin blurted out that she wanted to work there, wanted it badly. Erik sat silently, watching her face and loving the light that shone there.

That was seven years ago. Kristin now supervised the work in the orchard. She scouted and pruned to keep the peachtree borer population in check. When the pest pressure was particularly high, she resorted to an application of permethrin, but that wasn't necessary very often. She didn't worry about labeling, as nobody in this part of the country cared whether fruit was certified organic, only whether it tasted good. And these peaches were the best anybody could buy.

Erik did a number of jobs on their own homestead and up at the farm. Life slowed down for both of them. On the first warm night of spring every year, they put up their old canvas tent in the back yard and lined it with sheepskins and flannel blankets. The slightly musty odor of the tent brought back memories of all the other nights spent there, and a sweet urge to get naked and snuggle down. All summer they enjoyed each other against the hard ground, their noises joining those of the raccoons beyond them in the woods.

In the evenings the two of them could be seen on their porch, chairs tipped back, waving to the few vehicles that ever made it this far up the mountain.

Chapter 13 – Washington, D.C.

Vanessa Woodside's second week on the job as Task Force Lead for Operation NEVRR proved to be a challenge. She reviewed the material for the summit webinar that Mary gave her and it made no sense to her. Why had the FBI selected this problem as a priority? How did they even define the problem? Was there some sort of trend here, or was someone manufacturing a pattern out of random crimes, just to gin up some work? She viewed the PowerPoint that had been presented at the project kick-off; it appeared to be a hodgepodge of sophomoric conclusions without much grounding in data.

When she questioned Mary about it, Mary was noncommittal. "You'll need to talk that over with Mr. Williamson, I'm afraid. He's the one who set the strategic direction."

Vanessa had to wait another week for Williamson to have time for her. He had a busy travel and conference schedule, and normally only worked four days a week, so Fridays were out, too. Vanessa spent the days until her appointment with him digging into the data with the help of Samantha, Mary's friend, who worked in the Criminal Investigative Division. She could have gone the normal route of requesting crime data from the FBI Central Records Complex, but in her experience that never yielded much. Or rather, that usually yielded too much. There were far too many assaults and murders in far too many places to find patterns among them.

At any rate, her understanding now was that Operation NEVRR was established to create an enhanced security system, not to conduct a thorough criminal investigation. According to the material Mary shared with her, the problem had already been set in stone by Williamson, his boss, Associate Director Jones, and all the way up the FBI chain of command. They had decided that the challenge was a lack of coordinated control of attendance at conference centers. Criminals, probably radicalized foreign nationals, were finding their way through the lax screening stations and into the hotels and casinos where conferences took place. It was obvious from the presence of hecklers at speeches that subversives were sneaking in past the established perimeters. The challenge for Operation NEVRR was to identify and turn away those radical individuals before they found their way to the convention floor. The ultimate goal was to assure that these gatherings could take place with no threat of disruption. Solving the odd murder, theft or robbery outside the conference perimeter was not a high priority.

Samantha dutifully supplied Vanessa with data on individuals arrested for disturbing the peace at various political and business gatherings. Unfortunately, many of the incidents she looked into yielded no data, because the removals had been carried out by private security squads who did not coordinate with law enforcement. These protection services kept no records of encounters. They operated independently and often in direct opposition to local and state police. Therefore, despite Vanessa's diligent search, with Sam's help, she came up empty-handed at the end of the week.

The following week Vanessa finally got an hour with Williamson. Mary ushered her into his office, where he sat behind his imposing desk. He didn't bother to lift his bulk out of his chair, but motioned her to take a seat opposite him. She noticed the half-eaten jelly donut at his elbow and was glad she hadn't shaken his hand. He welcomed her with a hearty greeting.

"I hear that you're doing a terrific job, a terrific job. Keep up the good work."

"Thank you, I appreciate that. But I'm having a little trouble understanding the strategic plan for Operation NEVRR. Can you tell me what your vision for this initiative is?"

At that, he launched into a 10-minute monologue about "defending our way of life" and "zero tolerance for those traitors who want to destroy us."

Vanessa asked about the original impetus for the operation. "I was led to believe that there were some murders in and around convention centers. Isn't that what we're investigating?"

"Oh, yes, yes, that was the original problem, we thought. But not anymore. Now our directive is to secure these events so those damn demonstrators can't come anywhere near them. Every time one of these subversive groups gets into an audience all hell breaks loose. Before you know it, footage is uploaded and the press is all over it. It's time to shut this lawlessness down. Shut out the reporters and shut up the troublemakers. And make the entertainment venues safe again. There's a lot at stake."

Williamson paused and appraised Vanessa, who sat facing him, looking impeccable in a Dior suit. *She looks good for a colored woman*, he thought, *though she's a little old for my taste.* Still, he speculated that her being black might actually be a good thing. She'd be the perfect figurehead for the task force. *It'll blunt the criticism if the new security forces are, shall we say, a little too zealous.*

Williamson continued his monologue. "We received this directive from the highest authority, I don't need to explain to you who that is. A lot of money is going to be flowing through our agency and this task force in particular. The administration's goal to make our cities safer, and we need to strategically place those new resources where they'll do the most good. I'm talking the big entertainment venues, the big hotels, the Renaissance Center in Detroit, the Pru in Boston, McCormick Place in Chicago. You get the idea."

Vanessa kept a straight face. "Oh, yes sir, I agree with you there. That's where we need the forces on the ground. I understand how this lawlessness impacts both business and entertainment, in all these places you mention. You can bet we'll get this moving soon."

To herself she cautioned, *just don't say it.* You already knew there wouldn't be any more resources for crime prevention and neighborhood rehabilitation. You knew it, and there's nothing you can do to change it. Keep your head down and do what you can, in the job you've been assigned. Standing, she held out her hand toward the boss.

"Thank you so much for your guidance, Mr. Williamson. You'll hear back from me soon." He held her hand a moment too long, and she suppressed the impulse to pull back. *Goddamn it, don't these jerks ever let up?*

Walking back to her office, Vanessa started to get angry. Her old field training kicked back in and she wondered why none of it made sense. What was the original problem that got Operation NEVRR started? *I haven't learned a damn thing so far,* she thought, *and getting information around here is like wading through cotton candy. I'll bet Mary knows more than she's letting on. She's probably the only one who does.*

Back at her desk, Vanessa sat and thought it through. She vowed that one way or another she'd penetrate the invisible barrier that she sensed between herself and Mary. Something had to give.

A week later, Vanessa Woodside sat at her desk on a Monday morning. She had resolved to push harder on Mary and Samantha. She needed more than just the raw data they'd provided thus far. She needed to understand how Operation NEVRR had gone off track, and she believed these two women could answer that. Her repeated questions to Williamson had been met with blank looks and unease. He couldn't or wouldn't say anything except that their mission now was to protect rallies and meetings from "subversives and terrorists."

Mary came in at 8:00 a.m., and Samantha followed a few minutes later. Did Vanessa see a look pass between them as Samantha entered? She shook it off and proceeded to grill them.

"How did this Operation NEVVR get started? What was the evidence? What are we trying to uncover?" Vanessa looked at both of them in turn.

Mary and Sam answered Vanessa's questions straightforwardly but with no elaboration. Mary described how Operation NEVRR had begun in response to a triple murder in New Orleans back in February. Political pressure had been applied, due to New Orleans' dependence on tourist dollars, which would evaporate if people didn't feel safe.

"Mr. Williamson feels that visitors should be protected even if they are incapacitated and unwary," Mary began. "According to him, that's the whole attraction of places like New Orleans, New York and Las Vegas – they're places where people can leave their inhibitions behind and have a little innocent fun. If they get drunk and take off alone to some cathouse, well, they should still be safe from predators." Mary waved her hand airily, and her voice was only slightly sarcastic. She didn't let her face betray the contempt she felt for Williamson's opinions. Vanessa didn't say anything, and Mary continued.

"And somehow, according to Mr. Williamson, this assurance of safety has broken down in a few cities and resorts. Several men have been murdered, apparently while seeking female companionship. So far, the cases appear to be armed robbery, although there isn't much evidence, and apparently no eyewitnesses. Hence the crackdown and the launch of Operation NEVRR."

Mary summarized the work that had been done so far, the summit webinar that had taken place, and the recruitment of participating agencies in all the major cities.

Vanessa questioned Mary closely about how the focus had shifted from investigation of murders to perimeter security checks at rallies and conventions. And to investigations of leaks to journalists.

"What exactly is the aim?" she demanded. "Are we investigating, or are we just beefing up protection? And screening media coverage?"

"That's above my pay grade, I'm afraid," Mary replied innocently. "Only Mr. Williamson and Associate Deputy Director Jones know the strategy." She shrugged. "Or whoever they're getting their directions from. We're just here to follow their orders." There was no hint of sarcasm in her tone now.

At that, Vanessa dismissed Mary and Samantha and turned back to her computer.

As the women left her office, Vanessa's mood sank. The utter boredom of her new job hit her like a brick. That and the feeling of futility. Is this all the FBI does? Looks after fools too dumb to stay even a little bit sober and to keep their pants zipped, in a strange city? What about all the crime going on in the boroughs and East L.A.? And in Detroit, Chicago, Baltimore and D.C? Why do the folks in the inner cities deserve less protection than the new conference venues and Renaissance Centers? Why do only marble-lined towers get all of our attention and vigilance?

Vanessa's original sense of empowerment from being hired to lead the task force a month ago soured into cynicism, and she realized this was just one more dead-end job in a whole life of frustrating situations. She knew in that moment that she had been hired to fill a position with no real power, no pull, and no way out, and for less pay than the men around her. Hired to fill a quota.

Maybe I should go back to Afghanistan. At least my orders were clearer over there.

Vanessa almost smiled at the absurdity of that trade-off. Then she sighed and shut down her computer.

Chapter 14 – Ozarks

On the Barker farm, the newcomers continued to arrive in small groups. They were assigned to sleep in one of the bunkhouses or in smaller buildings. Some built their own cabins if they wanted privacy. The mountain had plenty of timber, and the old skills of log construction had been preserved here. A two-handled saw could be wielded even by teenagers of either sex. Working together, the youngsters learned to cut notches into the ends of logs. The corners of the buildings were dovetailed in opposing planes; such corners could never be pulled apart by bad weather or anything else.

The logging was done with chainsaws, but the logs were hauled down the mountain by a team of two horses hitched to a logging arch. The front end of a log would be caught between the large pincers of the arch, while the back end would drag along the ground behind it. The draft horses were large and had been well trained over many years. They responded promptly to signals given by a handler, who walked behind the logging arch. The handlers were surprisingly young, and thoroughly in charge. They walked on the left-hand side of the moving log, holding long reins attached to the horses' harness. "Gee!" the handler would shout, and the horses would turn right. "Haw," and they'd turn left. The horses could turn in a very tight radius, and as they passed through the dense woods they could squeeze together between the trees, through spaces that would barely have allowed a four-wheeler through. They easily traversed steep and difficult terrain, going places where a logging truck could never have traveled, even if the farm owned one.

In one of the barns, a small gas-fired sawmill was set up. It was used from time to time to cut logs into planks. These planks were used to line the walls of cabins, or were formed into tables, benches, beds and other sturdy furniture.

The larger bunkhouses held the families of single mothers. Up to four mothers and their children shared one large room. Over time these groups gained cohesion, with the children playing together and the mothers sharing chores and child care. Work took up a major part of each day, as electric tools didn't exist on the farm. After dark, the only light in the bunkhouses was from oil lamps or candles, so the families went to bed early. The newer children fussed at first, missing their electronic toys.

Some mothers, too, had a hard time without their smartphones. There were even a few who gave up and decided to leave. In these cases, Jim or Bonnie would drive them down across the valley and into town, where they could catch a bus. The ones who stayed, though, began to fit in with the rhythm of daily work. The children began to learn new skills from the older kids. Younger kids began to boast about how much work they could do, an attitude which astounded their mothers.

In May, a mother and her four-year-old daughter had arrived from a shelter in Commerce, a suburb to the east of Los Angeles. The mother was Alicia Lange, and while she had few possessions, her clothes were expensive. The story she told was that her husband Jeremy, the CEO of a young tech company, had abused her and their daughter until they escaped to the shelter in Commerce. He would hunt her, she said, and he had threatened to kill her. In Commerce, she had seen his car, a small black Mazda Miata, cruising the street where the shelter was, even though the place was supposed to be secure. She was sure Jeremy had tracked her to the shelter, but she didn't know how. She didn't realize it was because she had failed to surrender her smartphone when she came to the shelter, instead concealing it in a hidden pocket in her suitcase.

Alicia was afraid to send her daughter to preschool, as she was sure Jeremy would snatch her from the schoolyard. Finally, in May, when her friend at the shelter told her she was leaving to start a new life in a new state, Alicia had begged to go with her.

The two women and their children were picked up from the shelter by Ta'quisha Alberts and Jim Barker, who had traveled all the way from the Ozarks to get them. Ta'quisha was a young black woman with dreadlocked hair, dressed casually in jeans, a t-shirt and hiking boots. She had an exotic look despite her ordinary clothes, and the way she held herself conveyed a certain steeliness and self-control. She and Jim, Maybelle's husband, had volunteered to take this trip to the coast. They drove out in a small school van, making it across Oklahoma, Texas, New Mexico and Arizona in four days. When the van arrived in California, it was still covered with red Ozark dust.

Jim was at the wheel when they arrived at the shelter in Commerce. Ta'quisha sat in the seat behind him. She turned to him as she exited the van, and he waved her toward the door of the shelter.

"Go on in. They're expecting you. Right in that door there."

Ta'quisha rang the bell and announced herself through the intercom. "I'm Ta'quisha. From the Barker Farm."

Ta'quisha was buzzed in, and was gone for ten minutes. Finally, she emerged with the two mothers and three children they'd been sent to pick up. They walked out to the van together. Alicia Lange was pulling a large suitcase, while the other mother had her family's belongings in trash bags. Ta'quisha was carrying one of them. She hustled them along.

"Hop in. We've got a long way to go. Scoot." The other mother and her kids clambered in.

Alicia hesitated as she went to climb into the van – the seats were not clean and she would soil her pastel capris.

Her daughter Amy voiced her thoughts, "Mommy, this van is dirty!"

"Take it or leave it, ladies." Ta'quisha's voice was flat.

After a moment's hesitation, Alicia decided there was no alternative. She picked up Amy and put her in, then struggled with her large flower-patterned suitcase and attached carry-on.

Ta'quisha, expressionless, watched Alicia fumbling with her luggage. Then she opened the back door of the van and unceremoniously dumped the bags in. Alicia opened her mouth quickly, then after a tick said, "Thank you" in a small voice. She stepped into the van, sat down on the dusty seat, and gathered Amy close to her.

The van drove east that night, crossing California on I-40 and heading toward Flagstaff. Their route was carefully monitored by Jeremy, Alicia's estranged husband, seated at his computer in Los Angeles. It was simple for him to follow the tracking app he'd installed on Alicia's smartphone. He'd give them some time to feel safe and then, when the phone stopped moving, come after them. No problem at all. He'd follow them and kill them both. *That'll teach her.*

Chapter 15 – Washington, D.C.

The day after Vanessa met with Mary and Sam, she decided to call her old friend Mike Jenkins in Chicago. He'd been her platoon captain in Afghanistan through both deployments, and she trusted him probably more than anyone else on the planet. Especially now, since her parents were dead, and she'd lost touch with her sister. And since the people she worked with now, Mary and Samantha and Williamson, were so very unhelpful. Vanessa couldn't decide whether they were being deliberately deceptive or were just plain stupid. At any rate, she was getting no traction in actually leading this task force, and she needed some advice. Now that Mike was serving as Assistant Special Agent in Charge in the Chicago Bureau of the FBI, he was the logical one to go to for help. When they'd parted at the end of their last tour, they promised each other to stay in touch. And every once in a while, during Vanessa's ten years in the Intelligence Branch of the FBI, they'd call each other, or even meet up in Chicago or Washington, D.C., to talk over dinner. To Vanessa, it was like having a big brother she could lean on.

This morning she decided to call Mike on her secure line. She was aware that their conversation could be recorded, so she stuck strictly to business.

"Mike? I need your help."

"Vanessa? It's been a long time. What's up?"

"I'm in a new job. I'm supposed to be the task force leader of this thing called the Operation for National Entertainment Venue Recovery and Renewal and –"

"I've heard of that. Operation NEVRR." He chuckled softly. "It's a joke, right?"

"No, dammit, it's real, and I'm in charge of it. But I can't figure out what I'm supposed to be doing. I thought it was an investigation of some serial murderers. That's what I want to go after. Instead it turns out to be some kind of souped-up security detail for VIPs at conferences and arenas. What the hell is that all about?" She realized she was whining, and she took a breath and lowered her voice. "Have you heard anything about it?"

"Not a whole lot. I actually thought it was coming out of Homeland Security at first. You're saying it's an FBI thing? And you're saying there are serial murders?"

"Yes. At least I think so. That's why I'm calling you. I've been pulling records from the Intelligence Branch, and I'm having a hard time making connections between these murders. I can't find a pattern. And you're so good at that kind of thing. You've done so much with the gangs, you can tell when it's their work." She took a deep breath. "I need some fresh eyes on what I'm looking at. I need you take a look at these cases. Tell me what you think."

"Well, sure. I'm here for you, Vanessa." Mike meant to say more, but he didn't. Instead he said, "Send me your data."

"Thanks, buddy." She hung up abruptly. Then she wondered at herself. She hadn't even asked about his mom. What kind of a person was she turning into?

Vanessa decided to go over the cases she knew about again, one by one. Slowly and carefully this time. There was that case in New Orleans this spring. The Bourbon Street Slasher. He'd killed three people in the alley behind a bar with a knife. It seemed to be the same knife used on all three people, but how could one person take on three at once? What was missing here?

Hang on, maybe he didn't fight them all at once. Suppose it was one after the other. How would that have worked? How would he get them to come out the door one at a time? Suddenly the answer flashed in Vanessa's mind like neon. It wasn't a man, it was a woman. Someone they knew. Someone they would follow. Shit, that's it!

Vanessa stepped out to Mary's desk and asked her to call Samantha over as soon as possible. And to have her bring the file on the Bourbon Street Slasher – everything she had.

Mary complied, and Samantha showed up an hour later, carrying a banker's box. Inside it were several accordion files, each one documenting murders in New Orleans that had occurred in the past year. There were police reports, photos, and lab and autopsy reports in each file. They had been tentatively grouped together due to geographic proximity and a similar modus operandi – knife attacks or strangulations. All the victims were men. All had been alone. There were no witnesses, and no surveillance video. Clearly, these were carefully planned – and premeditated.

Vanessa shut herself in her office and spent the rest of the afternoon poring over the contents of the New Orleans box. She didn't notice when Mary and Sam stepped outside together for their customary smoke break.

Mary and Samantha sat on their usual bench on the plaza of Judiciary Square. Samantha displayed her irritation by smoking two cigarettes inside of five minutes, quite unlike her usual limit of two or three puffs.

"What's eating you?" Mary looked searchingly at Samantha.

Sam didn't answer right away. She looked in surprise at her lit cigarette and quickly extinguished it, then stomped on it.

89

Mary reached down, as she always did, and retrieved the butt, putting it in a sandwich bag she always carried for this purpose. When she straightened up again, she had a disgusted mom look on her face. "Okay, that's enough. What's going on?"

"Vanessa asked me for the Bourbon Street Slasher file. Everything. And she's smarter than all the rest of them put together. She's going to figure it out." Samantha looked panicky.

"Oh, I don't know. We've seen that file. There were no eyewitnesses in any of the eleven cases there." Mary paused. "I agree, there shouldn't have been such a cluster in one city. That's raising the risk a bit high. That's what I told Maybelle the last time I wrote to her. They need to tone it down some."

"No kiddin'," Samantha muttered under her breath. They sat in silence for another minute. Samantha stared across the plaza, her elbows on her knees.

"What's done is done." Mary gathered up her scarf and purse and stood up. "Now what we do is, we sit tight and don't complicate anything. Give Vanessa whatever she asks for. And without delay. She *is* sharper than anybody else. That's why I have hope for her." Sam looked at Mary questioningly.

"That's right," Mary repeated, "I have hope for her."

Mary reached down for Sam's hand, pulling her to her feet. "Relax, kiddo, we've been through things like this before. Breathe deep and smile." She demonstrated, puffing out her cheeks and rolling her eyes. Sam had to laugh. *What a silly old lady.*

At the end of the day, Mary poked her head into Vanessa's office.

"I'm leaving. Is there anything you need before I go?"

"No, I'm good. Thanks." Vanessa looked distracted and waved Mary off. When the door closed, she picked up her landline and called Mike. When he answered, she suddenly looked at her watch. "I'm not catching you on the road, am I?"

He chuckled. "No, Vanessa, we're on Central Time here. It's not quittin' time yet. And you called my office line. What can I do for you?"

"Sorry, Mike, I'm just tired. I've been trying to dig into some of these murders I was telling you about. And I'm not getting much of anyplace. Can I send some files to you? I want to see if you get the same impression I do."

"And what impression is that?"

"I'm not gonna say. 'Cause I can't prove anything. It's just a feeling I have, and I want to see if you get it, too."

"Um, okay." He sounded dubious. "What am I supposed to be looking at?"

"Everything. We'll start with this one case. It's called the Bourbon Street Slasher."

"It's one guy?"

"That's the assumption. But we don't know that. And I've said enough." She spoke briskly. "I'll see what's already uploaded, and anything that isn't, I'll scan for you. There are some crime scene photos and the autopsy report, and a lot of other stuff. I'll get it to you by the end of the week. See what you make of it."

"Fine."

"Thanks, Mike. I owe you one." Her voice softened. "And I've been meaning to ask – how's your mom?"

Chapter 16 – Ozarks

Alicia Lange, the young mother that Ta'quisha and Jim had brought to the farm from Los Angeles, had a hard time adjusting to life on the Barker farm. Her daughter, Amy, who was only four, fit in much better. There were a lot of kids there for the summer, and Amy joined in their work and play wholeheartedly. Alicia had never seen Amy tear around so much and eat so adventurously. She was a different girl from the whiny, bored, and picky kid she'd been.

But for Alicia the transition was harder. She hadn't brought clothes that held up to the elements. Her most sensible shoes, a pair of pink flats, had lasted one week and gave her fierce blisters. Jamie went to a storeroom and found a pair of secondhand sneakers that fit Alicia, and they gave her socks and t-shirts, a feed cap and work gloves. But her thin capris didn't protect against burrs and her drapy sweaters snagged on everything. And worst of all, there were only a couple of mirrors in the whole place. When she finally found one, Alicia saw that her chic blond haircut with the highlights was overgrown and faded now. Her pale skin had taken on quite a farmer's tan, leaving only her forehead white. She felt she was dissolving into some ugly drudge, and she had very little in common with the other women around her. What did they know about L.A. culture – the concerts and movie premieres she had enjoyed? She missed being tuned in to the latest music trends and the hysterical news feeds. She missed *life!*

Alicia began to wonder whether she should go back to L.A. Maybe the marriage could be patched up. Maybe she could change Jeremy, or just woo him again. Maybe the fights were her fault. *Could I just stop challenging him?* Yet even as she thought that, she knew she'd never be that nimble. His rages came out of a clear blue sky, like a lightning strike with no grumble of thunder or dark clouds ahead of time. She had made herself the lightning rod, for sure, but the storms were not of her making. Each one was more destructive than the last. She knew with certainty that if she went back, Jeremy would kill her.

Still, she missed her old world. Her smartphone was buried deep in her suitcase, in a pocket under the unused skirts and dresses. She knew she wasn't supposed to have it; Ta'quisha had made that quite clear. Before they even got into the van in California, Ta'quisha had said that any electronics would have to be left behind, in fact destroyed, before they left. Alicia's smartphone was tucked deep in the hidden pocket of her suitcase, not in her handbag, and she'd decided, right then, that wasn't going to let this smart-ass nigger take away her phone. She had said nothing. She had turned it off long ago, when she first went to the shelter, and she had concealed it. Amy begged to play with it a few times during the drive, but Alicia said she didn't have it anymore. Ta'quisha had repeated the rule once more before they crossed the state line into Arkansas.

Now, with the strength of a withdrawal spasm, Alicia wished she could open her smartphone and just watch the news, open Facebook, anything. That evening she snuck it out of her suitcase and took it to the privy in a pocket of her jacket. Sitting there, she pulled it out and found no signal. *Of course. We're in the middle of nowhere.* She stared blankly at it, then turned it off and pocketed it. Just then a mockingbird started a song right outside the privy, and further up the hill some kids, playing hide-and-seek, screamed with laughter.

Alicia came out of the privy, where she'd held her breath against the stink, and heard the mockingbird's variations trilling on and on. She breathed in the scent of sweet honeysuckle and the deep green vegetation beneath it. She saw the sun setting over the mountain and the mist moving in. She suddenly felt as if she'd been inserted into one of those tranquility messages people posted on Facebook, just missing the caption across the middle of it. She breathed deeply and listened and watched as the mountain cast its shadow across the farm.

Alicia took the useless smartphone back to the bunkhouse and tucked it away again into her suitcase. She was beginning to understand the reason for the ban, or at least part of it.

Feeling more peaceful, Alicia went out looking for Amy and found the bunch of kids tearing around the flat space between the hills. She sat down behind the other mothers watching the game. It seemed to consist of a lot of running and screaming, little knots of kids separating and coalescing like sparrows in a bush. The glee and silliness were almost too much to bear, and Alicia felt the tears welling up.

Another mom turned and saw Alicia's face, then scooted back and put her arm around her. She rocked her gently, as if Alicia were the little girl, crooning, "It's okay, it's okay." Alicia let the tears flow silently, until the other mom pulled out a bandanna. "It's okay, it's okay. Let it go." The rest of the moms sat and chatted quietly and watched the kids until it got too dark to see.

The other mom unwound her embrace and stood up. Alicia stood up, too. It was too dark to see any of the kids clearly. "Amy, time for bed!" she called out.

Amy came bounding up the hill, all energy, her face flushed and goofy-looking, her hair wild. Alicia hugged her hot little body, wondering at this changed child. Together they walked down the hill and washed up at the pump.

"Hold on a minute. We don't have to go in right way."

"Really, mommy? Can we stay up?"

"Sure. Let's look at the stars for a little bit. Come on." Alicia led Amy by the hand, back up the pitch-black hillside. They lay down on their backs on the hill, as the Milky Way took magnificent shape overhead. Amy nestled into Alicia's side, while Alicia stared up at infinity and felt a sudden giddiness, as if they could both float off the earth into deep space.

Chapter 17 – Washington, D.C.

As the weeks passed, Vanessa Woodside found it harder to get to work in the morning. She hadn't heard anything back from Mike in Chicago. She began to lose her earlier confidence that the murder cases could be solved. Instead she persevered at organizing the task force to increase security, but the work was uninspiring, routine. Mary was helpful and cheery always, but Vanessa sensed a little wariness, too. In turn, Vanessa didn't confide in Mary, didn't reveal her distaste for the task they'd been assigned. They worked shoulder to shoulder, contacting all the district offices and setting up security forces in each of the entertainment venues. The costs were skyrocketing, but it turned out that this didn't matter. Operation NEVRR had been granted a generous budget, and cost overruns could be solved by a phone call from Williamson to the Office of Federal Financial Management.

Vanessa estimated that, within six months, every entertainment venue and even some sports arenas, in every major U.S. city, would be equipped with more protection than they ever had before. These NEVRR squads could operate either with or without the cooperation of local police, depending on the locale. If a particular city did not get on board, the squads could work in an extrajudicial capacity and simply take anyone they arrested away in vans.

When Vanessa expressed doubts about the legality of these proposed operations to Williamson, he chuckled conspiratorially.

"Hell, our guys will be as free as ICE agents to pick up anybody, make 'em disappear. Who's going to shout habeas corpus about some crazy demonstrators? Don't let it worry you." Vanessa concealed her shock and returned to her office, walking past Mary without seeing her.

On Friday night, Vanessa, instead of driving straight home to her apartment, drove east along H Street toward Carver. It was the neighborhood she'd grown up in. Tonight, H Street looked worse than she remembered, with knots of young men standing on corners. Those tight groups alternated with conspicuously posed young whores of both sexes, spaced apart or in pairs, further down the block. Boom boxes competed with shouts and loud laughter that jarred her, even with all the car windows closed and the doors locked. What a difference an address makes, she thought. I work on 4th Street NW, and now I'm at 8th Street NE, only a mile and a half away. Might as well be another country.

She didn't slow down, but turned on Bladensburg Road and headed northeast in the direction of the Arboretum. Not that she planned to stop there, either. She passed a place she remembered, a side street where there used to be a small club. It used to have live music on Fridays. She drove past it, then thought, *what the hell, I could use some music and a drink.* Plus, as she recalled, they served some good barbeque, too.

She turned around and parked as close as she could to the club, a couple spaces down the street, and warily scanned the street before stepping out of her car. The nearest streetlight was out, of course. Would there ever be enough cops to protect patrons of a club like this? Or funds to invest in anything down here? Of course not. Nobody at the Office of Federal Financial Management would take a call from a police chief on this side of town.

Vanessa walked into the club and let her eyes adjust. She saw an empty barstool and headed for it. The barmaid was a sturdy young black woman with a great smile.

"What'll it be?"

Vanessa ordered whiskey with a beer chaser. She turned around on her stool to watch the band. It consisted of one old guy with a guitar and a girl with a saxophone. They were amazingly good, harmonizing on the vocals, playing slow blues tunes. They hardly needed to look at each other to pass signals, but they did anyway, sometimes with a wink and a little smile. Their music meshed so effortlessly that it was obvious they'd played together forever. Vanessa imagined that the young girl was the old guy's granddaughter.

Vanessa turned back to the bar. Somehow seeing the two performers pinched her heart. The mournful ballad didn't help any, either. She felt crushed by her life, by her stupid, meaningless job, by her loneliness. She ordered another whisky and beer.

The barmaid was busy for the next hour, but then the crowd started to drift out on the third set. Vanessa got up and made her way to the stage, where she slipped four twenties into the tip pitcher. She got a smile and a nod from the old guy. Walking back to the bar she realized she was drunk. *Damn. Better fix that.*

She decided she'd sit for a while and she ordered coffee and some food. A guy two seats down wanted to buy her a drink, but she turned him down cold. Suddenly she felt a tear roll down her cheek, a tear of anger, a tear of frustration, a tear of loneliness, she couldn't tell. She wiped it quickly and leaned her head on her hands.

"Here's your food, hon. Are you okay?" She looked up into the brown eyes of the barmaid.

"No, as a matter of fact, I'm not. But that's not your problem."

"Sure it is. I can listen."

And suddenly Vanessa found herself talking. Not revealing much, just saying her job sucked, and she was stuck in it for at least another couple of years. The barmaid asked her where she worked. Without thinking, Vanessa named the FBI Office of Public Affairs.

"Then you know Mary Anderson?"

Vanessa's head jerked up. "Who?"

"Mary Anderson. She's a secretary there."

"Yes. I do. She works for me."

"You must be Vanessa Woodside. Mary's mentioned you." She paused and nodded. "You're in good hands with Mary. She can be trusted."

Vanessa thought, *really?* For all her friendliness, Mary never let down her guard. What did this barmaid mean by "She can be trusted"? She puzzled over that for a few minutes and decided she'd said too much. Then her curiosity got the better of her, and she asked the barmaid's name and how she knew Mary.

"I'm Tracy Willis. We go to the same church, and we're in the choir together." That explained it.

"Well, I'll tell her you said hi."

"No, I'll tell her *you* said hi. We'll see each other on Sunday."

Yes, right, it's the weekend. Vanessa decided she could afford to sleep in tomorrow, not work remotely as she usually did. Still, it was time she got home. She finished the whole plate of barbeque even though she was full. It was as delicious as she remembered. She left a twenty-dollar tip and waved to Tracy.

"Thanks for listening. I'll be back soon." And she meant it.

Vanessa felt a little more buoyant as she left. Perhaps that's why she didn't notice the guy who followed her out, the same one who had offered the drink. As she opened her car door and slid in, he was suddenly there, pushing her down across the passenger seat.

"Give me your keys, bitch." She tried to push him off, tried to jab the keys toward his face, but he grabbed her wrist and wrung them from her fist. He punched her hard in the face and she blacked out for a minute.

She came to and found she had been pushed into the passenger seat. She didn't move. Through slitted eyes she saw him search for the ignition, and in that instant, she opened the glove box and pulled out her service revolver.

"Out. Get out or you're a dead man." He lunged for her and she fired expertly into his shoulder, then again into his leg.

"Want one in your head?" Her voice was steely.

"Shit, you bitch, you hit me."

"Get out now. You don't know who you're messing with." Her cold calm cut through his fury and he fell out of the car door. She slammed it shut and locked it, then grabbed her purse, slid over and eased out the passenger door, locking it, too. She dashed the few yards back to the club, grateful that she was wearing pumps and not spike heels.

As she slammed through the door to the club, everybody's heads jerked up. They stared at her gun.

"I'm FBI. Don't move," she shouted.

A second later she was surprised to hear Tracy echo her in a calm and commanding voice.

"She is FBI. Don't worry." Tracy's palms-down gesture brought the heat down in the room. Vanessa realized she could lower the gun.

Tracy was already on the phone with 911, which she had dialed as soon as she heard the shots. She reported a shooting and said the victim was still outside, and the shooter was FBI and was in the club, and there was no danger to anyone. She repeated that it was not an active shooter situation, and it was under control.

Vanessa, her panic calming, listened to Tracy's words. She guessed that Tracy was used to placing these calls. She sure knew exactly what to say. The barroom was hushed, listening, the patrons frozen in place.

"Agent Woodside?" Tracy's calm voice reached across to Vanessa. "Can you put your gun down?"

"Oh yes, sure. Sorry." Vanessa laid the gun on the bar in front of Tracy. No one else moved.

They waited 10 minutes, then 15 or maybe more, and finally heard sirens. Two cops came through the door, guns drawn. Everyone in the room raised their hands. The first cop shouted, "Where's the shooter?"

"I'm the shooter," Vanessa answered. "It was self-defense. My gun is on the bar there." Both cops grabbed her roughly and she suppressed the urge to fight back. They cuffed her before they led her out. The second cop bagged her gun.

"You need her purse," Tracy called out. "She needs her ID." The second cop came back, grabbed it, and followed Vanessa and the first cop out.

Outside, Vanessa glanced into the street where her attacker had fallen, but he wasn't there. There was blood on the street, but she couldn't see anything else.

"Can I look for my car keys?"

"No, you cannot. You're coming with us."

She knew better than to resist. "Yes, sir, officer. I understand."

They approached the squad car and the first cop opened the back door and pushed her head down. The second cop pushed her roughly into the seat. The wire mesh in the back of the squad car is what got her. She fought hard to stay calm, fought to hold down the puke that welled up. *Somebody help me!* she screamed silently.

The ride was a long one. This neighborhood did not have a local police station, and the 5th District Metropolitan Police Station was 20 minutes away. Vanessa looked out the window at the bleak streets, only slightly less populated than three hours ago. She ignored the jibes tossed at her by the cops in the front seat. She didn't even dare to look them in the eye, afraid that some of her fury would pierce through the wire mesh.

Finally, they pulled up to the station house. Vanessa climbed out awkwardly as the two cops pulled her out by the armpits. She walked between them into the lobby and faced the glassed-in desk sergeant's window.

"Excuse me," said a voice from across the lobby. And there was Mary! Mary, of all people, looking sharp in her business suit, with her carefully coiffed gray hair. Smiling, looking over her bifocals and holding out a handshake to the cops, thanking them for their cooperation. Showing her ID. Identifying Vanessa as her boss. Changing the whole atmosphere.

The two cops dropped Vanessa's arms and looked at each other. They turned to the desk sergeant, who vouched for Mary's identity. The three cops huddled together and held a hurried, whispered conference. One of the beat cops turned back to Vanessa. "We need to get a statement from you. Please step inside."

Mary stepped forward and asked, "Can you please uncuff her?" The beat cops looked at each other for a long second. Then the older one gestured with his head to the younger one, who quickly unlocked the cuffs. Vanessa rolled her shoulders and her neck, and shot a quick look at Mary. Then the older cop beckoned her through a door behind the sergeant's desk.

In the barren interview room, Vanessa found her voice. She described the incident and the shooting, making it very clear that she shot in self-defense. She suggested that they notify nearby hospitals to look for a man with gunshot wounds in his left shoulder and right leg. She described her assailant as best she could, a white guy with longish brown hair, but she couldn't remember what he was wearing. She told them that Tracy Willis, the barmaid in the club, could help identify him. The cops ran out of questions. They had her write out and sign a statement. Then they escorted her back out to the lobby.

Mary was waiting for her. She spoke up. "I believe you're still holding her purse. May we have it, please?" The younger cop was sent back to retrieve it. He returned and handed it to Vanessa, who fished around in it and came up with her badge and a business card.

Vanessa handed the card to the older cop. "Please call our office in the morning. We would like to help you coordinate the investigation."

He looked surprised, then sour. "Don't push it. You got lucky tonight. We're not booking you, and we're not making you post bail."

Vanessa smiled to herself. *Of course you're not. FBI trumps local D.C. police in this district.* Aloud, she said, "That's a good decision. Thank you very much."

"You're free to go. Get outta here." The cops and the desk sergeant huddled together again, their backs to Vanessa and Mary.

"What about my car?" asked Vanessa.

The older cop turned in surprise. "It'll have to be impounded. We'll go get it in the morning."

"The attacker grabbed my keys. His fingerprints would be on them. They're still in the ignition. They could be gone by the morning. In fact, the car could be gone by the morning."

"Ah hell, woman, we ain't drivin' all the way out there again tonight."

"But this is evidence. You need to collect it."

The cop glared at her. "Do you want us to book you? No? Shut up then and get out of here. I don't need you tellin' me my job."

"I need my gun back, too."

"You're not getting that either," the older cop snarled. "That's evidence, too. You better be damn grateful we're not keeping you tonight. Only reason we're not is we're a bit overcrowded, you'd have to sit there with the hookers and junkies. Which I'd be happy to do if you insist. You'd fit right in."

Mary took Vanessa's arm. "No sir, we don't want that," she said quickly. "We're just leaving. Thank you so much for your assistance tonight." She steered Vanessa toward the door.

Outside she found her car and helped Vanessa in. "Stay here and I'll be right back. I forgot something."

Mary walked back into the station. Luckily the two cops were gone. She smiled through the glass at the desk sergeant. "Could I trouble you for a couple of evidence bags, in case we find something on her person? I haven't heard her full story yet. Something could turn up." The sergeant grumbled, but found some bags and handed them over. She smiled brightly again, purred her thanks and left.

Back at the car, Mary opened her door, sat down in the driver's seat and held the steering wheel with a grip. She looked at Vanessa, who sat stonily staring forward. Mary's voice lost its softness. "Listen, we'll get through this. Think now. What's our next step?"

Vanessa, surprised by Mary's steely tone, turned to look at her. "How in the hell did you get here? And why?"

"I'll tell you later. Right now, we need to worry about evidence." She showed Vanessa the evidence bags. "Let's act like FBI. Where do we go?"

Vanessa stared at Mary. *What is this secretary doing acting like a field agent?* Then she found her voice.

"OK, let's go. Turn this way." As they drove, Vanessa filled Mary in on what had happened. "Sonuvabitch thought he could hijack me. Huh." She stared gloomily out the window at the sorry neighborhood. She wondered how she'd ever escaped. Wondered if she *would* ever escape.

Chapter 18 – Los Angeles

Many years ago, Jeremy Lange had installed a tracking app in his wife Alicia's phone. It struck him as funny that she never discovered it, but then she'd never been all that smart about tech. A couple months ago, when she left him, the app had allowed him to track her to the safe house where she and their daughter Amy had fled to. And now, it showed him that she had left Commerce and traveled east through Arizona, New Mexico, Texas and Oklahoma. He continued to watch the map and monitor her movements. For the past few weeks, though, the phone hadn't moved. It appeared to be somewhere in the northwest corner of Arkansas, in or near the Ozark National Forest. It was time to catch up with her.

Jeremy called his assistant, Barbara Edwards, into his office. She grabbed her notepad and came in quickly. She was a small, tidy woman in her fifties, wearing casual but crisply pressed slacks and a cardigan.

"I want you to let the staff know that I'll be gone for three weeks. I'll hiking up in Sequoia and Kings Canyon. It'll be a solo hike. Alicia isn't interested. She's taking Amy to Disneyland."

"Okay, then. How can you be reached?" Barbara asked

"Well, I'll have my cell phone, but there may not be any reception up there in the parks. But it's only three weeks. I'm sure you can carry on without me."

"Yes, of course we can. Thanks for the heads up."

More and more frequently these days, Jeremy was able to just leave for a week or two at a time, even a month or more, and the company would coast right along. *That's the advantage of hiring women,* he told himself. *They have more loyalty than men, that's for sure.* Especially if they don't have degrees or titles that they could offer to another company. And as long as he provided some health insurance, they might as well be indentured servants. Who can take the risk of switching jobs these days? Not these dames. But he was careful to screen them when he hired them. He made sure they weren't of childbearing age or inclination.

Barbara was Jeremy's second-in-command, a woman who had been with the company since its founding. In fact, she had worked there even before Jeremy had been recruited by the original owner. She had taught Jeremy the ropes and had encouraged his climb. Barbara knew all there was to know about running the business, which is why Jeremy let her do it. Of course, she wasn't eligible for bonus packages or stock options, and anyway she probably didn't even know that he took that kind of compensation. His accountant was the only one who needed to know that, and he was a whiz at devising tax-saving compensation plans. Jeremy made a big deal about annual Christmas bonuses to his staff – a hundred or two hundred dollars apiece. Barbara usually got two hundred, and in return she kept the company afloat through Jeremy's absences.

At the end of the week, Jeremy set out at dusk, driving east on I-40, not north toward Kings Canyon. He set his GPS tracker to locate Alicia's cell phone, and so far, it was telling him she was still in the northwest corner of Arkansas. *Did she really go there, or was her cell phone stolen by some hillbilly? Only one way to find out – track it and see if I can find her.* He couldn't imagine that she'd actually be out there, because she was such a city girl. But he knew she'd left Commerce, because he hadn't seen her at that shelter she'd been hiding at, and he'd tracked her route almost immediately. The fact that she'd gotten away was enough to ignite his mute anger, his cold determination to track her down.

He drove all night, stopping only for gas and food. He drove through Arizona as the sun came up, then on into New Mexico. Finally, at Albuquerque, his fatigue overcame his fury and he stopped to pick up a cold six-pack at a 7-11. He hunted for a motel, some little place where he could use cash and nobody would remember him. He kept his eyes open as he passed through Albuquerque and headed on east. A couple miles outside of town he spotted a club called Fantasyland. The logo on its sign was a classic mud flap girl silhouette, and he knew there had to be a motel nearby.

He found exactly what he was looking for, a scrubby little place with a faded vacancy sign over a painted concrete planter. The planter was filled not with live plants, but with plastic flowers and foliage leaning at odd angles. The motel was a single-story building with a concrete walkway shaded by an aluminum awning. A couple of faded metal chairs sat outside the office, but no one sat in them. At least the windows held AC units; he hoped they worked. The only vehicles were a couple of dusty pickups that looked like they'd been there awhile. As he checked in, he realized that his own late-model Miata stood out in this place. He'd have to fix that tomorrow.

He checked in and unlocked his room. The air was stale and hot but thankfully the AC grumbled to life. He turned it on full and lay on the bed for a minute. Finally he dragged himself to the shower, which refused to give him hot water at first. He turned it up higher and a thin jet of water escaped the nozzle and shot straight upward. As he adjusted the flow up and down, trying to get the temperature right, that errant stream of water arced over the shower curtain, finally landing on the bare light bulb above the mirror. Pop! it exploded, throwing shards of glass all over the bathroom.

"Jesus fuckin' Christ!" he bellowed. When he got out of the shower, he grabbed a towel and got down on his hands and knees to corral the glass into one corner. That left him with only a tiny hand towel to dry himself off with. Still cursing, he started to get dressed to march over to the office. Then he remembered that he was trying to travel under the radar, and for sure, making a stink about the goddamned plumbing would get him remembered. He stifled his anger and opened a beer, then lay naked on the bed to watch TV. Of course, the cable news pissed him off some more, so he shut it off. He drank three more beers and finally passed out.

When he woke, it was 4 o'clock in the afternoon. He left the motel, hit the road and drove east again through the Texas panhandle. On the outskirts of Oklahoma City, he saw a Thrifty rental car place near the airport. He parked his Miata in the long-term lot, then walked over to the Thrifty. He rented a Jeep which, he reasoned, would get him further on Ozark mountain roads than the low-slung Miata would. Assuming she was somewhere in the mountains.

To rent the car, he used his alternate ID, something he did seldom and judiciously. He put on a black baseball cap that hid his forehead, and sunglasses. He even added a fake mustache he'd picked up in a costume shop. This was a good time to disappear.

He checked the GPS tracker and it still showed her cell phone in the middle of nowhere, north of the Ozark National Forest. He zoomed in and added a topography layer to the map. *Where in hell is she?* Did she run off with some guy, some yeehaw who convinced her he could hide her in the mountains? Or did this yeehaw simply kill her and the kid, steal her phone and take off? Somehow the second possibility sounded more plausible, even satisfying in a way. The idea that she may have left willingly with another guy, might even be having fun with him, enraged Jeremy. His fury ground around in his gut like acid. He would find out and finish this thing. *Finish her.*

Chapter 19 – Washington, D.C.

Vanessa guided Mary to retrace her way from the 5th District Metropolitan Police Station back to the club. They drove slowly and silently through the darkened streets. Vanessa's old skills of navigation had never left her. Despite her panic, shackled in the back of the patrol car, she had memorized the route. Vanessa's experience as a field agent for the FBI had been gained before GPS was invented. In those days, she had to keep coordinates and distances in her head, memorizing landmarks, visual or auditory, for future reference. That habit served her well now, as she guided Mary back to her car outside the club.

The car had not been moved, and the small pool of blood was still there in the street. Vanessa directed Mary to use one of the evidence bags to protect her hand, while daubing a small bit of blood into the other two evidence bags. This would at least be something, if the car disappeared before morning. They could see the keys dangling in the ignition, but Vanessa chose not to open the car with her spare key, as it now constituted a crime scene, and not in her jurisdiction. She couldn't be, at the same time, victim and perpetrator and investigating officer. But she could document what she could reach, the blood in the street. So she had Mary collect it, and they drove back to the precinct house with it.

Vanessa and Mary walked back into the station and greeted the sergeant on duty. His surprise was obvious as they approached the desk and handed one of the evidence bags over. Vanessa made sure he logged it in and wrote a receipt. She told him that either she or a colleague would contact his office in the morning about her vehicle and her gun.

Mary and Vanessa left the station and got in Mary's car. Vanessa, her energy spent, slumped against the seat and laid her head back. Mary looked curiously at her and asked, "Is there somebody we should call?"

"No, nobody."

A pause. "Well then, are you allergic to cats?"

Vanessa rolled her head over and frowned. "Say what?"

"Are you allergic to cats? You're coming to my house."

"Why? I'm okay."

"If you say so. But it's a long way to your house and I'm right around the corner. Also, you need some ice on your face. And it's time we talked."

Vanessa turned to look at Mary and wondered again who she was. As before, she felt an odd disconnect, as if Mary were hiding something from her. It was a familiar feeling for an FBI agent like Vanessa, a suspicion and wariness toward everyone and everything. But Mary's reserve was so well masked by her cheeriness that most people didn't sense it. Or rather, men didn't sense it. Like Williamson, they took her cheerful servility at face value. To Vanessa, it felt strange. It made her wonder if she, herself, was overly commanding, and whether Mary's "Yes, indeed!" was her way of coping with an obnoxious boss.

And all of a sudden, Vanessa recognized what she was seeing – it was the same smiling, nodding acquiescence she'd seen her grandmother perform, back when her grandmother worked for Mrs. Whiting in Baltimore. It was a smile laid over a blank mask that revealed nothing. A sudden panic seized Vanessa, and her heart beat rapidly, as if she were looking over the edge of an abyss. Her instinct was to get out of the car.

Mary looked keenly at Vanessa and said again, "It's time we talked." Their eyes locked. They had never looked so directly at each other in the months they'd worked together. After an eternity, Vanessa saw Mary's eyes soften. "Don't worry. It's just us now. We either trust each other or we don't." Another pause. "What do you say?"

Vanessa put her head down, hand over her eyes. When she spoke, her voice was low and strained. "*Can* I trust you? Or are you just sayin' shit to throw me off again?"

"Throw you off how?"

"I know you know more about this operation we're supposed to be working on than you're lettin' on. You know more than Williamson. You probably know more than anybody in that whole damned agency. When are you goin' to let me in on it?"

"I might know something. But you do, too. You haven't fallen for his agenda, have you? You're too smart for that. I respect that. We can work together."

Vanessa looked stunned. Then she sighed and relaxed. This wasn't her grandmother talking to her domineering mistress in Baltimore. This was a sister talking to a sister.

After a long moment, Vanessa made up her mind. "Okay. We can work together. I'll come to your place tonight. Actually, I'd be really grateful. Thank you."

"You're most welcome." Mary smiled at Vanessa. Then she put the car in gear and started it up, headed for home.

Chapter 20 – Ozarks

Two days after Alicia had tried to get her smartphone working in the privy, her four-year-old daughter Amy found it. Alicia had neglected to tuck it into the hidden pocket as before, so Amy discovered it when she was playing around. She opened the suitcase, and there it was, peeking out of some pantyhose. She grabbed it and ran outside.

"Mommy, I found your phone! It wasn't lost!"

Alicia was working in the barn, helping to pack peaches into crates for shipment to Fayetteville and Bentonville. When she heard Amy, she looked up at Bonnie across the table, then set down her basket and ran out. Bonnie followed with a scowl on her face.

"What the hell?"

There was Amy, waving Alicia's phone, grinning from ear to ear. Alicia grabbed for the phone, but Bonnie got there first. She spun around with the phone in her fist.

"What the hell is this doing here?" Bonnie demanded.

"Excuse me, but that's my phone." Alicia swiped at Bonnie's hand but Bonnie yanked the phone out of her reach.

"What the hell is it doing here?" Angry, holding the phone above her head.

"I brought it," Alicia said defiantly. "It's mine. Give it back."

"Oh no, it's not. It shouldn't be here at all. Jamie Lynn, go tell Maybelle and Jim about this. And get Ta'quisha over here, too."

Alicia stood there defiantly, red-faced, muttering. Maybelle and Jim came out of the house, and Ta'quisha rounded the corner of the barn with Jamie. Someone was tolling the brass bell. Before she knew it, Alicia was surrounded by half the community. Maybelle stepped forward and asked what was going on.

"We have a cell phone here," Bonnie announced.

"So what? It's mine! Is that a crime?" asked Alicia.

"You damn straight it is." Ta'quisha's voice was low and strained. "You told me you didn't have any electronics on you. You told me that three times."

"So I lied," said Alicia, tossing her head. "What are you going to do?"

Maybelle stepped forward, motioning for calm, with a pointed glance at Bonnie and Ta'quisha.

"We're going to have to move you out. Someone could have traced you here. You've put this whole community in danger. Jamie, you go get some women to pack Alicia's stuff. It's got to happen now. Jim, take the cell phone. Bonnie, get a crew to get that truck ready to roll. And Arlene," she said, turning to the girl, "run down and get Erik back up here for me. The rest of you, go back to work but keep a lookout. Ring the bell if you see anyone."

Maybelle's calm directiveness settled the crowd, and the women turned away, staring at Alicia as they retreated. How could she have done such a thing, violated the primary rule around here? *Stupid, stupid, stupid.* Many of the women remembered the last time someone had been traced here. It hadn't ended well.

"Alicia, Bonnie, Jim, Ta'quisha, come with me," Maybelle commanded. She moved up onto the porch of the house. Alicia scowled at Bonnie but complied.

"We don't have much time," Maybelle continued. "Alicia, we have to assume your husband is coming after you. We know

115

he did it before. He'll do it again. You can bet on it. It's his strategy."

"His what?"

"His – how he operated. Chasing you. How do you think he found the safe house in Commerce? He's undoubtedly got a GPS tracker on you. He'll be here any time."

"Oh God." Alicia blanched and covered her mouth.

"Does he carry a gun?"

Alicia's head snapped up. "Yes," she breathed.

"Well, we'll do the best we can. The main thing, Alicia, is for you to stay calm, whatever happens." Maybelle took Alicia in her arms and patted her back, then held her by the shoulders and spoke straight to her. "We can't risk an out-an-out firefight, so we're going to have to take him by surprise. You have to play it cool. And we're going to try to get you out of here before he arrives. Go find your daughter and get packed. You're leaving right now."

Alicia looked wildly around. "Where? Where can I go? He'll find me anywhere!" She started to back off the porch, then slipped and crashed into the lilacs.

Ta'quisha pulled her out and growled, "Tough titties, girl. You lied to me. Now all of us are in danger because of you."

"Well I can destroy the phone, can't I?" Alicia begged.

"No, that will only tip him off that we know," Maybelle replied. "The best thing is to get you and it out of here right now. Later you can send it in a different direction to head him off." She turned to Ta'quisha. "Ta'quisha, get Kelly to help you and get her packed up. Including the phone. Let's hustle!"

Bonnie ran to finish loading the truck with the crates of peaches. Other women joined her and finished the job. Then she backed it out of the barn and parked it in the front yard, ready to go.

Arlene and Erik emerged from the path that was a shortcut down the mountain to Kristin and Erik's house. They huddled with Maybelle and Jim for a few minutes. Maybelle instructed Erik, "Watch for any vehicle you don't recognize. Then do the deadfall behind them. Be ready." Erik nodded and ran back down the path toward home.

Maybelle motioned Jamie Lynn over and they spoke in low tones. Jamie took off running toward her cabin. She came back through the yard carrying her bow and quiver, and followed Erik down the mountain.

It didn't take long to pack up Alicia's and Amy's stuff. The hard part was pulling Amy out of the group of youngsters in the garden. They were busy hoeing and harvesting greens, and Amy's basket was almost full. Her mother insisted that she leave it, and Amy wailed in protest. Then Amy turned and saw her mother's face, and recognized that old mask of barely-restrained terror, a look she hadn't seen in months. Alicia was carrying a suitcase. What was happening? Amy dropped the basket and scooted in front of her mother, as Ta'quisha and Kelly followed with the other suitcases.

The little caravan trotted down the hill and across the yard to where the pickup stood. The suitcases were tossed in the back with the crates of peaches, and Amy and Alicia climbed into the cab. Bonnie leaned out and spoke to Maybelle.

"I'll go on over to Fayetteville, then on up to Bentonville. Then I'll send the phone someplace and put these two on a Greyhound to St. Louis. They'll have to find their own way to the safe house. It's the best we can do in a hurry."

"Yes, it truly is," agreed Maybelle. "Good luck."

117

Bonnie had to ask Amy to move her knee out of the way of the stickshift. The pickup's old clutch ground as it shifted to low gear.

At that moment, before the pickup could get rolling, a Jeep rounded the corner and skidded into the driveway, stopping in front of the truck. A man jumped out of the Jeep with a gun, pointing it at the pickup's windshield.

"Get out. Right now. That's my wife." It was Jeremy. Alicia blanched and instinctively raised her arms to shield her face. Amy ducked and whimpered. Bonnie started to open her door and Jeremy fired into it, narrowly missing her. She slammed the door again, then tucked her body down over Amy and put her foot on the clutch. The truck rolled forward toward the Jeep. Jeremy jumped out of the way and fired again, this time through the windshield, right where Bonnie had been a moment before.

"Wait, wait, Jeremy!" A breathless scream came from Alicia. "Stop! I'll come with you!" Sobbing. Opening her door to step out.

Bonnie slammed on the brakes and stayed down. Alicia fell out the door and crumpled on the ground. Then she picked herself up and walked toward Jeremy, arms out, pleading.

"Honey, don't shoot. You know I was coming back to you. See, we're all packed up. We're coming back. Here, let me get my suitcase." She turned toward the back of the pickup.

Jeremy lunged and grabbed her arm. "Oh no, you don't. Get in the Jeep." He jerked her arm savagely as he dragged her back to the cab of the truck. "Amy, get out here." He kept the gun trained on Alicia and yanked the pickup's door open. Swung the gun toward Amy.

"Do what he says, Amy." Bonnie whispered. "Don't worry. Just go now." She forced a smile toward Jeremy. "This will save me a trip. Can I give you the suitcases?"

"Yes, you go get the suitcases, bitch." Waving the gun toward Bonnie, who hustled around back and brought them toward the Jeep. He swung the gun toward Alicia and Amy. "You two get in the back seat. I'm locking you in." He pushed them in and set the child-proof locks. He opened the hatchback and motioned with the gun toward Bonnie.

"Throw the suitcases in the back, bitch." Bonnie tossed them in and slammed the hatchback, then backed away with her hands raised. She said nothing but stared hard at Alicia for a second, willing her to be strong. She made a slight motion with her hand toward her own head, pushing it down.

"If anybody calls the police, this woman dies." Jeremy swung the gun toward Alicia and Amy. Amy ducked her head into Alicia's lap. Alicia leaned over Amy, cradling and stroking her silently. Jeremy jumped into the Jeep, not bothering with his seatbelt, and gunned the engine.

"We understand. Go ahead." Bonnie spoke for everyone.

The Jeep skidded out, heading out the drive and down the steep mountain road. Bonnie watched as billows of red dust hid the Jeep. Alicia looked up into the rear-view mirror, her eyes pleading with Jeremy. He grinned at her familiar panicked look. "Please, Jeremy, slow down. We aren't even buckled in." He just grinned again and accelerated.

She turned to Amy and latched her seatbelt, then buckled her own. Then she pulled Amy down onto the seat again, their faces close together. Alicia cradled Amy's chin, putting her finger on her lips. Amy saw a new light in her mother's eyes, a kind of grim determination. Then Alicia lay on top of Amy and braced her feet against the back of the front seat. She continued to stroke Amy's arm as the vehicle hurtled around curves.

On a curve halfway down the mountain the Jeep hurtled past the house it had passed on the way up. Again, no one was on the porch or in the yard. Jeremy smiled. He'd scared the shit out of those people up above, and nobody down at this place had seen him. *The first turn-off I see, I'm going to take it,* he thought, *and it'll be the last road Alicia will ever travel.*

Suddenly a huge branch blocked the road ahead. Jeremy braked hard but still crashed into the mass of leaves, sending the Jeep skidding sideways on the loose gravel and over into the ditch. He spun the wheels furiously and only succeeded in moving the Jeep further over the edge. He cursed and got out of the car. There was a thud, and his body spun, his face frozen in astonishment. Then another thud, and he pitched slowly forward into the dirt.

Alicia kept her head down, not daring to move for several minutes. She hugged Amy until she heard, "Mom – I can't breathe!" Alicia released her grip, but still didn't dare to sit up.

Then she heard Jamie Lynn's voice.

"Ha – that was easy!"

Alicia raised her head and saw Jamie standing outside her window. Uncomprehending, she looked for Jeremy and didn't see him. Jamie opened the driver's door and unlocked the childproof locks. Then she circled the car again and opened the back door on Alicia's side.

"Come on out, it's all over. Y'all are safe now." Jamie beckoned Alicia and Amy out of the car. They cautiously uncurled themselves, unbuckled their seatbelts, and stepped out into the road.

"What happened to Jeremy?"

Jamie grinned. "See for yourself. But maybe Amy shouldn't." Jamie reached out and took Amy's hand. Her other hand still held the bow.

"Come with me, kiddo," said Jamie. Wide-eyed, Amy obediently clung to Jamie's hand. Jamie led her back up the road toward Kristin and Erik's house.

Alicia watched them go, then circled around the Jeep to the driver's side. Jeremy lay face down in the road. A wooden arrow with a broad steel point had bisected his neck, and another protruded from his back. Blood pooled beneath his body and soaked into the red clay of the road.

Alicia dropped to her knees, but no tears came. Stunned, she sat there for several minutes. Then she began to laugh, hysterically.

Chapter 21 – Washington, D.C.

Driving toward Mary's apartment in Edmonston, neither Mary nor Vanessa spoke. The streets were dark but not deserted. Vanessa shivered. Why had she ever driven in this direction in the first place? Didn't she have any sense? She was a trained FBI agent, and she'd driven alone through a neighborhood she should have avoided. And then she'd stopped and parked and walked alone into a club. *Even if they catch that guy, a jury will say I asked for it.*

Vanessa thanked god the cops had decided not to book her. How had that miracle happened? Then she remembered: It was Mary who averted that, with her smile, her efficiency, her chatter. Vanessa looked over at Mary, puzzled.

"How did you happen to be in that 5th District station? Explain that to me now!"

"Tracy called me. Tracy, from the club." A pause. "My friend Tracy." She glanced at Vanessa, who seemed not to hear.

Then Vanessa remembered her conversation with the barmaid, and her unsolicited advice about Mary: "You're in good hands. She can be trusted."

"Okay, so you know this woman from the church choir," Vanessa ventured. "She somehow knows you can sweet-talk cops, and she calls you in the middle of the night to bail me out. Me, an FBI agent and task force leader. And you do it. As if you'd done it before. Explain that to me."

"There are many things about me you don't know," Mary answered. "Just as there are many things about you I don't know. And that's why we need to talk. Tonight is a good time to start."

"Yeah, hell, I guess so… I won't be falling asleep anytime soon, that's for sure," Vanessa acknowledged, shaking her head and looking out the window.

They drove in silence for another ten minutes, then pulled off 201 in Edmonston. Mary pulled into an underground garage beneath a modern apartment complex. She drove carefully, circled all the way around the structure before choosing a parking place close to the elevator.

"Got to be careful around here. There have been some armed robberies. I always swing around the structure twice just to check," Mary explained. Exiting the car, Vanessa noticed that Mary didn't drop her keys into her handbag, but instead held them in her right fist, sticking out between her fingers like claws. *Good training*, thought Vanessa. *When did I lose my vigilance?*

They walked to the elevator and Mary swiped a key card. They waited, Mary standing off to the side to scan both the structure and the elevator door. When it opened empty, they got on, Mary standing again near the front of the car. They stopped in the lobby to collect Mary's mail, then rode on up to the 6th floor. Mary unlocked her door and ushered Vanessa in.

"Can I offer you a beer?" Mary opened the closet and handed Vanessa a coat hanger.

"No, not this late. I don't think I'm gonna drink again ever, after what happened tonight. How could I have been so stupid?" Vanessa's hand trembled as she hung up her coat. "I don't think I'll be sleeping tonight."

Mary touched Vanessa's shoulder. "Turn toward the light." She examined Vanessa's face. "It's a little late now, but let's put some ice on your face there. Might keep some of the swelling down." Mary emptied an ice tray into a ziplock bag, then went into the bathroom and added rubbing alcohol to the cubes.

"This will feel nice and cold in a minute," Mary said, as she wrapped the ice bag in a dishtowel and handed it to Vanessa. It did feel deliciously cold on her cheek.

Mary offered a chair at her kitchen table, and Vanessa sank gratefully into it, resting her elbows on the table and her head in her hands. After a couple minutes of uncomfortable silence, Mary sighed and said, "Well, we have a big day tomorrow, we'd better try to get some rest. I'll make us some Sleepytime tea." Mary put the pot on to heat, then disappeared into the bedroom. She came back with some flannel pajamas, a robe, slippers and socks.

"Here – these are probably too short for you, but they'll be plenty big in the hips. Go on in there and take a hot shower. Grab a towel and a toothbrush from the cupboard. I keep new ones just for such emergencies."

"Emergencies like your boss getting arrested? That happens often?" Vanessa forced a laugh.

Mary chuckled lightly and waved her off. "That's better. Go on now."

After Vanessa went into the bathroom, Mary busied herself with unfolding the futon and fixing it up with bedding. She warmed her calico teapot and poured hot water over the tea ball. The soothing aroma filled the kitchen. She set out a plate of fruitcake and two smaller plates, along with two large handmade mugs. She was pouring the tea when Vanessa emerged from the bathroom, toweling her hair. She looked a little silly in the pajamas that barely reached past her calves. Mary hid a smile.

"Thanks, that did feel good."

"I'm glad. Sit down and try this fruitcake. I make it with almond flour and walnuts. You're not allergic to nuts, are you?"

"No ma'am. That smells good." Vanessa ate a small piece, then reached for another. "Wow, this reminds me of what my mama used to make, with those cherries in it."

Mary sat down and sipped her tea. There was a silence, which Mary broke. "Look, Vanessa, I'm going to be real honest with you now. I know you've had a hard time since you started working with us. It's not easy being a new hire, and it's really not easy to work for Mr. Williamson."

"You can say that again, sister. He doesn't have any idea what he wants. Hires me to do one thing and then completely changes course. But I know damn well that what he *doesn't* want is *me* working there. I'm about ready to quit."

"And I'm going to tell you why you shouldn't. At least not yet, not for this reason."

"What's your angle? Are you defending him?" Vanessa's look darkened. *What is this white woman manipulating me into?*

"Nope, that is not what I'm doing. I'm saying we can work around him." Mary leaned forward. "It doesn't matter what work you were assigned to do. Anything you give him, he will complain about and dismiss, even without reading or understanding it. So why knock yourself out? Give him something that looks plausible, or more important, that looks like what he imagines he wants. And spend your energy researching what *you* want to find out."

Mary let that sink in for a minute, then went on. "There are a lot of things that we have access to with our clearance. I should say, with *your* clearance – I'm just a secretary. Information that adds up to dynamite if we ever want to use it. Now, here, in this job, is your opportunity to learn, to collect, to arm yourself, to

125

build a case. An opportunity to avenge yourself someday for everything they have ever done to you. I know you know what I'm talking about." She paused and looked Vanessa straight in the eyes. "And in the meantime, an opportunity to help your sisters. Just like we helped you tonight."

Vanessa lifted her head and looked at Mary sitting across from her in a pink fuzzy bathrobe, her face pale, her gray hair a little windblown, her eyes tired. *This woman is a revolutionary, a radical, the leader of a spy ring?* She didn't believe it. And yet... she had sprung up out of nowhere tonight to save her ass.

"What are you asking me to do?"

"Well, nothing in particular. Just wake up and stop trying to please the man. Keep your eyes open. Know that you can trust me and Samantha. And Tracy. And many more. In fact, none of us knows exactly how many other sisters there are. But they're out there if you look for them. Listen to your gut and trust the ones who are awake, like you're going to be. And don't despair. Your job is not what the man tells you it is. Your job is whatever you make it."

Mary stood up and gathered the dishes.

"And now it's time for bed. Pick yourself out a book to read." She gestured toward the bookcase.

While Vanessa browsed the shelf, Mary ran hot water in the sink and opened two hot water bottles with pliers. She filled the bottles halfway and wrapped them in dishtowels. Then she brought a stuffed bear from the bedroom. As if she were Vanessa's mom, Mary directed her to turn off her smartphone. Then she turned on the small lamp by the futon and turned off the overhead light.

"I'll put a nightlight in the bathroom. Wrap yourself around this hot water bottle and this bear, and read. I guarantee you'll be asleep in no time." Mary patted Vanessa's shoulder, smiled and stepped back.

"We'll talk again tomorrow."

Chapter 22 – Ozarks

Slowly, Alicia got to her feet, pulling herself up by the Jeep's door handle. She felt a little dizzy as she looked at Jeremy lying in the dust of the road, the blood slowly spreading around his body. She tried to summon some feeling toward him – sympathy, friendship, even hatred. It was impossible. She felt nothing but a vast numbness. Her gorge rose, but she couldn't even puke. The world around her looked grey and dull, out of focus.

After an eternity, Alicia heard Ta'quisha calling her name and she turned toward her, surprised. Ta'quisha ran up and turned Alicia away from Jeremy's body. Then she steered her up the road.

"We're going to have to get out of here soon. But you and Amy need to eat. Come on."

Alicia stopped. "Wait a minute." She looked at her feet, then up at Ta'quisha. "I have to say something." She took a deep breath. "I know I've been nothing but trouble since I got here. When you and Jim first came to get me, I called you a smart-ass nigger."

"You did?" Ta'quisha's eyes grew hard.

"Well, not out loud. But I thought it. I didn't even want to get into the van. I didn't even like you. And I didn't listen to you. And now see what I did." Alicia teared up. She hung her head and whispered, "I'm so sorry."

Ta'quisha reached out and drew her in.

"Hush. The Lord works in strange ways. Now let's get going."

They walked together back up the steep road toward Kristin and Erik's house, Ta'quisha steadying Alicia, who walked as if in a dream. After a few hundred yards, the house appeared, with Kristin on the porch, beckoning them in. Inside were Jamie Lynn and Amy, already eating. Maybelle also sat at the table.

Kristin pulled out a chair and Alicia dropped into it. A bowl of stew appeared in front of her, and a plate of fresh bread. Alicia mechanically picked up her spoon and sipped at the stew. Kristin gave her a glass of milk and put butter on the bread. Alicia felt like a child. Slowly, like a child, she bit into the bread. The tastiness of the food penetrated her fog and she began to enjoy it. She looked over to see Amy doing the same.

What has changed? Why am I so hungry? Good grief – this is meat, and gluten, and lactose! I shouldn't eat any of those! Alicia pushed back her plate and started to stand up. Then, as if she saw the scene from above, she took in the women around the table, quietly talking and savoring the meal. Ta'quisha looked up at her, a question in her eyes. Alicia sank back down onto her chair and picked up her spoon. *How ridiculous. I'm alive. We're alive. I'll eat anything.*

After dinner, Arlene arrived. She told Maybelle quietly that she'd recruited a clean-up crew and sent them down the road. Maybelle grinned at Ta'quisha and Jamie, and nodded her head toward Arlene, as if to say, *This kid's pretty swift, don't you think?*

"Well, then, it's time for you to sit down and eat," said Maybelle. She sliced some bread while Arlene served herself some stew. "And after that, you can keep Amy occupied while we work out some plans."

Arlene looked around for a children's book to read to Amy, then took her stew and bread out to the front porch. The two of them sat snuggled under a quilt on the porch swing. Arlene read out loud between bites, while Amy turned the pages.

Maybelle, Kristin, Jamie and Ta'quisha sat with Alicia at the kitchen table.

"As soon as that branch is out of the way," Maybelle announced, "we need to get Alicia and Amy out of here."

Kristin turned to Alicia with a question. "Is that your husband's Jeep?"

Alicia shook her head. "Uh… no, I've never seen him drive anything like that."

"It must be a rental," Ta'quisha suggested. "I'll check the glove box. We'll get it back to where it came from and go from there." She turned to Alicia. "Don't worry, we'll get you to someplace safe."

"I know we will," Jamie agreed. "You know the safe places better than I do, Ta'quisha."

Maybelle leaned forward and took Alicia's hand. "Alicia, you need to go back to L.A. You need to reoccupy your house."

Alicia looked up, stunned. "I can't. I can't live there. Jeremy…"

"Jeremy is dead, Alicia. He can't hurt you anymore. But you need to be there when the investigation starts. You need to see it through. You need to have never even left the state. And you need to forget you were ever here." Maybelle paused and let that sink in. "We can send someone with you. We'll need two people. Who do you want to go with you?"

Alicia looked around in a panic. "Ta'quisha? And Jamie?" She reddened and looked down at the table again. Maybelle looked at each of them in turn, her eyebrow raised.

"Yes, okay. We'll go," Jamie agreed.

Ta'quisha shrugged. "How long do you think we'll have to be out there?"

"Long enough to head off an investigation. And long enough to get this woman title to her home." Maybelle looked from one to the other, gauging their agreement. "If you don't want to go, tell me now. Otherwise you need to stay long enough to get the job done."

Alicia sat staring at her folded hands. Then Ta'quisha's hand reached out to grasp hers. "We can do this, girl. I would have liked it if you'd ditched that goddamn phone. If he hadn't chased you here. But this may turn out for the best, and the sooner we're back there staking your claim the better."

Alicia looked up and met Ta'quisha's eye. Ta'quisha looked hard at her, then smiled grimly and squeezed her hand. "Come on, we don't have much time."

Maybelle stepped out to the front porch, where Arlene had just finished reading Goodnight Moon to Amy. "I'll take over here. You can be helpful down below."

Walking back down the road, Alicia, Ta'quisha and Jamie were met by Bonnie coming uphill. Bonnie handed a smartphone to Jamie. "This is his phone. Make sure it stays in the Jeep when you turn it in." She walked past them, then turned back to shout, "I'll bring the truck down soon."

The women continued around the curve, hearing the whine of a chainsaw. Down by the Jeep, Erik was cutting through the branch while several women hauled pieces of wood away. Arlene was picking up smaller branches and pulling them to the side of the road. Alicia glanced at the ground where Jeremy had lain, but there was no sign of him. Even the blood-soaked dirt had been scraped away, as if he'd never been there. The three

131

women joined the others in hauling the leafy branches to the side of the road.

Jamie inspected the Jeep, running her hand along the fender. Not a scratch. *How had they gotten so lucky?* Ta'quisha was leaning in the passenger side, pulling out the rental papers.

"It's a Thrifty place at OKC," Ta'quisha announced. "That's the Will Rogers Airport at Oklahoma City. That's a haul." She looked up at Jamie, questions in her eyes.

Jamie nodded. "Let's figure this out with Bonnie. She should be down pretty soon."

Chapter 23 – Washington, D.C.

Vanessa awoke in Mary's apartment, a little stiff and disoriented. A faint light was coming in around the window shade, but the window was in the wrong place. An alarm clock buzzed from another room and was quickly silenced. Then Vanessa remembered – she was at Mary's place. She sat up and looked around for her clothes.

Mary came out of her bedroom, yawning.

"I'm sorry, I forgot to turn off the alarm. It's Saturday. We can sleep in."

Vanessa stood up. She looked exhausted, and her face was still swollen.

"No, we can't sleep in. We have to find that shithead that tried to take me." Her voice broke and she turned away. Then she looked back at Mary. "'Scuse me, but that's what he is."

Mary hid her surprise at the crack in Vanessa's professional manner. *Could she be starting to trust me?*

"OK, then. After breakfast. What do you want? Eggs, bacon, oatmeal?"

Vanessa sat back down. "Actually, I'm not feeling so good. Maybe oatmeal. I've got one helluva headache."

Mary disappeared into the bathroom and came back with a glass of water and a tablet. "Here, take a rizatriptan. It's a silver bullet for migraines. And I'll get the ice pack for you again. Your face still looks a bit beat up."

Vanessa winced and looked up at Mary. "How could I have let that happen? Where's my training? I just let somebody just climb into my car and knock me out? Fuck..." She shook her head in disgust.

"Looks to me like you did okay. You shot him without killing him, and got him out of the car, didn't you?" Vanessa nodded. "OK, then," concluded Mary, "Your training was still there, you've still got it." She paused. "Don't start getting all vulnerable on me."

Vanessa took the towel-wrapped ice pack and lay back on the couch. Mary bustled around the kitchen getting breakfast. Finally she called Vanessa to the table.

As they ate, Mary asked, "So what's our first step today? Do we want to bother with the police we talked to last night?"

"Yes, we will," answered Vanessa, "but we're going to involve FBI also if we need them. Those cops can't just blow us off like they did."

"Okay, so what do we do first?"

"We go back up to the 5th District station and talk to the cops there. We figure out what to do with my car. Or what they'll let us do."

Two hours later, Mary and Vanessa pulled up to the 5th District Metropolitan Police Station, parked, and stepped out. They both had business suits on, every pleat in place. They walked together into the lobby and talked through the window to the desk sergeant.

"I'm here to discuss the incident last night," said Vanessa.

The desk sergeant looked puzzled. "What incident?"

"It was late last night. A carjacking and a shooting over on Meigs Place. Off of Bladensburg Road." When he still looked blank, Vanessa continued. "It was before your shift started. Do you have someone on duty who can talk to me?" She showed her FBI badge and the sergeant sat up.

"Yes, ma'am, just a moment, let me call."

"Please do." As the sergeant slid the window closed, Vanessa widened her eyes at Mary. Then she turned back to face the desk.

The desk sergeant picked up his phone. Two minutes later the hallway door buzzed and he ushered Mary and Vanessa through. They were met by the officer on duty, Lieutenant Abrams. He showed them to his office and gestured to seats.

Lt. Abrams smiled. "What can I do for you ladies today?"

Vanessa flashed her badge. "I need to get an update on the incident I was involved in last night."

"Yes, I was told about it."

"There should be a written report," said Vanessa. "If you haven't seen it, I can fill you in."

"That's okay. I got the gist of it. We haven't apprehended the perpetrator yet. But it's on our radar."

"I need to know when you'll be done with my car," Vanessa reminded him. "I can't be without wheels."

"Well, ma'am, that may take a while. You might want to rent a car for the next week."

"The next week?" Vanessa's voice was slow and deliberate. Mary recognized her growing irritation. "How long does it take you to dust a car's steering wheel?"

"Well, this case isn't exactly high priority," answered Lieutenant Abrams, with an apologetic shrug. "We've been called to add security to an event at the White House this week. You know, the parade."

Vanessa opened her mouth to speak just as Mary interjected, "Of course, Lieutenant Abrams, we understand. Can we get some idea of the progress of this investigation – aside from the car? Has the guy presented at any hospital for that gunshot wound? That would have required a police report, right?"

"Well, yes, it would have, under normal circumstances. But this week we're stretched so thin that normal procedures may not happen."

At that, both women just stared. Vanessa started to say, "Are you –" when Mary grabbed her hand hard and stood up.

"Well, we won't take any more of your time, Lieutenant. We understand the priorities, and we are grateful for any follow-up you can give us. We'll check back in next week. Thank you so much for your efforts with this case." She hauled Vanessa to her feet, smiled brightly at the Lieutenant and exited his office. Vanessa shook off Mary's hand, but followed her out the door.

Back in the car, Vanessa ripped Mary a new one. "What in hell was that about? I was about to give that idiot a piece of my mind. By the time they do anything the trail will be stone cold!"

"Yes, I know exactly what you were about to do," said Mary hotly. "You were going to pull rank and get that cop plenty pissed off at you. Not only would that not have helped, you could have wound up charged with something other than self-defense. And it wouldn't have speeded anything up."

"Goddamn parade," Vanessa fumed. "What does anybody need with a goddamn military parade? Is this a tinhorn dictatorship?"

"Umm, well, could be…?" Mary answered, as if it had never occurred to her. She gave Vanessa a sidelong look and then laughed. "Let it roll off, hon. We have to pick our battles. We can find this guy way sooner than they ever could have, anyhow. I just figured we should give them a chance to do it. Now that we know they won't, let's do it on our own."

"And how do you propose we do that?"

"I'd rather not say. And you don't need to know. But I'll let you know when I have an answer, probably this afternoon. In the meantime, let's at least go rent you a car."

With that, Mary put her car in gear and drove away from the station. She could feel the waves of heat coming off Vanessa, but she deliberately pretended not to notice. *No point in becoming a lightning rod myself,* she thought.

Chapter 24 – Ozarks

While Erik and the women finished cutting up and clearing the large branch and scribblage out of the road, Bonnie had been up at the farm, getting the pickup ready for a long trip.

Bonnie took a few minutes to round up several homing pigeons from the dovecote. She entered by the small door at the bottom of the structure and climbed up the interior ladder to where the pigeons were roosting. Gathering several pigeons, she carried them down the ladder and tucked them into two cages, each cage equipped with a feeder and a water bottle.

Crossing over to the barn, Bonnie collected tiny clips and canisters from the storage cupboard and packed them into boxes. These canisters were designed to carry messages, clipped to a pigeon's leg – messages too secret or too urgent to go by mail.

The homing pigeons were accustomed to being transported around the country. They were comfortable with their cages and familiar with the feeder, and the long road trips didn't seem to bother them. Bonnie nestled the cages in the back of the pickup under a heavy canvas tarp. The crates of peaches were rearranged so they wouldn't slide on the way down the mountain. She fetched a 6-person tent and four sleeping bags from the storeroom in the barn and packed them in under the tarp. Before she took off, Jim met her at the door with some food packed for the women, water in canteens, a bundle of cash, and a paper bag containing rags, plastic gloves, and a small bottle of ammonia.

By the time Bonnie came over the brow of the hill in the pickup, the remnants of the tree branch had been pulled aside. Erik was busy pulling a heavy rope down from an overhanging limb. Bonnie turned the truck around and backed it toward the Jeep. Erik hooked the rope to the Jeep's front bumper, then tied it to the pickup's trailer hitch. He put some of the smaller branches just in front of the Jeep's wheels for traction. Jamie got into the driver's seat and started the engine. Then Erik and the other three women got on either side of the Jeep, ready to push. One woman had gone to the back of the Jeep.

"No, never get behind a vehicle," Erik corrected her. "That's how to get hurt. Grab a door handle or the frame and push from the side." She moved around to the side and he shouted to Bonnie.

"OK, pull her out!" The pickup started up slowly in first gear and the rope went taut. The Jeep's wheels ground slowly and then caught on the branches under them. Without too much effort the Jeep rolled obediently up out of the ditch.

"Good job. Not a scratch. A little wash will take care of this dust." He lowered his voice and spoke to Jamie. "And be sure to get any fingerprints off."

"You bet I will," Jamie agreed quietly.

Bonnie turned the truck around to face downhill again, set the parking brake and climbed out, handing the keys to Ta'quisha.

Jamie pulled Alicia's luggage out of the Jeep and put it in the back of the pickup, under the tarp. The food went on the floor of the pickup, along with the bag of cash. Jamie kept the cleaning supplies in the Jeep, where she'd need them, along with another lumpy bag of clothes. As a final touch, she looped her hair into a bun, brushed off her jeans, and put on the baseball cap she'd taken off Jeremy. Into her pocket she tucked his ID and his fake mustache. *All set.*

Bonnie gathered Jamie, Ta'quisha and Alicia together and addressed them. She pulled two worn maps out of her back pocket and spread them out on the hood of the Jeep.

"OK, ladies, listen up. Does everybody have their ID? Let's plan your route now. Tonight, you'll drive as far as Eureka Springs, and you'll stay at a private campground there – the Washboard." She circled the location on the map. "Of course, you'll leave the Jeep outside the camp, and you'll pay cash. The tent and sleeping bags are in the back of the pickup there.

"Tomorrow morning you'll head for Bentonville. Jamie will stop to wash and detail the Jeep, while the rest of you deliver the first half of the peaches to the co-op there. The other half you deliver to Fayetteville, to the farm stand – you know where it is." She pointed again to the map and made another mark.

"You'll be coming down I-49 to I-40 to get to Oklahoma City. I know 412 is faster, but it's a toll road with cameras. You can't risk that. And you don't pull the Jeep into any of these stops. Ta'quisha, Jamie will catch up with you, OK?" She looked up at them and both women nodded.

Bonnie continued, "You'll get to Lake Eufaula State Park off 40 in time to camp. The day after that you'll deliver the Jeep to the Will Rogers Airport – Jamie, you'll do that. Ta'quisha will circle and pick you up at the exit ramp. It'll be a little cramped with all four of you in the pickup from there to LA, but you can do it.

"If you can get past Albuquerque that day, you have sisters in the Navajo Nation. They know Ta'quisha and Jamie, and you'll be safe there. Beyond that, you'll be on your own. When you get to L.A., deliver the pigeons to the safe house in Commerce – you know where that is."

Bonnie turned to Alicia and held her by the shoulders.

"Alicia, when you get back home, you'll just need to sit tight. Don't let anything surprise you. Remember, you don't know where your husband went. You need to reach out to his work friends to find out what he told them about this trip of his. Judging from the fake mustache and the fake ID, he was covering his tracks. And Jamie and Ta'quisha will be right close by, ready to help you, anytime."

She paused and looked around at them. "That's all I can think of. Now go collect Amy, and off you go. We'll finish cleaning up here."

In ten minutes, the caravan set off, with Jamie driving the Jeep and Ta'quisha behind the wheel of the pickup. Amy bounced with excitement in the middle of the pickup's grubby bench seat, thrilled to be riding in a big, noisy truck. Alicia stared out the window, wondering what her life had become, frightened of the future, but hanging on with a new, thin thread of courage.

Back up at their house, Erik and Kristin gave Maybelle a ride home. Tomorrow would be time to dispose of the body. And tomorrow he and Kristin would prepare another deadfall over the road. *You never know when you'll need one.*

Chapter 25 – Washington, D.C.

Mary and Vanessa drove by the club where the incident had happened last night. They had decided on the way over that, since the police were not going to secure Vanessa's car today, they had to do it themselves, even at the risk of appearing to tamper with a crime scene. So the first order of business was to retrieve the car keys and the fingerprints that were on them, and lock the car up.

Miraculously, Vanessa's car was still parked where it was last night, and even more miraculously, her keys were still in the ignition. Vanessa took the plastic gloves Mary offered her. As they drew abreast of her car, she slipped the gloves on, slid out the passenger door, and opened her own car door with her spare key. She reached in and took the keys out of the ignition, taking care to handle them only by the edges. She hit the lock button and closed the door quietly, then slid back into Mary's car. Mary drove on while Vanessa dropped the keys into an evidence bag.

They drove on back to the 5th District Station with the keys, and handed them over to the desk sergeant. He was surprised to see them again so soon.

"We understand that your staff is stretched thin today." Vanessa's voice was crisp and businesslike. "We took the liberty of bringing you these car keys. The last person who handled them is the carjacker who accosted me last night. Incidentally, I believe you should get some record of the injuries I received. Is your photographer on duty this morning?"

"Yes, but I think he's about to head out to the parade."

"Well then, it's a good thing we arrived just now. This will only take a moment. I need him to document this." She pointed to her left eye and cheek, still swollen and now very colorfully bruised. The sergeant, persuaded by her commanding manner as well as the badge she slid across the desk, called back for the photographer and opened the door for her to come through. He also accepted the car keys in the evidence bag and went to work writing a receipt.

A few minutes later, Vanessa re-emerged from the back room and winked at Mary, waiting in the lobby. As they left the station she remarked, "See, you're not the only one who can get things done. I don't lose my temper every time."

"I can see that. And I can also see that you have a whole lot more reason than me to lose it. Well done." She grinned over at Vanessa. Vanessa, this time, knew that Mary's smile was genuine, not a polite cover. Her old suspicion was fading.

As they drove to a rental car agency, Mary told Vanessa that she needed to do some work on her own today, but she invited Vanessa to spend the night again at her house. Vanessa declined, saying she had to go home to take care of things.

They pulled into the rental agency, and Vanessa got out. Then she leaned into the car and grasped Mary's hand. "Thanks for everything. Really."

Mary grinned at her. "Please think about coming back tonight. Even just for dinner. I'll be home by 6, probably."

"Well, maybe. I'll call you, at least."

After renting a Mazda, Vanessa found herself without plans for the day. She decided to go to the African American History Museum, a place she'd heard about but never taken the time to visit.

Mary, meanwhile, drove to the VA Community Resource & Referral Center on 15th St. NE, just north of the arboretum, figuring it's where a man wounded on Bladensburg Road might head to. She walked in to the reception desk and asked for her friend Jane, a nurse who worked there. When Jane appeared, Mary asked her to step outside. They walked a little way, while Mary described Vanessa's attacker, his appearance and his wounds. To her surprise, Jane confirmed that this guy had been there last night, and he'd been referred on to the Center for Medicare Advocacy for treatment of his wounds. Mary and Jane walked back to the clinic, where Jane discreetly looked up and wrote down the patient's name. Mary thanked her and jumped back in her car.

Mary drove straight down Rhode Island Avenue to the Center for Medicare Advocacy, less than four miles away. She pulled into the parking lot, parked and went into the hospital. This time she went to a hallway phone and called her friend Liz via the hospital's internal phone line. The two women met up in the cafeteria, where they spoke together in low voices. Mary explained the incident and her search for the perpetrator. Liz confirmed that the same guy had been treated early this morning for two gunshot wounds and was now on her floor.

"Then I've got something for you," Mary said quietly. "It's blood collected from the street where the incident went down. I want you to compare it to this guy's blood. Call me as soon as you match it – or if it doesn't match. I can be in touch with the FBI or district police right away. The 5th District Metropolitan Police Station also has this blood sample for cross-verification." Mary pulled the evidence bag out of her handbag, wrapped it in a napkin in her lap, and passed it across to Liz. Liz tucked it in the pocket of her lab coat.

On her way back to her floor, Liz stopped by the lab to fill out a requisition, requesting a STAT reading per law enforcement.

Back in her car, Mary called Vanessa. "We need to get together. Where are you?"

"I'm at the African American Museum – that's on the National Mall."

"Great, that's like a mile from where I am. I'll be right there. Where should I look for you?"

When they met up in the Sweet Home Café in the museum, Mary told Vanessa that she thought she'd tracked down her assailant, but was waiting for a blood match.

"Already? You think you found the guy already?"

"Yes. But from now on we have to play by the rules. I've submitted the blood sample we got from the scene. And remember that the cops also have the same sample. If we get a match, then we need to turn everything we know over to the FBI Lab Division. If they don't want to take the case on, then at least we'll have something more to go back to the local cops with. And with a little more muscle."

"You do work fast, Mary. How is it you're just a secretary instead of a detective?"

"Don't say 'just a secretary'. That'd be like saying Harriet Tubman was just a field hand. I get plenty of information, and I have plenty of power, right where I am, thank you!" Mary gave a sly smile that made her look like Margaret Rutherford, and Vanessa assessed her anew. She would never again underestimate this old lady.

"You astonish me, ma'am. And you know what? I think I will take you up on that offer to stay the night again. I think we both have a lot to learn from each other. Okay with you?"

"Absolutely! But first I'd like to take a look at this museum. Shall we?" And with that, they got up and, arm in arm, climbed the stairs to the galleries.

Chapter 26 – Ozarks

Halfway up the mountain road, below Kristin and Erik's place, two small houses sat near each other and too close to the road. In the old days, having a small front yard meant that a horse could be hitched right to the front porch rail. Nowadays, it meant that the front porch collected a new layer of red dust every time a vehicle went past. Still, the owner of the second house, a black woman named Susie, used the front porch as a haircut parlor. Susie, in her 40s, looked much younger to her customers. It may have been because of the dimples that appeared each time she laughed at their jokes, or perhaps the tunes she hummed as she cut their hair, or her seemingly boundless energy. She could be seen out there every day, sometimes with just one customer, sometimes with a few customers waiting on the other side of the porch. Even on rainy days, the wide porch overhang kept the operation dry. She had even rigged up a sink with a faucet at one end of the porch, while an extension cord ran out the window.

Susie considered herself lucky to have electricity. Her house was at the end of the power line that stretched up the mountain from the valley below. Everyone above her on the mountain – Kristin and Erik, and the whole Barker farm – did without electricity. Even so, her water supply was rudimentary, connected by pump to a well, and heated by propane. She still used a backyard privy, same as her neighbor Lisa did. Nevertheless, she managed to run her little barber shop, and she had a steady clientele. Her only advertising, aside from her presence on the porch and her friendly wave, was a sign:

Haircuts $4
Kids $3
Braids $6
Closed Sunday

People from a few miles around would come to get their hair done by Susie. She had a deft touch with the clippers, and her cornrow braid stylings were intricate and new. She made a small living from the hair business for herself and her 10-year-old son Cecil. She called him Ceci, and so did everyone else.

What Susie enjoyed most was talking with her customers when they visited. She collected their news and spread it to everyone else the same day. And there was something quite satisfying about being able to sweep all the cut hair right off the porch into the yard. Occasionally she would find a bird's nest with human hair woven into it. This made her laugh, and she'd take Ceci by the hand and show it to him.

Next door to her was another family, a white couple with a 9-year-old son, Jacob. The two boys, Jake and Ceci, were inseparable, usually running off together on the weekends to explore the mountainside. Both mothers were glad that the boys stuck together. It was safer that way, considering the feral hogs on the mountain – and the bears that had moved back in to prey on them. On weekdays both boys walked up the mountain to the Barker farm for school with Arlene and the other kids.

Jake's mom Lisa was disabled from a carpentry accident many years ago, but she managed to keep a large vegetable garden with Susie. Both moms demanded help from their boys, who were generally willing, especially if they worked together. The women shared garden produce and kept a small flock of hens and one rooster. The chicken pen and henhouse were behind Susie's place. They talked about getting a goat for milk, but that hadn't happened yet – the cost of fencing held that plan back.

Jake's dad Bob was pretty useless, usually hanging out at a bar in town, spending Lisa's disability payment on beer. When he drove down the hill around noon, Lisa and Jake were glad to see him go. In the evening, when they heard the truck chugging back up the mountain, they braced for trouble. Lisa hurried to get supper on the table and Jake sat on the front porch to greet his dad and absorb his mood. When he was younger, he would retreat to his bedroom or even out the back door to avoid getting punched. Now that he was nine, he thought he was big enough to protect his mom, or at least to distract his dad for a little while. Susie, on the porch next door, kept a wary eye on Bob. She also kept a pistol in the desk in her living room.

Today the boys were off in the woods and Susie had two customers, a mom and her daughter, both wanting braids. Susie shampooed and braided their hair, thinking that she ought to raise her prices, then dismissing the idea. She knew this lady would tip her generously on top of her $6 charge, and would take great pride in doing so. Raising the price would only diminish her customers' sense of generosity, and it would pinch those who couldn't afford to tip. Better to leave well enough alone. With the garden, she and Ceci did all right.

Susie glanced out at the road and noticed a man walking up the steep hill on the other side of the road. He wore a blue shirt and his blue jeans were dusty. In fact, he was dusty from head to toe, and Susie wondered how far he'd walked. He carried a jacket in one hand and kept his eyes on the ground. Perspiration had stained his shirt, and his dark face was shiny with sweat. As he got up opposite her porch, she called out to him, "Hey there – y'all want a drink of water?"

The man looked up, startled, then relaxed when he saw her. She beckoned to him. "Come on up and get a drink of water. Or I have some sweet tea if you want it."

"Just some water would be fine, ma'am. I thank you. It's a long way up here."

"Where are you headed? There's nobody up thataway except the Barker farm." Susie put the clippers down and filled a glass at her sink. She stepped down and handed it to him.

"That's where I'm going. I heard I could get work picking peaches up there." He squinted up at the sun, then shaded his eyes and looked up the steep road. "I've been out of work."

"Did somebody send you up here?"

"Yes, ma'am, it was Lurleen at the hotel in town." He looked up at Susie's face, suddenly wary.

"That's okay then… Lurleen wouldn't send you up here for no good reason. I'm sure they got work you can do." She paused and looked at his dust-streaked face and frizzled hair. She took the glass he handed back to her. "Would you like a haircut before you go on up there? I got nobody waiting after Eldon here."

Again, the man looked startled and started to turn away. Then he looked at her face and turned back. "Yes, ma'am," he said softly, "I guess I really could use a trim. I been traveling awhile."

She motioned him up and he took one of the chairs at the other end of the porch. He hung his jacket, the only thing he carried, on the back of the chair, and sat watching her, his forearms resting easily on his knees. She turned her attention back to Eldon and smiled brightly.

"You want a little shave today, too, don't you, dear?"

Eldon, an elderly man, smiled back at Susie. "Yes, ma'am, I sure do. My missus likes my face smooth." He chuckled at his own joke as she trimmed the edge of his hair. Susie knew his wife had died a few months back, and she admired his determination. He wouldn't let anybody think he was letting himself go. He held his grief in like the blue silk handkerchief in his pocket, only a corner of it showing.

In a few minutes, Eldon's grooming was done, and he paid Susie with a small tip. She thanked him profusely and told him not to be a stranger. He bowed and walked stiffly down the steps and out to his truck. He climbed in, ground the gears and eased it out, heading down the mountain.

Susie turned. "And now tell me your name, hon. I can't cut your hair if I don't know your name."

"I'm Tom. Tom Robbins." He looked over at her, then back down at the floor.

"And I'm Susie. So now we can get started. How short do you like your hair, Tom?" She ushered him into the chair and tied a cape on him.

He looked up at her. "Good and short. I'm goin' up there to get me a job. I'll be workin' hard, and it's hot. Cut it real short." He sat up straight as he said it.

"Well, that's good to hear. I know they always need pickers this time of year. You'll be working for Kristin?"

"Who's Kristin?"

"She's the boss at the orchard. Didn't Lurleen tell you?"

"Oh yeah, ma'am, I guess she did tell me. She told me to ask for Maybelle or Kristin."

"Well, I'll tell you something else. Kristin doesn't live all the way up at the orchard. She lives in the next house up from here.

Her husband's name is Erik. You just stop there on your way up and maybe you'll save yourself some time." Susie paused and hummed to herself as the clippers took off inches from Tom's hair. "And don't you worry about a thing. They're white folks but they're real nice." Another pause. "So tell me where you're from. And why you're walking."

There was silence from Tom. Susie looked down at him and his eyes were closed. She decided not to press. Instead, after she'd cut off the first layer of dusty hair, she had him lean back into the sink while she washed his hair. After toweling it off and trimming it again, she lathered up his face and shaved him. He still kept his eyes closed, but the tension had gone out of his face. She continued to hum.

She sat him up and he opened his eyes. Suddenly Tom spoke in a rush.

"Ma'am, I came from the Northwest Arkansas Community Correction – the prison up to Fayetteville. I walked because I ain't got no car." He looked at Susie warily.

Susie looked back at Tom, unfazed.

"What were you in for?"

"Burglary. But it wasn't me. Another guy finally confessed, after I'd been there five years. So they just let me out. But my mama had died while I was away, and her house and the farm got sold. What was left from that went to my sister… and she needs it. Where was I supposed to go?"

"Where did you go?"

"To the AME Church. Woman there talked to me, kept asking me what kind of work I like to do. I said farming, like I used to do. She finally told me she had a place for me to go, where they need help right now. And she sent me on up here. She told me to find Lurleen at the motel and she'd send me on."

Susie smiled. "So you were meant to come on up here. And get your haircut today." Unaccountably, she thought, she liked this man. "When did you eat last?"

He looked surprised. She looked back at him.

"Ma'am," he stammered, "it's been since yesterday. But I'm goin' on up the hill and I 'spect they'll feed me there. What do I owe you for the haircut?"

"Four dollars... if you have it."

"Of course I do, ma'am, right here." He turned toward the other end of the porch where his jacket hung.

"My name is Susie, not ma'am." She smiled at him. "And this here's my son Ceci." Ceci had come clattering up the porch steps and stood panting. She put her arm on Ceci's shoulder, patted him, then said, "Go wash up now, we're going to eat."

Tom picked up his jacket and reached into the pocket. Suddenly his eyes were startled. He reached into all the pockets in turn, then into his jeans pockets. He looked up at Susie. "My wallet's gone. I must have dropped it. For real, ma'am, I wouldn't mess with you." He looked down. "Jesus."

"Well, ain't that convenient," she answered. "I can see you don't have it." Her eyes were hard for a minute, then softened. "Look, don't worry about it. You can pay me when you see me next. You're getting a job, you know."

"I am, ma'am... Susie. I sure am. And I'll be back here with the money the first time they pay me. But now I gotta run down the road and see where I dropped it."

Ceci had been listening from the other side of the screen door.

"Mom, when are we having supper?"

Susie made a sudden decision. "Right now, sweetie. And Mr. Tom is eating with us. Set another place, please."

Tom looked at Susie and blinked. "Oh no'm, I couldn't eat with you. I need to get on up the mountain to meet them other folks. I 'spect they'll have something I could eat."

"Well, that's nonsense. It's past six now. It's another mile up to Kristin and Erik's house, and they'll be done eating by the time you get there. You're eating with Ceci and me, and you can't say nothin' about it." She said it with a firmness that surprised even her. "Now go in and wash your hands. I'm expecting you to say grace."

Tom started to protest one more time, then looked at Susie and surrendered. This woman is an angel sent to me, for real, he thought. She ain't young, but she's been awful pretty before and she still is. Then he stopped the thought and kicked himself for thinking it.

"Well, ma'am... Susie, I'd be mighty grateful for a bite. I've been on the road since yesterday."

She ushered him into the house and he washed his hands, then sat down at the end of the small table where Susie and Ceci faced each other. He folded his hands in his lap and recited a small prayer that he remembered from childhood – so long ago! Susie looked pleased and passed him a dish of beans.

Ceci ate voraciously and in the end so did Tom. The beans and squash were consumed and Susie's cornbread filled the chinks. Ceci was uncharacteristically quiet, thought Susie, but maybe it was the stranger's presence. That boy usually chatters all through the meal.

When the meal was over, Tom thanked Susie profusely, and promised to be back down within the week with the money he owed her. Or maybe sooner – he was going to try to find that wallet.

"Maybe it's on the road somewhere." A cloud passed over his face as he mentioned it, and she noticed.

"What else was in it, Tom?"

"My mama's picture. The only one I had of her. And a little piece of her hair. That's all I had, and now she's gone." His face started to crumple.

"We'll find it. We'll find it together. I'll ask the boys about it. They just came up the same road you did." She patted his hand and squeezed it. "Now go on up the hill and tell Kristin I said hello."

Tom turned obediently up the hill, swinging across the yard with an easy gait. His forearms, where they stuck out of his rolled-up sleeves, showed his strength. She remembered his closed eyes and calm face, and how soft his black hair had been under her hands. He's not young, Susie thought, but he's still easy on the eyes. She watched him until he disappeared, then turned toward the house with a sigh.

Chapter 27 – Los Angeles

The drive from Arkansas to Los Angeles went smoothly. After delivering the crates of peaches at Bentonville and Fayetteville, Alicia and Amy, along with Ta'quisha and Jamie, camped the first night at the Lake Eufaula State Park, as Bonnie had advised. The next day, Jamie put her hair up and dressed in jeans and a loose flannel shirt, disguising her shape. On the outskirts of Oklahoma City, she took the Jeep to a car wash and carefully wiped down every surface with ammonia, inside and out. She also wiped off Jeremy's cell phone, then put it back in her pocket. Satisfied with the detailing job, she discarded her plastic gloves and put on a pair of leather driving gloves. Using the vanity mirror, she attached Jeremy's fake mustache, put on sunglasses, tucked her hair in his hat, and pulled the hat down over her face. Then she drove to the Will Rogers Airport and returned the Jeep to the rental company, handing the key to the teenage attendant who barely looked at her. She gathered up the paper bag with her cleaning supplies and walked toward the terminal.

Outside the terminal, Jamie walked slowly toward the arrivals area, carefully scanning for surveillance cameras as she strolled. Seeing none, she sat down on a bench near the Trailways bus stop. After a minute, she pulled Jeremy's phone out of her pocket. Still wearing the driving gloves, she turned it on, launched Google Maps, then navigated to Location Settings. She selected "Delete all location history" and shut the phone down. She pulled a newspaper out of her paper bag, casually folded the phone into the paper and set it down beside her. Watching to make sure any other passers-by were distracted, she turned on the bench, knocking the newspaper and phone off the back edge. Then she stood up and walked further down the sidewalk, crossed the road, and set off for the meeting place she had arranged with Ta'quisha. Before she got there, she took off the mustache and let her hair down. She took off the flannel shirt, turned it inside out and tied it to hang from her waist. Suddenly her silhouette, in a flattering tank top and flared hips, was no longer male. Ta'quisha and Alicia were relieved to see her finally appear around the corner of an airport building.

The pickup truck, with the four of them crammed in the front, headed west from Oklahoma City on I-40 toward L.A. They drove 11 hours, taking turns at the wheel, because neither Jamie nor Ta'quisha thought it would be smart to risk being seen staying in a hotel. Late at night, approaching the New Mexico-Arizona border, they turned north on 491, then wound their way northwest toward the Navajo Nation in Arizona. It took another hour and a half, driving through Window Rock and Fort Defiance, before they finally reached their destination, a small mobile home inside the reservation.

As they approached the mobile home, a dog ran out barking. They stayed in the truck until the door of the home cracked open. Ta'quisha rolled down the truck window and called out.

"Yatahey! It's Ta'quisha and Jamie!"

At that, the door swung wide open, yellow light spilling out onto the dark yard. A bulky woman stepped out onto the porch and called the dog to heel.

Ta'quisha stepped out of the truck.

"Ama!" she called, waving. Once the dog was under control, she ran up the steps and hugged the woman. "So long since I've seen you!" She turned and waved to the others. "Come on out!"

Jamie, Alicia and Amy climbed stiffly out of the truck and joined Ta'quisha. Ta'quisha introduced them. "Haseya, this is

Alicia and Amy, and of course you know Jamie. Alicia and Amy, this is Haseya, my Ama. Well, not really my Ama, my mother, but she might as well be."

"Ah yes, your friend Jamie." Haseya opened her arms to Jamie, then turned to Alicia and Amy. "Welcome, friends. Come in."

Everyone trooped in the door of the tiny mobile home. Haseya invited them to sit on the sofa, which was barely bigger than the truck seat had been. She bustled around the kitchen and emerged with a tray that held cookies and mugs of steaming tea.

"You'll stay here tonight, yes?"

"I hoped you'd say that… yes, we need to. We drove a long way today," Ta'quisha yawned. "We have sleeping bags. Can we just roll them out in here?"

"Of course, you can. I'll bring in some more blankets." Haseya looked around at her guests. "But tell me, where are you headed?"

"We're on our way to L.A.," Ta'quisha answered cautiously. "Family business."

"That's good enough for me," Haseya chuckled. "You know I look for you when I see you coming."

In a few minutes, tables were moved out of the way and handwoven blankets were laid down over the rugs. Jamie and Ta'quisha brought the sleeping bags in from the truck and unrolled them on top of the blankets.

Amy crawled in her bag and fell asleep almost instantly. Jamie brought the cage with the pigeons in, placed it in the kitchen and restocked it with food and water. Soon everyone settled down and slept in the safety of the warm room.

In the morning, Ta'quisha and Jamie carried a small, heavy box into the kitchen and set it down. From the weight of it, Haseya knew it contained gold and silver ingots to share with her circle of craftswomen. The money earned from the sale of their jewelry would improve the lives of many in their community. Haseya quietly thanked Ta'quisha. "And please – thank your blacksmith for melting it down for us. It's safer this way."

Haseya made eggs and frybread for breakfast and the women ate sitting at her table and in the living room. Amy's appetite amused her.

"You need to feed this young one better," Haseya chided. "She's growing." Alicia smiled at that, and vowed to herself that she'd better learn to cook.

After breakfast, two of the pigeons were moved to Haseya's coop. Ta'quisha gave Haseya a couple of leg canisters for the birds. If she needed to send an urgent message to the Barkers, she would roll the paper and insert it into the canister, attach it to the bird's leg, and set the bird free.

"You let us know when supplies run out. Our forge is busy, we're always melting stuff down. I don't mind running over here more often."

"I will do that. Thank you again."

The women packed the sleeping bags back into the truck, hugged each other, and started up the truck. As it rolled out the dusty drive, the dog accompanied it for a while, trotting on its long legs. Eventually, winded, the dog changed its mind and turned back.

The next day the pickup rolled into Los Angeles. Their first stop was at the shelter in Commerce, where they delivered the last two pigeons, as Bonnie had directed them to. The women shared a meal there, catching up on news.

After dinner, they switched Alicia's luggage from the battered pickup truck to Alicia's car. Her car had been kept at the shelter all along, ever since Ta'quisha and Jim had picked her up there a month and a half ago. Alicia retrieved her keys from the women who ran the shelter. They thanked her for the loan of her car, and hugged her with feeling.

"Don't be a stranger. Come on by anytime."

"I will, I promise," Alicia said, and she meant it.

Ta'quisha and Jamie accompanied Alicia and Amy out to her car. There they made plans for the next day.

"We'll be by around 10 in the morning. Can you turn off your security cameras before we get there, please?" asked Ta'quisha. "We don't want this old wreck to show up on 'em." She pointed at the pickup, which looked out of place even in Commerce.

"Oh, yes, of course. Thanks for reminding me. And look, I hope you'll think about staying with me for a few days. Please?" Alicia reached out toward them. "Will you?"

"Maybe. We'll play it by ear. We need to figure out a game plan." Ta'quisha looked at Jamie, who nodded. Then she turned back to Alicia. "But yeah, we can stay. Can we pull this old truck into your garage?"

"Of course!" Alicia laughed. "I'll make sure there's room."

Alicia drove home with Amy, feeling strange about driving through her old neighborhood again. It was a nice neighborhood, and her expansive house was well screened from the neighbors. Alicia knew her neighbors wouldn't have noticed her absence, since she rarely interacted with them. And since it was summertime, Amy hadn't been missed at preschool, either. Alicia and Amy walked into the house and settled in as if they'd never been gone. But after two months away, the house felt too big, too sterile. And not nearly so safe as a certain farm nestled in the Ozark mountains.

Chapter 28 – Ozarks

Susie watched as Tom disappeared around the bend in the road, then turned back to the house. As she came back through the screen door Ceci was still at the table. He looked up at his mom and back down at the table.

"What? What is it?" She frowned at him.

"Mom, I know where his wallet is."

She crossed her arms. "You do?"

"Yeah, Jake and me were in the woods. That guy – Tom – was sleeping by the road. Then we saw Jake's dad take his wallet."

"You saw what?"

Ceci looked up at Susie and spoke quickly. "Jake's dad went by him in the truck. Then we heard the truck stop and he came walking back up the road. He stopped by Tom and reached down and took his wallet from his jacket. We saw him."

"And then what?"

"Then Jake's dad went back down the road. And we heard the truck start up."

"So then what did you do?"

"We just run off. We didn't want to get in trouble."

Susie sat down and gazed at Ceci, shaking her head. A single tear rolled down his cheek.

"We didn't know he was gonna stop here. And not have the money to pay for the haircut. I'm sorry, Mama." Ceci started to cry in earnest.

"Hush. You and me are goin' to go over now and talk to Lisa and Jake. And Jake's story better match yours. Hush now. Blow your nose." Susie handed Ceci a bandanna and pulled him up gently. "Come on now."

They walked hand in hand over to Lisa's house and went in without knocking. Lisa looked up in surprise, seeing Susie's set mouth and Ceci's tear-stained face. She turned to Jake and asked, "Are you in trouble?"

"No ma'am. I don't think so." Jake caught Ceci's eye.

Lisa turned to Susie. "What's going on?"

"I need to ask Jake something." Susie turned to him. "Jake, a gentleman came and got a haircut from me today. When he went to pay me, he couldn't, because his wallet was missing. What do you know about that? No, don't look at Ceci, look at me," she commanded, clapping her hands.

Jake looked from Susie to his mother and back again.

"Dad took it! We saw him take it. We were in the woods down yonder." Jake's eyes were wide with earnestness and he waved toward the road.

"Well, okay, that's the same story I got from Ceci," Susie sighed. "You boys can relax. But you should have come and told us."

"I was going to, Mama," Ceci pleaded. "Me and Jake stayed in the woods and we talked about it for a while. Then when I ran home the guy was right there. I couldn't tell you right in front of him. I didn't know what to do." His voice had a righteous tone.

His mother looked askance at him and frowned, but with a smile starting to show.

"Okay, okay, I get it. Tell you what – you boys go over to my house now while I help Lisa with the dishes. Scoot."

Jake and Ceci, glad to be out from under their moms' scrutiny, didn't need another prompt. They scooted.

Susie turned to Lisa. "So now what? Bob's going to come home stinking drunk. Do you want my gun?"

Lisa stood with her hands on the back of the chair, making up her mind. She looked up. "No, Susie, I don't. I can handle him. He doesn't swing as fast as he used to." She paused. "But I don't want Jake here. Nor Ceci neither."

"Let's take them up the hill," suggested Susie. "They can stay at the bunkhouse up to Maybelle's and get to school early. OK with you? I'll take them up."

Lisa looked at Susie gratefully. The women both knew the coming danger. Their minds worked in sync – their first instinct was to protect the boys. Lisa fetched Jake's sleeping bag and came back to the kitchen.

"Leave the dishes. Let's go." Lisa's voice was tense.

Back at Susie's house, the moms hustled the boys and their sleeping bags out the door. They didn't give them much explanation, just said they wanted them to stay at Maybelle's tonight. The boys, sensing their moms' mood, didn't object. Lisa saw them and Susie off in Susie's truck, then turned back to the dishes.

When Susie returned, she and Lisa had a tense conversation over the kitchen table. Lisa was frightened, but she was determined to face Bob.

"I need to see if he's got that wallet. I don't know what I'm gonna do after that, but I'll be ready."

"I'll be ready, too. With my gun. Ain't nothin' goin' to happen to you, girl."

Lisa grasped Susie's hand. "It won't come to that. And he's not worth goin' to jail for, remember that." She paused and squeezed Susie's hand again. "But thank you just the same." She turned and left, and the screen door closed softly behind her.

Chapter 29 – Ozarks

It was many hours later when Lisa heard Bob's truck struggling up the mountain. She lay in bed pretending to be asleep, but with her hand near a small baseball bat on the floor beside the bed. The truck stopped and the door slammed. Then the front door bumped open and Bob clomped in. Lisa heard him open the fridge, slam it again, and pop a can of beer. In bed, she gripped the bat with one hand.

After five minutes, she heard another beer can pop. Then Bob belched and shuffled into the bedroom. His pants dropped to the floor. Lisa held her breath and kept her eyes closed. When he dropped across the bed and lay still, she finally exhaled.

Bob's breath finally slowed and grew even. Lisa waited another five minutes, then slithered out of bed. She reached for his pants on the floor and went through the pockets. She found a wallet that wasn't his. She took it out into the kitchen to examine by the moonlight flowing in through the window over the sink. It held four dollars. It also held a photo in a plastic sleeve, a photo of an elderly black woman. Behind the photo was tucked a small lock of hair tied with a piece of yarn.

In the bedroom, Bob rolled over and found Lisa gone. He dragged himself up and stumbled through the doorway, eyes reddened and angry. His eyes went to the wallet.

"What the fuck are you doin' with that? Give it here!" He took a swipe at Lisa. She dodged and put the table between them.

She had suddenly had enough.

"You stole this wallet, didn't you? It wasn't enough to just spend all our money? You had to steal someone else's? How much money did you spend on drinkin' tonight? Huh?" She defied him to reach her.

He circled the table, swinging for her again. His arm hit the beer can still in the middle of the table and it spilled. Instantly, she grabbed it up, ran to the door and out onto the porch. The screen door hit the wall with a bang. She threw the can out into the yard.

"There! There goes your stupid beer!"

He flew out past her, chasing the beer. The can landed with a fizz, and Bob hurtled over the porch rail headfirst. She jumped back into the house, slammed the inner door and threw the deadbolt.

She fully expected to hear him come back up onto the porch, slamming the door and breaking windows. Instead all she heard was silence for several minutes. She stood there in shock until a soft knock came on her back door. She started with fright.

"Lisa? Are you okay in there?" Lisa crept to the back door.

"Yes, I'm okay," Lisa whispered through the door. "But Jesus, you shouldn't be here, Susie!" Lisa cracked the door and pulled Susie through, then closed and locked it again. "Bob's out there and he's going to kill me!"

"No, he ain't." Susie showed Lisa the gun in her hand.

"What? Did you shoot him?"

"Didn't need to. He broke his fool neck, it looks like. He's lyin' out front, and he ain't movin'. What the hell happened?"

Lisa gasped and her hand flew to her mouth. She went to the front door, unlocked it, and stepped cautiously out onto the front porch. She sidled to the railing and looked down at Bob, who lay oddly crumpled in the dirt. She stood there a minute and saw no movement. Then she turned to Susie, her face blank.

"Guess he just likes his beer too much. He went flying out after it. I tossed it out the door. See it out there?"

"Oh, yeah, I do." The beer can lay in the middle of the dirt yard, in a pool of liquid that looked like blood. "Huh, that's somethin'."

"Sure is." Lisa breathed deeply. Then she grimaced and shook her head. "That man loved his beer." She began to laugh hysterically.

Susie reached over and pulled her in, wrapping her arms around her.

"I'm sorry."

"I ain't. It was gettin' to the point where either he was goin' to kill me or I was goin' to kill him. He just saved me the trouble."

"I know *that's* true. Why do you think I brought the gun over?" Susie sighed. "Well, now what? Are we goin' to get the sheriff?"

"Yes, I guess we better. Just a minute, I want to give you something before we go." Lisa went inside and emerged with Tom's wallet. "Put this somewhere really safe. I don't want nobody finding it now. And put your gun far away, too. Let's not complicate this thing."

Minutes later, the two women were winding their way down the mountain in Susie's truck, headed for the police station in town.

After the long trip down the dirt mountain road, and back up north on the twisting highway, Susie's truck rolled into town and stopped outside the police station, which was dark and closed at two o'clock in the morning. Lisa jumped out and pushed the call button that was mounted outside the door. After a couple minutes, a voice crackled over the intercom.

"Arden County Sheriff. What's the trouble?"

"My husband fell off the porch. I think he's dead."

"He fell off the porch? Where?"

"Up on Baskett Mountain Road. My name's Lisa Sims. My husband is Bob Sims."

"Oh yuh, we know Bob. Where did you say he is?"

"Up to my house. On Baskett Mountain Road. He fell over the railing and I think he's dead."

"Okay." The voice sounded more awake now. "Where are you right now?"

"Right by your station. Can you meet me here?"

"You'll have to give me a few minutes."

Five minutes later Sheriff Campbell showed up in an AWD vehicle. Susie stood with her arm around Lisa. Lisa, looking distraught, had managed to summon some tears. She talked to the sheriff briefly before the two vehicles pulled out and headed back up the mountain.

It took them 25 minutes to get back to Lisa's house. As they pulled into the yard, their headlights swung over the still form of Bob in front of the porch. Sheriff Campbell left his lights on and went to examine the body. He felt for a pulse and noted the odd angle of the man's neck. He turned his attention back to the women.

"What happened here?"

Susie stepped away from Lisa with a shake of her head.

"She'll have to tell you. I didn't see it."

"He flew out after the beer," said Lisa in a strangled voice. "I threw his beer out the front door and he ran out after it. There it is." She pointed to the can spilled in the dirt.

"Y'all were having a fight?"

"Yes, we were. He was circling on me. I put the table between us, and then I just threw the beer out the door and he went after it. I locked the door behind him. I didn't dare look out for a while."

"Well, that somehow doesn't surprise me. Any of it. But we'll have to do an investigation, and we'll have to get the coroner up here. I'm going to call him right now."

The women huddled on the porch while the sheriff went to his vehicle and called the coroner on his radio. After he'd done that, Lisa offered him some coffee. He accepted and sighed, "Lord, what a night. First that dustup at the bar, and now this."

Lisa pulled more chairs out onto the porch, and the three of them sat there silently. Lisa was curious as hell about what had happened at the bar, but she dared not ask. Then Susie asked for her. Just making conversation, she ventured, "So what happened earlier – at the bar, you said?"

"One of them brawls. I got there too late to stop Bob – he'd already left. They said he spent a lot of money tonight, got good and loose, and ended up giving Billy Ray a black eye. It was all I could do to keep Billy Ray or some of them others from chasing Bob home. I am not at *all* surprised that Bob came home and started that mess up again with you." He paused and turned to Lisa. "Excuse me for sayin' this ma'am, but your husband got what he deserved. Breakin' his fool neck diving off the porch after a beer is divine justice. 'Scuse me again." He sat shaking his head. The women exchanged a look.

Some time later the coroner arrived with an assistant and a van. They examined Bob and concurred with the conclusion the others had come to: Bob had broken his neck in his headlong dive over the railing and off the porch. When they were done with their examination, they offered to take the body back to town and deliver it to the funeral home. Lisa spoke up for the first time.

"No, leave him here. I'm going to take care of him myself. We'll bury him on our own land – we don't need nothin' fancy. I'll get Maybelle and them to help me with everything. Now if you could help me load him into the truck, I'd be grateful."

So the five of them picked the limp form of Bob up and carried him to his own truck. They slid his bulky body onto the bed of the pickup. Lisa went into the house and came out with an old quilt, which she spread over his form. She looked sorrowful as she slammed the tailgate.

The coroner spoke up. "I'll get the paperwork done today, ma'am, and you can pick up the death certificates the next time you're in town."

"Thank you kindly. Thank you all. You don't know what a comfort you've been to me just now." Lisa looked like she was going to break down, and the men turned away hastily.

Once the men had driven off, Lisa turned to Susie with a look of relief, then her mouth twisted in a grim smile.

"Good thing they're gone. I wasn't sure how much longer I could have kept that act up. Am I bereaved? Hell no, you know I ain't. In fact, I haven't felt this free in a *long* time." Her voice had risen to shrillness. "Hell no!"

Susie shushed her. Lisa subsided. They sat back down on the porch for a while, not speaking, but holding hands and sharing the same thoughts. They were two women alone, with boys to raise, but they knew they could lean on each other. They also knew they had sisters up the mountain. They'd survive just fine.

In the early dawn, Lisa turned Bob's truck up the mountain and drove up to Maybelle's place. She brought Tom's wallet with her, giving it to Maybelle with the story that the boys had found it in the road, almost empty of money. Maybelle promised to get it to him.

"And there's something else. Bob is in the back of the truck. He's dead. He broke his neck fallin' off the porch last night." Maybelle was startled and turned to Lisa, a question in her eyes. Lisa patted her arm and continued, "Don't worry, the coroner already examined him and it's ruled accidental. All I need now is to get rid of his damn body. Quickly and quietly." A look passed between them and Maybelle nodded.

Maybelle called Bonnie in and explained about the body. Bonnie fetched a stretcher and a length of rope, and asked Babs and Kelly to come along. They piled into the truck and drove further up the mountain on an old logging road, finally reaching a place where the road ended. From there, they placed the body on the stretcher and continued to carry it upward. At a certain point they left the trail and pushed through the low brush. After another ten minutes of hiking and scrambling they reached the lip of a sinkhole. Looking down into the hole, they could see a floor about 15 feet down.

Babs and Kelly tied the rope to a tree and looped the other end under Bob's arms. They played the rope out a little at a time. Bob's body twisted slowly as it descended to the floor of the sinkhole. Then using the same rope, they climbed down themselves, and helped Bonnie and Lisa climb down to join them. In the vertical walls of the sinkhole were dark open holes, a few feet across. A pebble tossed into one of those holes would fall for several seconds before finally – *ploosh!* – hitting water far below.

Bonnie and Lisa unceremoniously stripped Bob of his clothes. Then three of the women wrestled his body through the aperture in the wall and let it fall. It dropped for several seconds, finally landing with a splash in the water and settling to the bottom of the underground river, where it joined the remains of Jeremy, tossed there a few days earlier.

Chapter 30 – Los Angeles

Now a week after they'd left the Ozarks, Alicia and Amy Lange were settled back in their L.A. home. They'd been glad to get back to the relative luxury of private bedrooms and abundant running water. But they had changed. Alicia relaxed her rules about Amy's friends, and within a few weeks the house filled up with neighborhood kids. Alicia found joy in cooking for the crowd. The kitchen became a boisterous place, with kids jostling each other at the table, or pulling up chairs to stand on, at the counter. Amy loved to help Alicia with her newest culinary experiments. Usually, but not always, the experiments were greeted with shouts of enthusiasm. It was a new kind of life for both of them.

Jamie and Ta'quisha stayed at a safe house and met with Alicia occasionally. The first thing they had done when they arrived was to show Alicia how to erase the location history from her phone.

"Let's look at your call history, too," Ta'quisha suggested. "How often did he call you?"

"Never. He never called," said Alicia. "He could be gone for a week, and he never tried to reach me at all. He'd just show up randomly. I never knew when he'd appear, or what kind of a mood he'd be in. Though it was usually bad." Alicia's voice dropped as she remembered.

Ta'quisha also took care of Jeremy's computer, erasing the memory completely and rebuilding the computer's operating system from scratch with factory defaults. Ta'quisha coached Alicia through each step.

"You don't want to leave anything that will point to you, or anything about what happened in the last two months. That needs to be completely gone from all devices." After two days of intense work, including replacement of the hard drive, Ta'quisha declared the job done, and Alicia breathed a sigh of relief.

The two women coached Alicia in her story. Ta'quisha had a plan. "You need to go to Jeremy's office. Do you know anybody there?"

"Well, yes, his assistant is Barbara Edwards. I know her a little bit."

"Good. Let's think of a script." Alicia looked blank. Ta'quisha explained. "A reason for you to be looking at his work computer. Some questions to ask."

"Umm, let's see. I can say I need to find his mother's new phone number."

"Excellent. That will work. Now let me teach you what you need to do once you're in."

The next day, when she got to the office, Alicia asked for Barbara Edwards.

"Please, come in! It's been a while since we've seen you." Barbara got up from her desk and gave Alicia a hug.

Alicia stuck to the story that she'd worked out with Ta'quisha and Jamie.

"Well, we've been at Disneyland for a few weeks now. That sounded like more fun to Amy than hiking in the wilderness."

"Well, yes, I can see that. How old is Amy now?"

"She's just four. She loves Mickey and Minnie."

"Of course. Well, what can I do for you today?"

"I need to see if Jeremy stored his mother's new phone number in his computer. The one I have written down doesn't work anymore. I think he bought a new phone for her, and maybe she couldn't transfer the number. Can you get me into his computer?"

"Be happy to." They walked into his office. Alicia sat down in his office chair. Barbara leaned over her shoulder to type in his name and password. Alicia, as she had been coached, memorized the keystrokes.

"Thanks so much. I won't be long." Barbara left and Alicia quickly wrote down the name and password she had seen Barbara use. Then she cleared Jeremy's search history and erased any emails pertaining to herself. She also uninstalled the tracking app that Jeremy had used to follow her phone to Arkansas. Ta'quisha had taught her quite a bit in the last two weeks. Alicia took notes after she completed each step, to show to Ta'quisha when they got together.

Alicia left Jeremy's office and stopped by Barbara's desk again. On an impulse, Alicia invited her out to lunch. Barbara was glad to go, and she found herself warming up to Alicia again. Alicia had been out of touch with the office for a while now, and it was great to see more of her. They chatted over lunch, and Alicia casually probed for information. Barbara supplied her with all the details about Jeremy's trip to Sequoia and Kings Canyon. She said he told her he's be back in another week.

"Oh yes," replied Alicia. "I'm going to give him a week to rest up, and then we're going out to Terranea, just the two of us. Amy will be staying with his mom. That's why I needed her number."

In talking to Barbara, Alicia confirmed that Jeremy had never told anyone that she had fled to a shelter after their last fight. In fact, at one point during the meal, Barbara remarked that she

175

envied Alicia and Jeremy's solid marriage. Alicia smiled and did not correct her opinion.

When she got home, Alicia made the reservation at Terranea for three weekends from now, and she called Jeremy's mother to ask her to take Amy for that weekend. As she described her plans for a romantic weekend with Jeremy, she listened carefully to her mother-in-law's voice.

"Oh honey," his mother chirped, "I'm glad to hear you're going to have a special weekend. You certainly can afford it. I'm sure it'll be exactly what he wants after he gets back from that silly hike. Sometimes we just have to remind our men about the good things in life, you know?" She chuckled at her own joke.

Alicia laughed and told her mother-in-law that she'd call again soon. As she hung up the phone, she realized that her own reluctance to reveal her marital troubles would serve her well now. She hadn't told a soul about Jeremy's abuse, preferring to present an image of normal family life to the outside world. No one had known when she escaped to the shelter, and no one knew of her trip east. All to the good.

At home, Amy occasionally mentioned the adventure at the farm on the mountain. After a few of these conversations, Alicia realized that while Amy chattered about all the fun things she had done, she never mentioned the harrowing ride down the mountain in the Jeep. Or so it seemed – but Alicia was wary. *Suppose Amy started to talk to her friends? Or a teacher?* Amy asked Jamie and Ta'quisha for advice.

"The best thing you can do, girl, is to plant a more exciting memory in her head," Ta'quisha answered. "Make that Disneyland trip you've been talkin' about real. Do it quickly."

A week later, Jamie and Ta'quisha met with Alicia one last time. At this meeting, they suggested that Alicia really could pick up the reins now. They had introduced her to sisters in L.A., women she'd never met before, even though some of them lived nearby. At this last meeting Ta'quisha helped Alicia formulate her plan. She would wait three more weeks, then file a missing person report on Jeremy with the information she'd learned from Barbara. She could use her considerable acting skills to exhibit genuine distress when questioned. Then she'd work to remake her life.

"Are you okay now? Do you think you can do this?" Ta'quisha questioned.

"I think so," nodded Alicia. "Can I get in touch with you if I need help?"

"Well, not immediately. Write a letter to Maybelle if you have to. But you have some other sisters out here now. And you might find out that Barbara is a sister, too. Sound her out, but go slowly." Ta'quisha paused. "You have more sense than you give yourself credit for."

"Well, now I do." Alicia smiled wryly. "Doing without plumbing kinda beats that into you. That and good hard work." She grinned at Ta'quisha, then reached out for her hand.

Reassured, Ta'quisha and Jamie headed for the door. They hugged Alicia, then climbed into the truck and drove off. Jamie had volunteered for the first shift, and Ta'quisha let her take it. It'd be a long drive home.

Alicia and Amy left for Disneyland that afternoon, for an exciting two weeks together. Alicia showered Amy with souvenirs and toys to haul home. When they got back to L.A., they spent a week painting and decorating Amy's room. They ran a wallpaper border of dancing dwarves around the ceiling, pasted other Disney characters on the walls, and hung a mobile of waltzing princesses from the fan. The memorabilia became Amy's new focus when her friends came over.

The following week, Alicia threw away her smartphone and bought an old-style flip phone. Then she left it on her dresser, turned off most of the time. She bought squash, bean and tomato seedlings at the farmer's market, and rototilled a large garden plot in the back yard. Together, she and Amy spent two days putting in their vegetables. They wore their grubbies most of the time these days, intent on their work and looking forward to harvest.

A week later, they drove to the Humane Society and adopted a golden retriever puppy, who proceeded to wreck Alicia's stylish home in various ways. And she couldn't have cared less.

Chapter 31 – Washington, D.C.

By July, the FBI Division of Public Affairs was deep into its work on Operation NEVRR – the National Entertainment Venue Recovery and Renewal Operation. There had been a couple of video conferences since the first one. Vanessa Woodside, in charge of the task force, had collected evidence from all over the country. It demonstrated a pattern of incidents at entertainment centers and conference venues that was hard to interpret. There had been some instances of drug overdose deaths, some involving illicit drugs and some involving prescription medicines. There had been some unfortunate cases of cardiac arrests in hot tubs. There had also been outbreaks of salmonella as well as legionnaire's disease at some of the larger conferences, such as the NRA Convention in Dallas.

Vanessa had been in regular contact with Mike Jenkins in the Chicago Field Office. He called her a month after she sent him the information about the Bourbon Street Slasher.

"Hi Vanessa, Mike here." He launched right into his findings. "We now know it was a female prostitute that killed at least five of the New Orleans victims. We have her on one surveillance video walking with one of the victims. In another, she's getting into a car. Similar clothing each time. Long black hair. Very heavy makeup. We can't see her face well, but we're presuming Hispanic for now."

"Where does that leave us? That's one case."

"Actually, it's not just that one case. What we're seeing, more and more, is that there are a number of prostitution rings that cater to large conferences. Especially in Las Vegas, Miami and Atlantic City. These guys walk right into it. Alone."

"And they wind up dead."

"But here's the thing, Vanessa. The only reason we're looking at this now is because men are getting killed. The real crime has been going on for a lot longer than that. I'm talking about the trafficking of these women."

Vanessa didn't expect him to say that.

"So what are you saying? Should we not investigate the murders?"

"No, that's not what I mean. We should, of course, and we'll keep doing that. But they're just little pinpricks inside a whole cloud of barbarity, of exploitation. You know. You've seen it. Up close."

Vanessa's face grew hot. What did he know about the streets of Washington, D.C.? Had he heard about her arrest? No, of course he hadn't. *Oh, hell.* She kept her voice level. "We need to keep at it. On both fronts. The murders *and* the prostitution."

"I was hoping you'd say that. We've sure got a lot of both in Chicago. And say," his voice changed. "do you have any plans to come out this way?"

"I – I hadn't planned to."

"Well, think about it. We could put our heads together and you could meet my team." Again his voice changed. "And you could meet my mom."

Vanessa felt another flush. *Could he see her, right now, over the phone line?*

"Ah, we'll see," she said airily. "Gotta go now." She hung up abruptly.

The next day, Vanessa and Mary pulled all their information together and presented a report to Williamson. He mulled it over for a week, then asked Mary to convene yet another video conference with the regional directors of the FBI. He asked

Vanessa to do the presentation, while offering to introduce her. She agreed, and did her best to summarize everything they had collected.

In her presentation, without mentioning Mike Jenkins specifically, she touched on her office's coordination with the Chicago FBI Field Office. She described their efforts to focus on the cases that were clearly violent crime. She offered to involve any other regional FBI offices that would like to join their probe.

"So far," she admitted, "we haven't made much headway in solving the murder cases. Furthermore, the obvious murders are only a small fraction of the incidents occurring in and near convention centers." She put a pie chart up and pointed to it. "One third of the cases have been attributed to natural causes – heart attacks and insulin shock, for instance. Another quarter of the cases have had something to do with drugs. The remainder were either accidents or violent crime, but it's difficult to sort out one from the other. A man falls from a hotel balcony. A man steps in front of a bus. A man suffocates in an elevator. The only statistical thread is that the victims were all male." She paused and let that sink in.

"Why do you think that these unusual deaths at conference sites are all men?" she insisted. "I do hope our audience today will be able to suggest ideas as to why this is happening. Please click on the link on your screen to submit your comments. Or you can ask your questions at the end."

Hoping that some suggestions might be coming back to the moderator, Vanessa proceeded with her presentation. She presented evidence that showed that, in general, over half of conference attendees in the U.S. were male. However, the

181

predominance of attendance by gender varied, depending on what the subject of the conference was.

"Business and finance conferences, as well as auto shows, boat shows and gun shows tend to attract more men. Conferences focused on education, public policy and local politics are predominantly attended by women." She put up graphs illustrating these trends, and continued, "Gatherings of various medical and scientific specialties were split about equally between men and women.

"What we've found out in our investigation is this: All but one of the deaths at conference venues in the past three years has occurred at gatherings predominantly attended by men. I would like to ask you, the regional FBI directors, to propose a theory about why this is happening.

"And with that, we'll go to the phones," she concluded. "Thank you for your time and attention."

Williamson came back on and thanked Vanessa for her work. The phones were unmuted and the moderator proceeded to handle the incoming calls.

The regional director for New York spoke up.

"The attacks at the International Trade Finance Conference were clearly aimed at their top talent. Three of their featured speakers died during the conference. And it was a weekend conference. How do you explain that?"

"How did they die?" Williamson asked.

"One apparent overdose. One hit-and-run outside the hotel. One was knifed in an alley. This looks like some terrorist organization to me. Especially since the conference was promoting foreign investment in Africa."

"Why is that important?"

"Because they were talking about mines, rare earth mines. There's a fortune to be made for the right players there. And there are forces allied against this mining. Wasn't it Al Jazeera that published that article *Blood and Minerals: Who Profits from Conflict in DRC?* In my opinion, it's probably Al Qaeda behind these murders."

"That's something to consider." Williamson hesitated. "Anyone else?"

Another director spoke up.

"What I want to look at is why so many of these murders are happening in private. Why are these men getting into compromising situations and clandestine hookups just because they're at a conference? I mean, why are they doing it at all? Are there that many rotten marriages? Or is this just our culture – a conference is where you can run off and do anything you dang please?"

"And it seems like the more important a man is the more likely he is to get offed," chimed in another director. "Just look at who's been killed in the last year – more CEOs than you can count."

"I agree, this is troubling," commented Williamson. "This is something I plan to take up with the White House in the near future. I will be meeting with FBI Director Trent next week, and we'll decide how to proceed." He wrapped up. "I want to thank you all for your participation today, and I'd like to keep the focus on this problem. I will follow up with you in a couple of weeks after I brief the administration."

As soon as the videoconference was shut off, Williamson turned to Vanessa.

"They're right, you know. This is obviously the work of foreign terrorists. We need to involve Homeland Security on this."

"How can they help?" Vanessa questioned. "Do we know who we're looking for?"

"It's a bunch of anti-American jihadists." Williamson was sure. "They're trying to limit our access to those minerals. I know something about this. They're connected to Al Qaeda and ISIS, I know it. This will be something the president wants to hear about." He strode to the door.

"What do you want me to do?" Vanessa looked puzzled.

"You work on keeping the lid on this story. We're the Office of Public Affairs, remember? I don't care how you do it, but the message has to continue to be that our casinos and conference centers are safe. If we have to patrol them with Homeland Security guards, we will. If we have to deputize local police to do it, we will. Whatever works. That's your assignment."

"But we still don't know –" Vanessa started to say. But he was out the door already.

Later over lunch Vanessa and Mary compared notes. Mary had been tasked with setting up a meeting with the Director of Homeland Security for Williamson. Vanessa described her assignment – a vague directive to keep every venue in the U.S. safe, while not alerting the public to the danger. But what kind of danger? What was going on?

Mary's face reflected Vanessa's puzzlement. She knew what was going on, but she also had a lifetime of practice in keeping her mouth shut.

"And the worst part of it is this," Vanessa continued. "Williamson is just aching to bring this issue to the president's attention. He wants to get Director Trent's backing, and he wants to march into the Oval Office and get noticed. And as soon as he does that, the threat is going to be all out there. This president just can't resist a chance to be the tough guy. And his *aim* is to scare people. I don't have a chance in hell of keeping a lid on this."

Mary nodded. She couldn't argue with that.

Chapter 32 – Ozarks

Summer brought sweltering heat to the Ozarks, but the higher up on the mountain people lived, the less they suffered. The Barker farm lay mostly on the bench, a broad, flat ribbon of land that circled the mountain. A steep bluff lay below the bench on one side, and another steep bluff towered above it on the other. The contour of the bench followed the pattern of erosion that had carved out the flat-lying limestone plateau eons ago. Since the farm was halfway up the mountain, there was at least some breeze blowing in the morning and the evening.

The peach harvest wouldn't end until August, but some of the earlier varieties were ripening now. The Barker farm delivered whole fruit to local and not-so-local markets. The remainder of the fruit was put up as jam. Peaches were not the only fruit the farm grew, either. There were plenty of raspberries, strawberries, and a few plum trees as well. In addition, the farm produced an astonishing variety of vegetables, everything from broccoli to tomatoes to sweet potatoes.

The women on the farm canned the perishable vegetables and fruit and then stored them in a root cellar that was built into the side of a hill. The temperature in the cellar, like in a cave, remained a steady 55 to 65 degrees Fahrenheit, regardless of how hot or cold it was outside. Potatoes, carrots, rutabagas and squashes were also stored in the root cellar, where they remained fresh all winter.

Workers on the farm also collected and packaged many different kinds of seeds, primarily herbs, wildflowers and vegetables. At the moment, the seed business was run out of Maybelle's kitchen, but it was apparent to everyone that a larger space would be needed soon. Bonnie was working on plans for a new building adjacent to the barn.

Once a year, the farm published a small seed catalog and sent it to an exclusive mailing list. The distribution list was carefully curated, not purchased from another source. Each subscriber to the list had to have been introduced by a previous subscriber, and vetted by Maybelle and her committee. If someone failed to make an order or write at least once a year, their name and contact information were deleted from the list. All orders were read carefully by Maybelle, and she occasionally wrote short notes back. Usually Maybelle's responses accompanied seed orders, and her notes were concealed inside the seed envelopes.

Once a week, several women loaded up a pickup truck and carried produce down the mountain to the farmers' market in town. One of the women would go over to the post office to collect the mail and send out seed packages. The other women would unload the fruit and vegetables at the market. They served customers from 8am and until 5pm, even in winter. Theirs was a popular stand, as they smiled and bantered with everyone who stopped by.

On this particular Saturday, Irina and Malik Varayeva, the sister and brother from Chechnya, were on the farmers' market crew. This was their first foray into this enterprise, and Malik was excited. Arlene, his friend and mentor, was on the crew also. Today she taught him and Irina the techniques of counting change and bagging produce. By noon, Irina and Malik had gotten over their nervousness and were enjoying the challenge of the new job. They began to chatter and laugh with customers.

Halfway through the afternoon, two local men wandered into the market and spotted Irina. Being tall, graceful, dark-haired and dark-eyed, she drew their eyes immediately. She wore a sweatshirt, jeans and work boots, but the men stared at her anyway. She glanced at them and turned quickly back to the lady before her, smiling and nodding. When she finished with that customer, the men approached. Irina sensed them coming and reflexively stomped her feet. This was a signal to Malik, one that went back to their teenage years on the streets of Newark, and before that to their childhood in Chechnya. It meant danger was coming.

Malik tensed and moved closer to his sister, scanning the crowd. Irina didn't look at Malik, nor did she look at the approaching men. Instead she stepped back behind Arlene and Bonnie, going back to the truck's tailgate to fetch another box of peaches. The men walked up and started fingering the vegetables, leering at Irina and making rude comments. Malik turned red, and Arlene noticed. She stepped in front of him, turned to the men and asked, "Can I help you?"

"Yeah, I want a piece of that." The man nodded at Irina, who was coming back with the box of peaches. "That looks just peachy." He and the other man laughed drunkenly.

Malik challenged them. "Get out of here."

"Oh, what do we have here, a little Russian? A little Russian boy?" Their faces turned ugly and they took a step closer.

Suddenly Bonnie was around the table and in front of the men. She stared straight into the men's hostile eyes. Her hand rested on the hilt of a knife tucked in a sheath at her waist. "I'd suggest you walk away very quickly. Now!" she hissed quietly.

The men backed up, then turned clumsily and stumbled away.

"Goddamn foreigners. We'll get them, dammit. Fuckin' illegals. Fuckin' think they can come down here and fuck with us."

Irina brought the box of peaches up to the table and set it down. Her hands were trembling and Malik reached out to grasp one.

"It's okay, it's okay, they're gone. They can't hurt you," he whispered.

Irina's eyes were wide as she looked at Malik, then at Arlene and Bonnie.

"Thank you. Thank you." That was all she said.

A minute later, the four of them resumed their chatty and friendly demeanor and finished out the day. At 5 o'clock they packed up the empty crates and the table and drove back up into the mountains.

Later in the afternoon, Bonnie stopped into Maybelle's kitchen and related the whole incident.

"Irina and Malik might need some help. They were really frightened."

"Yeah, it sounds like it. Those goddamn yeehaws. Sometimes I hate that town, you know that?" Maybelle looked up. Bonnie nodded silently.

The next day, Maybelle came to seek out Irina and Malik, to find out from their perspective what had happened at the market. She invited them into the kitchen for some tea and asked about yesterday.

"Nothing happened that we couldn't handle." Irina lifted her chin. "Malik and I can take care of ourselves." She looked at Maybelle defiantly.

"Hang on, I'm not trying to scold you. I'm trying to help you. Tell me about what happened." Maybelle reached out and took Irina's hand.

"Irina signaled me," Malik spoke up, "and I saw the men standing there. They were after her. I told them to go away and they called me a little Russian boy."

"Hmmm, that's not good. We're going to have to keep a watch out," said Maybelle. "For now, it's best if the two of you don't go down to town."

"That's fine with me," agreed Irina. "It wouldn't be our turn again for a few weeks anyway."

Maybelle turned to Malik. "That's fine with you, too, isn't it? I don't want you to go down there and get hurt."

"Yes, okay," he mumbled. When Maybelle reached for his hand, he looked up at her. After a moment he squeezed her hand back and said more audibly, "Yes, ma'am. I know you are trying to keep us safe."

"I sure am," agreed Maybelle. She held their hands for a minute more, then leaned back in her chair. "OK, then, finish your tea. Relax. You know you're safe here."

Irina and Malik stared at the table and finished their tea. Maybelle wondered what was going through their minds. *How do you unwind trauma? What's the best thing to say?* she asked herself. In the end, she decided silence was as good as anything else. As they stood up to go, she ushered them to the door.

"You be sure to let me know if you need to talk, you hear?" Irina and Malik looked at her and nodded. As the screen door slammed, Maybelle watched them go, walking swiftly across the field as if they were being chased.

Five minutes later Irina was back. Her face was red and tear-stained. "I need to talk to you, ma'am. I don't know who else to talk to."

"Come in, then." This time Maybelle led Irina to the sofa by the woodstove. Maybelle sat her down and asked, "What's troubling you, child?" She held Irina's hand and stroked it.

For a minute the tears rolled down Irina's cheeks silently.

"My uncle, my mother's brother - he raped me," she finally choked out. "I never told anybody."

She started to sob now, her head on Maybelle's shoulder, while Maybelle cradled her.

"Shhh, shhh, now. It's okay. It's okay." Maybelle lifted Irina's chin. "It wasn't your fault. Tell me what happened."

Irina dried her eyes and blew her nose, then started talking fast.

"I was seven years old. I didn't have anybody to play with. We lived out in the country. There was nobody else around. I went into my uncle's room to see what he was making. He was working on a windmill that had a wheel that turned around. He showed me how it worked and then he told me we'd play a game. He took me into his bedroom and took my pants off. Then he – " She started to sob again.

Maybelle held her and stroked her back.

"There, there, it's okay. You're okay. You're safe. It's okay." Gradually Irina's sobs slackened, and she drooped and sat still. After a few minutes she spoke again.

"You don't understand. I thought it was fun. I thought that was what I was supposed to do. I came back to him. And I went to other men, later. I was never a little girl again." She paused. "I sinned." She stared at the floor, lost in memory.

After a few minutes, she continued.

191

"When the war came, everyone was killed except me and Malik. We had to run. We had to survive. We got on a ship and came to America. And we lived in Newark." She sighed and shrugged.

"I made him go to school. And I supported us... the way I knew how." She paused again. "And that's where Angela found us. She brought us here."

"Yes, I know." Maybelle looked Irina in the eye. "And this is where you can stay. You're safe here. We are your new family."

"My family. This is what you don't know yet. I have an aunt here in this country. She is my mother's sister. Her name is Dannika. She is married to the man in charge of immigration in this country. You know, George Townsend."

Maybelle had to suppress her astonishment.

"Dannika Townsend is your aunt? I didn't realize – she's from Chechnya?"

"Yes. She left when she was 18. She became a model in Paris. That's the last we saw of her. Then a New York modeling agency recruited her, and she got a U.S. visa. A few years later, we heard she married George Townsend. He had plenty of money, so after a while she got my grandparents to join her."

"Does she know where you are?"

"No, I never was able to get in touch with her, even after I got to Newark. And she doesn't know my mother is dead. My mother, my father, my whole family. Even my uncle. Damn him." Irina sighed with a shudder, but she didn't start crying again.

Maybelle took a minute to collect her thoughts. She spoke slowly.

"This is difficult. But maybe it's good news. You know we filed for asylum for you, but your hearing isn't until December.

Now, maybe, we can get your aunt to sponsor you instead. That might be more certain than an asylum claim. There is still such a thing as chain migration, you know. In fact, your aunt must have used it to bring your grandparents in. And now they are citizens. If your aunt can't sponsor you, maybe your grandparents can." She thought a minute.

"This is good, this is really good." She held Irina by the shoulders and looked straight into her eyes. "Don't say anything to Malik yet. I'll get to work on this."

Irina breathed in deeply, then blew out her cheeks. "There's one more thing. Malik doesn't know what my uncle did to me. Please don't tell him. He liked my uncle." Her voice sank, "Let the dead rest in peace."

"I understand. I won't say a word." Maybelle stood up and put her arm around Irina's shoulder. "Go now, and don't worry about anything."

"Thank you, ma'am. You are so kind. We are lucky we came here." Irina stood up straight and lifted her head. Then she turned and walked out.

Maybelle sat down and wrote a quick note to Mary. She placed it between the pages of a small seed catalog. She addressed the envelope to Mary Anderson, Office of Public Affairs, FBI Washington Field Office. She would mail it tomorrow from town.

Chapter 33 – Washington, D.C.

Doug Williamson, Assistant Director of the FBI's Office of Public Affairs, accompanied FBI Director David Trent to a meeting at the White House. Aside from President Angus Betrog, the other attendees included Vice President Clay Dowd, the president's daughter and son-in-law, and a couple other minor functionaries. Also present was the Assistant to the President for Immigration Affairs, George Townsend, or as the president liked to call him, "my immigration czar."

The topic at hand was the unusual incidence of deaths at conference venues all over the United States. Williamson passed out copies of Vanessa Woodside's report. He emphasized the year-over-year increases in deaths at conferences, pointing to a chart in the report.

The president interrupted him. "Are these shooting victims? Are you making some point about guns? Because I don't want to hear any more about that. I support the second amendment."

There was a brief silence.

"No," Williamson answered slowly. "In fact, none of these were shooting incidents. Not a one. They died of other causes, and that's the –"

"Well, good. Because I sure don't want to hear anything more about guns."

Another silence. No one ventured to say anything.

The president crossed his arms and looked around the table. "So what's going on? Why are you here?"

"We're worried about security at conference venues," ventured Williamson. "We were hoping to involve Homeland Security. It could be some terrorist group behind these deaths."

"Murders, you mean?"

"Well, some murders... some we don't know yet. We're still investigating. But in the meantime, we think we need some protection, some dedicated manpower."

The president's eyes lit up and he nodded. "I can see that. ISIS – and those Mexican gangs – infiltrating deep into our cities. Or maybe those Antifa terrorists. This is a crisis. A real crisis. You can be sure we'll get Homeland Security on it. And this is another reason we need that wall."

"Please, sir," interjected Director Trent, "We need the utmost secrecy on this. We don't want to scare the public about this. Imagine if people were afraid to attend conferences. Business would grind to a halt. Places like Vegas would go broke."

"I see what you mean. Well, we'll take care of it." Turning to his Assistant for Immigration Affairs, George Townsend, the president spoke with authority.

"George, take this report over to Homeland Security and tell them to get on it." He handed his copy of the report to Townsend.

Another silence.

"That's all. We're done. Thank you very much." The president turned his back and the room emptied.

The president turned the TV back on.

Later that afternoon, Dannika Townsend, George's wife, waited for her husband to come home to the estate they owned on Chain Bridge Road in northwest Washington, D.C. She had spent the past year decorating it, while her husband traveled to the Mexican border states, to Europe, and to China. She had also converted one of the outbuildings, a former carriage house, to be an office for herself and her staff. Her staff consisted of three female aides, who helped to coordinate her work with various charities in both Washington and New York. She also still served on the board of Townsend Model Management in New York, although her work there had diminished with their move to Washington.

Dannika was a tall, slender, attractive woman of middle age, with light brown hair swept up in a chignon, usually. She dressed impeccably and conservatively. She was conscious of her position, conscious of her responsibility to be an asset to her husband's career. Her presence on his arm at any Washington gathering always turned heads. He knew it, too. The image the couple presented to the public was one of grandeur and good breeding.

George Townsend had been appointed by President Angus Betrog to oversee all aspects of immigration. As an appointee to the Executive Office, Townsend had not been confirmed by the Senate, nor did he need to be. He served at the whim of the president. His mandate was to coordinate policy between several agencies: the Department of Homeland Security, the Department of State, the Department of Health and Human Services, the Department of Education, and several others. Within these agencies, he also touched sub-departments such as ICE and U.S. Customs and Border Protection.

In short, George Townsend wielded enormous power, and had almost exclusive access to the ear of the president. The president had plucked him out of a Fox News panel after watching his lengthy and animated opinions about immigration, and had brought him to Washington as his advisor. President Betrog liked George Townsend's look. He was a late-middle-aged, formerly handsome man, now grown rather chunky and awkward. Still, his expensive tailored suits fit him fairly well, and his thinning hair was not yet too noticeable.

In his new life, Townsend was an extremely busy man, and thus was rarely home. The only time he spent much time with his family was during rare vacations at their New York penthouse, or at their Florida winter estate.

George Townsend's family fortune had come from his father, a successful real estate developer. He had inherited the Florida estate from his father, as well as several New England properties. With so many residences to choose from, the family had its choice of vacation spots, but they preferred Florida or New York. George used all the residences in rotation, and his wife Dannika suspected that he had mistresses in various cities. Since his appointment by President Betrog, however, his schedule was considerably busier. *That must cut into his free time a bit,* she thought with satisfaction.

Due to Townsend's extensive travel requirements, as well as his high profile, President Betrog had extended the use of executive limousines, jets and helicopters to Townsend. Then in the spring Betrog imposed the Muslim ban, and protestors filled the airports. When family separation policies were initiated at the southern border, protest demonstrations swelled across the country. George Townsend began to get death threats, so President Betrog provided him and his family with Secret Service protection through an executive order. This round-the-clock presence rankled his wife Dannika, who previously had been able to run her own life, to step out with girlfriends or attend their son James' tennis matches. Now everywhere she went she was accompanied by at least two Secret Service agents, and she resented it.

Tonight was a homecoming of sorts, though. George had been down in Texas for two weeks, meeting with border agents and mayors, touring the detention facilities, writing up his observations to bring back to the president. Dannika looked forward to seeing him after his absence, so she spent some time downstairs in the kitchen arranging a special meal with the chef.

"I really would like some healthy meals upstairs," she instructed the chef. "Can we get more vegetables? And salads?"

"Certainly, ma'am," the chef responded. "We'll bring you whatever you want."

"I'd like more fish and more vegetables. And some whole grain bread, please."

"Of course."

That evening, the meal served in the dining room was fresh grilled trout with dill and lime slices, served with roasted parmesan kohlrabi, whole wheat rolls and tossed salad. Dannika and their 11-year-old son James waited patiently for George to join them, but after half an hour it was clear he wasn't coming. So Dannika and James enjoyed the meal alone. Dannika had just suggested to James that he bring his homework to show her, when George walked in. Suddenly the mood shifted.

"What's this stuff? Fish? I don't eat fish." George sniffed and turned to the steward. "Get me a burger and fries." The steward exited and George turned back to the table with a frown.

"James, are you a fish-eater? A little tadpole? A floppy little fishy?"

The boy stared at his plate, and Dannika's eyes narrowed. "Don't you talk to him like that. He's not your plebe to push around."

"Well he's pretty easy to push. Aren't you, Jimmy? Jimmy mommy's boy!"

"Stop it! Stop it right now!" Dannika stood up and her chair fell over. "I'm leaving. Come on, James." She marched out with James on her heels.

George switched on the TV and sat in front of it with his meal. He ordered a second burger after the first one, washing it down with a Diet Coke. He watched his former colleagues praise the president's latest tweets. Then he watched CNN, which enraged him. He decided he needed dessert, so he called the steward back and ordered a piece of chocolate cake with ice cream. He turned back to his own station, Fox News, and relaxed. Then he picked up his phone and called the director of ICE.

Dannika and James, meanwhile, retreated to Dannika's private living room. James asked to continue watching the documentary about the Civil War. Together they settled into it. James had a piece of paper and a pen, and Dannika noticed he was writing notes.

"What are you doing, James? Are you making notes for school?"

"No. I'm writing down the battlefields. I want to see them someday. Do you think we could, Mom? Some of them are pretty close to here."

Dannika sat up. *That would be a wonderful idea!* They could, just the two of them, go on a trip to see the battlefields. They could get out of Washington, and they'd have a real reason to go.

"I love that idea! You're on vacation in two weeks. Let's go!"

James looked up at his mother.

"Really, Mom? I want to go to Gettysburg. I want to take some maps. And can we find a guide?"

"Of course, we can. It will be our own trip. We can ask for anything we want. I'm afraid your dad will be too busy to come with us." Dannika and James shared a look. She nodded. "Let's do it before school starts again."

"Then can I bring a friend along?" James begged. "Maybe two?"

"Of course, sweetheart. This will be a vacation just for you. You decide."

Two weeks later, Dannika and James and two of his friends from school left Washington, D.C. in a limousine, escorted by a second vehicle. They started in the morning and headed north toward Gettysburg. Aside from their Secret Service detail, the group was unimpeded with onlookers or press, as Dannika had requested. Their visit to Gettysburg had been unannounced except to the Park Service personnel assigned to meet the small group. After getting out of Washington traffic, it took only an hour more to reach the park. On the way, James had chattered about the battle, surprising Dannika with his knowledge and impressing his two friends.

At the visitor center, the group was met by park personnel. The young woman assigned to lead their tour was Kiara Jefferson, a short young African American woman in a crisp uniform, with a quick stride and a voice that carried. She led them on a hike from the museum, out past Meade's headquarters to a spot from which they could see almost the whole battlefield.

Kiara pointed south toward Little Round Top and Big Round Top, toward Devil's Den and the Peach Orchard, outlining the Union positions. Then she pointed west across the low farmland to the Confederate line on Seminary Ridge. She asked the group if they were ready to hike, and the boys eagerly assented, hopping around in their enthusiasm. Dannika was pleased to see how well they were getting along. James was usually shy and unassertive, but now he fit right in. In fact, he seemed to be leading the others, answering their questions. What a surprise!

They set off on a long loop to the west, turning south on Confederate Avenue and following the rebel battle line. Finally, they turned back east, leaving the safety of the forest's edge and setting out across tilled fields on a small pathway, aiming for the copse of trees that was the goal of Pickett's charge.

As the boys and Dannika walked across the wide fields with Kiara, their guide, they looked up the long slope toward Cemetery Ridge and imagined the artillery aimed down at their defenseless position. There wasn't a single place to hide in the three-quarters of a mile that they had to march.

Pointing toward the Union position, Kiara described the different types of artillery rounds that would be coming at them. The boys followed her every move.

"First there will be solid shot aimed at your line. You are the infantry, and you're marching side by side. When one of those solid cannonballs come in, you can't dodge them. They come in low, and they can take your leg clean off. When someone beside you falls, you close ranks, move in closer to the next guy." Kiara gestured toward the boys. They obediently closed the gaps.

The group kept walking, shoulder to shoulder, toward the copse of trees, and Kiara continued.

"Now you're about 400 yards from the Union line. Now the Federal guns will start firing canister shot. Canister shot explodes when it gets to you. Shrapnel shoots in all directions.

Dozens of your soldiers fall at once. The troops that are left have to close ranks again.

"Now look up ahead. What's up there? There's a low stone wall, and the Union soldiers are behind it, four lines deep. They can fire over the wall with their muskets and rifles, then fall back to reload while the others fire. Volley after volley of musket fire comes at you.

"Their ammunition is minie balls, which are made of soft lead. When they hit you, they spread out to make a massive hole, not a simple little bullet wound. The exit wound from a minie ball is huge. If you catch one in a limb, that limb will be amputated. If you catch one in your chest, you're dead." The boys looked at each other, their faces pale.

Finally, the boys, Dannika and Kiara reached the stone wall. Kiara made them climb over it.

"Here is where you meet two Pennsylvania regiments. You're climbing over this wall onto their bayonets, and you're stabbing with your bayonet. If you lose your weapon, you're slugging it out with your fists." She turned around and pointed back across the field they'd just crossed. She paused a moment for dramatic effect.

"You started out with General Pickett and 12,500 men in the tree line back there. By the time you got here, you had only 2500 men, no match for the 6500 Union soldiers waiting for you here. This was the end of the battle. This was as far north as the Confederacy got in this or any other battle of the Civil War. This was the high-water mark." She continued in a lower voice.

"The war went on for two more bloody years, through many more horrible battles. But the bloodiest four days of fighting in the war happened right in this valley, and the highest casualties were right here where you're standing."

Kiara finished. There was no sound. Dannika was thinking about her own family and the war in her homeland of Chechnya. The boys were stunned into silence.

Walking back to the Visitor Center, Dannika asked Kiara how she knew all this history. Kiara explained that she was finishing a graduate degree in Civil War history at Temple University. She had just completed her master's thesis and would be looking for an internship soon.

Dannika thought quickly, then spoke.

"An internship? Would you like to come to work for me in Washington?"

Kiara was surprised. She hesitated for a moment before she answered.

"I – I don't know. I thought I'd be going to work here, or maybe at another national park."

"But suppose you could get a paying job, and still be close to all of these places. And you could have access to archives in Washington that most people don't get to see."

"Oh my gosh." Kiara's hand flew to her mouth. "You mean I could get into the National Archives? Mrs. Townsend, you could make that happen?"

Dannika lifted her chin. "Well, if I couldn't, I don't know who could. I would like to invite you to join my staff. Will you think about it? You know where to reach me." She opened her purse and pulled out a card and handed it to Kiara. "Now give me your last name."

"My last name is Jefferson, Mrs. Townsend. And I thank you ever so much for your offer. I need to think about it. But I will be in touch, certainly."

As the group walked back to their vehicle, James looked at his mom with sparkling eyes. He glowed with an excitement that Dannika hadn't seen in a long time.

"Do you think she will come, Mom? That'd be really fun!"

Dannika smiled down at James.

"Well, we can hope so."

Chapter 34 – Ozarks

It had been a week since Maybelle had written to Mary
Anderson in Washington, telling her about Irina and Malik
Varayeva and their relationship to Dannika Townsend. In her
letter, she asked Mary to work through discreet channels to
reach Dannika. Maybelle figured it would take some time to get
through, but in the meantime Irina and Malik were safe here on
the farm.

She was wrong. It was still early on Tuesday morning when
two black vehicles roared up the mountain road. Kristin had run
up the shortcut path from her house to Maybelle's, dashing into
Maybelle's kitchen just ahead of the arrival of the vehicles.

"It looks like ICE. The windows are all black," Kristin
whisper-shouted to Maybelle. Both women stepped out onto the
porch. Maybelle locked the door behind them, and she and
Kristin sat down in the chairs there. Maybelle even tipped her
chair back and put her feet up on the rail. She had grabbed her
coffee cup on the way out of the kitchen, and she placed it now
on the railing in front of her. At that moment Kristin saw Arlene
out of the corner of her eye. Arlene had left the house by the
back door and was sprinting around the corner of the barn
toward the bunkhouse. The black SUVs roared into the yard.
The women on the porch didn't move.

Nine armed men jumped out of the vehicles and moved
toward the porch. The captain reached the porch first.

"Where are they?" he demanded. "Where are the workers?"

Maybelle turned languidly to face the captain. "Excuse me,
sir, can you tell me who y'all are?" She smiled and picked up
her coffee cup.

The officer pulled up short and started over. "Where are your workers?"

Maybelle smiled at him more fixedly. "May I see some ID, please?" She tipped her chair down and reached out a hand.

The officer pulled out a badge and thrust it toward her. She took his hand and perused the badge, slowly moving her glasses down on her nose.

"I see. You are an ICE Special Agent. Captain Andrews – may I call you by your name?" She looked at him intently and he nodded. "What is it you want?" She ignored the large lettering on all of the agents' jackets.

"We've been informed you're harboring illegals. We got a complaint from someone down in town." The captain's voice boomed louder. "We're here to inspect the premises and to detain any illegals we find. We need to see your workers' documentation. And we need to see your records."

"I see. I'll need to see your search warrant." Maybelle was unperturbed.

The captain patted his pockets, then turned to another agent. "The warrant – where is it?"

The agent ran to the first vehicle while the captain fumed. The agent trotted back with a paper.

"Here it is." The captain grabbed it and shoved it toward Maybelle.

Maybelle took the warrant and unfolded it, moving her head up and down and adjusting her glasses again.

"I see. This is my name and address, but I'm looking for a signature. Who issued this warrant?"

"United States District Court in Fayetteville. That's the court for the Western District of Arkansas. And the signature is at the bottom there. Judge Arthur Hanson." The captain pointed. "This authorizes me to search all your premises. So tell me where the workers are."

Maybelle got up with a grunt, pulling herself upright with a grip on the porch railing.

"Well. Please come with me." She moved slowly to the steps of the porch. As she stepped down the first step her knee buckled and she reached for the captain's hand. He jumped forward and grabbed her hand to steady her. She flashed him a grateful smile and patted his hand. Then leaning on his arm, she slowly descended the steps, favoring her bad knee.

Kristin moved quickly down the steps and took Maybelle's other arm. Maybelle's grip on the captain's hand tightened as he half-turned to summon the other men.

Maybelle moved forward at a glacial pace, her grip on the captain's hand surprisingly tight. Her steps were halting and she grunted a little as she moved forward.

"Where are we going?" the captain demanded.

"To the bunkhouse. It's six o'clock in the morning. That's where everyone is."

At that point the captain wrested his hand away from Maybelle and gestured to the agents.

"Where is the bunkhouse? Point the way. Quit messing around," he demanded. "You –" he pointed to Kristin. "Show me the way."

Kristin kept hold of Maybelle's hand. She gestured in the direction of the barn.

"Back behind there, across the field."

The captain set out at a trot, and the other agents followed him. As soon as they rounded the corner of the barn Maybelle dropped Kristin's hand and picked up her pace. Kristin ran to the bell at the corner of the barn and hauled on the rope. Peal after peal rang out over the hillside.

Arlene, trailed by three women, was making her way up the mountain trail toward the orchard. They heard the bell ringing down below and sped up. At the orchard they turned up another path that wound up the side of the upper limestone bluff. Halfway up, there was a thicket of tall bushes. The women squeezed between the bushes and the rock wall and then through a crevice in the face of the bluff. In another moment they were inside a cave that led deeper into the rock formation. Near the entrance was a cache of candles and matches in a glass jar. They each lit a candle, and Arlene led them deeper into the cave along a narrow pathway. They came to a larger room with a sandy floor. There they sat down to wait. They blew out two of the candles and sat silently watching the third one.

Meanwhile, down below at the farm, the agents surrounded the bunkhouse. Maybelle shouted to them to wait for her. She resumed her slow pace across the field, limping painfully, until Kristin caught up with her. Captain Andrews marched back to confront Kristin.

"What's with that bell? Why did you ring that bell?"

"Why, because it's 6:00 in the morning. It's the wake-up call." Kristin stared at him blankly, then smiled. He looked down at his watch. It was exactly 6:00.

Kristin and Maybelle continued to move slowly, arms linked, across the field, with Captain Andrews dogging their heels. Eventually they reached the bunkhouse and Maybelle knocked on the door.

"Ladies?" she shouted through the door, "I need you to get dressed and open the door. There's nothing to worry about."

Maybelle turned toward the captain and smiled.

"Give them a minute to get dressed, and then y'all can go in." She paused, crossed her arms and waited. She yawned widely, and then, as if she'd just thought of it, she asked, "Howcum you're here, anyway? Who sent you?"

The captain stifled his own yawn and answered her.

"Got the complaint from somebody in town. Somebody who saw your people at the farm market. We have to follow up on every tip nowadays."

"Well, hon, I'm afraid y'all are gonna find you've wasted your time." Maybelle smiled sweetly. "Everyone here has the proper papers." She turned as the door opened and spoke to the woman who opened it. "This gentleman here has a search warrant for our premises. I'm sure this won't take any time at all. And I'm sure he's going to be real polite about it." She flashed a penetrating glance at the captain as she said it.

"Yes ma'am," he answered, ducking his head in agreement.

Maybelle stepped out of the way and the captain entered the bunkhouse. She stepped back into the way of his agents and stared them down.

"One is enough. These are ladies here. And families." They stepped back and waited for a signal from their captain. He stuck his head back out the door and came face to face with Maybelle.

"Well shit. Some of you go inspect the other buildings. That barn. That privy." He waved his hand vaguely and ducked back out of her gaze.

After ten minutes Captain Andrews opened the door and stepped out with a grip on Malik's upper arm.

"We're bringing in three of them. The rest are all from around here. You –" he motioned with his chin to the nearest agent. "Take this kid to the van. Cuff him."

Malik started to protest, but Maybelle shook her head.

"Don't worry, Malik, we'll get you out. Don't you worry about a thing. Just do as the officer says." She pleaded with him with her eyes and he relaxed. Even when the agent roughly handcuffed him, he didn't resist.

Another agent entered the bunkhouse and a minute later emerged with Bianca, a Hispanic woman. The captain ushered Irina out in front of him. Both of the women walked submissively ahead of the agents, and the captain ordered them cuffed.

Maybelle stepped up and her voice was calm.

"There's no need to arrest these folks. They're all here legally, and we can show you their paperwork."

"You're going to have to show us your paperwork anyway. Where is your office?" The captain turned toward another agent. "Get these people in the van."

"My office is back at the house. I'll show you." Maybelle reached out for the captain's hand again and leaned heavily on him all the way back to her porch and up the steps. She unlocked the door and ushered him in. She pointed to a small teacher's desk with two drawers. "There's my files."

He looked around. "Where's your computer?"

"My what?"

"Your computer. I'm authorized to take your equipment."

"I ain't got a computer," she laughed. "What would I need that for? There's no electricity here." Then her face grew serious. "I have ledger books. And a pen. And an oil lamp. What exactly do you want?"

"I want your employment records. I want your copies of your workers' legal papers."

"That I do have." She pulled out a folder from one of the drawers. "Let me show you. Irina and Malik and Bianca, those three you have in the van, here are their papers. Irina and Malik have applied for asylum, and their interview is in December. Bianca has also applied for asylum, and her interview is coming up in September." She pulled out copies of documents to show the captain. He grabbed them.

"I'll take these, but I'm not the one you have to show them to. You're going to have to show them to the judge. In Fayetteville."

"Is that where you're taking them?"

"No."

"No? Then where are you taking them?"

"I can't disclose that. You'll have to talk to the judge and then he may let you know. There's a process." He turned his back on her.

Maybelle started to get angry now, but she hid it as she tucked the folder away in the drawer. She followed him out the door and leaned heavily on the railing as he slammed the van door. The vehicles pulled out fast, turning down the dirt road in a cloud of dust.

"You can't take them away!" Tom came running around the corner of the barn, yelling at the departing vehicles.

Out of nowhere, Bonnie grabbed him and pulled him back out of sight.

"No! Don't do that!" She held onto him with an iron grip. "This isn't your fight. You'll only get hurt. And it won't stop them. Please." Tom succumbed and stepped back. He breathed heavily.

Bonnie soothed him. "You're new here. I know you want to help, but you just came from prison. I know you don't want to get hauled back there." She turned him around and put her hands on his shoulders. "I'll tell you what you can do, Tom. You can go up to the cave and tell those ladies they can come down now. Be sure you call out to Arlene when you get up there – she's in charge and she knows you. And ring the all-clear on the bell on your way up."

A few minutes later Maybelle, Kristin and Bonnie were in the kitchen making a plan. After breakfast, Kristin and Maybelle headed down the mountain with their folder of papers. They stopped at the motel in town to see Lurleen and to make more copies, then headed west to Fayetteville to see the judge.

Chapter 35 – Washington, D.C.

It was three weeks since the meeting in the oval office that Doug Williamson had attended. George Townsend, the immigration czar, had taken Vanessa's FBI report to Homeland Security, where it was passed up the chain of command. It was met with some skepticism. Those who were allowed to see it expressed doubt that Antifa had anything to do with individual murders in American cities. That theory was being circulated by the White House, but it wasn't reflected in Vanessa's report.

Closed-door meetings were held between the FBI and the military, working on some way to tighten security at conference venues. It was agreed that more could be done to screen people entering conferences. However, it would be much more difficult to protect conference attendees as they went out clubbing in the evening. Or as they left during the day to go shopping, play golf, or go to the beach. And most of these reported murders had taken place in locations that no one would want surveillance of – strip clubs, exclusive nightclubs, hotel suites. The discussions went nowhere as the difficulty of the task became clear. No one could think of any good solutions.

This evening, Dannika Townsend was still away with James and his friends at Gettysburg. George Townsend sat in front of a TV, watching his favorite team of pundits. They were reporting on an incident in Orlando, Florida. The senior senator from Idaho, David Bayard, had been found strangled to death behind a strip mall. He had last been seen entering a day spa and massage parlor at the other end of the mall. The anchors reported that he had been attending a business conference in Orlando. The scene shifted to a newscaster standing outside the strip mall, describing the scene, while police lights flashed in the background. Then it shifted to the senator's home in Idaho, where his family was refusing all interviews. Reporters were pestering neighbors instead, and serving up tasty tidbits of gossip.

At the White House, the president was riveted to the same show. He knew exactly what was going on. He reached for his phone and put out a tweet:

> Antifa attack on Senator Bayard in Florida! Our Conference Cities are infiltrated by Foreign Operatives. FBI and Military will be deployed to keep our Cities Safe!

Five minutes after the tweet appeared, the phone rang in Townsend's home. Townsend picked up the phone. It was FBI Director Trent.

"Can you get him to take that tweet down?" The director's voice was urgent. "This was supposed to be kept quiet."

"What does it say?" asked Townsend.

Trent read it off to him. "Where does that Antifa stuff come from?" he asked.

"Don't you remember?" Townsend reminded him. "That Williamson guy from your Office of Public Affairs said something about terrorists at the meeting in the Oval Office. It wasn't in the report, but he said it. And the president took that to mean Antifa." Townsend paused. "So now it's my problem, huh?"

"Please. See what you can do. He listens to you more than he does to us. You know that." Director Trent was practically pleading.

Townsend called President Betrog's phone and got shunted to voicemail. He tried again in two minutes and still couldn't get through. He decided he'd better just go see him. *Great. Another fun night.*

Townsend changed into a clean shirt, whistled up his limousine and driver, and rode over to the White House, trying to come up with an approach to use. He asked to see the president and was grilled by the chief of staff. He was left waiting for twenty minutes before the chief of staff came back and ushered him upstairs to the residence.

Townsend found President Betrog dressed in a bathrobe, sitting in his private office, TV remote in one hand and smartphone in the other. He looked up briefly as Townsend entered, then looked right back at the TV. Townsend cleared his throat.

"What do you want?" Betrog barked.

"Sir, we're concerned about leaking the intent of Operation NEVRR. If it's going to work, we need to keep it under wraps." He paused. "We need to ask you not to tweet about it."

"I tweeted about it?"

"Yes sir. Your tweet about Senator Bayard. You claimed Antifa was behind his murder."

"Weren't they?"

"We don't know that. We don't know anything yet."

"Well, I have a pretty good hunch it was them. Either them or MS-13. They work together, you know. I have a feeling – you watch, I'll be right." The president stared at Townsend, his jaw set.

Townsend decided that talking sense was useless. *Try another tack.* "Sir, you may be right. And if you are, we don't want to alert them that we know their strategy. It will blow our operation. You understand." He gave Betrog a conspiratorial look.

"Yeah? So?"

"So we need to ask you to take down your tweet about Senator Bayard. It will compromise our pursuit." He paused. "Please."

"Oh, hell." Betrog was indignant. "If I do, will you get out of here?"

"Of course. Yessir."

"Then I will. Good night."

Townsend turned around and left. As he got into the limo to go home, he realized he didn't even care if the tweet came down. In fact, he didn't care about much at all. He was tired. He had been so glad to get this job, so proud of the title Assistant to the President for Immigration Affairs. But tonight it was wearing him down. When he got home he poured himself a double whiskey, undressed and fell into bed.

The next day Vanessa Woodside and Mary Anderson were in Vanessa's office, going over what they knew about the conference venue situation. Mary asked Vanessa if she'd seen the newest tweet from the president. Vanessa hadn't, so they both looked. There it was, along with several follow-ups, each more inflammatory than the last.

"I guess there's no such thing as a covert operation anymore." Vanessa looked disgusted. "Not if you have to report to the president. I'm done with this job."

"Oh no. You're not thinking of quitting, are you?" Mary was alarmed. "We need you."

"No, I mean I'm *done* with this job of trying to protect conference sites. They took my report and made it about gangs or terrorists. Clearly, it's not that. But you know what?" Vanessa stood up and flung up her hands. "I don't care. I'm here to do what I can to stop crime. And the crime of human trafficking, including at conferences, is bigger than a few murders. That's what I'm going to focus on." She stabbed the air with her finger.

Mary kept her face impassive, but inwardly she was jubilant. She stood up. "Can I get you some tea? I'm getting some for myself." She walked out of the office toward the lounge, using the moment to collect her thoughts.

Vanessa thought back to her last conversation with Mike Jenkins. *I'm starting to sound like him*, she thought. *Why is that?* She sat back down, deflated.

When Mary came back, she brought the tea and some papers in her hand. She settled into her seat across from Vanessa. "Can we move on to something else? I have a personal favor to ask. I've gotten two letters from a friend in Arkansas."

Mary handed across the letters she'd gotten from Maybelle Barker. In the first one, dated two weeks ago, Maybelle described Irina and Malik Varayeva's relationship to the wife of the immigration czar, Dannika Townsend, their aunt on their mother's side. Then, Maybelle asked Mary to help expedite Irina's and Malik's applications for asylum. She explained that they had sent Form I-589 two months ago to the USCIS Nebraska Service Center, but they hadn't gotten a receipt back. She outlined Irina's and Malik's grounds for seeking asylum: their Russian heritage, the fact that their parents were murdered by Chechens during the uprising, and the fact that they had been trafficked to Newark and rescued from a pimp there.

Then Mary produced Maybelle's second letter, received yesterday. In it, Maybelle described the ICE raid and the detention of Irina, Malik and Bianca, despite Maybelle's efforts to demonstrate their legal status. She said she couldn't find out from the judge in Fayetteville where the three of them had been taken.

Vanessa sat and looked over the two letters, then handed them back. "I don't know if we should get involved in this. This isn't an FBI matter, it's a Department of Homeland Security matter."

"Really? We're going by the book now?" Mary crossed her arms and sat back, disgusted. "After you've seen how we can kick ass when we don't follow the rules? Who caught your attacker the other day anyhow? The D.C. cops or a secretary and a nurse?" She paused a moment. There was silence as the women stared at each other.

Vanessa blinked and adjusted in her chair. "Well. You've got a point." Her brow drew down. "But we have to be careful. Work under the radar."

"That's all we do, lady. I'll get on it, and if I need your access, I'll ask you."

It took three days, but by perusing Department of Homeland Security records, Mary and Vanessa found where Irina, Malik and Bianca had been taken. They were being held at the Farmville Detention Center in Farmville, Virginia. This was only three hours south of Washington, D.C. Mary wrote back to Maybelle that they would work on getting the three of them released.

Then the real underground work began.

Chapter 36 – Washington D.C.

A week after their trip to Gettysburg, Dannika Townsend received a letter from Kiara Jefferson, the young student guide whose stories had so captivated James and his friends. She wrote to say she was honored to have been offered a place on Dannika's staff. Her letter inquired as to her duties and her proposed salary.

At first, Dannika was a little put off by the boldness of Kiara's questions. As she thought about it more, though, she realized that this young lady was right to ask. In fact, she probably could have taught Dannika a thing or two, in her younger years, about how to approach a new job offer. Dannika wondered, if she had known something about negotiating a salary, how different her own career might have been.

So Dannika consulted with her chief of staff, and they decided that an appropriate title for Kiara Jefferson would be Staff Historian. And an appropriate salary for someone with a master's degree would be just over $60,000. Dannika was pleased with this decision, and she wasted no time in having her executive assistant draft an offer to Kiara.

Kiara arrived in Washington in the middle of July. She joined Dannika Townsend's staff, who were engaged in a study of the history of women's suffrage in Britain and the United States. The end result would be school curriculum plans and materials that middle schools throughout the country could use. Since it was summer, James wasn't in school, so Kiara met with him several afternoons a week to discuss American history. Often Dannika sat in on the sessions. She enjoyed seeing how James dug into the subject under Kiara's tutelage. He hadn't shown this kind of interest in any other area.

"You know what, Mom? This stuff makes sense to me."
Dannika had entered the room as Kiara was gathering up her
books. James continued, "It's starting to hang together. I can see
how the arguments started. I can see why nobody would back
down. I can see how money was all tied up in it. And how white
people used blacks in all kinds of ways. In the South, to pick
their cotton and make them rich. And in the North, to get all
righteous about slavery. But nobody really wanted to mix with
them or actually give them rights. Am I right?" He looked at
Dannika defiantly, hands on his hips, then turned to Kiara. "Am
I right?"

"As a matter of fact, you are." Kiara said cautiously,
watching Dannika's reaction. Then more emphatically, "I'm
impressed. You're really picking up on some of the nuances.
You'll be a good historian someday, kiddo."

"Mom, can we go to out to Virginia again, to some of the
other battlefields and museums? I really liked that trip to
Gettysburg. Please, can we, mom?"

"Why not? Do you think some of your friends would want to
come, too?"

Kiara set her books back down, and for the next half hour the
three of them were deep into plans for later in the summer.

Over the following few weeks, Kiara took James and his friends
to exhibits in Washington: the National Museum of American
History and the African American Civil War Museum. Her
stories brought the exhibits to life, and the boys clamored for
more. Kiara approached Dannika about taking James and his
friends out of the city on day trips, and Dannika agreed. She
liked the idea of accompanying them, especially since it got her
out of a number of events that her husband wanted her to attend.

Let him take his daughter as an escort, she thought. S*he's more at ease at those ceremonies anyway.*

This is how Dannika, Kiara, James and his friends wound up attending an event called "Mystery & Myths of Lee's Lost Orders," at the Monocacy National Battlefield in Frederick, Maryland. After that program, they visited the National Museum of Civil War Medicine in Frederick, where they learned more than they wanted to know about amputations.

The following day they toured the battlefield at Antietam. The ride back home to Washington that evening was quiet. The boys were tired and subdued. Each boy, in his own mind, was imagining lying on the ground under fire, or charging toward the sunken road, or battling through the cornfield in confusion.

The school term for James didn't start until after Labor Day, so the group made plans for a long trip in August. They would travel first to Fredericksburg, Virginia, the site of Lee's decisive victory in 1862. Then they would visit Richmond, the Confederate capital. Finally, they would travel all the way over to Appomattox, where Lee finally surrendered to Grant and the war ended. In planning this route, Kiara had another agenda in mind.

Several weeks earlier, Kiara's old friend from college, Tracy Willis, had contacted her to ask for a favor. Mary Anderson had approached Tracy at church with a problem. Mary knew she could count on Tracy's help. After all, Tracy had saved her boss Vanessa's hide that night a couple months ago, when she called Mary from the bar and told her the police were hauling Vanessa in.

A month after that incident, Mary had a favor to ask of Tracy. The story was long and complicated, so the two of them went to Mary's home to talk it over.

"There's a lot to explain," Mary began. "I'm trying to find a way to get a message to Dannika Townsend."

"Who's that?"

"She's the wife of George Townsend, the Assistant to the President for Immigration Affairs. She has a niece and nephew who are in danger, but she doesn't know it."

"Um, okay…"

"And you went to school with Kiara Jefferson."

"Yes, I did. We roomed together." Tracy looked puzzled. "What does that have to do with anything?"

"Well, Kiara now works for Dannika Townsend. She is her staff historian. One of the things she does is to plan trips to historic sites, mostly for Dannika and her son and his friends."

"I still don't see –"

"Hang on, you will. Dannika Townsend has a niece and nephew who were scooped up by ICE. They're now being held in a detention center in Farmville, Virginia. I know that there's a lot of media attention on Mrs. Townsend, so this isn't going to be easy. But here's what I want you to do: Can you and Kiara and figure out some way to tell Dannika about her niece and nephew? Maybe even arrange a way for Dannika to meet them?"

"Huh, you don't ask for much!" Tracy frowned. "I'm supposed to figure out a way to get past ICE?"

"Well, you don't have to figure it out alone. Get ahold of Kiara and see if she has any ideas. But do your talking in person. Call her and tell her you heard she'd moved to Washington and you want to have lunch."

"Well, I guess I could do that. What are the names of Mrs. Townsend's niece and nephew?"

"They are Irina and Malik Varayeva. Their mother was Mrs. Townsend's sister, Galina. She was killed in the war, but Mrs. Townsend may not even know that much." Mary paused. "I'm betting that she doesn't know what happened to them."

"Well, I'll get in touch with Kiara. Maybe she can figure something out."

Now several weeks later, and a few days before their trip to Appomattox, Kiara approached Dannika in her garden. She felt her heart beating fast as she began.

"I have something important to tell you. It's about your sister Galina. The one who died in Chechnya." Kiara was speaking quietly, but Dannika startled. Then she recovered her poise.

"My sister? Yes, she was murdered," Dannika stopped and turned to face Kiara. "How did you know? Why are you telling me this?"

"Because her children, your niece and nephew, Irina and Malik, are in trouble. They are here in the United States, in ICE custody. In Virginia, in a place called the Farmville Detention Center. We're trying to get them out."

Dannika was stricken. "How do you know all this? I thought Irina and Malik were dead! Where have they been?" She paused and, with an effort, lowered her voice. "And what do you mean 'we'? Who is trying to get them out?"

"Their friends. My friends. People who care about them. Does that include you?"

"Of course it does!" Dannika, her face pale, reached for Kiara's hand. "Of course I care about them. They are all I have

of my sister. And I didn't know what happened to them." She
paused. "Tell me what I can do."

"We can stop at the Farmville Detention Center on the way
home from Appomattox. Maybe you can see them." Dannika
slowly nodded. Kiara continued. "Can you figure out a way to
do this? I don't think we can bring the kids along to the
detention center, it'd be just too weird."

"Give me a little time to think about it. Let's talk tomorrow."

By the next day, Dannika had come up with a plan, which
she explained to Kiara as they walked in the garden again. They
could bring two vehicles for the trip to Appomattox. On the
final day, she would send the boys and one of the Secret Service
crew home in one vehicle. She and Kiara and the other Secret
Service officer would use the second vehicle to stop at the
detention center, which was directly on the way between
Appomattox and Washington. She would come up with an
excuse for the visit, and they would try to connect with Irina and
Malik without divulging their relationship. Dannika couldn't
think beyond these bare-bones logistics, and she dared not
imagine how the meeting would play out. *Could she bluff her
way past ICE? Would Irina give it all away, would she cry out?*

Dannika forced herself back to the present, and spoke to
Kiara in a calm and level voice.

"We have to make this work. We have to be strong. And it
must be kept secret." Kiara nodded, but she looked puzzled.
Dannika realized she'd have to explain. "My husband must not
know. I can't trust him. Not with something like immigration."
She smiled grimly, looking away. She did not elaborate, and
Kiara did not ask.

Later that night, Dannika prayed she'd have the guts to see
the plan through. She hadn't laid eyes on Irina and Malik in

fourteen years – would she even recognize them? Would they recognize her? And would they forgive her for believing they were dead?

Chapter 37 – Virginia

Dannika and James Townsend, along with their entourage, started out for Fredericksburg on the morning of the first Saturday in August. It was a beautiful day, a little cooler than normal for Virginia at this time of year. A brisk breeze was blowing, and it felt like a lazy summer day once they got out into the country. Since they had all week for the trip, Dannika and James added another destination: Manassas Junction. Kiara readily agreed. The two limousines set off from Washington, with James, his two friends, and Kiara in the first, driven by the male Secret Service officer. Dannika's female Secret Service officer drove the second vehicle, with Dannika as the only passenger.

In the hour that it took to reach Manassas Junction, Kiara kept the boys occupied with stories of the battle. "Take a look out the window," she directed them. "We're driving 25 miles from Washington to Manassas. Imagine, now, that you're marching on this same road, except it's a dirt road. It's a hot day in the middle of July, and you're carrying weapons and ammunition, and heavy backpacks and blankets. There are 35,000 of you on this road, and the dust is rising from all those marching feet. You don't know exactly where you're marching or why – all you know is that you're excited to be going, because this is going to be a quick and glorious victory. The battle cry you hear all around is 'On to Richmond!'

"The actual objective of this march, under General Irvin McDowell, is the railroad at Manassas Junction, Virginia, where the Orange and Alexandria line connects to the Manassas Gap line. If the Union troops – that's you – can seize this railroad, they will have a direct route to Richmond.

"But it takes you two whole days to reach Centreville, and that's still five miles away from Manassas Junction. That gives Confederate General Beauregard two whole days to call for reinforcements, and two whole days for Confederate General Johnston to bring his army up the railway to his aid. To make things worse, between your army and the railroad you're trying to seize, there's a creek called Bull Run. That creek is difficult for an army to cross, with a bridge and fords well guarded by Confederate troops.

"So the battle takes place, and at first the Union side is winning, until they come up against the troops of a Confederate brigadier general known forever after as Stonewall Jackson. And then, at the end of the day, a well-coordinated Confederate counter-attack sends the Union soldiers back across Bull Run Creek. By the end of that long day, 5000 soldiers have been killed or injured, and 3000 of those casualties are on the Union side. How many is 5000?" asked Kiara. None of the boys answered. "Have you ever been to the Kennedy Center?" James and one of his friends nodded. "Imagine the audience at the Kennedy Center, times two. That's 5000 men." The boys looked at each other in shock.

Kiara continued. Her hand ticked across the seat with a regular beat. "The Union army retreats in an orderly way at first. But pretty soon the troops just panic and start running!" She flung her arms out and the boys jumped. "To make things worse, the roads are clogged with broken-down carriages." She pointed out the window. "People, picknickers from Washington, for heaven's sake, all over the road. The army can't get past them.

"The Union soldiers run for their lives, dropping their weapons and backpacks. They run all the way back to

227

Washington in one day – the same distance it had taken them more than two days to march out. Imagine that." The boys looked stunned and stared out at the landscape. Suddenly each rolling hill became an obstacle to them, each barn a place to hide.

Before the two vehicles reached Manassas Battlefield Park, they stopped for lunch at a pizzeria. Each place that the limousines stopped had been carefully screened, and the small group was always given a private dining room, with the family at one table and the Secret Service officers at another. Dannika's staff had planned the entire trip itinerary in advance, with major input from James. This is why lunch was pizza rather than Greek cuisine, which had been Dannika's choice. She decided to let James choose the menus. This was going to be a great week, she decided, and there was no need to inject food battles into it. *God knows there are enough of those with his father,* she thought.

As they sat around the table waiting for their pizza, the boys begged Kiara for more stories. She decided to tell them the story of Rose O'Neal Greenhow, a well-connected Washington socialite in the 1860s, who cozied up to presidents, generals, senators and other high-ranking officials in the capitol city.

"Rose Greenhow controlled a pro-Confederate spy network in Washington," Kiara explained, "and she managed to collect and pass on strategic information to the Confederacy before the battle of Manassas, the battle I just told you about. She drew maps of Union fortifications, and she found out General McDowell's plans to attack Manassas Junction. She passed this information to General Beauregard, on the Confederate side, before the battle. After the battle was over, the Confederate president, Jefferson Davis, ordered a telegram of thanks sent to her. The telegram concluded with these words: 'We rely upon you for further information. The Confederacy owes you a debt.'"

"Did the Union side catch her?" asked James.

"Well, yes they did, eventually, but it took them awhile. She was imprisoned, along with her youngest daughter, who was eight years old. She was a widow, and before the war, she had sent all her older daughters away, because it was too dangerous for them to stay in Washington. So when they caught her spying, she went to prison. But after five months the Union authorities released her, and deported her and her daughter to exile in the South. Back then, women, even women spies, were not considered true combatants. So they got off a whole lot easier than male spies, who were usually shot.

"Well, Rose didn't quit then. The Union had blockaded all the seaports of the Confederacy, but somehow Rose Greenhow got on a ship that ran the blockade. She sailed to England and France on an official diplomatic mission from the Confederate States of America. She cut quite the figure in London. She even published a popular book of her memoirs there. She met Emperor Napoleon III in France and Queen Victoria in England. She even got engaged to an English earl.

"In the long run, though, she never could feel at home in England. She finally sailed back to America in 1864, carrying diplomatic papers and $2000 worth of gold sewn into her undergarments. But her ship ran aground off the coast of North Carolina, and the rowboat she tried to escape in was chased by a Union gunboat. The rowboat overturned and she drowned. It didn't help that she had so much gold sewn into her clothes."

The boys were silent, digesting the story.

"What happened to her daughter?" James wanted to know.

"Well, I don't actually know the answer to that," admitted Kiara. "We'll have to research that together. Later, when we get back home. Okay with you?" James nodded.

The waitress came in with the pizzas, and the boys clustered around, leaning across the table to get their favorite toppings. Kiara turned to Dannika and spoke under her breath.

"So you see, if you're glamorous enough, you get invited to the best parties. You can hide in plain sight and hear all kinds of things." Kiara chuckled. Then she sobered and said, "But spy missions are dangerous, of course." Dannika looked slightly nonplussed and nodded. The boys, preoccupied with their pizza, missed the point.

After lunch they were off to the battlefield, where they learned on the ground how the battle played out. Kiara and a local guide took them through the movements of the various regiments of both sides. The guide described the two historical firsts of this battle: the first movement of troops to the frontlines via railroad (on the Confederate side), and the first aerial reconnaissance by balloon (on the Union side). He described the throngs of day-trippers from Washington, who rode buggies and horses, and carried picnic baskets and spyglasses to observe the action. "And guess what?" he concluded. "The guy who shouted 'On to Richmond' the loudest, Congressman Alfred Ely of New York, was captured by the rebels and went to Richmond, sure enough. He spent the next six months there, in Libby Prison." The boys cracked up at the end of that story and begged the guide for more. Even Dannika found herself caught up in the drama.

By the end of the afternoon they were exhausted by all the walking and ready to retire to their hotel. It was not quite the level of luxury that Dannika was accustomed to, but the boys enjoyed the pool, and Dannika was too tired to care. In a strange way, she realized that this anonymous style of travel was fun. She hid behind shades and a large hat, and her Secret Service staff were dressed down in order to blend in. Still, they maintained a perimeter around her and she couldn't have mingled if she'd wanted to. But she didn't want to. She was happy just talking with Kiara.

The next day, with a different guide, the group learned about the second battle of Manassas. Listening to the story, Dannika began to have a strange feeling, almost as if she were watching the battle at first hand, at first alarmed at the death and destruction, but then developing a strange sense of numbness as the numbers of casualties mounted and mounted. She wondered what it was about men – that they would fling themselves at each other with such fury.

All of a sudden, a scene came back to her, a memory of answering a phone call in her college dorm room, hearing on the other end the boom of artillery and shattering glass. It was the last time she had heard from her sister Galina. She felt like fainting, and it was all she could do to remain standing. Kiara noticed her pallor and stepped up, signaling to the nearby Secret Service woman. Together they walked Dannika to a bench under a tree, where they sat her down. Kiara brought some water to Dannika, then sat beside her and waited for her to talk.

Dannika was not forthcoming. She had learned, above all, to keep her mouth shut. To not reveal anything about her past before she came to New York.

Kiara worried that night about the wisdom of sending Dannika to try to find her niece and nephew at the Farmville detention center. She began to watch Dannika closer for signs of

231

strain. The next morning, though, she was glad to see that Dannika was once again cheerful and poised.

The group went to Richmond, the onetime capital of the Confederacy, to visit the two museums there, but the boys were restless indoors. So they wound up walking along the riverfront, where Kiara got them to picture the Confederate retreat in April of 1865.

"Right across here is where the trains crossed the James River. First they took President Jefferson Davis's wife and children and servants away. Then a few days later, when General Grant and the Union army were approaching Richmond, Lee ordered his Confederate army to evacuate. It took all night to get President Davis and all the soldiers across the river. During that last night, there were two Confederate warships in the river, downstream of the city." Kiara pointed downriver. "Those ships were loaded with munitions, and the Confederates didn't want the Union army to get their hands on them. So in the middle of the night, the Confederate navy blew up the warships. The explosions rocked the city and rattled windows."

Kiara turned toward the town, and her arm swept in a great arc.

"There were three tobacco warehouses here, and the Confederates didn't want the Union army getting that tobacco, either. So they set fire to them, too. After they got across the river, they burned the bridges behind them. And that tobacco warehouse fire spread to the whole downtown. By the time the Union army came into Richmond and put the fires out, a thousand buildings had been destroyed. Many people were homeless and destitute, and they huddled together on the courthouse lawn."

That evening, as Dannika and the boys sat around the hotel pool, the boys begged Kiara for more stories. Kiara decided to tell them the story of the rich old spinster of Richmond, Elizabeth Van Lew, who was a successful spy for the Union.

"Elizabeth came from a rich family, and she lived in a mansion in the middle of Richmond. She never married. When her father died, she freed the family's slaves, and when the war came, she acted as a spy for the Union side. She used her own house to hide escaped slaves as well as Union officers."

"On top of this, Elizabeth had a farm outside Richmond. By late in the war Richmond was surrounded by the Union army. She sent coded messages out to the Union army by using her farm workers, who were allowed through Confederate picket lines. The messages were concealed inside eggshells and hollow shoe heels. Nobody challenged a couple of innocent-looking black women with muddy shoes, carrying baskets of greens and eggs.

"Elizabeth's van Lew's most brazen plan involved a former servant. Years before the war, Elizabeth had arranged for one of her former slaves, Mary Bowser, to get an education in Boston. Then during the war, Elizabeth asked Mary to return to Richmond, where Mary became a dining room servant in the household of Confederate President Jefferson Davis. She quietly served the important men who dined with President Davis, listening intently to their strategies. To the men, Mary was just a black servant, too uneducated to worry about. They had no idea she was a spy who reported back to Elizabeth regularly.

"Elizabeth, too, had her own disguise. She was known around town as 'Crazy Bet,' the old spinster. She had a slightly frowzy appearance and nutty mannerisms, talking to herself in public. Her abolitionist views were well known around Richmond. However, in spite of her public opinions, or maybe because of them, nobody took her seriously. And nobody noticed Mary, the quiet, obedient dining room servant in the home of the Confederate President. Between them, they conveyed war secrets to the Union army with a regularity that Elizabeth joked 'beat the Confederate postal delivery.'"

"Elizabeth's final triumph was on the morning when General Ulysses S. Grant's Union army entered Richmond. She helped her servants raise a smuggled American flag above the Van Lew mansion. This was too much for the mob in the street below, and they threatened to burn down the house. But Elizabeth stood on her balcony and pointed at them. 'I know you, and you and you!' she yelled. 'General Grant will be in this city within the hour. If this house is harmed, your houses shall be burned by noon!'" Kiara waved her arm over the boys' heads and they laughed. She nodded. "Uh-huh, they backed off."

Dannika smiled. The mood of feminine rebellion was contagious. She suddenly felt lighter than she had in a long time, and thoughts of a different life crowded into her mind. *Suppose I could act on my own, do things on my own, be more than just an ornament on George's arm? What if I could get James away from his scorn and ridicule?* Dannika thought about it, and suddenly froze with the old fear. She could never divorce George. Never. That way lay deportation – followed by disgrace and poverty. She could never leave.

Then she looked at the laughing group of boys and realized she was already free, at least a little bit, just by taking this trip. And that feeling she owed to Kiara.

After another two days spent visiting Appomattox and watching a reenactment of the final confrontation of Lee and Grant, the boys were exhausted and ready to head home. They stayed the night at an elegant bed and breakfast inn, then left mid-morning for the return trip to Washington. The boys were excited about getting back home to see the latest superhero film, and they pestered Dannika to get them back in time. Realizing this worked to her advantage, Dannika instructed one of her Secret Service officers to leave with them right away. She and Kiara and the other guard would stop at an antique store for a little shopping and would follow shortly.

"I do not want these boys in a shop with stained glass lamps!" Dannika laughed. Then she turned to them. "Boys, get your bags to the car."

"Well, that was smoothly done," whispered Kiara. As soon as the first limousine pulled away, Dannika turned to her female Secret Service officer. She spoke in a low voice.

"I am going to ask something extraordinary of you. This is a strictly confidential request, and it must remain so. I want to visit a federal detention center. I am determined to learn the truth about my husband's policy on immigrants. There is an ICE detention center in Farmville, which is on the way home from here. I want to stop there just briefly, to see with my own eyes how these people are being treated. And this stop must never come to the attention of anyone. Not even George."

This speech was delivered quietly, but with a firmness that couldn't be challenged. The officer nodded. She put the bags in the limo and opened the door for Dannika and Kiara. As the two women settled into the back seat, Dannika reached out for Kiara's hand and squeezed it, not looking at her.

It took only half an hour to reach Farmville. As they
approached the detention center, a long, low metal building,
Dannika felt a chill of fear. She looked at Kiara and met her
eyes, and Kiara nodded imperceptibly. When the limousine
pulled up and stopped, Kiara stepped out, holding Dannika's
I.D. She beckoned the Secret Service officer to accompany her,
and the two of them strode toward the door while Dannika
watched from behind the tinted windows of the limo. Kiara
spoke to the officer who came to the door, then all three of them
disappeared inside. A few minutes later, they returned to the
limo. The Secret service guard opened Dannika's door, and the
ICE agent stepped back. Dannika stepped out regally.

"They have told you why I'm here, I presume? I do not want
to stay long, but I want to see your facility. And I want this visit
to be kept secret. Do you understand? Please take me to your
commanding officer." As she said this, Dannika was tying a
kerchief around her hair and putting on a pair of dark glasses.

The ICE agent nodded and gestured toward the door. He led
them through it, down a long hallway, into an office. "Director
Davis," he addressed the uniformed man behind the desk, "this
is Mrs. Townsend, wife of George Townsend." Dannika was
already handing her I.D. across the desk and pulling off her
sunglasses.

"I am here on an informal visit. I hope you will allow me to
have a look around and report back to my husband as to the
conditions here. May I see the families you have in custody?"
She reached to retrieve her I.D., which the director hastily
handed back.

"Yes, ma'am, of course. Ted, please show Mrs. Townsend to
the rec room." Dannika put her sunglasses back on and turned
toward Ted.

"Please." She gestured and he almost bowed, then quickly led the three women down the hall. They entered a common room full of tables and chairs. Children were underfoot, playing games or sitting quietly. Women and a few teenagers sat around the tables, looking subdued. At a table in the corner, Dannika caught sight of her niece Irina, sitting with Malik, their heads bowed in quiet conversation. She recognized them instantly, although it had been over a decade since she'd left them in Chechnya. She nudged Kiara, who followed her nod and looked in the same direction. Then as Dannika questioned Ted about the nutrition plan for the detainees, Kiara approached the corner table. She spoke in a low voice to Irina, who looked up in surprise. Just at that moment, Dannika removed her sunglasses and stared directly at Irina. Irina's hand flew to her mouth, then instantly dropped back to her lap. She looked down at the table again. Kiara spoke to her quietly. Irina answered in a whisper.

Kiara moved away from the table, circled the room, and arrived back at Dannika's side. Dannika, meanwhile, had been grilling Ted, the ICE agent, on the subject of medical care afforded to the inmates. He answered stumblingly under the glare of her interrogation. Kiara turned to Dannika and spoke up.

"Ma'am, there are some people who would be willing to speak to you. That young lady in the corner, and her brother." Kiara motioned with her eyes in their direction, then turned around to face Ted.

Dannika addressed Ted. "I would like to know something about the length of stay, and about legal representation for your detainees. Please describe these things to my assistant, while I do a little interviewing." She stepped away and walked slowly around the room, stopping to talk to several of the women and leaning down to greet their children. Finally she reached the corner table, bent down and spoke softly to Irina in Chechen. Her smile was fixed.

"Don't look at me. You are….?"

"Irina and Malik Varayeva," Irina whispered, her head down.

"And your mother is…?"

"Galina Varayeva."

"Very good. I am your aunt Dannika. I will get you out of here. Do not worry. Do not tell anyone I have been here. Understand?" Irina nodded and Dannika straightened up. She shook Malik's hand and he nodded slightly, looking at the table. Dannika strolled around to some other mothers and engaged them in conversation. Finally, she approached the group at the door. Kiara had a notebook out and was still grilling Ted. Dannika addressed him.

"May I see Director Davis for a moment more, please?"

"Of course, ma'am, right this way." Ted escorted them back down the hall.

Ted knocked and ushered Dannika into the office. He started to leave, but Dannika motioned him back in. "You need to hear this as well." She turned to Director Davis. "Sir, I am very impressed by what I have seen today, and by what your agents have told me. You are to be commended, and I will be making a favorable report to my husband. I appreciate your hospitality, and I will also count on your discretion. The fact that I have visited you today is not to be leaked to the press or to anyone else. This is strictly confidential. Is that understood?"

Director Davis stood and extended his hand. "Of course, Mrs. Townsend. We appreciate your report to your husband. Thank you for coming."

Back out in the hall, Dannika motioned to Kiara and her Secret Service agent, and they turned toward the door. She put her sunglasses back on as Ted escorted them outside.

When they reached the limousine, Kiara circled around the car and got in. Dannika shook Ted's hand. "Thank you again for your time, and your discretion."

"Of course, ma'am."

Dannika's Secret Service agent closed her door, then took the driver's seat. The vehicle turned around and sped off. In the back seat, Dannika reached for Kiara's hand and squeezed it. The two women shared a sigh of relief, not looking at each other.

Chapter 38 – Washington, D.C.

The limousine with Dannika and Kiara pulled up to the central entrance to the Townsend mansion on Chain Bridge Road in McLean, Virginia, a little after noon. The two women stepped out and stretched. Dannika turned to her Secret Service agent and asked if she'd enjoyed the trip.

"Yes ma'am, I really did. I learned so much." She paused, then decided to be bold. "Please take me along if you do any more of these Civil War trips. They're so much better than riding around a golf course!"

Dannika laughed and pointed toward Kiara. "This is the lady we need to thank. She makes it all worth it."

Then she turned back toward her agent. "And we need to thank you for keeping us safe. And for being discreet. Do you understand?"

"Yes, ma'am, I do."

Dannika and Kiara went upstairs to the dining room. Dannika found James and his friends sitting around the dining room table, eating pizza again. She negotiated with the boys and agreed that they could stay long enough to see the movie in the screening room, but only if they called their parents first. And they'd have to go right home after that. Inwardly, she was pleased that their friendship with James was so solid. It wasn't quite like living a private life. The boys weren't free to just camp out at each other's homes for days on end, but taking these trips was the next best thing.

Dannika and Kiara took some salads from the dining room and retreated to Dannika's suite. They sat down and ate in silence for a minute or two. Then Kiara spoke quietly.

"Mrs. Townsend – you spoke to Irina. What did she say?"

"I wanted to be sure it really was Irina – it's been so long since I've seen her. So I asked her who her mother was, and she said Galina Varayeva. I told her we'd get her and Malik out of there. I didn't dare say anything else."

"Well, at least she knows we're working on it. And she's being discreet. That's good." Kiara paused and looked at Dannika. "But what's our next step?"

Dannika didn't answer, and the women ate in silence. Finally Kiara sat back and put her napkin down. "I'll tell you what. I'll talk to some people. Do you want to sponsor your niece and nephew?"

Dannika considered that idea, her brow knitted. "Is there any other way to get them visas? Here's the thing: my husband keeps yelling about chain migration and how he wants to end it. We got my parents in, but this is even more of a stretch. If the story got out, it'd be bad for him politically." She paused and studied her hands, then shook her head. "And I just don't want to owe him anything. Is there any other way?"

"They have already applied for asylum. They did that before they went to Arkansas. They have a good case, and their interview is scheduled for next December. They came from a war zone where their parents – your sister and brother-in-law – were killed. That ought to qualify them."

"Ought to, but will it really? I heard that it's really hard to get asylum these days."

Kiara looked grim. "You're right there. Thanks to a certain asshole." She winced and looked at Dannika. "I'm sorry. I didn't mean to say that. I'm sorry."

"Yes, I know," Dannika answered quietly, looking down at her hands. "There are a lot of things my husband decides that

241

are just plain evil." She looked up. "But what can I do? He doesn't listen to me."

"He doesn't listen to anyone," Kiara muttered. "That's the trouble." She paused. "But look here. For Irina's sake, and maybe for yours, he shouldn't hear anything about her and Malik. We'll support them in their asylum claim. And we'll get a lawyer for them – a good one. Don't worry. Just be glad they're coming from Europe, not from Central America."

They sat in silence for a few moments. Then Kiara stood up and gathered her things.

"I'm headed home. I'll let you know tomorrow what I find out. Don't worry." She reached out and squeezed Dannika's hand. It was a gesture she wouldn't have ventured even two weeks ago.

The following day, Kiara met with Mary Anderson and Vanessa Woodside over lunch. They had left the FBI Washington Field Office and picked up sandwiches in the National Building Museum. Now they sat on the stone wall at the Darlington Memorial Fountain, speaking quietly. They discussed the different routes they could take to get legal status for Irina and Malik. The first thing to try, of course, was political asylum. The problem with that would be proving that their parents had been murdered. They might even have to reveal how Irina and Malik had been trafficked, how Irina had wound up as a sex slave in Newark. Mary shook her head.

"I was hoping that wouldn't come to light. That would be painful for both of them. If only there was another way…" Her voice trailed off. Then she sat up straight and spoke briskly.

"In the meantime, it's important to get a lawyer assigned to the case. I have a contact at the Immigrant Advocacy Coalition.

I can visit her this afternoon. What can I say about their case? All I know is what I got from Maybelle in those two letters. Kiara, do you know anything else?"

"No, I'm sorry, I don't. Dannika couldn't tell me anything. She hadn't heard from them at all, and it had been years since she'd seen them. And their mother, her sister, is dead. Dannika managed to get her parents out of Chechnya, but they had lost track of Irina and Malik by that time. I'll tell you, though, Dannika was overjoyed to know they are alive, even if they are in custody. She will help us in any way she can. Well, any way that doesn't involve her husband." Kiara looked like she'd tasted something sour.

"Okay, then." Mary gathered up her lunch bag. "I'll do my best to get help for them. And for Bianca as well. She was captured along with them." She frowned. "Getting three people out of ICE custody, that's gonna be hard. And it's really just a drop in the damn bucket." She stood up. "But I'll let you know what happens."

That afternoon, Mary found herself cooling her heels for an hour in a waiting room at the Immigrant Advocacy Coalition office. She finally met with a legal aide, who said she could give her five minutes. Mary summed up the case as quickly as she could, but did not divulge Irina's relationship to Dannika. She did say that Irina's friends could afford to pay a private attorney.

"In that case, you want Courtney Sims. She's expensive, but she's the expert in immigration cases. I'll give you her contact info." The legal aide consulted a Rolodex and wrote out a note. "And that's all the time I have. I'm sorry." She stood up suddenly, and Mary quickly gathered her coat and left.

Mary exited through the waiting room, more crowded now than when she had come in. Seeing all the tired waiting faces made her hate the men at the top of this wicked system. Especially George Townsend. And his boss.

Back in her office, Mary made an appointment for two days hence with Courtney Sims. As she hung up the phone, she wondered, *This attorney – can she work a miracle?*

Chapter 39 – Washington, D.C.

Mary had to do some homework to prepare for her meeting with Courtney Sims on Irina and Malik's immigration case. In the meantime, Mary and Vanessa toiled on with Operation NEVRR. FBI agents were dispatched to major cities to work with local police bureaus. Federal grant funds flowed to cities, linked to mandates to guard the most prestigious conference centers. The money didn't begin to meet the need for genuine security upgrades, but it did allow each city to hire a few more cops.

These additional patrols weren't usually integrated with the rest of the force, however, due to two factors. The first was that the conference venue detail was considered to be a plush assignment, not suited to regular beat cops. Only the most polished, nonthreatening, obsequious individuals, men as well as women, were hired for these positions.

The second reason why these new positions were not integrated into regular police forces had to do with funding. Police chiefs were not at all confident that the federal funds would continue for long, so they were hesitant to make changes to accommodate the new mandate. Why introduce complications and upset routines for a flashy new initiative that would disappear in six months? Most police chiefs had lived through dozens of political shifts and campaign promises, and they'd learned to patiently outwait policy changes by not changing anything.

Williamson called Vanessa in to explain the federal grant program for additional security at conference venues. Vanessa almost shrugged at this announcement, but resisted the impulse. She knew that her influence was minimal. She would only be assigned to flesh out the tactics, the details of how-do-we-accomplish-this? The overarching goals and strategy were the purview of Williamson and higher pay grades. In fact, they originated at the White House. *Heck*, Vanessa admitted, *they probably started at the very top, with Fox News.*

After patiently listening to Williamson's explanation of the grant program, Vanessa posed a question.

"Are we – the FBI – being directed to analyze the string of deaths we've been seeing? Am I coordinating that?" she asked. Williamson looked surprised at her question.

"Why would we need to? We know where the threat is. It's foreign terrorists."

"No, we don't. We have no proof that these murders are a terrorist plot. In fact, we don't even have proof that they *are* murders."

Williamson snorted. "Oh, don't start down that path again. Who are we to challenge the White House? I don't have time for this."

"Please, Mr. Williamson. Are we working on this or not?" Vanessa sat forward, pleading. "If we're serious about solving this problem, we need to invest some time and some manpower. Do we have a budget?"

At the word *budget*, Williamson blinked. "Well, as a matter of fact, we do. And if we don't use it, it won't get renewed. All right, go ahead. Check with the budget director to see how much Operation NEVRR has to spend. Do whatever you want, but don't exceed that amount." He waved his hand in dismissal. "That's all."

Vanessa left his office, thinking *He really doesn't give a shit. He's so close to retirement he doesn't care what happens.* She decided she wasn't going to give up so easily. First she'd talk it over with Mary. And with Mike Jenkins in Chicago.

Vanessa's strategy, as she explained it to Mary, was to use undercover agents to penetrate the mystery of the murder epidemic. So far, with the exception of the Bourbon Street Slasher, the FBI had not been able to define a pattern to the murders – no particular location, no specific weapon, no surety, even, that murders rather than natural deaths or accidents had occurred. But Mike Jenkins had raised Vanessa's suspicions. He claimed that sex trafficking was at the root of it all. She was beginning to agree with him. The one crime wouldn't get solved without the other.

But Williamson was convinced that the problem lay in the venues, the conference sites and their host cities. Vanessa had presented her research to him, the research that showed that the murders were much more widespread, and sometimes seemed to be connected to prostitution. Williamson didn't want to hear it, though. He was unwilling to contemplate the enormity of what Vanessa described. He preferred to adhere to the administration's theory that the threat was from foreign-born terrorists, whose targets were businessmen at well-attended conferences.

After several nonproductive sessions with Williamson, Vanessa was ready to admit defeat. She opened up to Mary as they sat together on a bench, eating sack lunches.

"He doesn't want to hear it. He thinks he already knows why this is all happening. All he wants me to do is to prove him right, so he can polish the president's apple. I'm ready to give up."

Mary suppressed a snicker at *president's apple*. Then she sobered and challenged Vanessa.

"So how is this different from several months ago? You knew then what they wanted you to find. They're not going to change their opinions. Don't take them so seriously. Remember? Your job is what you make it." She pivoted and looked Vanessa in the eye.

"I guess you're right," Vanessa sighed.

"So what's your plan?"

"Well, I want to try to at least find out what's happening at these conferences. That's why I want to hire undercover agents who don't look or act like FBI. I want them to look like grad students or interns – you know, young folks who naturally would be networking like crazy at these events. That's my idea. They'll be able to infiltrate and get to the bottom of what's going on. If anything's going on." Vanessa shook her head and her voice trailed off.

"Sounds good to me," Mary agreed. "One step at a time."

"Anyway, it makes a whole lot more sense than posting armed guards at the doors. I know that's going to happen also, but I know for sure they'll never catch anyone that way. And if they do, I know for damn sure it won't be foreign terrorists."

And so, under Vanessa's direction, and with Mary's help, Operation NEVRR installed an elite cadre of specialized agents in cities like New York, New Orleans, LA and Las Vegas. Vanessa was careful in the selection of these agents. They were not drawn from the usual pipeline for beat cops, nor were they veteran FBI agents. They weren't even given much in the way of security training, and they didn't carry weapons. For the most part, they were college-educated, urbane young women, who

248

were selected to fit in well with the conference crowd. They would be able to stroll through an exhibit hall in a suit or business casual clothes, or linger in a hotel bar over drinks, and blend right in. Their job was to observe and report back to the Washington office.

Vanessa had no illusions that they would be able to prevent a murder, at least not at first, but they would be on hand to see clearly how it had happened and to provide context. Vanessa hoped that somehow a pattern would emerge, something that would explain the whole trend, some brilliant answer that would prove Williamson wrong. And that she could take back to Mike Jenkins.

Chapter 40 – Washington, D.C.

On Wednesday, Mary Anderson met with Courtney Sims, the attorney recommended by the Immigrant Advocacy Coalition. Attorney Sims' office was among the cluster of immigration law offices on I Street, a mile and a half west of the FBI Washington Field Office, just past the White House. Mary sat in the waiting room for a few minutes before a young woman in a no-nonsense black pantsuit strode through, stopping at her aide's desk briefly. Her blond hair was pulled back in a neat ponytail at the nape of her neck, her glasses bore heavy black frames, and she carried a large leather briefcase. Mary guessed that Courtney Sims' appearance was a deliberate effort to make herself look older than she was.

A minute later, Mary was ushered into her office. Courtney greeted her with a businesslike handshake and motioned her into a chair. Mary began by describing the reason she was seeking help – the three detainees in ICE custody in Virginia. She did not divulge to Courtney that Irina and Malik had any relationship to Dannika Townsend. She only reported that the three of them – Irina, Malik and Bianca – had been apprehended during a raid on a farm, and were now being held at the Farmville Detention Center in Virginia. She told Courtney that Irina and Malik were from Chechnya, while Bianca was from Guatemala. She explained that all three had legitimate grounds to ask for political asylum. Irina and Malik had survived the war in Chechnya, while their parents were killed, and had subsequently been trafficked to the U.S. Bianca had joined a caravan that had walked all the way to the U.S. from Guatemala, and had also been caught up in a sex trafficking ring.

Mary did not tell Courtney exactly how the three of them had been rescued from their traffickers. She didn't even know, exactly, but she suspected that the traffickers were dead now. No one at Maybelle's end had told her more than she needed to know, and she, in turn, didn't divulge any extraneous information either.

The sisters, including Mary, adhered to an unspoken rule: the less known and the less shared, the better. This came as second nature to them. Growing up, they had learned that divulging secrets or expressing feelings often led to punishment or humiliation. In the present day, they had a constant, acute sense of the danger involved in their exploits. These were not women who gossiped. These were not women who posted online – or if they did, it was to create an alternate persona, a pet-loving, baby-doting grandma, for instance, or a fashionable young selfie-snapper.

Mary had no knowledge of the women beyond her small circle of confidants, but she sensed that she was part of a vast informal network, one as compartmentalized as the cells of French resistance fighters. Mary guessed that their network was probably more efficient than anything the FBI or CIA could set up. *Oppression has always bred secrecy and sabotage,* she thought, *and it's no different today.*

At the moment, though, Mary's aim was to give Courtney enough information to start working on the case, and to arrange to pay her, in cash. Mary left a retainer of several thousand dollars with Courtney, making up the name of a GoFundMe group as the source of the money.

"Okay then, I'll get right on this," Courtney reassured her. "I have a reason to go out to Farmville on Friday this week. I'll add this to my list of things to do. I'll meet with all three of them and restart the applications for amnesty."

"Thank you. I'm glad you can make the time. Thank you again." Mary shook Courtney's hand with feeling.

A week later, Mary and Courtney Sims spoke again. Courtney reported that she had met with Irina and Bianca separately at Farmville. She had listened to Bianca's story, and she was in the process of getting her released, pending her asylum interview in September. She felt confident about winning the case, because Bianca's was a classic case of persecution.

"She told me the whole story. She said she'd been raped as a child by soldiers who came to her village. She'd gotten pregnant, and her family made her carry the baby. The baby was born prematurely, and it died. Bianca's family turned against her, in fact her whole village turned against her. Her father claimed she was a whore and threatened to kill her. She finally ran away to join a caravan that was traveling north, with little but the clothing on her back." Courtney related this story dispassionately. She had heard every bit of it before, in similar cases that she had handled. She continued.

"That's why I'm pretty confident that I can get Bianca's application approved – because she was threatened with death. Still, it'll be several months until her official asylum interview. I'll see what I can do to get her released from Farmville between now and her interview."

"Will she need a place to stay? I can probably find a place for her," Mary offered.

"Yes, she will. That'd be helpful. See what you can do." Courtney turned over a page of her legal pad and continued. "I'm not so sure about the asylum claim for Irina and Malik

252

Varayeva. They didn't or wouldn't tell me much about their experiences in the Chechen war, although it's clear their parents were killed. Still, the war is over now. It'll be a little harder to prove that they're running from a tangible threat.

"Irina seems very bright. She told me that she wants to continue her studies in mathematics. There's a possibility that she could qualify for an H-1B visa if a job could be found for her. But unfortunately, she doesn't have a bachelor's degree yet, so she isn't qualified for the H-1B." Courtney paused, then continued. "But she's also an extraordinarily beautiful girl. It so happens that the degree requirement for a H-1B visa is waived for fashion models. All they have to demonstrate is "distinguished merit and ability." I wonder…." Courtney frowned.

Mary blinked. Why hadn't she thought of this? *Dannika Townsend has connections in the fashion world! She could help Irina get a job.* A glimmer of a plan began to take shape in Mary's mind.

"How long do we have to wait for the asylum hearing for Irina and Malik? Can you get them out in the meantime?"

"Their interview is in December," Courtney reassured Mary. "But as soon as you arrange a place for them to stay, I can apply to get them released. This is never a quick process. Let me know what you can find." Mary thanked her and left the law office.

Back at her own office, Mary called Kiara and arranged to meet her after work. They got together that evening and Mary laid out her idea. If they could get Dannika to use her connections to get a modeling job for Irina, then she would qualify for the H-1B visa. Malik's status would be more of a problem. But they had some time to work on it.

253

A week later, Irina and Malik were released from detention at Farmville, and had been driven to Washington, D.C. Mary arranged and paid for the transportation. In Washington they were welcomed into a safe house that Mary had connections to. Mary went to some trouble to find nice clothes to outfit Irina. She hoped to boost her confidence for her visit with Dannika. Of course, Mary's second aim was to convince Dannika to help her niece and nephew.

Mary had met with Courtney Sims again two days before, to discuss Irina and Malik's chances of obtaining asylum. Courtney's advice was straightforward – and discouraging.

"I don't think it's going to happen. There is a lot of legal precedent that weighs against them. Not only that, we have to assume that their parents might have had some connection to the rebellion in Chechnya – after all, why would they have been killed? If we try to use that as a reason to prove a threat against them, then we really get into the thorn bushes. Right now, as you know, the administration is siding with Russia against the Chechen claim to autonomy. So refugees from that conflict are even more likely to have their claims rejected. I'm sorry."

Mary stood up. "Well, I know you've done all you can, for now. I'll get back to you about the other angle we discussed – the H-1B visa. I'll be in touch, Courtney."

If asylum wasn't likely, Mary wasn't going to wait for the ruling and deportation. She'd take the risk of asking for help, through Kiara, from Dannika. She met with Kiara to float her idea.

"Under immigration law, Dannika can't directly sponsor her niece and nephew for entry. She could have sponsored her sister, who in turn could have sponsored her children. But her sister is dead, so that cuts off that avenue. And for another thing, if she tries, somebody will leak that story. Her husband will find out, or the media will find out, or something. Dannika is caught between her husband and her niece, and the wider world is watching her every move. There has to be another way." Kiara looked confused, and Mary continued.

"Courtney told me about the H-1B visa. It's a visa that allows somebody to work in the U.S. temporarily in a 'specialty occupation', but your employer has to apply for you. Normally you would need at least a bachelor's degree, and specialized knowledge in biotech, engineering, medicine or something like that. But there is one exception – fashion models. They just have to be 'of distinguished merit and ability.' That's where we can fit Irina in. At least I truly hope so."

Mary went on to explain the strategy. "Dannika has connections to the fashion industry in New York. She might be able to help Irina find a modeling job. Irina is extraordinarily beautiful – she has the same tall, exotic look as her aunt. If Dannika can pull some strings and get her an audition, without revealing her relationship, Irina would have a job – and an H-1B visa. In fact, I'm pretty sure that's the same visa Dannika used when she first came here."

Kiara agreed that it was worth a try. But the effort would depend on Irina's skill and appearance, and on Dannika's commitment to the idea. The first step was to arrange a meeting between Irina and Dannika.

Kiara brightened. "I'll ask Dannika tomorrow. I have a tutoring session with James tomorrow. You know, this just might work!"

The following day, Kiara and Dannika strolled in Dannika's garden, looking at the summer flowers, and absently plucking a few dead blossoms. Their conversation was serious, but anyone watching wouldn't have thought so. Every once in a while, one of them would laugh or gesture. Then they'd stroll and think some more. Together they laid a plan.

It took some imagination, but Kiara had come up with a ruse to get Dannika and Irina together, unobserved. Over the past few months, Kiara had become a trusted confidant, with access to Dannika's calendar. They planned the meeting at a school in D.C. that Dannika was scheduled to visit on Constitution Day. Irina would accompany Kiara, who was scheduled to give a lesson to the kids, with Dannika in the audience. Afterward, the three of them would convene in the teachers' lounge for a quick meeting.

On the day of the meeting, Kiara picked up Irina at the safe house. Before they left the safe house, they sat a while talking. They had gotten to know each other a little over the past three weeks, since Irina and Malik came to Washington. Kiara had explained the plan to Irina, and Irina embraced it. She had spent her time, since then, studying videos of models. She had carefully chosen an outfit for this meeting, something slouchy but chic, atop a pair of 4" heels. Not exactly one of the outfits Mary had given her to wear.

Kiara was impressed with Irina's presence today. She looked glamorous, with carefully applied makeup and an air of slinky seductiveness. However, as they talked, Irina confessed to Kiara that she was nervous about meeting Dannika. Kiara tried to reassure her.

"Do you remember when we all came to Farmville? That trip was Dannika's idea, and she went to great lengths to get there. She cares about you and Malik, very much. But she also has to be very careful. A wrong move could be dangerous for all of you. So it's not Dannika you need to be nervous about. It's the rest of the world... including her husband. Do you understand?"

Irina looked puzzled, but accepted Kiara's assessment. Kiara went on to review the strategy to get the H-1B visa. Her employer would have to apply for the visa, and the process would require that she and Malik return to Chechnya briefly to get their passports, but this time they'd be escorted and protected. Then once Irina had secured the H-1B visa, she could bring Malik with her, as her dependent, on an H-4 visa. This would buy them three years, or maybe six, in the United States. By the time those visas ran out, Irina could be eligible for an EB-1A visa, with any luck.

"It all depends on how good you are at the modeling. I'm sorry that this means putting off the mathematics for a while. But think what you could do for Malik. And you wouldn't be running from ICE any more. If your boss thinks you're good, he'll support your application. The EB-1A visa is your ticket to full citizenship... and Malik's, too, through you."

Irina squared her shoulders. "Then it's worth a try. I do have some ability, you know." She stood up and slung her coat over her shoulders. Instantly she affected the gangly, disdainful look of a fashion model. As she walked across the room, she tossed her hips and wove her ankles like a pro, her face expressionless. She stopped, thrust one hip out for a second, turned around and strutted her way back. She did the turn again, face deadpan. Then she turned and laughed at Kiara. "What do you think?"

Kiara was stunned. "Well done, girl, well done. You're a natural." She grinned. Then she looked at her watch. "Let's get going. We don't want to be late."

The drive to the elementary school took half an hour. Kiara had planned to arrive well before Dannika, and she spent the extra time meeting the principal and teachers, introducing Irina as her assistant. Irina carried the box of Kiara's props, consisting of hats and wigs and 18th-century clothing, along with a large parchment replica of the Constitution of the United States.

Kiara and Irina went to the classroom where the lesson was to take place. Today desks had been shoved to a wall and extra chairs brought in to include the other 6th grade class. Kiara started by quizzing the students on their knowledge of the Constitution and the Continental Congress. She had them volunteer for roles in her impromptu reenactment, while directing Irina to hand out different props, costume pieces, and speeches written on cards.

The lesson was well underway when Dannika arrived. When she entered the classroom, Kiara halted the proceedings and led the class in welcoming Dannika. Then she and the students started the reenactment over. Kiara played the part of James Madison, drafter of the Constitution. Bewigged kids read their parts with melodramatic seriousness, but before long the improvised play devolved into silliness and hilarity, and Dannika enjoyed every minute of it.

After the play was over, Kiara and Irina collected the costumes and props onto a cart. Since Dannika still had questions, Kiara invited her to come with them to the teachers' lounge, where they could work on sorting the stuff out. As soon as the door closed behind them, Dannika embraced Irina for several long seconds, then held her out at arms' length.

"You look just like your mother, my sweet Irina. What a beauty! Ah, I mourn her, I miss her! Let me help you now." She released Irina and stepped back, her eyes glowing. Kiara spoke up.

"Look what she can do. Show her, Irina." Kiara gestured, and Irina did a repeat performance of her model's walk to the other end of the lounge and back. Dannika watched with surprise in her eyes, her hand over her mouth.

"Oh, you will slay them. It will be no problem to get you an audition in New York. Kiara, you and I will work on this tomorrow. But remember, Irina, you never mention that you are related to me. Luckily our last names are different. We keep our secret. And you will be a citizen one day!"

That was the end of their conversation. Kiara and Irina packed up the props and took them out to Kiara's car. Dannika nodded to her Secret Service detail, who had waited in the hall, and they escorted her to the limousine. Kiara and Irina drove back to the safe house. They parted with a hug, and Kiara promised to report back soon.

A week later, Irina was on her way to New York City, with appointments for auditions with two major modeling agencies. Malik and Briana were still at the safe house, waiting for the next moves in their respective journeys toward acceptance into the land of the free. Mary Anderson and Courtney Sims managed their progress through the system, and kept their spirits up with visits and updates. Courtney often thought how fortunate these two were, to have friends and supporters in their quest for citizenship. Their situation was better than that of many other refugees she had seen over the years, people without resources or advocates, risking all to come to the United States. Only to find themselves and their children trapped in a Mexican border town, alternately pitied and reviled, pawns in a larger political game.

Chapter 41 – Washington, D.C.

Summer stretched out in Washington, hot and humid. Congress had recessed and most legislators left town. Stuck in her office, Mary mused about why the nation's capital was located at the head of a tidewater river, in former swampland, with a mosquito problem that welled up every summer. Like so many other unfortunate decisions, it was the result of a political compromise that no one living in the present day can remember. *How many decisions made today will haunt our children's children?* Mary wondered. *Will they look back in disgust at the level of discourse we have today?* Mary shook her head when she thought about it.

Still, it was turning out to be an exciting time in the capitol. Candidates for this fall's election were popping up, exciting new faces, many of them women. Political races nationwide were heating up, although Mary tried to limit the time she spent paying attention to that. She was something of a cynic, even though she voted in every election. But she'd seen a lot of how Washington worked behind the scenes, and it wasn't edifying or even rational most of the time.

For her part, Vanessa was beginning to make headway in her investigation into the random deaths at convention sites. She would have preferred to be an investigator herself, rather than directing other agents in the field. Still, she was beginning to get a sense of competence in this supervisory role. She was enjoying the challenge of collecting field reports and sussing out possible patterns.

Vanessa and Mary had worked together on recruiting agents for the investigation. They had discussed it in Vanessa's office one day, two months ago, before the hiring began.

"I'm not sure it's really FBI agents you want to hire," ventured Mary. "They're a little too stiff for this job. Male or female. They just don't look the part. Or act it."

"Oh? What part's that?" Vanessa was a little miffed. "What's wrong with good posture?"

"I'm not talking about posture. I mean attitude. Upright and virtuous. That's not going to work."

"Not going to work how?"

"Come on, I don't have to spell it out for you, do I? We're trying to find out what's happening to men in clandestine situations. Places where they shouldn't be. Do you think your buttoned-up FBI agents are going to be invited out on those escapades?"

"No, I guess not. I see what you mean. So your suggestion is…?"

"Get some actresses. Or if you want to go cheaper and even more authentic, find some college students or interns. They'd naturally be trying to network at these conferences. They'll blend right in."

"If you say so."

"I know so."

The investigation proceeded, and the patterns that Vanessa found were increasingly ugly. In New York, LA, Los Angeles and Chicago, the increased police presence allotted to conferences was making no dent at all in the death rate. Vanessa became more and more convinced that there was something unseen, some web of evil right under the surface of American business-as-usual. The more she investigated, the more corruption and excess she saw.

It turned out to be advantageous that Vanessa had hired young, untrained students and interns as observers. Their unsophisticated perspective helped them notice things that older, jaded investigators would accept as normal. Something as simple as the price of drinks in a swanky hotel bar was noted by these new agents, who went on to observe how much money changed hands in the course of one evening. Then they noticed who spent money on whom, and who left with whom at the end of the evening. They also noted the clustering of hangers-on around men of immense wealth and influence. In some cases, Vanessa's agents were invited to join these exclusive little groups. Being younger, more attractive, and mostly women, they were picked up like baubles by the older men. They noted and reported on what was novel to them: the assumption that wealth and power would make an older, paunchy man attractive to, even deserving of, a nubile, beautiful young woman.

They also noted how seldom there was any real content to these after-hours conversations. This was as true at scientific or medical conventions as it was at machinists' union get-togethers. Of course, this made it easier for the agents to blend in. They realized that they hadn't needed to bone up on neuroscience or business jargon ahead of time, because no one asked for their opinions, ever. In fact, they found that the more heated the conversation, the more they themselves melted into the background.

As a consequence, Vanessa's agents were witness to an astonishing variety of informal business deals, some legal and some not. It appeared that these men routinely boasted and bullied their way into agreements, completely unaware of

263

observers. All the young women had to do was keep smiling and sipping their drinks. Two of these young women had actually gotten in touch with Vanessa to ask if she'd like them to wear a wire. Vanessa decided against that idea, first because it was dangerous, and second, because nefarious business deals were not what she was investigating. Yet.

It was enough to learn about the routine and expected diversion of resources by the conference industry. If conferences were ostensibly held to unveil new research, or to promote the professional exchange of ideas, in reality they were all too often just elaborate parties, financed by taxpayers. Travel and entertainment costs were wholly reimbursed by the conferees' companies or universities, with rarely any cap on the expenses. Liquor and game tickets were considered legitimate business expenses, even for public universities, as long as the purpose of the event was "development" or "recruitment." All of the guidelines used by sponsoring institutions and companies were underwritten by tax law, such that every dollar spent by conferees could be written off by the institution. Ultimately, working class taxes and student tuition paid for the lavish lunches and entertainment of well-heeled businessmen. The more Vanessa learned about this system, the more her blood boiled.

But the worst discovery of this probe so far was the close connection between conferences and human trafficking. Vanessa's agents reported back that they were often pressured to have sex by men they'd just met at these conference venues, men who should have been colleagues or mentors. They found that a conference badge worn prominently was no protection against unwanted advances. If the conference badge was not worn, the assumptions were even more blatant: that the woman was simply a whore catering to the conference crowd. They observed many women who apparently were prostitutes, openly haunting the hotel bars. Of course, these were not the thigh-boots-and-fishnet-stockings archetypes of city streets, but more sophisticated women who could banter with intelligent small talk, and who were very discreet in their hookup arrangements. Nevertheless, the traffic was brisk.

Directly outside the conference venues, Vanessa's agents found even more evidence of trafficking. Within a couple of blocks of any large conference complex were strip malls with massage parlors, and small bars with pimps and their protégés hanging around. These groups of women, some of them quite young, appeared timid and cheerless. Their pimps did the talking for them.

As Vanessa did more research, she found that the number of massage parlors in any given area was directly proportional to the tourist and business conference traffic. This was true of Las Vegas, Detroit's Renaissance Center, the Baltimore Convention Center, anywhere that had an influx of out-of-towners. Even Orlando, home to Disneyworld, hosted dozens of brothels masquerading as spas and bodywork venues. Worse yet, as Vanessa's team dug deeper, they found that local police were often complicit in these trafficking rings and accepted tribute from their owners.

Vanessa called Mike Jenkins more and more frequently these days. She even flew out to Chicago to meet with his team. And, she had to confess, to meet his mother. His mom lived with him these days, as she needed care. It was just the two of them, in a brownstone on the west side.

Vanessa realized, sitting across the kitchen table from this guy, that she really hadn't gotten to know him at all in

Afghanistan. There he had been the captain. She saluted him and she obeyed him. Now she saw a completely different side of him. He looked a little more worn, a little more paunchy, that's true. His hair was no longer closely buzz cut, but stuck out a bit. His sideburns were graying. But his dark face creased into a grin much more often, especially when she was around. Or maybe it was because of his mom.

"Mom, can I get you some sugar in that coffee?" he'd say. Or, "Mom, is it time for bed?"

Each time, his mother would smile sweetly and say, "Okaaaaay, honey. I miiiight." He would roll his eyes at Vanessa and escort his mother upstairs. Vanessa just loved it.

But – at the moment – Vanessa didn't dwell too much on Mike and how he treated his mom. She needed to concentrate on the task at hand. For now, she knew she needed Mike's smarts more than his sweetness.

The scope of Vanessa's investigation grew, involving other FBI branches, and expanding well beyond what Williamson originally authorized. Williamson tried to regain control, but he was overruled by the Deputy Director, who involved the Intelligence Branch as well as the Criminal Investigative Division. Soon there were a number of FBI probes taking place in major cities all over the country, aimed at cracking down on sex trafficking everywhere, not just at conference venues.

The press started to get wind of the FBI investigation, especially when prominent men began to be swept up in sting operations. Overnight the press on both sides of the political divide jumped on the story. Several newsrooms excoriated the men who had been caught patronizing the illegal massage parlors. Other news outlets focused on the vast network of

266

trafficking rings and their owners. They exposed the overseas sources of trafficked women – China, Korea, and several South American countries. A few investigative reporters dove into the relationship between police and trafficking rings. A few even wrote about the role of restrictive immigration laws in keeping women subjugated by their traffickers.

Then the news of the deaths of prominent men began to gain coverage. This reporting was all over the map. Some deaths were attributed to natural causes; others were investigated as suspicious. A few were obviously murders. The only elements in common were the ones that Vanessa had pointed out months ago: the men were attending conventions, and they had put themselves in harm's way by going out alone at night, or by consorting with strangers. Vanessa didn't talk to reporters, but somehow they caught onto the story. Fox News started promoting a conspiracy theory about terrorists murdering these men, but they alternated between saying that the perpetrators were Iranian and declaring they were MS-13. It didn't really matter – the point was that everyone should be terrified.

At that announcement, President Betrog unleashed a set of tweets:

> Islamic Terrorists infiltrating our wonderful
> Hotels and killing Patriots. This will not be
> tolerated. I am ordering the Military to
> investigate. FBI is not performing, under weak
> management. Some Heads will roll!
>
> Gangs crossing our Southern Border, bringing
> Drugs and Murderers. Our cities and Conference

Centers aren't safe. What is FBI doing? Dems in control. Pathetic! Build the WALL!

Later that day, Vanessa was called into Williamson's office. She found him seated with the Deputy Director of the FBI. Together they grilled her for an hour about the direction of the investigation. She maintained her cool with difficulty, just resisting the impulse to shout at Williamson.

They want me to quit, she thought. *They want to drive me out.* And then she realized she didn't care. She was done trying to fit her findings into their presupposed verdict. If they had decided they knew the answer to the whole investigation, so be it. From all she had seen of the convention industry, it was not something worth saving. She really didn't give a shit anymore.

That sudden realization freed Vanessa of the anger that had been building up, as these two men grilled and berated her. She remembered the playwright Lillian Hellman's advice, "If you are willing to take the punishment, you are halfway through the battle." She smiled to herself as she imagined stalking out, just quitting this damn job. Then she laughed out loud, which startled both of the red-faced men.

"What's so funny?" Williamson demanded. Vanessa sobered and answered him.

"Just the thought of you losing my agents. If I decide to go, they'll go with me. And you'll lose your inside scoop on just about everything." She stood up. "You let me know."

Vanessa turned on her heel and strode to the door. She walked out without a backward glance. The door slammed.

Behind her, the men looked at each other, stunned.

Chapter 42 – New York City

It was late August in New York City, a time when most people, who could afford to, escaped the heat by going out to the Hamptons, up to the Catskills, or out to Martha's Vineyard. A few even went to their families' lavish cottages in Newport. For those stuck in the city, it was a time of heat and stink, when subway platforms became ovens and even Central Park steamed.

After Dannika Townsend placed a few discreet phone calls to old acquaintances, Irina Varayeva was called to interviews at several of the top modeling agencies in New York. She was quickly signed to Townsend Model Management, who hoped to use her during New York Fashion Week in September.

Mary alerted Courtney Sims, who worked fast with the Townsend agency to get the H-1B application through. A week later Irina and Malik flew back to Chechnya to obtain their visas. Dannika paid for their airfare and lodging through back channels, not revealing to anyone, even her parents, what she was doing. For Irina's sake, she hoped to keep as much distance as possible between herself and the two of them.

As soon as Irina and Malik made it back to New York, Irina was swept up in preparations for Fashion Week. Being one of the youngest models, and newly signed, the Townsend agency hoped to use her a lot this year. The agency sent her out to small design houses at first, Livini and Tao Ming. Soon she caught the eye of Kory Bank, who signed her to perform at her show at Summer Studios. Scouts for Matthew Kane saw her at the Tao Ming show and contacted the Townsend agency as well. There was something magnetic about this tall, young, defiant girl that drew the eye.

Inwardly, Irina shrank from the attention, but observers saw only her bold, self-possessed stare and her confident posture. When she walked, their jaws dropped. One of her handlers at Townsend joked that her looks were actually a liability, in that nobody in the audience even saw whatever it was she was wearing.

The September issue of Vogue featured a spread by Halston, in which Irina was featured alone, as well as in groups of models, usually front and center. Dannika saved this issue of Vogue, keeping it in her sitting room. She secretly celebrated Irina's rapid rise in the industry. Meeting with Kiara one day, she showed her the magazine.

"I want to thank you for helping me to find my niece Irina. And for whatever you did to get her through immigration. I know it wasn't easy."

"Actually, I didn't do much. I had friends who made it happen. We help each other."

Dannika looked puzzled, but didn't pursue the question.

Later that day, in a meeting with another aide, Dannika mentioned New York Fashion Week. She talked about attending some of the runway events. That would be a welcome diversion, after James was back in school.

The aide advised against the idea.

"I'm afraid that if you attend the runway events, the media will be all over you. And the security logistics would be a nightmare. It would be more discreet if you invited a designer to send samples to your home. Sort of a private event."

"To my home? You mean here in Washington?"

"No, I meant at Townsend Tower in New York. That could be arranged, and I'm sure they'd accommodate. Would you like that?"

"Really – they would do that?"

"Of course. You are their idol. They all want to see their fashions on you. It's excellent publicity for them."

Dannika was touched. "That would be very nice. I wish I had some friends I could invite. But I don't know anyone. Even in Florida, I don't have any lady friends." She shook her head. "Maybe it's not such a great idea."

"We would come." The aide paused. "Us – your staff. It would be fun. I know Kiara would love it."

Dannika brightened. "Well, then, let's see what they'll do. Maybe a week or two after Fashion Week, give them time to catch their breath. What's on my calendar for that time?"

"Actually, nothing, the third week in September. At least so far. Anything could come up, but that's only three weeks from now, so I think we're pretty safe." She gestured toward the copy of Vogue that Dannika held. "Let's sit down and decide which designers you'd like to invite."

Two weeks later, Dannika and her staff were treated to a private fashion showcase that lasted the whole afternoon. It was held in the penthouse at the top of Townsend Tower, overlooking Fifth Avenue. Four designers brought samples from their collections, which were shown off by at least a dozen models from various agencies. The audience was small, consisting of only Dannika and her staff of four women, including Kiara.

The fourth designer was just getting set up when into the room walked George Townsend with his daughter, Jackie. Dannika started, stared for a split second, then coolly stood up to welcome them.

"How nice of you to come! I didn't think you'd have the time."

"That's because you didn't bother to invite us. Isn't it?" George Townsend fixed his wife with a steely look. She paled, but did not recoil.

"I thought that you were busy at the U.N. all day today. Did they finish early?"

"I finished early. I left before the photos. Can't stand that crowd." He frowned and sat down heavily as a staffer quickly vacated the seat next to Dannika.

"Well, I'm so glad. You're just in time to see the Matthew Kane collection. Tell me what you like. You too, Jackie," Dannika smiled and gestured toward her stepdaughter. Jackie stared right through her and turned away to a seat.

The show began, with models coming out from the anteroom in ones and twos. The presenter described the fabrics and pointed out details of the design. The audience began to relax after the tense interchange between George and Dannika, who sat stiffly next to each other, eyes fixed on the models. After a few minutes George started commenting on the outfits, although his eyes mostly tracked the models' legs.

The show lasted another fifteen minutes. Kiara had been taking notes whenever she saw Dannika look with interest at a particular design. She hoped to salvage this event for Dannika, to bring it back to what it should have been, before the unexpected intrusion of George and Jackie.

Suddenly she was aware that one of the models was Irina. Dannika saw her in that instant, too. Irina blinked and averted her eyes, adopting the haughty pose she was becoming famous for. She paused, turned, and wove her way back for another costume change. Kiara glanced at Dannika and saw that her hand was shaking, but she otherwise betrayed no recognition.

When the show wrapped up, George stood up and announced that he'd like to meet all the models.

"That's why I like these events, you know."

Dannika decided not to argue, and turned to ask the presenter to bring them in when they'd dressed. She tried to engage George in chat about the outfits, but he couldn't remember any that he'd particularly liked.

"You get what you want," was all he said. His jaw jutted forward and he did not look at his wife.

After ten minutes the models started to return to the room, dressed in their street clothes. George immediately started smiling and shaking hands, asking the girls' names and who they worked for. When he got to Irina, he gripped her hand with both of his, pulling her toward him.

"And where are you from?" he asked.

"I live here in New York City," she answered.

"I mean which agency do you work for?"

"Townsend Model Management." She tried to retrieve her hand, but he wouldn't let go.

"Then you work for me." He grinned. "Didn't you know, I own that agency!"

"No, I didn't know. How nice." Inwardly, she thought, *Was this a set-up? Did Dannika do this to me? Is she trying to control me?* She didn't dare glance in Dannika's direction, but continued to try to withdraw her hand.

"How would you like to visit Washington, D.C.?" He sounded excited. He released Irina's hand and turned to Dannika and the show's presenter. "Why don't you set up a visit for all of my models to come down to Washington?"

"They could give you some tips." He addressed this last comment directly at Dannika.

He turned back to Irina. "I'm sure you'd all have a great time. The agency will pay for your plane fare." He paused. "And your time, of course."

Irina had regained her composure. "We would be flattered, I'm sure." She kept her eyes down.

He pointed at Dannika. "Make it happen." His smile didn't reach his eyes.

Townsend left, and the others began to drift out. Eventually, it was just Dannika and Irina standing near the door.

"Did you plan it this way?" Irina whispered hoarsely. "Did you want me to work for your husband?" Irina's hand shook and her voice grew louder.

"No, I swear I didn't. I never called Townsend Model Management. I called other people. I don't know how this happened. I wouldn't want you to work there – for many reasons." Dannika was earnest. "I'm so sorry." She reached out for Irina's hand. Irina did not pull back. Dannika continued to plead with her.

"I didn't want this to happen – I didn't want him to see you." She looked away, then back at Irina. "Can we make the best of it, though? If you come to Washington, we can spend a little time together. Please think about it. It wouldn't be the end of the world."

Irina saw the pleading in Dannika's eyes and thought, *How lonely she must be.*

"All right, I'll come. But please keep him away from me."

274

Chapter 43 – Ozarks

Summer was waning in the Ozark mountains, and life got busier on the Barker Farm. The harvest of root vegetables began with the carrots, which were pulled and brushed and stored in barrels of sand in the root cellar. Next the potatoes were dug up, after the vines had died back. They were left to harden in a dark corner of the barn for two weeks before they, too, were packed in sand in the cellar. Last of all, the winter squashes turned darker and their vines wilted. They were carefully cut off and stored on shelves in the root cellar. The brussels sprouts were left in place to sweeten with the first frosts later in the season.

The women on the farm planned a harvest festival on the September equinox. Visitors from distant states drifted in for a week before the festival and set up tents. They brought news from other parts of the country. There were many late-night confabs in Maybelle's kitchen.

Babs and Kelly were kept busy at the forge, melting down metals that were brought in, molding them into ingots for distribution next summer. Arlene begged Maybelle daily to let her spend more time at the forge. Finally, Maybelle surrendered to the girl's pleas.

"All right," Maybelle announced one morning. "I've talked it over with Babs and Kelly. Babs is very impressed with you, and she says you're tall enough now to stand at the anvil, and you've pumped the bellows enough to work up your arms. She's willing to take you on as a part-time apprentice – if you keep up with your schoolwork. And we've even worked out some new subjects for you. We'll start with mechanical drafting and geometry. And then chemistry and metallurgy. And Babs brought this up – would you like to learn how to blow glass?

Arlene clapped her hands and whistled. "Oh, Gramma, would I! Let me show you something!" She ran back to her bedroom and came back with a pair of denim coveralls.

"Look, Gramma, look what I did. I cut them down to fit me. Babs told me that I couldn't roll the pants legs up, because sparks would land in the cuffs. And she told me the sleeves couldn't drag. So – see what I did? I used your sewing machine." She climbed into the coveralls and turned around.

"See? A perfect fit. And to be extra safe I can put an apron on over these."

Maybelle fingered the new seams and sat back.

"Well, I'll be. You even flat-felled the seams. Nicely done! Where'd you learn to sew like that?" she asked with a wink.

"You taught me, silly. And you know that old machine of yours sews right through four layers of denim. You said yourself that a treadle machine can do anything. So this is what I did! I wanted to surprise you."

"Well, I am surprised. And I can tell there's nothing that'll keep you out of the forge now. I see you have your boots on. Don't forget your face mask, and your gloves. You'll do fine. Go on now – take the whole morning and –" The door slammed on Maybelle's words as Arlene dashed out.

As the month of September rolled on, each new carful of women who arrived followed the protocol of checking in with Lurleen at the motel in town. They'd leave their cell phones with her, if they had any. Many would also leave their cars parked back behind the motel. They'd join together in carpools, using the most rugged vehicles to make the steep climb. Or they'd or get a lift up the mountain from Jody. Some even chose to walk, just for the challenge of it.

Ta'quisha and Jamie had returned from Los Angeles a few weeks back. Bonnie and Maybelle had welcomed them home. The four women sat on the porch, chairs tipped back, glasses of mint lemonade in their hands.

"So what's happening with Alicia? And how's Amy doing?" Bonnie wanted to know.

Jamie let out a sigh, shaking her head. "Well, you're not gonna believe this, but they're doing just fine. That woman has a backbone after all. Or she's growing one."

"Don't worry," added Ta'quisha, "we left her in good hands. There's this woman named Barbara. She runs Jeremy's company – not in title, but in fact. She knows everything about the company. I'll bet she knows more about Alicia's finances than she does herself."

"Barbara is tutoring Alicia," added Jamie. "She's stepped right up to help. She's a real ally."

"But how is Amy doing? That kid's been through some pretty rough stuff," Bonnie asked again.

Jamie smiled at Bonnie. "Again, you're not going to believe this, but the kid is just fine. She doesn't even talk about her dad. She has so many new friends now that, I guess, she doesn't have time to remember what happened. Maybe she's suppressing it, or maybe it never got a foothold at all. You can tell she admires her mama. And you know what? I saw her teaching her little buddies some campcraft – they were making stuff with sticks. And digging up her mother's lawn to plant some vegetables. With trowels. And the other day I heard her telling them about climbing mountains. It was all a big adventure to her, I guess."

"Well, kids are resilient. We can be grateful for that," Maybelle agreed.

Bonnie and Jamie were happy to be back together. Maybelle forgave them for running off in the afternoons to swim in the stream and lie on the rocks. After a week, though, she suggested they get busy planning the harvest festival.

Bonnie and Jamie recruited other women to help plan the feast and music. The food would consist of two lambs, spitted and roasted over coals, along with summer squash, breads, new potatoes, fruits and greens. The music didn't take much preparation. Many women had instruments, and everyone had voices. There was even a children's choir which had been rehearsing in secret, led by Arlene.

For some of the residents, this event would mark the end of their stay here. After the festival, they'd head out to other communities, to new lives, taking with them the healing and connections they had known here. Other residents would stay the winter and make plans next year.

During the week leading up to the festival, several business meetings were held on a hillside overlooking the broad common area. To an observer, such a meeting would look like three or four women sitting on blankets having a picnic. Their voices were low, but every once in a while, one of the women would throw her head back in laughter.

Mary Anderson had come down from Washington, using the vacation time she'd arranged last spring. Her boss, Doug Williamson, was with his wife in the Bahamas. They'd taken the cruise suggested by the pamphlets that Mary had scattered around the office, way back in the spring. Now Mary met with

Maybelle, Bonnie, Jamie and Ta'quisha, who were eager to learn what the FBI knew.

Mary started by telling them about Operation NEVRR, and why it was set in motion.

"I hate to say it, but this operation is headed up by my second boss, who is pretty darn astute. Her name is Vanessa Woodside, and there is nothing that gets past her. She knows that a lot of men have been dying at conference centers and corporate meetings. She's starting to pick up on the pattern. The investigation has broadened to Chicago, to Denver, to Las Vegas, to New Orleans and L.A. The FBI is closing in, and my boss is in charge." Mary looked around at the group, her face stern. "We need to close the operation down."

"Really!" It was Jamie. She looked disgusted. Mary ignored her.

"For now, anyway. It's getting too dangerous. We don't need to blow the whole thing. And we don't need to get caught." Mary paused and spoke to Maybelle. "But the good news is that Vanessa is finally seeing the sex trafficking problem for what it is. And she is resolved to fight it. She's networking with other branches of the FBI to really shut it down. With her leading this effort, it just might have an impact. And that was our goal in the first place, right? Right?" Mary stared pointedly at Jamie.

"Yeah, okay. I'm not the vicious bitch you think I am, Mary. I'm okay with not murdering my quota of assholes this year. Fun as it was." Jamie grinned at Mary, then sobered. "No really, I was getting sick of it. Ask Bonnie."

"How much does the FBI know, though?" asked Maybelle. "What has your boss Vanessa figured out?"

"Well, I would say that we don't need to worry too much," Mary ventured. "They don't have enough physical evidence or eyewitness testimony to follow up on. All they have is the circumstantial evidence. Although they do think the New Orleans stabbings were done by a woman, a Hispanic woman with heavy makeup and long black hair." Mary deliberately did not look at Jamie.

She continued. "In many cases they don't even suspect murder. We've been lucky. But Vanessa has been working with agents in Chicago and those other cities, and they're beginning to draw some parallels. We can't push it any further right now. But – as for the upper hierarchy of the FBI – they're busy falling over their own feet. They really, really want to find some terrorists to blame. Iran is the latest target. Or was it Mexico?"

At this, all of the women cracked up. Jamie thumped the ground.

"This is too damn easy, ladies." Jamie caught Mary's eye. "Yeah, okay. Okay."

"Alright then," Maybelle said briskly. "We lay off the pimps and the johns. We need to get the word out. We'll work on writing out the messages. Can anyone think of a good euphemism for "Quit killing"?

Jamie put up a V sign. "Peace now!"

"The heat is on. Cool it!" hissed Bonnie.

"Do not plant until further notice."

"Live and let live."

Maybelle rolled her eyes. "How about 'Due to the recent heat wave, planting should be postponed. Stay tuned for our spring gardening tips.'"

"That sounds pretty good. They'll get it," Jamie agreed.

"Okay, let's get at it. The sooner we get this shipment out, the better."

The women picked up the blanket they'd been sitting on and strolled back down to the house. Ta'quisha, the fastest typist, typed the message many times onto a few sheets of paper, then cut the paper into strips. In the meantime, the others were putting spring flower mixes into seed envelopes. One of the message strips went into each seed envelope. These were sealed and enfolded into a one-page ad for spring seed varieties. The ad started with the sentence, "Open our complimentary gift of seeds and enjoy springtime all year long!" Then the women addressed envelopes to the three dozen recipients of this mailing. They finished the task in time for Bonnie to carry the outgoing mail down to town before 5 p.m.

Over the next week, many meetings were held on the hillside. Different groups of women attended different meetings, and the topics ranged all over the place. The aspirations these women held were high, and their plans were audacious. They discussed how they could help trafficked women in Los Angeles, Las Vegas, and New York. They plotted to help teachers in Kansas unionize. They planned to lobby for a higher minimum wage in Michigan. They talked about distributing a windfall of money that had come from the Caribbean or someplace.

The decisions these few women made were not difficult or complex. They were agreed to without fanfare or posturing, as the women shared common sensibilities of charity and practicality. Nor were the decisions recorded in any way. Nothing was signed or even written down. Among these lifelong friends, and by the credo of their loosely-woven organization, a woman's word was good enough.

The women came up with some clever ideas, adopting tactics from all over. They talked about the schoolkids' campaign of truancy on Fridays to protest the world's inaction on climate change. Suppose both teachers and students stayed out sick on Mondays until such time as teachers were paid a professional wage? Or imagine if all of New York's waitresses stayed home just one day in protest of their subminimum wage? Such a campaign would be easy to do, even without the internet.

"No fuckin' problem, ladies – look at how far we can make a *little* piece of gossip fly!" Jamie sent a spitball arcing high out over the field. The rest of them shrieked with laughter.

At the end of the week, the festivities began. Two days of gathering and cooking led into a night of feasting and music. A bonfire was lit in the middle of a soft, groomed expanse of sand, and the women danced around it, barefooted and with swirling skirts. Musicians were grouped off on one side, and the clarinet, guitars, drums and fiddles together wove an intricate pattern. Improvised percussion joined in – sticks, spoons, clapping, and the dancers' finger cymbals. Sometimes the music became quiet and soft, with a single soprano performing an aria. Other times the whole crowd joined in to sing a raucous old sea shanty. The silliness rose to a crescendo, sending a wild harmony flying upward with the sparks from the bonfire.

On the last night, the dancing didn't stop until almost dawn. The next morning, the women reclined on their blankets on the hillside, the children snuggled among them, watching the sun rise over the misty plateaus. A flute played softly as the women hugged one more time and went to gather their luggage. Another harvest had been blessed and stored away, and another set of plans had been laid. The women left with high energy, and with renewed purpose to face the challenges of the year ahead, until they could meet again.

Maybelle walked Mary to Bonnie's truck. Mary swung her small satchel into the back of the truck and turned back to Maybelle.

"It's been fun. You take good care of yourself, okay? I'll be in touch, and I'll let you know if there's anything to worry about."

"Thank you, Mary." Maybelle kissed her on both cheeks. "And I wonder – do you think you can get Vanessa to come down next year?"

"Ho ho! That'd be something! She's a very righteous woman." Mary laughed out loud. "But then," she continued slowly, "she *is* a very righteous woman. We'll see. I won't promise anything. But we'll see."

Chapter 44 – Washington, D.C.

In early October, George Townsend reminded his wife Dannika that she had agreed to invite the models from Townsend Model Management to Washington for a visit. By this time, the event had taken on larger form in his mind. He proposed that they would benefit from a week of inservice training in customer service, combined with some dance or fitness instruction. He had asked one of his aides to recommend employee development programs that could offer workshops. Then he pressured his wife to bring all the details together, to work with Townsend Model Management staff to set it up as soon as possible. He pointed out that his models were underutilized following Fashion Week – what better time to give them a refresher course and a change of scene? He began to imagine a few gala events, perhaps even a gathering at the White House.

Dannika began to warm to the idea, especially since it took her husband's mind off the immigration crisis for a little while. She realized that his mood was brighter and he was obsessing less over the caravans approaching from Central America. For a little while he was not inventing new punitive measures to enforce, and that was a good thing. So she played along, and set up a week's worth of workshops and training sessions for the thirty models that comprised Townsend Model Management. She fit in ample free time so the women could explore Washington. And she arranged a small fashion show to take place in the White House, for the entertainment of the first lady and her staff. *Maybe this will turn out all right*, she thought. And of course, she looked forward to seeing more of her niece Irina.

The whole event was scheduled for the second week in October, and to her surprise, Dannika heard from several of the models that they were looking forward to this escapade. They considered it a vacation from the daily grind of modeling work, which often involved enduring long commutes, or uncomfortable exposure in temperatures not suited to the scanty clothing they were modeling. And of course, the prospect of being paid for an entire week of work, instead of the piecework shoots they usually were assigned to, lent an air of relaxation, even gaiety, to the assignment. Hearing this, Dannika was happy for them. But she still harbored an uneasy feeling about George's involvement – why had he come up with this idea in the first place? Was he after one of the women? Dannika vowed to keep an eagle eye on him all week.

The week of the Washington visit arrived, and the women arrived in a chartered bus to a conference center in the northwest quadrant of the city. Dannika met them on their arrival and helped orient them. The conference center included a fitness center with a studio, where the dance and movement classes would take place. Dannika was touched by the women's excitement about doing something together, an activity that for once was stress-free. She had gone to some lengths to engage a few out-of-the-ordinary trainers – a belly dance teacher and a West African dance teacher, for instance. If this was an obligatory assignment, she could at least make it fun. In fact, she planned to join in the classes herself, along with some of her own staff. The classes would begin the next day.

This evening, Dannika hosted the group for dinner at a restaurant close to the conference center. She welcomed them with a brief speech.

"It's good to see so many of my friends again. You make me wish I were back in New York with you. Well, except – I know how hard you work, and I just don't think I could keep up. And on top of that," she said, pointing to herself, "this mom is much, much too old to be modeling!" Her audience laughed. "But please, accept this week off the schedule, and let's get together to dance! And later this week, we will visit the White House together. In fact, we'll be giving a little private fashion show, just for the first lady and her staff. No pressure!" Dannika waved a hand airily, and they laughed again.

After dinner, they all returned to the conference center, where Dannika and Irina finally got a chance to chat. Together, they retired to the hot tub in the fitness center. They talked for an hour and a half, catching each other up on family news. Dannika wept when she heard the details of how her sister died so many years ago, and she wept again when Irina told her how she and Malik had survived their teenage years in the U.S. Irina glossed over the details of their rescue and where they ended up, in the Ozarks. She had been drilled enough about the secrecy of that location to ever reveal it. She also knew not to name her rescuers or reveal anything about the structure – or lack of structure – of how they worked.

Dannika in turn told Irina how she had left Chechnya. Her departure was between the first and second Chechen wars, in 1998.

"I was lucky to get out at all. And then I was lucky to survive my journey to France. I still remember saying goodbye to Galina. Well, I knew it was goodbye, but she didn't. I couldn't tell her my plans, all I could do was hug her." Dannika grasped Irina's hand beneath the roiling water, and Irina's eyes filled with tears.

Dannika told Irina how she had traveled south through Georgia and Azerbaijan to Turkey, where she was granted asylum. From there she had journeyed all the way across eastern Europe to France.

"It was not easy to get into the modeling business in France. I got a couple of lucky breaks. But I paid for them…" Dannika's voice trailed off and she looked away. Irina could sense her unease, and she could guess pretty well what that payment had been. Both women had endured shame and exploitation on their way here, and neither wanted to dwell on it. Dannika wrapped up her story with the triumph of acquiring an H-1B visa and making it to the United States. Oddly, she said nothing about her marriage to George Townsend, and Irina had the good sense not to inquire.

At the end of their talk, they rose up out of the hot tub, two pink and sweaty girls with limp hair and pruny fingers and toes, laughing at themselves and at each other. Dannika robed up and rejoined her Secret Service agent, waiting for her in the hallway.

Over the next week, George Townsend found reasons to visit the conference center. He loved interrupting the discussions or dance classes. The women stopped dancing when he walked in, but he waved his hand and said, "Go on, go on, don't mind me!" while he took a chair. He sat hunched over with his knees spread, staring at their bodies, while they tried to ignore him.

At the end of one class, he approached Irina. "How would you like to go get a drink with me?"

"No, I'm sorry," she demurred. "I need to shower and catch up on my reading."

"Do you know who I am?" he practically growled at her.

"Yes, of course – you are George Townsend."

287

"And – ?"

"And you own Townsend Model Management."

He grinned blandly. "Which means – I own you. C'mon, what do you say to a drink?"

Again she declined, dipping her head. "No, thank you. I appreciate the offer, but I can't tonight. Thank you so much for asking, though." She quickly grabbed her towel and walked away.

Flushed with anger, he turned toward another of the models. This time he was more successful. The model he approached agreed to join him for drinks after she freshened up.

It was several hours later that George Townsend's new conquest, Trixie, returned to the conference center, to the room she shared with Irina. Irina looked at her with a question in her eyes, and Trixie related in graphic detail his boorish come-on.

"He ordered dinner catered to his room. I was hungry, so I didn't object. And that was okay." She paused and her face grew dark. "But after dinner, he came on to me like a fuckin' bulldozer. He wouldn't take no for an answer. I just managed to get out of the room because I'm faster than he is. What a fat, arrogant bastard! I'm probably going to get my contract pulled because of this, but you know what? I don't care. There are other agencies to work for."

"That's easy for you to say," Irina said softly. "My visa depends on the petition from my sponsor – and that's Townsend Model Management. I'm scared."

"You should be. He kept asking about you. I could have slapped him for that, too."

"Why me? Does he know me?" Irina looked terrified.

"No, he's just smitten with your looks. Something about that disdainful attitude of yours just drives him crazy. That or your accent. Worse luck for you."

"They taught us not to smile. What are we supposed to do?" Irina was genuinely distressed. Trixie reached out for her hand.

"Don't worry about it. Just keep dodging him like you're doing. And start sending your resume around. You can find another sponsor, I'm sure you can."

"Maybe. I'm going to try, anyway." Irina looked worried. "Thanks for the warning."

The next day, George Townsend was back at the conference center, watching the dance class. No one quite had the courage to ask him to leave, until Dannika walked in. She sat down beside him and whispered in his ear, smilingly at first. His face took on a scowl and he wouldn't look at her. She took his hand and he yanked it away. She gave up and sat beside him passively, but she didn't leave. As the class broke up, she stayed by his side. She caught a few *thank you* glances from the models, as they ducked out.

Back home, George pounced on Dannika. "You interfering bitch. Who told you to babysit me?"

Dannika feigned surprise. "Babysit you? I came to enjoy the dancing with you. It was like a date." She smiled her most radiant smile. "Come, honey, don't be mad. We don't do so many things together, I thought it would be fun to watch the class."

"Sure you did. How in hell did you even know where I was?"

"I – I guessed," Dannika faltered. "After all, it was you who invited your company to visit here. But I was in charge of arranging their activities. I even gave you the schedule, remember?"

"Oh, yeah, that's right," he conceded. "But that doesn't give you the right to follow me around."

"I wasn't following you around. I could care less what you do." She turned her back on him, hiding her anger. Then suddenly a dam burst, and she whirled around to face him, her cheeks flushed. "But I have a duty to protect those girls. From you!"

At this, he chuckled grimly, his triumph complete.

At the end of the week in Washington was the White House fashion show, planned for the benefit of the president and first lady. Dannika was nervous about this event, hoping that it would go smoothly. George took every opportunity to remind the president's chief of staff about the event, talking about 'my girls' as if they were a harem. At one point, George Townsend was invited into the Oval Office to pitch the event to the president himself. President Betrog listened eagerly.

"This sounds like fun," the president agreed. He turned to his chief of staff. "Don't put anything else on my schedule for Saturday evening. Then, impulsively, he turned to George Townsend. "How would you and your wife like to join me and the first lady for dinner before the show?"

Townsend reddened with pleasure. "We'd be honored, sir." He bowed slightly.

On the night of the show, George and Dannika arrived to dine with the president and first lady in the private residence of the White House. George could hardly contain himself. He was even gallant to Dannika, waiting for her to take his arm as the chauffeur let them both out of their limousine. Dannika was stunning in a deep blue silk gown, understated but clingy, and George looked pleased to show her off. The models arrived shortly after George and Dannika were ushered upstairs to the family residence for dinner.

Dannika had surrendered the choreography of the show itself to the White House protocol staff, who worked with the Townsend Model Management staff to plan the show. The models, all thirty of them, were shown into the state Dining Room, where stacks of boxed Big Macs and sleeves of french fries were spread out on a table, along with tacos, burritos and CrunchWraps. Accompanying these food choices were soft drinks nestled into ice in large steel pans. The models, looking a little confused, hunted through the choices for anything like a salad. Not finding any, they contented themselves by nibbling on burritos and sipping a little soda. Soon they were ushered into the Green Room, which had been set up as a temporary changing room. Racks of clothing were arranged around the room, and mirrors were set up, but no chairs. They got busy dressing for the first round of the show.

The room next door, the East Room, was set up with chairs facing in toward a catwalk space that ran the length of the large room. Within the hour, the invited guests began to arrive. They were greeted with flutes of champagne and trays of hors d'oeuvres. The guests included some members of the House and Senate and their wives, as well as members of the president's cabinet with their wives. Everyone was dressed to the nines, excited to be part of this unusual event.

President Betrog and the first lady entered ceremonially, followed by George and Dannika Townsend and George's daughter, Jackie. When they were seated, the presenter introduced the first collection, featuring Jane Taymore and L'Arlesien day dresses. Designers invited to this show, fully aware of the immutable conservatism of Washington, had selected the more conventional items in their collections to exhibit today. Among the business suits and cocktail dresses, there was little to surprise and nothing to shock the audience. Nonetheless, there was a distinct air of glamour in the air, lent by the lithe young models sashaying down the aisle.

Irina appeared in the second wave of models, showing off Sensei's creations for spring. These were a little edgier than L'Arlesien's had been, and there were some murmurs and frowns among the audience. George Townsend's eyes followed Irina as she strutted toward the guests of honor. Irina stared coldly and fixedly above the heads of the audience, her face betraying no flicker of recognition.

The show concluded with a collection of evening gowns by Patricia Rolemy and Rachel Zarista. Again the models floated down the room with lanky grace, and each woman in the audience vowed to take off ten pounds and buy one of *those* dresses for next summer. The applause at the end of the show was decorous and short. The models retired to the Green Room to change into street clothes before boarding the bus to go back to their hotel. They left in a group within twenty minutes, eager to escape the stuffy atmosphere of the White House. They were laughing as they exited.

George and Dannika stayed a little while longer, then left for home. When they got home, Dannika changed into a peignoir and slid into bed. She heard George moving around in his dressing room.

"Are you coming to bed, sweetheart?" Her voice had a purr to it.

"No, I'm going to watch TV. Don't wait up." He headed downstairs. Dannika smiled grimly. At least she'd tried. She picked up her novel from the bedside table and read herself to sleep. Dannika did not hear George leave the house again, twenty minutes later.

Chapter 45 – Washington, D.C.

On a Monday in mid-October, Kiara Jefferson and Dannika Townsend were working together in the office, designing a new series of field trips for schoolkids. Their idea was to take kids from some of the underachieving schools of Washington, D.C. out to visit Civil War battlefields, as part of a comprehensive history curriculum for grade school and middle school students. At one point during their work, Dannika looked down at a folder that Kiara had handed her. Kiara signaled with a blink of her eyes. Dannika opened the folder and saw that it held an envelope with a sticky note on it. Kiara's writing on the sticky note said, "PRIVATE – open later, then destroy." Dannika slid the folder into her briefcase along with other homework.

At home that night, Dannika retreated to her bathroom to read the letter. On the envelope, Kiara's name and address were typed, but there was no return address. She looked at the postmark – it was from Palm Beach, Florida. The envelope had been opened. Inside it Dannika found a single page folded together and sealed with wax. On the flip side was written, "Please deliver to Dannika Townsend." *So Kiara doesn't even know what's in this,* she thought. *Who sent it?* She broke the wax seal and opened the page. She glanced at the bottom of the page and read the closing, "In distress, Irina." *Irina's in Florida?* She read the letter quickly.

> Dear Aunt Dannika,
>   I hesitate to write to you but I must. I have been fired from my job in New York. I was unable to pay the expenses that were charged to my account at the agency. They said I owe for

my plane tickets to Chechnya and back, and for Malik's as well. I also owe for my head shots, my website profile, and even legal and accounting charges. All of this comes to far more than I was paid during Fashion Week. I even owe for the classes we took in Washington, and the hotel there, and the food I ate. I thought that was being offered for free. I didn't understand that the agency keeps track and takes it out of anything I am paid. Why didn't you tell me this? You must have known it. You were a model yourself. Should I have trusted you?

Now I am in Florida, working as a chambermaid in the Townsend Resort. I am here because I had no other choice. My visa has been changed from H-1B to H-2B. Your husband threatened to deport me immediately unless I went to work for him in Florida. And the H-2B visa means my employment is temporary. I can be deported at the end of the season. All of this is because I would not sleep with your husband. Was this your plan? I trusted you.

In distress,
Irina

Dannika let her hand drop and stared blankly across the bathroom. How could this have happened? She let herself feel frightened for one minute. Then her mood shifted to a cold fury. Because she was not surprised. Not surprised at all. But this time, she swore, he would not get away with it.

Dannika quickly tore the letter and envelope into tiny pieces and flushed them down the toilet. She washed her hands and splashed her face with cold water. Then she quickly repaired her makeup and brushed her hair.

Dannika joined James in the dining room and they waited for George. He came in twenty minutes later. She greeted him with a smile as usual, and they sat down to eat. As usual, he was served his cheeseburgers while she and James ate salad, followed by braised chicken with vegetables. Dannika asked George how his day had gone and he grunted but didn't answer. James started to chatter about school and George barked at him to shut up.

"Honey, what's the matter?" asked Dannika. She seemed genuinely concerned. "Are you feeling all right?"

"No, goddamn it, I don't feel all right. Damn doctor has me on these damn pills, but they don't do a damn thing. I – oof!" He winced and moved his left arm around at the shoulder. "Shit."

She stood up. "What's going on, George? What's wrong?" When he didn't answer, but continued to look distressed, she said, "Honey, I'm calling Dr. Bornsweig." She didn't wait for him to answer, but ran out the door.

Soon she was back. "He's on his way over. You should lie down." She took his arm.

He shook her off savagely. "Get the fuck away from me. Goddamn bitch." He looked at her through narrowed eyes. "I don't know why I ever married you. I want a divorce."

She willed herself to look stricken. "Honey, you don't mean that. Please lie down." She didn't approach him again, though. Instead, she turned to James. "James, let's give your dad some space. Come on." She gestured with her hand and he scooted out of range. They both left the dining room.

Outside in the hall, Dannika took James' hand. "Don't worry, kiddo. No matter what happens, we'll be okay. Now go start on your homework." She spoke to the first staffer she saw. "Go keep an eye on George. He's in the dining room. The doctor will be here soon."

When Dr. Bornsweig arrived, Dannika met him at the door. She ushered him quickly into the dining room, where George sat stiffly in his chair. He gripped his left arm with his right hand and struggled to remain upright. Dr. Bornsweig convinced him to try to walk to his bedroom. Finally, George managed to shuffle down the hall, with Dr. Bornsweig on one side and a male staffer on the other. Dannika followed, trying to summon up some feeling of sympathy. In his bedroom, she sat at his side while Dr. Bornsweig gave him a nitroglycerin tablet under his tongue, then checked his blood pressure.

He turned to Dannika. "I want him to come to the hospital for an EKG. And blood tests. Then we'll go from there." George started to protest, but couldn't because of the tablet under his tongue. He lay back, defeated.

The ambulance arrived and the EMTs loaded him onto a stretcher. The stretcher was put into the ambulance, and Dannika, ever the doting wife, joined him. The Secret Service detail followed in the Townsend limousine.

Once at the hospital, Dannika stood in the back of the room while the EKG was done and the blood was drawn. As they waited for the results, she ventured to approach the bed and hold her husband's hand. This time, exhausted, he didn't shoo her away. She stroked his hand and whispered, "Shh, shh."

Eventually, Dr. Bornsweig came back and announced that the EKG did not show any damage. The blood tests also came out normal. Nevertheless, he would like to keep George overnight for observation. "And I might keep him tomorrow as well. You should go home," he advised Dannika. She feigned reluctance, but she was only too glad to go.

Out in the hall, Dannika headed for the elevator. Dr. Bornsweig caught up to her and asked her to step into the residents' room for a moment. She followed him into the room, and he waved her to a chair. They both sat down. He cleared his throat.

"Mrs. Townsend, we need to talk. Your husband is in a precarious state. He has chest pain – angina – which is why I've had him on the Elantan LA. I'm going to raise his dose to 50 mg for just this week, and then we're going to titrate him back to 25 mg."

"Wait a minute. What is this Elantan LA?"

"It's a nitrate. Something like the nitroglycerin I gave him when I got to your house this evening. It calms down the angina, the chest pain. The LA version is long-acting, so he takes it once a day, and it keeps the angina under control. But since he had the attack tonight, that's why I'm doubling the dose to 50 mg for a few days. By Sunday he can go back to the 25 mg. Do you understand?"

"Yes, I understand. Will he be released tomorrow?"

"That's my plan. Be here by 10 a.m. and I'll get him out of here by noon. I'll send you home with the 50 mg tablets and you are to switch back to the 25 mg on Sunday. But keep the 50 mg in case we need to raise the dose again. Got it?"

"Yes, doctor, I understand. Thank you so much." She stood up.

"Wait, Mrs. Townsend… there's one thing more." She sat back down. "Does he still use Viagra?"

It was all she could do to stop herself from saying, "Are you kidding? We don't have sex at all." Instead she said, "No, doctor, we don't need anything like that."

"Good, good. That's fortunate." He stood up and turned to go. She almost asked for an explanation, but he abruptly left the room. She laughed to herself at his embarrassment. Then she looked around the room. It was lined with bookshelves, many of them containing textbooks and medical journals. She was curious about the Viagra thing, and she wondered if she could look it up. Her eye fell on a row of small booklets, about the size of old Reader's Digests. She picked one up. It was a monthly publication called PDR – Physician's Desk Reference. The one she had in her hand was current, from this month. She thumbed through it and realized it had all the details on the latest drugs, including drug interactions. Just the thing!

The door to the room opened and she froze. As she turned, she slipped the booklet into her coat pocket. The resident who entered looked surprised to see her.

"I'm sorry, I was just leaving." Dannika walked out and asked her Secret Service agent to take her home. She thought about saying goodnight to George, but decided against it. *I'm done pretending for tonight.*

When she arrived back home, Dannika checked in on James. She found him deeply involved in a video game that he didn't want to abandon. He listened to her with half an ear as she told him not to worry about his dad. His blank look told her that hadn't even crossed his mind. *Oh well,* she shrugged, *that's no surprise.* She kissed the top of his head and left the room.

Dannika pulled the Physician's Desk Reference out of her coat pocket and took it to her bedroom. She found Elantan LA in the index and turned to the page that contained detailed prescribing information. She confirmed that it was used, as Dr. Bornsweig said, to keep angina under control. Then she scanned down the page to the section titled "Interaction with other medicinal products and other forms of interaction." She read down to this paragraph:

> Concurrent administration of drugs with blood pressure lowering properties and/or alcohol may potentiate the hypotensive effect of Elantan LA. This may also occur with neuroleptics and tricyclic antidepressants.
>
> Any blood pressure lowering effect of Elantan LA will be increased if used together with phosphodiesterase type-5 inhibitors which are used for erectile dysfunction. This might lead to life threatening cardiovascular complications. Patients who are on Elantan LA therapy therefore must not use phosphodiesterase type-5 inhibitors (e.g. sildenafil, tadalafil, vardenafil).

She turned back to the index to look up sildenafil, tadalafil and vardenafil. There it was: Sildenafil is the same as Viagra.

She sat back, stunned. She remembered that his habit, back when they used to have sex, was to take two Viagra at once, even though he knew the doctor didn't approve. She knew he still kept some in his suitcase.

Elantan plus Viagra plus alcohol. Imagine.

The next day, Dannika took the copy of Physician's Desk Reference and put it in the outgoing trash pickup. She'd gleaned all the information she needed.

Chapter 46 – Florida

Two weeks later, on the weekend of Halloween, Dannika and James were in Florida at the Townsend Resort. George stayed in Washington, claiming work demands. Actually, he preferred to avoid the nonsense of Halloween and the noisy kids' parties it entailed. So Dannika and James flew down together, accompanied as always by their Secret Service guards.

James had invited friends to a Halloween night party in his suite at the resort. Dannika had allowed him, at age twelve, to have his own space, although he was still under the watchful eye of the Secret Service. She had hired a nanny service to help supervise and cater this party. She retreated to the spa for the morning, planning to join him in the afternoon.

Dannika had just arrived back at her suite and showered, when there was a knock on the door. She opened it and found Irina there with a cart.

"Your lunch, ma'am."

Dannika glanced at the Secret Service guard in the hall.

"Yes, yes, come right in. Thank you." She closed the door behind Irina and the two women squared off. At first nothing was said. Irina's face was a cold mask of anger. Dannika tried to think of what to say. Finally, she looked into Irina's eyes and her voice came out in a whisper.

"I'm so sorry. This shouldn't have happened." She reached out to take Irina's hand, but Irina flinched away.

"You planned this," Irina hissed. "You just set this up so he'd have a plaything."

"No, no, I didn't," protested Dannika, still whispering. "I didn't intend for you to work for his company. I didn't think he would ever see you. This is all a mistake."

"Well, he has seen me, and apparently he can do what he pleases with my visa. So now I'm stuck here. I am his captive – until he decides to deport me." Her face crumpled and she turned away. "What will happen to Malik?"

"Don't worry, I'll protect him."

"Like you protected me?" Irina challenged Dannika in a fierce whisper. "Is that what you call protection?"

"I didn't know. Tell me what happened. Please." Dannika was almost in tears. A tense moment passed as the women stared at each other. "Please – we don't have much time. Come." Dannika gestured toward the far side of the room, toward the table in an alcove by the window. Irina pushed the cart across the room. Then as she placed the lunch on the table, she recited the story, her voice low.

"He came back to the hotel that last night. The night after the show at the White House. He found me and demanded that I go with him. When I refused, he grabbed me. I started to scream and he pushed me back against the wall and covered my mouth. Then he said he would ruin me. He told me I owed thousands of dollars to his company. And if I didn't go with him, he would take away my visa. And I that's when I bit him."

"Oh my god." Dannika's hands flew to her mouth.

"Yes, I bit him and I got away."

"Did you tell the police?"

"I didn't tell anyone. Who could I tell? Who would listen to me against him?"

"Jesus." Dannika stood with her fists on the table. She looked up. "Then what happened? How did you come here?"

"I went to work the next day. They told me I'd been fired. And that I owed all kinds of money. Everything they had paid

303

for me, it was on my account. I went back to my room and I called Courtney Sims."

"Who is that?"

"That's the lawyer who got me the visa. Don't you know her?"

"No, I don't. Kiara did all that work."

"Courtney looked into it. She called me back the next day. My visa had been downgraded to H-2B and my new sponsor was the Townsend Resort. She said the order came from high up. She said she'd work on it, but I'd better comply for now. So here I am – a maid in your resort."

Dannika sat down, her head in her hands. Then she hit the table with her fists, making the silverware jump.

"This is the last time," she growled. "This is it. We are going to end this now."

"What do you mean?"

Dannika looked at Irina, her face grim. "I mean I'm going to kill him."

Irina met her eyes. "You have to. We have to."

"We can. And we will."

And Dannika explained how.

Chapter 47 – USA

It was early November, and election fever gripped America. Politicians with outsized personalities were posturing in front of crowds, repeating phrases they knew would get a reaction. The crowds were all dressed the same and held the same signs up on cue. They hooted at the same lines and chanted the same chants.

Cameras followed these gatherings in fevered pursuit. Mikes were shoved in faces to collect the same hardwired opinions. All over the news stations and all over the web, pundits were predicting results based on online polls. Campaign contributions were counted as proxy votes.

Everybody knew who would win.

It was the guy who considered women expendable. Who vetoed the UN resolution to allow women raped in war to get medical support. Who vowed to outlaw and defund Planned Parenthood. Who advocated the overturn of Roe v. Wade. Who took every opportunity to undermine and belittle every female candidate for any office. Who cut off food aid for seven hundred thousand Americans.

Everybody agreed this guy would win.

Except the women who met in churches and schools, planning voter drives. And the women in book clubs. The women in offices. The women with clipboards standing outside public libraries. The women who held bake sales and visited each other's yard sales. The women working at homeless shelters. The young women in exercise classes. The old women at stitch-and-bitch sessions.

The waitresses.

The teachers.

The administrative assistants.

The bus drivers.
The nurses.
The students.
The mothers.
The sisters.

They met in small groups, not in large rallies. They talked to
each other over backyard fences and over cafeteria tables. They
met in living rooms and drew handmade signs. They talked to
fellow workers and posted notices on union billboards. They
instructed voters on absentee ballots. They laughed over beers
and they grew determined.

Determined to vote.

Election day came, and all over America, workplaces went
empty. Women lined up at the polls in queues that stretched
down city blocks. They stood in dusty roads in rural towns, and
under umbrellas when the rain hit. They stood and waited for
hours before the polls opened. Their vast numbers forced the
polls to stay open hours after they should have closed. They
worked as election observers and election officials, and they
made sure the count was right.

And the count was right. The guy that everyone said would
win... lost by a landslide. And the men who claimed to support
him lost. All over America, empty balloons of hot air popped.

Women walked into state legislatures, into governor's
mansions, and into Congress in unprecedented numbers, vowing
once and for all to clean this shit up. To expose corruption and
exploitation. To treat people fairly. To frame a future for
everybody's kids.

January would bring a new beginning for America, after its long nightmare.

In the Townsend household, the mood was subdued. George knew he'd be out of a job come January. The current administration would be out on its ear, along with all its appointees. In a way, George looked forward to shucking off the yoke of public service. Let somebody else police the damn border and issue the damn visas. He didn't care. He'd go back to his many businesses in New York, including Townsend Model Management. Especially that. He'd been away too long.

In the meantime, Dannika was asking him about Christmas vacation plans. For once, he didn't have to stick around Washington – what was there to do, anyway? They'd head down to Palm Beach and he'd get some golfing in. He told Dannika to plan for two whole weeks. She looked thrilled and grateful. He seemed to have forgotten his threat to divorce her. For her part, Dannika pretended she had never heard it.

One thought was running around George's head, as he contemplated the upcoming Christmas vacation: *Maybe I'll have some better luck with that little Irina. She knows I carry out my threats now. Let's see if her attitude has changed now that she's a maid.* He smiled grimly in anticipation. He packed his own suitcase, including the little bottle of Viagra.

Chapter 48 – Florida

The flight to Palm Beach was uneventful. President Betrog insisted that the Townsends accompany him on Air Force One, since they were all going down for the Christmas holidays at the same time. This time there were no reporters on the plane.

Dannika had begged her husband to try to relax this week, to have a private vacation alone with her.

"Not much chance of that," he countered. "I'll be playing golf with the president. Probably every day."

"Oh, honey, really? I hoped we could spend some time together. You know –" She smiled seductively and approached him, and he almost wavered.

Then he turned his back. "I don't think so. Forget it."

She forced herself not to react. Keeping her voice level, she asked smoothly, "May I come to watch you play, then? It would be fun."

"Yeah, sure. Whatever." He shrugged and left the room.

That's okay, she thought. *I can be decorative. Whatever you want.*

Dannika had arranged for a nanny and of course the Secret Service to watch over James during the vacation, but she had given him permission to invite friends to stay over. James was given a suite of his own that opened onto the pool complex. He was thrilled to have a little more freedom than last year.

For three days the same routine was followed. Dannika and George slept in separate bedrooms at opposite ends of their expansive suite. The room between them featured a wet bar, a huge fireplace, and a few leather armchairs and side tables. There was also a small table surrounded with gold brocade chairs, in front of a leaded-glass bay window. Outside, two stories down, the Secret Service patrolled the sidewalk. Agents were also stationed outside in the hallway leading to the suite.

Each morning George stayed in his bedroom past eleven o'clock, watching TV. Dannika called down each morning for a breakfast cart loaded with bacon and eggs, pastry and fruit and coffee. The maid who brought the breakfast rang the bell to the central room of the suite and was met by Dannika. The maid was always Irina. Each morning they exchanged no words while Irina served Dannika's breakfast at the table by the window. When that task was done, Irina knocked and entered George's bedroom with the heavily laden cart.

For three days, the time that Irina spent in George's bedroom lengthened each morning. When she emerged, she exchanged a look with Dannika, who always sat quietly by the bay window. Irina retreated to the hallway by way of the central door, coming back a couple hours later to retrieve the cart.

Around noon each day, Dannika knocked on her husband's door, feigning sleepiness. She sat on the bed next to him and made him take his daily medications. He continued to watch the TV as he did so, or he would have noticed the very slight difference in the Elantan LA capsule. It was no longer the 25 mg sustained-release dose, but the 50 mg. But for three days, his eyes glued to the TV, he didn't notice. In fact, he felt energized and ready for his golf game.

Each day at 1 p.m., a small coterie of business partners and civic leaders gathered on the golf course and waited for President Betrog and George Townsend to show up. Dannika Townsend also rode up, sometimes accompanied by the first lady.

Betrog and Townsend played nine holes over the course of a few hours. They were accompanied by the usual group of burly Secret Service men, looking formal and overheated in their black suits. George, too, looked overheated. Dannika trailed along with the Secret Service, keeping an eye on her husband and posing for occasional photos. She discouraged photos of her husband, as he didn't look his best climbing in and out of the golf cart. She thought he looked sloppy and overweight, and increasingly flushed in the face. She noted that once or twice he held onto the handle of the golf cart to steady himself as he stood up.

On the second day, she saw him stand up, wobble, then sit down again suddenly on the golf cart bench. She rushed over, concerned. He waved her off, but she sent one of the caddies for some ice and a towel. When the ice came, she wrapped it in the towel and caught up with George's cart. She insisted that George wear the ice against the back of his neck. He growled at her, but then acquiesced. The look he gave her warned that she'd better not approach again. She turned away, worry written on her face.

"He gets so overheated," she commented to one of the Secret Service guards. "It's not good for him. But he doesn't want to disappoint the president, you know."

After each day's game the group retired to the club for dinner. Dannika sat next to her husband and ordered expensively, encouraging him to indulge himself with the best brisket and prime rib. She sat quietly while he expounded on the news, the latest from Sean Harrington, his favorite pundit, and what his opponents were saying. His golf partners nodded and agreed, but didn't interject. Dannika ordered dessert for both of them, and sat picking at hers while he devoured his own.

On the evening of the fourth day, on their way upstairs to the suite, Dannika took the stairs as usual, followed by her Secret Service bodyguard, while her husband rode up in the elevator with his own guard. Dannika turned a corner in the hall to see her husband talking to Irina. Irina's eye flicked to Dannika for a split second, then went back to George's face. Before he could turn around, Dannika had disappeared back into the stairwell. Her bodyguard was just emerging, and she told him that she must have dropped her scarf in the dining room.

Dannika returned to the dining room. Her bodyguard trailed a respectful distance behind. She circled the table where dinner had been served, lifting napkins and peering under the table. The bodyguard joined her to help, but they found nothing.

Finally, looking unhappy, she said, "That scarf was my mother's. I'd so hate to lose it. Perhaps the waiter picked it up. I'm going to go ask the kitchen staff." She turned and strode off down the hallway and asked one of the receptionists how to find the kitchen. Her bodyguard caught up to her and they both went down the stairs to the kitchen and pantry suite.

In the kitchen, Dannika found the supervisor. She described the missing scarf – a small beige silk scarf with red edges. The supervisor walked her to the kitchen. She clapped her hands and raised her voice, and the noise stopped.

"Did anyone pick up a small beige scarf off Mrs. Townsend's table?" The waiters looked at each other with blank stares and shook their heads. The supervisor apologized to Dannika. "I'm sorry. Perhaps a maid picked it up."

"And where can I find the maids?"

"Their central office is just down the hall. I'll take you." The supervisor walked Dannika and her guard further down the hall to another door.

Dannika entered the large room that was the housekeeping area, and spotting Irina, she asked if she'd seen a small silk scarf in the dining room. Irina shook her head, but when Dannika summoned her with her eyes, she took a step forward.

"Perhaps I can help you to search for it."

Together Dannika and Irina walked back up the stairs to the dining room, with the guard following.

When they reached the table where the Townsends had dined, Irina and Dannika continued the search, under napkins and under chairs. They bent down together, and Irina whispered into Dannika's ear.

"He asked me to come tonight, 10 o'clock."

Their search failed to turn up the scarf.

Finally, Dannika sat down, defeated. Then suddenly she had a thought. She opened and searched her own handbag – and there was the scarf! She waved it and apologized to Irina and her bodyguard.

"I'm so sorry!" she laughed, embarrassed. "Silk is so small! It was here all the time."

Chapter 49 – Florida

At 9 p.m. that night, Dannika changed into a peignoir and walked into her husband's bedroom, carrying her sleeping pills. She offered him one but he waved her away. He was dressed in the pair of silk pajamas she'd given him for Christmas instead of his usual underwear. *A good sign*, she thought.

She got a glass of water from his bathroom and pretended to take her own pill. She needn't have bothered with that act, as his eyes were glued to the TV screen. She kissed him goodnight, told him she wanted to sleep late in the morning, and left the room.

At exactly 10 p.m., Dannika heard her husband open the door to the hallway from the central room of the suite. A service cart rattled into the room, and the hallway door closed. Voices murmured in the next room, and a girl giggled. The voices and the cart disappeared into his bedroom, and the door closed behind them. Two minutes later a champagne cork popped and there was more muffled giggling.

Ten minutes later, Dannika came out of her bedroom and sat in one of the brocade chairs by the bay window. She didn't turn on the light, but remained in the shadows. It was almost quarter after 10 when Irina came back through the door from George's bedroom, pushing the service cart, and smoothing down her uniform. Dannika stood up and approached Irina, her hands outstretched. Her eyes held a question that she didn't dare speak aloud. Irina reassured her with a smile and a slight shake of her head. Dannika clasped her hands together in thanksgiving. *She didn't have to give in to him.*

Irina took a champagne flute from the cart and set it on the bar's counter. Dannika washed the glass, dried it, and set it down. A grim smile was exchanged between the women, but no words.

Irina pushed the empty cart to Dannika's bedroom at the other end of the suite. Dannika walked past her to the bathroom, took a vial from the cabinet and flushed the last of the Elantan LA 50's down the toilet. She handed the empty pill vial to Irina.

Irina pocketed the vial, washed her hands, then scooped up an armload of towels. She loaded up the service cart and proceeded out into the hallway. She nodded at the Secret Service officer in the hallway.

Meanwhile Dannika entered her husband's bedroom with a handful of wet wipes, swabbing surfaces of door handles and the bedside table. She scanned the bed and under it for stray fibers, hardly glancing at the softly snoring form of her husband. In the bathroom, she found the open container of Viagra and a water glass by the sink and didn't touch them. *So he did take one – or probably two. Excellent.*

Dannika stepped out to the bar in the central room of the suite and retrieved the second champagne flute – the one that she'd washed earlier. Back in his bedroom, Dannika used her husband's hand to hold the champagne bottle and pour the second champagne flute full again. His skin felt cold and clammy when she touched it, although his face was flushed. She noted that his breathing was slowing and would occasionally stop for half a minute at a time. She sipped a little of the champagne, leaving lipstick on the rim, and set it down. She pulled back the bedclothes on her side of the bed and lay down for a while, being sure to place her own hair on the pillow as she indented it. Finally, as his breathing continued to slow and began to rattle, she picked up the wet wipes and went back to her own bedroom.

Dannika flushed the wet wipes down the toilet. She went to bed with a book and slept peacefully until morning. Early in the morning she carefully made up her own bed, smoothing the coverlet and plumping the pillows. She walked into her husband's bedroom and saw that the flush had drained from his face. His skin looked yellow and waxy. She felt for a pulse and found none. She kicked her slippers under her side of the bed and lay down again until the covers warmed around her.

Finally she sat up, then got out of bed. She smiled down at him, took a deep breath and started to scream.

Chapter 50 – Cayman Islands

It was a Tuesday afternoon in January in George Town, Grand Cayman. Sandy Smith and Maria Cruz emerged from a small banking establishment on the main boulevard. They had spent the morning visiting various banks, transferring funds from Flight Incorporated's accounts to banks overseas. At the receiving destinations, women were standing by to withdraw the funds in cash and reinvest it, in smaller amounts, in many different repositories. In some places, purchases of property would be made, creating new housing for homeless families. In some places, cash was hidden for a time before being used or distributed. The plans for the distributed cash were as varied as the recipients, and Sandy and Maria didn't need to know, or even care, what they were. The vetting of the recipients had happened long ago, and what happened from now on was beyond their reach.

"So – don't you feel about 20 pounds lighter? Sandy asked Maria as they walked out of the last bank.

"I would if I weren't wearing this body padding. It'll be good to get it off," whispered Maria. Both women wore hats, wigs, sunglasses, body padding and dowdy clothing. They hailed a cab and drove to Owen Roberts International Airport, where they tipped the driver and watched him drive off. The private hangar was a short walk away from the main terminal, and they hustled down the sidewalk toward it, about a quarter mile away. While they walked, they pulled off the wigs and stowed them, wishing they had time to take off more in this heat. At the hangar, a small private plane with a discreet pilot, already well rewarded, awaited them. Maria's family was there, ready to board. The plane taxied and took off, headed southwest toward

Belize. Before they even touched down, the news of Flight Incorporated's liquidation had reached the New York offices of BGS Capital Advisors.

Rick Gregory, Sandy's boss at BGS Capital Advisors, was on vacation, skiing in Utah, so it took a while for his office to reach him. It was mid-afternoon before he decided to stop skiing and go back to the hotel suite. He still had his ski boots on when he picked up the phone.

His boss was shouting at the other end. "All of the assets of Flight Incorporated have been disbursed to banks in Panama, Switzerland, Ireland and Hong Kong, and a bunch of other places. Then they tell me they were immediately collected and cashed out or moved, who knows where. What the hell is going on? Aren't you in charge of this enterprise?"

"Yes, sir, I am. How much is missing?"

"How would I know? Don't you know?" The boss's voice was suddenly suspicious. "And where are you right now?"

"I'm in Utah, sir. But I'll be back to New York by the first flight. And I hope to have an answer for you when I get there."

Rick hung up and frantically tried to reach Sandy. She was supposed to be at a music festival in Vegas. She didn't answer her phone.

He dialed another number, the guy in the office next to his in New York. This guy had no reason to be nice to Rick, as Rick had usurped the position he was aiming for two years ago. His voice had a tinge of sarcasm as he described the situation to Rick. The entire haul had been huge, tens of millions of dollars. It vanished into thin air, apparently. Rick felt the heat rising in his face as he absorbed the magnitude of the situation. He promised to come straight back to New York.

Rick started to pack his bags. Then he stopped. He stood there and stared into his future. He saw courtrooms, lawyers, and judgments. He didn't want to imagine what lay beyond that. Never in his life had he looked at poverty. Never in his life had he suffered a setback that he couldn't just slide over with his confident business jargon and his charming personality. The abyss he was looking at was so deep that he couldn't imagine how to get out of it. Even if he did, his reputation would be ruined forever. This was the end of the line. And the maddening thing is, he couldn't imagine how it had happened.

Rick picked up his bottle of oxycodone from the bedside table. He took it into the suite's bathroom and held it up. He looked at himself in the mirror and a ghost stared back. He started to turn on the faucet to get a glass of water, then went back out to the kitchenette and grabbed a bottle of water from the fridge. *You never know how clean tap water is.* He shook the pills into his hand and drank them down with the water.

Knowing he didn't have much time, he put his coat back on and grabbed his skis and poles. He trotted down the hall to the elevator, rode to the first floor, and exited the building. He realized he'd forgotten his gloves and helmet and he almost went back for them. Then he laughed – what difference would it make?

The ski lift was just a few hundred yards away, and it was still running even though it was late afternoon. He put on his skis, got into position for the lift, let it catch him up, and rode it to the top of the slope. He dismounted and started down the mountain. His hands were getting numb, and he wondered if he could hold his poles for long. He saw an opening into the trees at the side of the run and headed for it. Already he was feeling loopy from the oxycodone. *This makes it easier,* he thought. *It will really look like an accident. Maybe my parents can collect some insurance. Did I put them down as beneficiaries?* That was his last thought before he aimed straight downhill into a tree, crouching so that his head would hit first.

Sandy and Maria, with Maria's family, left the airport in Belize and took a taxi to a hotel for the night. The next day, they boarded a flight to Bogota, Columbia, the last time they would use their old identities. In Bogota, they boarded a bus traveling south toward Brazil. From that point on, they disappeared into their new life. They were never heard from again.

Chapter 51 – Ozarks

Early winter visited the Barker Farm by way of a thunderstorm that brought high winds. It had been building up in the west all day, and Maybelle was worried that the livestock wouldn't be brought back down from the pasture in time. She needn't have worried. Arlene and Malik had it under control, and they got the cattle and sheep under cover in plenty of time.

Malik had arrived back at the Barker Farm in September, after Courtney Sims had taken charge of his and Irina's immigration case. Courtney had sent them back to Chechnya to get their proper visas, which were granted within a week. As Irina's dependent, Malik was given an H-4 visa. Irina's new employer, Townsend Model Management, had exerted pressure and provided bribes to get the process completed quickly.

As soon as Irina was back in New York, she put Malik on a plane to Little Rock, where Bonnie met him and brought him home. Irina knew he'd be safe and welcomed at the Barker Farm. He spent the rest of the summer fitting back into his old routine, working with the livestock. By the time Arlene begged to spend more time in the blacksmith shop learning to forge, he was ready to take charge of the animals. He recruited some of the other teens to join him in the barn and pasture, and together they shared the animal husbandry duties: milking, herding, mucking out the stalls, spreading manure. Malik trained a black and white shepherd mix dog to round up the livestock, and the two became inseparable. When Malik whistled, Shep was instantly at his heels, eager eyes watching for his signal.

Malik never knew that his sister had run into trouble with George Townsend, that she'd been fired from her modeling job, and that her visa had been downgraded. He never knew that she'd wound up in Florida, working as a hotel maid. Irina purposely didn't communicate with him except to send a note that she might not visit at Christmas. Instead she wrote to Courtney Sims, and she wrote to Dannika through Kiara Jefferson – the letter that drew Dannika to Florida.

After George Townsend was found dead in his bed, with Dannika beside him, the situation in Florida was tense for a few days. Investigators arrived and questioned Irina, Dannika, and the Secret Service detail to determine a timeline of the events the prior evening. A coroner's inquest was called, and an autopsy was performed to determine the cause of death. George's physician in Washington, Dr. Bornsweig, was called in to testify.

"We've heard the medical examiner establish the time of death as 5:00 a.m." The coroner addressed Dr. Bornsweig. "We have also been told that there were traces of isosorbide mononitrate and sildenafil, as well as alcohol, in the deceased's blood. The official cause of death is said to be cardiac arrest. Can you shed any light on this combination of facts?"

"I'm afraid I can," responded Dr. Bornsweig. "It's well known that the medication Mr. Townsend was prescribed for his angina, Elantan LA – that's the isosorbide mononitrate – is not to be taken with other hypotensive medications. Specifically, Viagra – that's the sildenafil – is contraindicated. As is alcohol."

"Yet the investigators found an open bottle of Viagra, that Mr. Townsend had handled, in the bathroom. And Mr. and Mrs. Townsend had shared some champagne that evening. Was Mr. Townsend aware of these contraindications?"

"Yes, he was. Or at least I think so. I know I explained it to him. But he was a difficult patient. I'm not sure if he was compliant. I was not aware that he used Viagra anymore – in fact, I asked Mrs. Townsend about it, and she said he didn't need it." Dr. Bornsweig glanced at Dannika, who was sitting stiffly in the courtroom pew, her face pale and puffy. She shook her head. "I surmise he simply obtained it on his own and took it without telling her. Men do that."

"Thank you. That'll be all." The coroner turned to Dannika. "Please step forward. Raise your right hand. Do you swear to tell the truth, the whole truth, and nothing but the truth?"

"I do."

"Were you aware that your husband had taken Viagra on the night of December 22nd?"

"No, your honor, I didn't find that out until afterwards."

"And were you aware that he shouldn't be drinking alcohol while he was on Elantan?"

"No, sir, I didn't know that. He often had beer with his meals. That or Diet Coke."

"Who ordered the champagne?"

"He did, your honor. But I drank some with him." She started to tear up.

"That'll be all, Mrs. Townsend. Thank you." The coroner wrapped up hastily. "I'm ruling that Mr. Townsend's death was due to his underlying cardiac condition, complicated by adverse drug interactions due to his noncompliance. Court is adjourned."

The following day, Dannika and James flew back to Washington with George's body for his funeral. George Townsend's funeral was a lavish affair, befitting a high government official. During the wake, Dannika appeared to be

322

barely holding up, and James was subdued. At the funeral itself, Dannika looked frail and somber in her black veil and black suit. She held James' hand the whole time.

Once she returned to Washington, Dannika picked up the reins of managing Townsend Model Management, and one of her first acts was to re-hire Irina as a model. That allowed Courtney Sims to get Irina's visa reclassified back to H-1B. Irina flew back to New York for a few weeks, before asking for some vacation time. Dannika also took charge of the human resources operations at Townsend Model Management. No longer would models be charged for expenses related to their work. They would be salaried, not paid piecework, and they'd be covered by a new health insurance policy. She instituted these changes within the first month, and she was soon deluged with applicants to the agency. Other modeling agencies, under pressure, started to follow suit.

Late in January, Irina flew to Little Rock, and rented a car to drive to the Ozarks. She spent the night at Lurleen's hotel, then was driven up the mountain by Jody. Arriving at Maybelle's, she was greeted by a joyous crowd. She spotted Bianca and ran to her.

"I'm so glad you're here! How did you get out?" Irina was practically crying with joy.

"Ms. Sims – Courtney – got me out." Bianca grinned. "And I think you must have had something to do with that. No?" Irina shrugged, noncommittal. "And the best thing is, she thinks I can get asylum."

"Really? That's wonderful!" Irina looked around. "But where is Malik? He got out also. Didn't he?" She looked at Bonnie, her face suddenly anxious.

"Ah, he's where he likes to be. Where we can't watch him. He's up in the pasture. Go on up."

At that, Irina left her bags sitting in the dirt and took off running. She ran up the dirt path in her dress shoes, not minding the mud and the burrs that caught at her skirt. Breathing hard, she mounted the last rise before the fenced pasture. Within the fence, cattle and a few sheep were intermingled, still managing to find forage under a light dusting of snow.

"Malik! Malik! Where are you?" She stood still under the winter sun, suddenly chilled.

"Irina!" The voice came from the woods at the upper end of the pasture. "I'm here!" Malik was jumping like a puppet, waving his hands. He dashed down the slope, alarming a few of the cattle on the way, then galloped over the stile and into his sister's arms.

"Oh, my sweet boy. You're safe."

"Of course I am. You can stop worrying. And you can stop calling me *boy,* you know. I do as much work as anyone else around here."

At that, she ruffled his hair and hugged him again. He stepped back, looked at her short jacket and skirt and shook his head. "You go back down and get some proper clothes on. It's getting cold." He glanced over her shoulder at Arlene, who had just arrived at the edge of the woods. "My help is here. We've got work to do." He winked at Arlene.

"Well, okay, I'll go." Irina turned downhill, hugging Arlene as they passed each other. When Irina was gone, Arlene and Malik exchanged a look and laughed. Shep ran circles around their legs until Malik shushed and petted him. At Malik's signal, Shep circled the herd and drove the sheep down the slope to the gate, where Malik met them. Arlene took hold of the tether on the oldest cow, and the others followed obediently. Together they walked down the mountain to the barn in the deepening twilight.

Chapter 52 – Washington, D.C

Toward the end of Christmas break, as Congress was about to reconvene, Mary Anderson and Vanessa Woodside sat in Vanessa's office, enjoying a rare moment of relaxation. They decided to go out for lunch, where their gossip wouldn't be overheard by others.

Settling in at a picnic table at a nearby park, they talked about the election and what it would mean for staffing in Washington.

"Probably no change in our hierarchy. We'll still be doing the same-old same-old, I guess," Vanessa suggested. "I'm still thinking of moving on."

"Really? Aren't you happy with what we've been able to do?" Mary asked. "Think about it. Remember last summer when we tracked down the guy who attacked you? A week after we caught up with him, he was behind bars. Three months later he started serving a 10-year sentence for assault. And then it turns out his DNA was linked to an unsolved murder."

Vanessa considered that.

"Yeah, that did feel good."

"And then," continued Mary, "when Center for Medicare Advocacy really started cooperating with the 5th District Metropolitan Police, they found five more crimes committed by this one man. Which he confessed to, you know.

"Well, just suppose we could encourage more cooperation between local police and FBI. The way it works now, it's a turf war. Once the FBI steps in, local cops are shoved aside – not to mention local medical facilities, nurses – everyone who helped solve your case. Why does it have to be that way?"

"It doesn't. And you're right, that's something we can encourage." Vanessa paused. "But whatever we do, let's keep it casual. Don't call it a task force. And don't bring it up to Mr. Williamson, whatever we do! All he'll want to do is slap an acronym on it." Both women laughed out loud.

Then Vanessa got serious, and her voice dropped to barely above a whisper.

"I did want to talk to you about something else. Remember how, in the beginning, Operation NEVRR was about investigating a cluster of deaths? Maybe murders? Well, I've been working on this all year, even after they told us the focus of the operation had shifted. I got some help from a guy in Chicago. His name is Mike Jenkins, and he's the Assistant Special Agent in Charge in the Chicago Bureau. We've been digging into the cases, and we finally found a pattern."

Mary looked startled. "You did? Like a connection? I thought the causes of death were all over the place. All different."

"Yes, you're right. There was no identifiable modus operandi. At least nothing we could pinpoint. But there was a pattern to the cases we looked at."

Mary said nothing. Her brow drew down and her eyes were questioning.

"The pattern had to do with who died. Every one of the prominent men who died was hated. Sometimes not even mourned by his own family. This complicated the investigations a lot, let me tell you. For each case, we had to look at everyone, inside his family, at his company, at every contact he had. Because there were so many reasons to kill him." Vanessa paused and looked across the park. Her shoulders slumped with weariness. She went on, her voice rising.

e were guys who cheated on their wives, who trampled coworkers, who ruined their children's lives. And at the ighest levels, they were titans of industry who beggared whole regions. Billionaires – whose work forces lived in poverty. Slumlords. Thieves. The common thread was that they used other human beings to enrich themselves. Period." She paused again, leaned forward and put her fists on the table. Her voice drew down to a whisper.

"And now I'm gonna confess something to you." Vanessa closed her eyes and opened them again, looking straight at Mary. "I really don't care whether we solve those cases or not. If it were up to me, I wouldn't pursue them. And now you can turn me in for violating my oath of allegiance."

There was a long silence. Mary looked up at Vanessa, then reached out and laid a hand over one of Vanessa's clenched fists.

"I'd have to turn myself in, too," Mary said softly. "I don't care either. I care more about *their* victims. Especially the girls they used. Which is what we've uncovered, right?"

Vanessa nodded. "That – that's a good thing. That's worth doing."

"Okay, then, let's get back to it." Mary sat back on her bench.

"But I might have to do it from Chicago."

Mary had no answer to that.

Back in her office, Vanessa decided there was something she needed to do before anything else. She picked up the phone and called Mike.

"I'm coming out to Chicago this weekend. I mean tomorrow. Tomorrow at 7 p.m. United flight 3455 from Washington."

"For what? You have a meeting?"

"Yessir. A meeting with you."

There was a silence on the other end of the line.

"I'll be here."

And he was. He stood there waiting for her at the gate, a dozen long-stemmed roses in his hand.

This time she slowed down and read him with her heart. And she liked what she saw.

Chapter 53 – Los Angeles

Lange and her daughter Amy had been home in L.A. for months when the police informed Alicia that her husband .my's Mazda Miata had been located at the Will Rogers .rport in Oklahoma City. They had traced Jeremy by his credit .ard receipts that far, and found he had rented and returned a Jeep. They even found that his cell phone had been picked up there and turned in to airport security. Beyond that the trail had gone cold.

The police came to interview Alicia repeatedly. The first time they arrived at the house without warning, and Alicia prayed silently that Amy wouldn't say anything. As soon as she got an opportunity, she shooed Amy next door to her friend's house. Fearing another encounter, she shipped Amy off to another friend's house for a week.

The cops also interviewed staff at Jeremy's company. All of them repeated Jeremy's story of planning a hike in Sequoia and Kings Canyon. There was speculation that Jeremy had lied to all of them and had flown off to South America.

It was discovered during the investigation that Jeremy had withdrawn large amounts of money from his firm just before he left, and the funds were untraceable. This news came as a shock to his assistant Barbara Edwards. Barbara called Alicia about the issue and the two got together the next day. Barbara brought over the company books and explained the whole situation. Alicia could offer no clarity, as she hadn't even handled their household finances.

In going over the company records, Barbara discovered that loans had been taken out using Jeremy's home as collateral – except that the home appeared to be in Alicia's name. This prompted more searching through county title records. Barbara and Alicia went down to the courthouse together. After a bit of confusion, and with the assistance of a very helpful clerk, the women discovered that the title was, in fact, in Alicia's name. The real estate tax bill address, however, was the firm's address. Barbara peered skeptically at Alicia.

"So why would the house be in your name, not his?"

"I – I don't know, honestly. No wait, I do remember. When we got married, he switched the house title to me. He said he wanted to protect it, in case he ever got sued. Imagine." Alicia smiled ruefully. "And now he's embezzled and run off and the firm is going down anyway."

"Oh, not necessarily," countered Barbara, "We have a few cards yet to play. But how could the house be used as collateral on this loan if you didn't know about it?"

Alicia peered at the loan papers. "That's my signature, all right. But this was 10 years ago." She re-read the papers. "Oh, now I know – this was the home improvement loan we got. Or at least that's what I thought it was. Damn, I should have been paying more attention."

"Well, it looks like this was really a home equity line of credit," said Barbara, "and it's been stretched pretty far. Did you know you were $150,000 in debt?"

Alicia blanched and her hand flew to her mouth. "No. My god. How am I going to pay that back? Will I lose the house?"

"Relax, kiddo. The house is worth probably $900,000, maybe over a million. You won't lose it as long as you can service this loan. What's your income like?"

Alicia was embarrassed again at her own ignorance. "I get an annuity check from my parents' estate – that's $7000 a month. I don't know what Jeremy earned."

enough. I suggest you start paying down this loan as
⟋s you can. What does your budget look like?"
⟋get?"
⟋hat you have to spend on other things – taxes, Amy's
⟋ol, food, utilities, all that stuff."
Alicia was ready to cry.

"I don't know. I didn't do any of that except the food
shopping. And clothes. I used my annuity money for that. All of
the rest of it, Jerry took care of."

Barbara blew out her cheeks with a sigh of resignation. "I
can tell there's some education that needs to happen here. Let's
plan to get together once a week to work on this."

"Work on what?"

"Your money management skills. You are a very wealthy
lady and you have no idea how to manage your own money. If
Jeremy's gone from your life you need to take charge.
Otherwise you will blow your own future and Amy's, too. I'm
going to be pretty busy just trying to keep the company on its
feet, so give me a couple weeks to get back to you."

Over the course of the following months, Alicia and Barbara
worked together to pull the firm back from the brink of
bankruptcy. They used the fact that Jeremy had, long ago,
designated Alicia as his durable power of attorney for financial
matters. That document was part of a whole package of estate
planning papers that Jeremy and Alicia had completed early in
their marriage. At the time, estate planning was deemed
essential to avoid certain taxes, so Jeremy was all for it. Neither
of them quite understood the need for all the documents, but
they followed the lead of their attorney.

Now Alicia and Barbara were grateful that all of these safeguards had been put in place. The attorney who had done the work was a woman who was well versed in all the events that could take place over the course of a marriage, including the birth of children, separation or divorce of the couple, and finally the death of one or both partners. Every contingency had been anticipated in the documents, and the attorney led Alicia and Barbara through the choices that had been made, and the implications for the present situation. Since Jeremy had disappeared and was unable to sign legal documents, Alicia was empowered to do so in his name, up to and including managing his firm.

One of the first decisions Alicia made was to promote Barbara to the role of CEO of the company, with commensurate raises in pay and perks. Then together they worked to redefine the goals of the company, reorganize staffing, and explain the changes to the staff. The process took the rest of the year. At New Year's, the whole staff celebrated with a party.

At the party, some speakers briefly mentioned Jeremy, but most celebrated the company's accomplishments since he'd been gone. Alicia and Barbara accepted these speeches for what they were, genuine and heartfelt endorsement of their leadership. Alicia realized how much she had grown under Barbara's tutelage.

"I am so grateful to Barbara. You all understand that she has saved this company. She saved it for you, the team that supported her. She saved it for me, too, and I can't thank her enough. Here's to Barbara!" Alicia raised her glass and drank to her friend.

"And from now on, this company is going to work like a family. You all can expect some raises very soon. We are going to do great things together."

The photo that was taken then showed Alicia and Barbara with their arms around each other, grinning from ear to ear.

After the next year spent revamping the company, Alicia found herself less in demand and more in search of a new pursuit. She started working more with the parent-teacher organization at Amy's school. She had decided to send Amy to public school while she was so busy with company work. Also, she was able to save the private school tuition and put it into a college fund. Now, as she looked back at the year, she was glad of the grounding that Amy was getting, and the diversity among her friends.

In working with other PTO members, Alicia began to understand that even in her relatively wealthy neighborhood, there were instances of domestic violence that were just beginning to be acknowledged. As she thought about it, she recollected her own years of hiding Jeremy's abuse because she was ashamed. She proposed in one meeting that parents should take a role in protecting one another from abusive situations. Almost before she thought about it, she volunteered her own home as a safe place for any woman to bring her family.

Three years after her decision in that PTO meeting, Alicia was sitting with Barbara and two of the sheltered women in Alicia's living room. Amy, now in 5th grade, was working in the other room on a science project, along with several other kids. Alicia suddenly thought back to that long-ago day in the Ozarks, sitting on a hill at dusk and watching the kids run around. She realized that she had created another community, right here in L.A. From her despair and fear had grown a fierce determination to smooth the road for other women, and she had done it! She reached out her hands to the women seated on either side of her. Silently they closed the circle and lowered their heads in gratitude.

The next day, Alicia took out her seed catalog and placed her spring order. Enclosed in it was a long letter to Maybelle, and a large check written out to Barker Farm.

Chapter 54 – Epilogue

It had been three years since the last presidential election, and the mood in the country was entirely different from the last time around. This time, people had real jobs, and were finally being paid real wages. The wage disparity between CEOs and rank-and-file workers had come down considerably, from 270 times the average worker's wage to something nearer 85 times that wage – still not good enough, according to some in Congress, but an improvement.

At the same time, the pay gap between men and women was narrowing, too, as was the pay gap between whites and minorities. Congress and the new president had moved mountains over the past three years to redirect money from the military to civilian infrastructure, and to reinstate progressive taxation. The ripple effects of improved roads, rebuilt bridges, and fully funded schools were being felt from inner cities to small rural communities.

As a side effect, some studies even showed that the gig economy was slowly drying up, with more people finding full-time, permanent jobs with benefits. The new medical system was taking shape as well, resulting in fewer bankruptcies and healthier populations. Oddly enough, there were few, if any, celebrations of all the improvements in the economy and way of life. Senators and congresswomen didn't spend time congratulating themselves or lambasting their opponents – they just got on with the job. It was as if the country were breathing a huge, quiet sigh of relief.

Lucy Blaylock, the former homicide autopsy transcriptionist, had moved with her boys from Utah to Las Vegas, where she was now second-in-command of medical records at a large hospital. Her ex-husband didn't even try to chase her, not after the last time she'd taken him to court, and the judge heard what her kids had to say about their dad. Lucy was awarded full custody, and soon after that, with the infusion of cash that came in a wildflower seed packet, she packed them all up and moved.

Back at the Barker Farm in the Ozarks, Tom Robbins had proven himself indispensable in the orchard and the carpentry shed. He liked being the one the women came to when a job was just too heavy for them to do. He was even forgiven for showing off his strength, as he heaved logs and split rocks.

He made more and more frequent visits down the mountain to Susie's barber shop, until she finally told him, "You know, I really can't cut your hair any shorter. Are you wantin' me to shave you every morning, too?" She chuckled and gave him the side-eye.

At that he grabbed her hand and knelt down.

"Would you? Would you marry me, and shave me every morning?"

"Oh for heaven's sake, the idea! Get up now!" She turned away quickly, and out of the corner of her eye, she saw Ceci duck behind the edge of the house. Then his head stuck out again slowly, and the look in his face said, *please, Mom!*

Susie turned back to Tom. "Are you serious, or are you just funnin' me?" Her voice had an edge to it.

Tom stood up and dusted off his knees. He met her eyes with a directness she had never seen in him before.

"Susie, I couldn't be more serious. Will you marry me? Why do you think I keep comin' down here for these haircuts I don't need? I want to feel you touch me. I want to hear you hum. And

I want a lot more than that. Please, Susie." He took her hand and looked into her eyes. "Please."

"Humph." Susie shrugged. Then she paused, still caught in Tom's gaze. "I'm gonna have to think about it." She turned and gestured toward her house, then toward the house next door. "I'm gonna have to talk it over with Ceci. And with Lisa."

After an awkward moment, Susie took Tom by the elbow and steered him off the porch. "You go on now. Leave me alone. Don't bother me for a week."

Tom walked away then, and Susie, as she always did, watched him go.

Five days later, Tom was back. As he walked up the porch steps and caught Susie's eye, a jubilant grin crept onto his face. Businesslike, she pretended not to see. Instead she sat him down and draped the cape around his shoulders. Carefully pretending to give him another unnecessary haircut, she started to hum a song. He joined in on the chorus.

"So darling, darling, stand by me – oh, stand by me," he sang in a rich baritone.

"Yes, Tom. Yes, I will." And she laid down the clippers and kissed him.

THE END

338

CPSIA information can be obtained
at www.ICGtesting.com
Printed in the USA
FSHW010051261120
76185FS